KATE
SCHUMACHER

A SONG OF MAGIC

THE GRAIL CYCLE
2

A SONG OF MAGIC, BOOK 2: THE GRAIL CYCLE

Copyright © 2024 Kate Schumacher

Paperback: 978-0-6454030-7-7

Ebook: 978-0-6454030-9-1

Hardcover: 978-0-6454030-8-4

First paperback edition: 2024

Edited by Danikka Taylor

Cover design by Franziska Stern

Map created by Rachael Ward

For more information, please visit https://www.kateschumacherauthor.com/

For the misfits and the ones who haven't yet found their place
Be yourself
And place will find you

TO THE READER

This story has been written for an adult audience. Within these pages you will find content that may be triggering, including physical assault and violence, death, emotional manipulation including grooming behaviours, torture, and discrimination against those from different backgrounds and those from LGBT+ communities. People who have suffered religious trauma may also find some of the story content distressing.

A NOTE FROM THE AUTHOR

Welcome back to the world of Teyath, and to Jenyfer, Ordes and Arthur's journeys. By the end of this book, all the cogs will be in place and the wheel will begin turning. But in what direction, you shall have to wait and see.

I hope you enjoy where this story is going.

You will meet a lot of new characters and travel to different lands.

Merlin's prophecies will begin to unfold.

Some people will learn who they truly are, and some will be still working it out.

But all will be thrust right into the middle of a game that has been set long before they were born.

Pronunciation Guide

People

Jenyfer - Jennifer
Ordes - Or/dez
Lamorna - Lar/morn/a
Jalen - Jar/len
Iouen - I/oh/an
Carbrey - Car/bray
Ulrian - Ol/re/ann
Bryn - Brin
Niniane - Nin/ee/aine
Aelle - Ay/la
Tahnet - Tar/net
Katarin - Kat/ar/en
Tregarthen - Tree/gar/then
Ankou - An/coo
Ophine - O-feen
Andromache - An/dro/ma/keh
Halymere - Hal/e/meer
Ethinne - E/thee/en
Morgause - Mor/gowz
Goerika - Gor/e/ka
Melhala - Mel/hal/ah
Ereshki - Ee/resh/key

Asrai - As/rye
Boggarts - Bog/arts

Carlings - Car/lings
Colpach - Col/pack
Sheleitari - Shay/leet/ar/ee
Syhren - siren

Places

Teyath - Tae/ath
Cruithea - Crew/i/the/a
Mahwenia - Mar/when/e/a
Kernou - Ker/know
Calledun - Cal/ee/dun
Sacellum - Sack/ell/um
Lyonesse - Lie/on/ess
Dinas Emyrs - Din/nass Emm/riss
Malist - Mal/iss/t
Kunis - Koo/ness
Ossuary - Oss/you/airy

THE LANDS OF
TEYATH
—— MAPPED ——
IN THE PRESENT AGE

CARINYA

CELIVALE
GROVE

NEWLYN

THE
FAIR WATERS

VIDARRA
FOREST

AVALON

KERNOU

BAY OF
CALLEDUN

LYONESSE

MAWHENIA

ABSHAW
WOODS

BANSTEIN RIVER

ARCDON

PORT
LEORE

SKOVER'S BAY

SEA OF ANDRED

THE TEETH

THE ROOST

GREENSTONE SEA

THE MOON'S BITE

NIMUS ARBORES

THE DEAD WOODS

HUNTER'S FOREST

CRUITHEA

KUNIS

THE CATIGERN SEA

FEY HIGHLANDS

CAMLANN PLAINS

DINAS EMRYS

LYSEIGN RIVER

NEMHAINS MOUNTAINS

MALIST

BAY AN ANAON

FAERY FOREST

VINIAY RIVER

REDCANA FOREST

BAY OF SHADOWS

THE VALE

SKULL'S REST

CHAPTER 1

Travelling all the way from Avalon to Cruithea in the arms of a storm demon had left Arthur's stomach in knots. At least the trip didn't take long, he thought, wiping his sweaty palms on his trousers.

Jalen planted his hands on his hips and gazed up. The trees that stretched above their heads created great cathedrals that captured the light, holding it in the canopy and slinging it between the branches, as delicate and strong as spider webs. The treetops were a flourish of red, gold, and green, the colours of a turning season, and a chill clung to the air.

Four times the moon had shifted from full to dark since Arthur had fled his father's house but, in many ways, it seemed much longer than that … and much shorter. For a brief moment, Ulrian's face floated into Arthur's mind as he had last seen it – broken and bleeding, the skin on one cheek strangely twisted by the magic that had been unleashed on him. He hadn't remembered that fact until much later, and part of him was sickened by what he had done.

'Tell me what you remember about this place,' Jalen said.

Before the journey, Arthur had spent days cloistered away in Avalon's great library, towering shelves of books, of knowledge, surrounding him, and he knew he'd never have enough time to absorb it all. There were books on every conceivable subject, and Arthur had to regretfully set his desires to learn everything aside, focusing on one topic – Cruithea. Jalen had lazily thumbed through books containing information he already knew, while Arthur crammed as much knowledge about the place they would be visiting into his head.

He wished they'd been able to stay in that library, with the warm light and apple-scented air waltzing into the room through wide, stone arches. Jalen had sat with him day after day, their arms touching, Arthur's skin burning. Whenever he managed to tear his eyes from the pages, it was to find Jalen watching him, one corner of his mouth turned upwards, his expression soft. That look always led to kissing, which led to something more, which meant less time reading, which, in the end, meant they had left Avalon later than originally planned.

Arthur didn't mind. Anything to hold off this great destiny he supposedly had. He realised with a jolt that while he had been in Avalon he had not dreamt of the Grail or the Fisher Queen; he wondered what that meant. Would the dreams return now he was back in Teyath? Or had the Fisher Queen given him all the information she was going to, leaving him with a patchwork of visions and phrases that mostly made no sense?

He toed the ground with his boot, glancing again at the trees that towered above them, aware Jalen was still waiting for a response. 'They worship the goddess of war and fertility, Inanna, and live their lives by the turning of the Wheel.' Once, Cruitheans had practised a different sort of magic to the elemental magic they used now – blood magic.

Inanna had once been worshipped alongside her sister Goddess, Ereshki. Ereshki was a dark goddess, who brought forth death and destruction and, together, their worship was associated with blood and death-twisted magic. This was where Cruithea's bloodthirsty reputation came from – the one Ulrian and the rest of the continent believed. But, one of the books Arthur had read had told him worship of Ereshki had ceased many years ago. Although they still followed Inanna, there was no more blood magic, no more sacrifice. The High Priestess had seen to that, determined that Cruithea would have a different future to the one the rest of Teyath had written for her.

The Priestesses of Inanna began their training young, and the Temple of the Goddess – the World's Door – was hidden by magic. Only the Priestesses could find it and only a Priestess could open it.

'The High Priestess?' Jalen asked.

'Morgause,' Arthur replied, a tingle travelling down his spine. 'My aunt.' He paused, shooting Jalen an apprehensive look. 'Will she know who I am?'

The storm demon nodded, but said nothing. Apart from Katarin, Morgause was the only family Arthur had left in the world, as far as he knew. His father had kept so much from him he couldn't be certain what was true and what was not. Were his grandparents on his mother's side alive? Did he have aunts and uncles, cousins – family? Ulrian had been an only child, and his parents had died before Arthur's birth.

'Where do we go?' Arthur asked, glancing around. 'Which direction?' He could not imagine his father in this place, with its towering trees draped in moss and the air filled with the scent of decaying vegetation.

'They'll come to meet us,' Jalen said softly.

'They know we're here?'

Jalen smiled. 'No one enters these trees without anyone knowing. There's a magical warning system in place, and the Inborn would have noticed us the moment we arrived.'

'What are they like? These people?' Arthur asked, drawing closer to Jalen. 'I know I read the texts, but there's a difference between words on the page and reality.'

The storm demon slipped his arm around Arthur's shoulders and gave him a squeeze. It made Arthur's blood sing – that Jalen was able to touch him so easily, that he didn't need to fear discovery anymore, but still, the instinctual need to glance over the shoulder was like an omnipresence. 'They're straight to the point, fierce and strong, Proud of who they are and their land. But,' Jalen added, pressing a kiss to Arthur's temple, 'they're your kin. You will be welcomed here, Arthur, especially now. The Cruitheans know of the prophecy, and they have been waiting for the time the visions of the Myrddin promise. There is nothing to fear.'

Arthur nodded. The weight of the task that had been set for him threatened to send him tumbling to the ground. He was supposed to be the King of Teyath. It had only been yesterday that he'd once again insisted everyone was wrong, and Niniane, as frustrated with him as Katarin was, made him look into the surface of her mirror. Arthur had seen the same vision the Fisher Queen had shown him – the Grail, a crown on his head, and a sword between his hands, a sword he had never seen anywhere else, while a battle raged around him in a place he did not recognise.

There was a castle in the mirror, he remembered suddenly. Nothing but a ruin, but a castle all the same, overlooking a vast, barren plain. It had to be Camlann, and the castle, Dinas Emrys, the castle of Enyon and Eseld, ancient rulers of old, and the only castle he knew of. Arthur wished he had had the time to read more about Enyon and Eseld and their reign.

Lying in the darkness, curled around one another, white curtains shifting in the warm breeze and Avalon sleeping around them, Jalen had told Arthur he needed to trust in himself, believe in himself, but Arthur wasn't sure how he was supposed to do that when he didn't know who he truly was. Maybe here, in this wild land where magic was part of life, he would find some answers.

'When will I meet him? The Myrddin?' Arthur asked now.

'I don't know exactly,' Jalen replied. 'When it is time, he will find you.'

'Have you met him?' Arthur rested his head on the muscle of Jalen's shoulder.

Jalen chuckled. 'Yes, I've met him. He's … Those who are connected to the world between the worlds like he is are often different to the rest of us,' he said. 'It has been a long time since I have seen him and the last time …'

'What?' Arthur asked, lifting his head so he could see Jalen's face.

'He told me it was my destiny to serve the Once and Future King.'

Arthur's smile froze as self-doubt and fear and all those things he thought he was slowly shaking off leapt to swallow him. 'Is that why you're—'

'No,' Jalen cut in quickly, his voice sharp. He took Arthur's face between his hands. 'No one told me I would come to care for you like I do, Arthur. That is all me. You need to believe that.' Jalen kissed him softly but even that could not tease the smile back to Arthur's lips. 'You aren't alone in any of this, know that as well. It's not just your destiny that is tied up in prophecy,' Jalen reminded him. 'There are two others who will join you on your quest, remember?'

Quest. It sounded like something out of one of the story books he had thumbed through in Niniane's library; but Arthur was no hero, and the stories always had heroes in them. Maybe it would be one of the other two mysterious people the prophecy mentioned.

They waited, the canopy above them strung with pieces of light that winked like jewels. Like the forests near Kernou, this one was alive with the sound of insects, and Arthur could hear small feet moving through the thick bushes that clustered around the bases of trees. He could hear water in the distance but whether stream or river or ocean, he couldn't tell. He'd never glanced for more than a second at a map of Teyath before his father had snatched it from him, as if he didn't want his son to see how vast the world was and be tempted by it.

It wasn't long before three people stepped into view. Arthur blinked. He hadn't heard them approach, hadn't sensed them at all. It was as if they'd appeared out of thin air. They were tall and slender, well-muscled, a man and two women. Two of them had swirling tattoos marking their exposed arms – arms that were carrying weapons.

5

They walked with the same gait – long, strong strides, perfectly in time with one another. The man was taller than the women, but only just. He had a thick beard and hair the colour of the sky on dusk, worn in braids that dangled down his back and over his shoulders like snakes. There was a marking between his deep brown eyes; Cruithean Magic Wielders were marked with glyphs that signalled which element they were strongest in. The glyph on the man's forehead marked him as an earth elemental.

The women were of equal height, both with dark hair. Arthur wondered if they were sisters, but as they came closer, he could see the differences in their faces. They stood close together; one rested her hand on the weapon at her hip. She also bore a glyph between her eyes – the sign of water – where the other woman's forehead was clear, and she was unarmed.

Jalen bowed his head.

The man laughed heartily. 'A demi-god, bowing to us?'

The weapon-carrying woman smiled, a flash of white teeth in the darkened world beneath the trees. 'We've been expecting you,' she said, her eyes passing over them both. 'Come,' she commanded.

Jalen grinned at Arthur as the Cruitheans turned and headed back the way they had come. Arthur's mind was a swirling mass of questions, so many questions, but they would have to wait.

Introductions were made as they walked, Arthur taking care not to stumble over tree roots and rock. The man was Halymere, and the women were Melhala, a water wielder, and Ethinne, a Priestess in training from the Temple. The Priestesses, Arthur had read, were skilled in more than one element, and in other magic besides that, which was why they bore no markings on their foreheads – their marks were on their bodies, hidden from human sight so only the gods could see them.

As they made their way deeper into the trees, Arthur heard a voice in his head, a whisper. He heard it move through the branches above them. He heard it in the leaves that crackled and crunched beneath the beat of his feet – the pulse of life through the earth itself.

Up ahead, Halymere stopped. He waited until they caught up, before reaching out to lay a hand on the trunk of the nearest tree. The skin on his hand slowly morphed into the colour of bark. He closed his eyes, and around them, the air shifted. Arthur's blood sang and his head spun as the very air parted like a curtain, pulled aside by the invisible hands of the forest. Behind Halymere, where before there had been layer upon layer of trees and leaf covered ground, was a settlement that appeared to grow from the landscape itself.

'Welcome,' Melhala announced, 'to Nimus Arbores.'

'Place of Trees,' Jalen translated.

There were no cottages in the village. No guild houses or paved market square, no real order to anything at all, although there were laneways of varying widths between the tent-like structures the Cruitheans lived in. Some were small, barely big enough for a few people, where others were large, with dome-like roofs. Arthur wondered if the larger ones housed important people. His home in Kernou had been extensive, too large for his father and himself, too obviously different from everyone else that he had often wondered if anyone thought about the inherited wealth of the Tregarthen family compared to the men who worked hard every day of their lives to feed their families and perhaps leave a little aside for whatever their futures may be.

'They're called kibitkas,' Melhala explained, indicating the tents with a sweep of her arm. There were dozens upon dozens of kibitkas. Smoke crept into the air from chimneys in the roofs of the larger ones, the smell of burning wood mingling with the scent of damp earth and sunlight, herbs and roasted meat.

Arthur followed the Cruithean Magic Wielder deeper into the village, Jalen walking behind him. He could feel Jalen's eyes on his back, the warmth of the other man's gaze a security, a surety, in this new world. He wanted to turn and glance over his shoulder, but didn't, keeping his eyes fixed ahead of them as they wove between tents, following laneways that reminded Arthur of tree roots, all leading back to one place – a large kibitka in the middle of the village, bordered on one side by a circular space clear of trees.

'What is that one for?' Arthur asked.

'You'd call it a tavern,' Halymere said. 'It is the place where we gather to hear news, to celebrate. We call it the Meeting Place, and this cleared space is a communal cooking area. We share meals here, and other things besides. There are rules,' he added, shooting Arthur a quick look, 'that you will have to learn.'

Arthur nodded uneasily, wondering what these rules could be, if they were similar in their severity to the rules of his father. The villagers were watching him, some pausing in their tasks. Their open curiosity made his blood twitch. He was used to people staring at him, but this was different. Here he was a stranger, a nobody.

Until they found out who he was.

Unless they knew already. People were whispering behind their hands as he passed.

They continued past rows and rows of kibitkas. So many. Arthur had no idea how many people actually lived here and realised he hadn't asked. He stored the question away for later, where it sat at the top of a very long list of questions that had been brewing and breeding since he arrived in Avalon. Some had been answered through the books he had read but, more often than not, those answers led to more questions.

Up ahead, Halymere had stopped in front of a large kibitka that was part of the landscape. Tree branches draped over it protectively, the branches dripping with autumn colours. The air around the kibitka shimmered and pulsed in the wane light. Arthur could feel magic thrumming through the ground beneath his feet.

He did not need to ask who this kibitka belonged to.

People had followed them through the village and were standing behind them. The hair stood up on the back of Arthur's neck. He did not turn to look at them, unable to take his eyes from the entrance to the kibitka.

He could barely breathe as Halymere entered the tent. No voices eased through the canvas and Arthur wished he knew what was being said behind that flap. Halymere emerged suddenly; the warrior gave Arthur a brief nod before he stepped aside, making way for another figure as Arthur's heart seized.

The High Priestess of Cruithea was as tall as Arthur and as slender as a reed. Her hair, pale as moonlight, was bound in a series of intricate braids and wound around her head in a complicated design. Bright blue eyes appraised him. Her skin was darker than his, but her full lips ... they were familiar. Her smooth forehead was marked with an intricate glyph that Arthur knew from his books indicated both magic and her status as a leader.

He stared and stared at her. She was dressed in dark orange, the colour of a muted flame, the gown she wore belted at the waist with a thick band of leather. There were at least three daggers attached to that belt, and the skirt of her dress was slit thigh-high on each leg, revealing bark-brown trousers fit close to her skin, and boots that reached below the knee. Her arms were exposed, tattoos cresting each wave of muscle beneath her skin. Each arm bore a band of silver above the elbow, and the leather cord around her neck held a collection of feathers and crystals.

She was his aunt, his family. Arthur searched her face eagerly, looking for something else in her features he could claim as his own. Her face was perfectly composed, as regal as a queen, the hem of her dress trailing along the ground, leaves caught in her wake, as she approached him. The air around her shifted as she moved. Arthur opened his mouth, his greeting dying on his lips as she drew one of her blades and ran it swiftly across her palm, turning it towards the earth. Blood dripped to the ground at her feet. Before Arthur could say anything, she dropped to one knee before him. Around him, people copied her actions.

'Grail bearer,' she said softly, reverently. 'I welcome you. By my blood, the earth beneath me knows you have come. By my blood, I pledge my people, my land, and myself, to your quest.'

Arthur was shocked into silence, his cheeks burning at her words, at the implication of them, of the weight that they carried. That weight rushed forward to heap itself onto his head, almost bringing him to his knees. Eventually, he swallowed tightly. 'Please don't.'

Morgause straightened. 'You are what you are, Arthur.'

He shook his head. 'I …'

With a nod from their High Priestess, the people gathered around them rose from their crouched positions and melted away, until no one else remained. Even Jalen had vanished and Arthur felt a stab at the storm demon's absence. Morgause reached for Arthur's hands; he took them, held them tight, feeling the blood on her palm coat his skin, and her voice was soft when she spoke.

'You want to know about Igraine.'

'Yes.' It was a whisper. 'Yes, I do.'

'Then I will tell you,' Morgause said simply. 'My memories of her will become yours. And then, you will train.'

'Train?'

She nodded and squeezed his hands; he felt her magic beneath his skin, sliding through him, before it withdrew. 'Your magic is strong, as your mother's was – I can feel it – but you have only begun to learn to use it and you don't understand it. Here, you will master your gift, and you will learn to use a weapon. You will discover your warrior's heart.'

'My warrior's heart?' A flash of memory – his father, face-down, blood leaking from his head. 'I don't think—'

The High Priestess smiled. 'The heart of a warrior lives in all of us – this is what we believe. This is Inanna's gift to us. You will need your warrior's heart, Arthur, for once you have the power that has been foretold, there will be those who wish to take it from you. We shall make a warrior out of you.' She smiled, and warmth spread through him at the sight of it. 'Welcome home, Arthur, son of my sister, born of her blood.'

Arthur pushed out a shaky breath. 'Thank you.'

CHAPTER 2

The *Night Queen* sliced through water that sparkled like crystal. There was nothing but the sharp bite of the sun and the dry kiss of the sea breeze on Jenyfer's cheeks. She licked the salt from her lips and continued to watch the horizon, where the ocean merged with the sky in an unending realm of dazzling blue. She'd been a month on *The Queen,* a month with the notorious pirate Captain, Katarin Le Fey, and in that time Jenyfer had earnt blisters, rope burn, and dehydration. Katarin did not allow anyone who was not prepared to work on her ship.

Jenyfer could still barely believe the bold words she'd spoken that day in the tavern in Newlyn, words that had led her to her place on this ship. After stepping from the sea and onto the beach, dripping with water and wearing scales across her skin, Jenyfer hadn't seen any other option. She was a syhren, dangerous and to be feared, and she had no idea how to control the magic in her voice. Every time she'd used it since leaving Kernou, mostly by accident, sometimes on instinct – like with the Konsel man – someone got hurt. At least here, on *The Queen,* she couldn't hurt anyone. Katarin's crew were all female, and everyone knew syhren magic only worked on men.

Jenyfer needed answers. She needed to know how to control her voice, what to do when she felt it creeping up her throat, her palms tingling with magic. The last syhren she had encountered had tried to drown her. Jenyfer had thought back on that night over and over, wondering what would have happened if Ordes had not pulled her from the ocean. She had sung that night, her voice blending effortlessly with the syhren's, the magic in her veins alive, but the moment she'd been dragged beneath the water, she fought, and the next she knew, she was lying on the sand with Ordes.

Ordes was one more thing in the long list of things swirling around Jenyfer's head. He was the one thing she didn't want to think about, and the one thing she couldn't help thinking about. If she stilled her mind, she could feel the touch of his hand on the back of her neck, the gentle press of his lips against hers, the beautiful weight of his body.

Inside Jenyfer's chest, buried deep within the beating of her heart, was another heartbeat, steady and strong. She'd been trying to ignore it, but whenever the heartbeat that was not hers thumped alongside the steady rhythm of her own heart, regret threatened to sweep her away, so she shut it out, until she couldn't, and the cycle started again, leaving her biting her lip in her hammock while the other women slept around her.

It was better to keep busy, and there was plenty to do here. Jenyfer pushed all thoughts of Ordes from her mind, pushed everything that had happened between them aside, and focused on the things she had discovered about herself. She could breathe underwater, something she would never have believed until it happened, and she now knew she could swim. She glanced down at her thighs, wondering at the silver and blue iridescent scales that had flecked her flesh after she'd crawled from the water in Newlyn. They weren't there anymore – she checked her legs almost every opportunity she got, terrified she'd wake up and her skin would be covered with them and if that happened, there would be no denying what she was, not to anyone, even herself.

Finding Katarin was another thing Jenyfer thought about constantly. *The Excalibur* had been down the coast, close to Port Leore, but, somehow, Jenyfer had ended up in Newlyn.

Just like Tymis said she would.

She rubbed at her face and sighed. Gods and prophecies. Old Ones and syhrens. She had no answers, no idea why the God of the Earth had commanded Ordes to rescue her from Kernou, and no idea why Tymis thought she was part of some prophecy.

The Night Queen was headed south and was somewhere in the Fair Waters, Teyath to one side of them, Avalon to the other. The magical island could not be seen, but a permanent haze of mist lingered over the horizon to the west. Soon, they would sail past the Bay of Calledun – and Kernou. Where was Lamorna? Jenyfer had failed to find her sister – that had been her goal when she dove from *The Excalibur* into the sea. But instead of Lyonesse, where everyone seemed to think Lamorna had been taken, Jenyfer's magic had led her to Katarin.

Jenyfer had listened for any talk during the three days and nights they had spent in Newlyn, and the old fisherman in the tavern had laughed and told her she was mad if she thought anyone returned from beneath the waves. She'd asked countless questions of Kat's crew, but no one could give her any clear answers, and, Jenyfer suspected, were sick of hearing about it. If there was one thing that bound all the women of *The Night Queen* together, it was loss. Tahnet had told her that everyone on board had lost someone, and it was up to Jenyfer to decide if she would let her loss eat at her, or if she would take steps to move beyond it.

Jenyfer could not return to Kernou and would probably never see her aunt Tamora again, so she clung to the tiny slice of hope that, somehow, she would find her sister. She could not bring herself to believe Lamorna was dead.

And if you find her, then what? a voice asked.

Lamorna would want to return to Kernou, and her life there, but for Jenyfer that was not an option. Sometimes she wondered why it was so important. Lamorna hated that Jenyfer had magic. Jenyfer didn't expect a heartfelt reunion if she managed to find her sister, but she wanted to know *what* had happened once Lamorna vanished beneath the waves. After all, it had been Jenyfer's magic that had called the syhren to the beach. It was her magic that had seen Lamorna taken beneath the water.

Jenyfer was determined to make things right: find Lamorna, return her to her life, and then ... with a sigh, Jenyfer rubbed at her eyes. She had no clue and she hadn't asked Katarin if she could stay on *The Queen* indefinitely.

Katarin emerged from her cabin and made her way to the helm, where the quartermaster, Aelle, stood with her hand resting lightly on the ship's wheel. *The Night Queen* didn't need steering, but Jenyfer suspected Aelle liked being behind the wheel. She was in charge of navigation, and could read the waves and the water as easily as others read ink on a page. Aelle was blunt, demanding, and tough, but Jenyfer liked her. With someone like Aelle, she knew where she stood. If the quartermaster wasn't happy with something Jenyfer had done, she let her know, as she did anyone.

Aelle and the boatswain, Tahnet, were often with Katarin, the three of them talking in low voices. Jenyfer liked Tahnet as well – the blonde woman had kind eyes and a warm smile. While the rest of the crew had treated Jenyfer well enough, she couldn't help but wonder how they actually felt about having a syhren on board. Jenyfer was here because Katarin had allowed it, and the crew would follow their Captain.

With Katarin, Jenyfer had learnt how long she could let her eyes linger before the Captain turned her burning gaze on her face. Like Ordes had, Katarin had copied the map from Jenyfer's skin and had been able to fill in some of the gaps. Beyond that moment, no one had mentioned Ordes, and Jenyfer was glad, afraid that if someone said his name, it would be an acknowledgment of what she had lost, but was it even possible to lose what had never truly been hers?

Tymis thought his son had been under a spell – Jenyfer's spell, something her magic had done that she could not control, and that she had no idea how to undo. That was one of the reasons why she left. She'd spent her life under the control of others. She didn't want that for anyone else, especially Ordes.

'Little Morsel,' Katarin called, and Jenyfer repressed a sigh at the nickname. She left her place at the railing and made her way up the ladder to the helm. Katarin scared her, there was no denying it, and she didn't even bother to try and hide it. Jenyfer did what she was told, when she was told. She had nowhere else to go, and was well aware of her unimportance on *The Queen*, so she obeyed every command, every request, and never questioned anything.

Her obedience would make Lamorna proud.

Katarin was watching her curiously.

'Yes?' Jenyfer asked softly.

The Captain tipped her head to one side, a bemused expression on her face. 'I'm not going to bite you, you know,' she stated, then flashed perfect teeth in a brief smile. 'Hard, anyway.'

Aelle chuckled. 'Sleep well, Tidbit?'

Tidbit. Jenyfer hated that more than Little Morsel. It was the crew's nickname for her, one that she heard every morning when she woke and struggled her way free of her hammock. Unlike on *The Excalibur*, on this ship she didn't have a private cabin. She shared a sleeping space with the crew, spread out in the belly of the ship. It wasn't so bad, she supposed. At least on *The Queen*, she was in the company of women like her – hunted and despised, feared for being what they were, and hated for being what they were not.

Subservient.

Normal.

Jenyfer forced herself to meet first Aelle's sharp gaze, and then Katarin's. 'Yes,' she answered eventually, but it was a lie. Jenyfer had been sleeping terribly since leaving *The Excalibur*. Her dreams were scattered things, full of water and music, and of two sets of hands that were not hers holding the Grail between them; of a cave and a woman with pale skin and sorrowful eyes, the landscape around her dead and dying. And a man with dark hair wearing a crown of bones. She knew instinctively that the crown in her dreams had nothing to do with the Grail. It was something for her alone, but she hadn't worked out what. There were no clues for her to follow, nothing but her inner song, which rang with power when she dreamt of that crown.

'Where are we going?' she asked.

Aelle ran her eyes over Jenyfer's exposed forearms, where the inky lines of the map stood out against the milk of her skin – it didn't matter how long she spent in the sun, Jenyfer was still pale. Katarin and Aelle exchanged a glance, as if deciding between them whether Jenyfer was worthy of sharing knowledge with.

'I've had a message from Niniane,' Katarin said. 'She's told us to go to Carinya.'

Jenyfer's heart began thundering. 'Why? What's in Carinya?'

Katarin gestured to the lines on Jenyfer's skin. 'A Treasure. Maybe.'

'But … none of Tymis' crew could work out this map.' Jenyfer said, examining her arms and the inky lines that ran along both forearms to disappear beneath her bunched up sleeves.

Aelle smiled. 'They're men and they're idiots.'

Katarin shielded her eyes from the sun as she scanned the horizon. 'Let's get turned around and go Treasure hunting, shall we?'

Slowly, the ship began to change her bearing. 'I still think we should be headed for The Vale,' Aelle muttered, one hand on the wheel. 'It looks like the coast around The Vale to me.'

'Carinya first,' Kat said firmly.

Jenyfer tried desperately not to think of the last time she was in The Vale. She bit her lip, cursing her memory, which was crystal clear about that particular incident. She swallowed it away, aware the others were watching her.

Kat and Aelle exchanged another meaningful glance.

'What?' Jenyfer asked.

'You-know-who is useless at magic, but did he ever try to work this map out?' Katarin asked. 'Even a little?'

'I'm not sure, and you can say his name,' Jenyfer said. No one said anything. Water lapped at the sides of the ship, gentle and strong at the same time, creating its own music that settled alongside the music in Jenyfer's head. 'I don't know what to do,' she admitted. 'About him.'

'What you do,' Aelle said simply, 'is get up each day and move forward. I'm not saying you put the past in a box and forget about it. I'm saying you need to find a way forward, to not let it weigh you down.'

'I'm not sure how,' Jenyfer said quietly. 'My whole life was controlled, even though I didn't want to acknowledge it. But it was. What we wore, what we ate, what we spoke about, what we did or didn't do. I wasn't the best at following the rules but I still followed them, in a way.'

'Freedom is a thing people don't realise they need until they get it, and then most don't know what to do with it,' Aelle said.

Katarin had been silent, but now, she turned her sharp gaze on Jenyfer. 'You can be yourself here. No one will judge you for it. You can't hurt any of us with your voice, even if you wanted to.'

'I don't want to use my voice ever again,' Jenyfer said.

'You can't not, Little Morsel,' the Captain told her, not unkindly. 'It's part of you.'

'Ordes said something similar,' Jenyfer replied.

'Well, he was right about that. Just as Aelle is right. You can't forget what happened to you in Kernou – in fact, you shouldn't ever forget it – but you can either let your past consume you or you can use it to shape your future,' Katarin said.

Silence dropped between them, but it was a companionable silence. Jenyfer felt lighter somehow, as if the women's words had lifted something away from her. They stood and watched the water together, until Katarin sighed.

'I wish Arthur was here.'

'You miss him?' Aelle teased, giving Katarin a nudge and making her grumble.

Arthur Tregarthen was in Cruithea. Jenyfer's head still spun when she thought about what she'd learnt about him – not only was he a Magic Wielder, like her, he was Katarin's brother. He'd attacked his father and fled Kernou, much like Jenyfer had, and ended up finding his way onto *The Night Queen*. But it wasn't that information that left Jenyfer's head spinning. Arthur was destined to be a King, caught up in these prophecies everyone was talking about. She couldn't reconcile the Arthur she knew – quiet, reserved, timid – with the Arthur Katarin believed he would become.

He'd been gone by the time she'd ended up sailing with Katarin, so now they were left with nothing but half a map, and Niniane's orders. If a Goddess couldn't find a magical artefact, Jenyfer could not see how any of them were supposed to find it.

'If we find nothing in Carinya?' Jenyfer asked.

'Then we return to Avalon,' Katarin said.

Jenyfer turned her gaze west, where the sun reflected off the ocean. By morning, the mist would be thrown over the ocean like a pale grey blanket. Tamora had told her to go to Avalon, that Niniane would be able to help. Perhaps that was why Jenyfer had found Katarin and not Lyonesse – maybe her magic knew what it was doing after all.

'Tidbit,' Tahnet called from the deck. 'This isn't a holiday. There's work to do.'

Jenyfer smothered her groan.

CHAPTER 3

Ordes put his feet up on his desk and used his teeth to pull the cork free of the bottle. He took a long drink, barely noticing the taste of the rum as it slid down his throat. A half-eaten plate of food rested near his feet. He couldn't remember who brought it to him and he couldn't remember eating any of it, just like he couldn't remember sleeping.

Everything since Jenyfer had vanished was a blur of anger and pain. Everything since his father had revealed the truth about himself, about Ordes' mother, seemed unimportant. At first, he'd tried not to think of any of it, tried to keep himself busy, but as days bled into night and he was alone, there was nothing he could do to stop what was churning through his brain.

Two empty bottles of rum sat on the floor. He had another drink.

This wasn't the way he usually dealt with things. He was aware, somewhere in the tangled mess of his mind, that he should sober up and think, but the will to do that was buried deep. It was easier this way. The drink didn't stop the pain, but it quenched the anger and, if he drank enough, Ordes could forget, just for a moment.

Part of him knew he couldn't avoid it forever, but he mostly ignored that part.

The door eased open, but Ordes didn't turn from his seat, giving his father the finger over his bare shoulder before Tymis could say a word. Ordes glanced down at his chest, where the map was scrawled, clear as the clearest sky, across his skin.

A map that was missing its other half.

His insides twisted. He had another mouthful of rum.

'Have you found the bottom of that bottle yet?'

Ordes said nothing.

'You've been drunk for a month.' Tymis sighed. Ordes glanced at his father long enough to watch him kick the door shut. 'You're my quartermaster,' the Captain reminded him, his voice hard.

Ordes raised the bottle to his lips, and drank. 'I quit.'

'You can't quit,' Tymis snapped wearily. They'd had this conversation multiple times already. 'The men need you.'

'Get them to vote for someone else,' Ordes mumbled, ignoring the twinge of guilt that snaked through him. The last time Iouen had come to see him, he'd told his friend to piss off.

Tymis sighed. 'All this over a girl.'

Ordes was out of his seat with his hands fisted in his father's shirt before he could blink. His magic curled from his fingers and for a moment he couldn't speak, couldn't find the words as anger surged through him. 'Don't. You. Dare.'

'At least you're not stuck to that fucking chair.' Tymis shoved him away.

'You don't have the right to lecture me about women,' Ordes snarled. 'You've spent your life running from your mistakes. Should I be running as well? Steal a ship and hide away on the ocean and never have to face up to anything, oh great and powerful one?'

'This isn't about me,' Tymis said.

'You lied to me,' Ordes whispered. 'You told her to leave, didn't you?'

'She made her choice,' his father snapped, then ran his hand over his face. He shoved the mountain of clothes off the armchair and sat heavily. 'Go and see Katarin,' he suggested.

'You really think that will help, do you? Is that how you got over my mother?'

'I never got over your mother.'

Ordes laughed, then stopped at the look on his father's face. 'Is that why you've been such a grumpy bastard my whole life? You want what you can't have.'

'I can have her,' Tymis said softly, his eyes on his tattooed knuckles – the same symbols were replicated on Ordes' hands. 'But I chose you, Ordes. I chose to give up my magic and to protect you, over being with her.'

Ordes was suddenly very sober. He sat down, his legs heavy. 'Protect me from what?'

'From what's to come,' Tymis said, standing and kicking the legs of Ordes' chair; the chair collapsed, leaving Ordes in a heap on the floor. 'Get your shit together. Go and see Katarin and I don't know, talk to someone.'

'You think talking to Kat will help? You have met Katarin Le Fey, haven't you? She's less likely than you to give me any sympathy. She'll probably give me a black eye,' Ordes added, lying back in the wreckage of the chair, blinking at the ceiling as *The Excalibur* rocked gently beneath him and something sharp stuck into his side.

'That's the point,' Tymis said. 'You need to hear it from someone else.'

Ordes did not want to see Katarin. 'No.' He waved his hand – the bottle of rum rose from the table and floated towards him, but his father snatched it swiftly from the air.

Tymis glared at him, the bottle tucked under his arm, then his expression shifted and when he spoke, his voice was soft. 'You need to wash and sleep, Ordes. You need to eat and you need—'

'If you're about to say what I think you're about to say—'

'You need to get out of this cabin and get your life back,' Tymis finished calmly. 'Things happen and we can't change them.' He held up his hand when Ordes glowered at him. 'Yes, alright, maybe that's a bit callous,' he said loudly, drowning out whatever protest Ordes was about to make, 'but she isn't dead, you know that. So she's somewhere and, when the time is right, you'll find her, or she'll find you, or some other lovey-dovey bullshit.'

Ordes rubbed at his face wearily.

'When you've got your head on straight, I have a job for you.'

'Oh wonderful,' Ordes said darkly. 'Can't wait.' Then, because his father was giving him the sort of look that used to see him sent to his cabin for misbehaving, 'What is it?'

'You're going on a treasure hunt.'

Ordes groaned, rubbing at his eyes, so hard colourful spots danced behind his lids.

Tymis smiled and left, leaving the door open and taking the rum with him.

A wash, some food, and a change of clothes did absolutely nothing to dampen the anger that lived in Ordes' blood. He wasn't sure who he was most furious with – his father for his lies and bullshit, Jenyfer for leaving him, or himself for being such a bloody fool. He thought he'd known what he was doing. He thought he'd had a handle on it, that he was in control of it, as much as his head felt like it was filled with clouds whenever Jenyfer was near him. But he'd been wrong in that as well; and now … he placed his hand over his heart, feeling two heartbeats thundering beneath his palm.

The drinking was an attempt to block out the absence of her, the absence of feeling, that emptiness of his arms, while all the while her heart was still beating alongside his and he was two steps away from losing his mind.

But there was nothing else for it – he was going to have to get up off his arse, go above deck, and face the world. Or face the crew at least. His father was right in that.

He'd start there – the rest of the world could wait.

Ordes found Iouen directing the repair of a sail. His friend gave him a long look.

'I'm not drunk,' Ordes said.

'Well, that's something different,' Iouen shot back. 'I can't pretend to know what you're going through at the moment, Ordes, but there was no need to hide it, from any of us. We've all lost people. That's why we're here, living this glamorous life on the high seas with a grumpy bastard for a Captain and a lovesick fool for a quartermaster.'

'I know,' Ordes said quietly. He looked past Iouen, to the horizon, a perfect line of deep blue water cut across a paler sky, wondering where in this world Jenyfer was at the moment, and if his father was right and he would find her again. His eyes found Iouen's; there were so many words he needed to say, but none of them made their way up his throat and onto his tongue.

A sly grin crawled over his friend's face. 'Do you need a hug?' He held out his arms. 'Come on, faery. Rest your pretty head on my very manly shoulder and—'

'Fuck off,' Ordes said, laughing.

Iouen punched him lightly in the shoulder, then turned away, back to his job, silently reminding Ordes that he had a job to do as well. He glanced around for his father and, not finding him on deck, headed for the Captain's cabin.

Tymis was sitting at his desk, his expression closed, and Ordes wondered what was going on in that head of his. But he said nothing, going to stand by the window.

'Where do you propose I start?' Ordes asked, gesturing to the world of water outside the window. 'Where does one even begin looking for the Treasures of the Gods?'

Tymis unrolled a large piece of paper; Ordes turned from the window, recognising the map inked on his skin, and Jenyfer's. He ignored the pinch of his heart and made himself focus. 'Carinya,' Tymis said. 'The Sea Caves.'

'Why there?'

'Call it intuition.'

Ordes folded his arms. 'Do you know where they are, oh wise one?'

'Don't start that shit with me,' Tymis said. 'That crap is precisely the reason I don't tell people who I am.'

'Fine. I'll go look at your caves.'

His father's voice stopped him at the door. 'There is something you need to know.'

'Gods, what now?' Ordes joked, his smile freezing at the look on his father's face. His stomach dropped, then twisted so fiercely it hurt. 'What is it?'

'You were born between the worlds, in the place where magic comes from. You are a part of my prophecy,' Tymis told him.

Ordes returned to the chair, sitting before his knees gave out.

'You already knew this,' his father said. 'You felt it. Whenever I told you stories, when you were a tiny thing hanging on my every word, you wished it was you.'

'I was a kid – what kid doesn't wish they had some great destiny?' Ordes managed.

'Look back on those moments, and remember how you felt. Remember how every part of you tingled, and how your magic would sing. You knew,' Tymis repeated.

'How can you know that was what I felt? I never told you,' Ordes breathed. His fingers flexed and silver light crept over his knuckles to curl along his forearms; his body felt light and heavy at the same time, burdened, but free, because here was more of the truth of himself.

'I knew your face before you existed, Ordes, just as I knew Jenyfer's and Arthur Tregarthen's. And you're not just looking for treasure because I'm asking you to – you're looking because one of them is yours,' Tymis said. 'Close your eyes and tell me what you see.'

Ordes took a deep, shaking breath. He closed his eyes. Immediately, his brain filled with mist, and from within, something took shape. He opened his eyes. 'A bow.'

'Yes,' Tymis said. 'You need to find the Bow of Mists.'

CHAPTER 4

Lamorna tucked the basket of linen caps against her hip. No one had noticed her yet; the shadows wrapped around her were thick and deep. She knew this place between the buildings on the edge of the market square was the best to keep out of sight because it was Jenyfer's favourite spot.

It was early; the town square was bustling with people. Lamorna reached up to make sure her cap was in place and every strand of golden hair was tucked securely beneath it. Tamora had offered to go into town this morning, but Lamorna had refused. She couldn't stay hidden forever, as much as the idea appealed to her. Normally, she'd have been up before dawn in preparation for the trip into town. The market was often the highlight of Lamorna's day, and she had never been able to understand why Jenyfer grumbled her way out of bed … Lamorna swallowed, giving herself a mental shake. Later. She'd think about her sister later.

Everyone had known she'd returned from the ocean by the time she left the Chif's house a month ago, still damp and wrapped in one of his woollen blankets. He'd led her through the streets, one arm around her, the other held out in front of them, a signal for everyone to stay back. The crowd gathered in the square had parted for them and Lamorna had heard their whispered awe in her dreams for a week. They had wanted to touch her, and some had – earning them a reprimand from the Chif. But it hadn't stopped others from following them all the way to her aunt's cottage.

Tamora had met them at the gate, her face blank with shock, and the rest of that day and the next was a blur.

Lamorna had slept on and off for days, plagued with nightmares that only went away after her aunt made her drink a bitter tonic. Lamorna had recognised the smell – Jenyfer's tonic – and she'd asked after her sister again, only to be told Jenyfer was gone. Tamora did not believe they would ever see her again and would not speak any further about it.

There had been people gathered outside their cottage. Lamorna did not see them, but she heard her aunt telling them to go away. Only when they were gone did Lamorna venture outside into the sunlight to sit in the garden, watching her aunt tend to the beehive and the vegetable patch. She had wanted to help – she was supposed to help – but her limbs had been as floppy as wet straw and her head ached constantly.

When her aunt had asked where she had been, Lamorna could only shake her head. She didn't have the words to describe it.

Lamorna had slowly regained her strength and her wits – the dreams floated away, until nothing remained but scattered visions, filled with water and screams, music ... and a man, with hair like black silk and a voice that could make her weep from listening to him speak. But she did not know who he was and could not clearly recall his face. She could live with that, she'd decided, trusting that the Chif was right – the One God had returned her to them for a reason, only she did not know what that reason was.

Now, as she stood and watched the world that used to be hers, her palms were sweaty and her breathing short and sharp. She needed to visit the fishmonger and the butcher, and they needed milk and flour.

She peered into her basket. She had more than enough to barter with – six caps and three jars of honey, and a small amount of coin – but she didn't step from the safety of Jenyfer's hidden place in the shadows. She could hear the lapping of the waves on the shore and the sound made her shudder as a memory of water and darkness ripped through her before vanishing into the morning light.

Lamorna knew she couldn't put it off any longer. She took a deep breath and stepped into the sunshine, making her way purposefully towards the fishmonger. She would get what she needed and leave, not linger and not let herself be engaged in any conversation about where she had been. She had no answers for any of their questions.

The fishmonger did not want any caps or honey or coin. The fish was a gift, he said, his eyes wide as he looked at her. It was the same at the butcher and by the time Lamorna was approaching the bakery she was trembling. She could feel eyes on her as she walked, so kept her head high and her chin lifted, concentrating on her breathing.

As she was about to step into the bakery, a group of older women spied her and hurried over. Lamorna's heart sped up. She wanted to go home. She could see their reverence, their awe, from where she stood frozen with her hand on the door. One of them gripped a battered copy of the Decalogue in her withered hands.

Before they reached her, the door to the bakery opened and a hand shot out, closing around Lamorna's forearm and pulling her inside to safety.

Bryn locked the bakery door and shook his head at the women crowded outside the windows, straining for a peek at Lamorna. He stood in front of the glass-panelled door, the bulk of his body blocking her from view. He glanced at her over his shoulder and his voice was rough when he spoke. 'They need to leave you alone. You've been through enough.'

'Thank you,' Lamorna breathed. The baker was watching her from behind his counter and she was relieved to see a neutral expression, then she remembered the baker was not a believer and nerves flooded her again. She cleared her throat and approached him. 'I need flour, please,' she told him softly, keeping her eyes lowered, as was proper.

He chuckled. 'You need more than flour, girl,' he said, placing a small sack on the counter. He took a jar of her honey and a coin as payment. Lamorna could feel him watching her and lifted her eyes. 'You met him, didn't you?'

'Who?'

'The Master of Songs and Death,' the man said simply. 'Those of us who still believe in the truth of things discussed it. Some thought you'd been taken to Avalon, to the Witch of the Mists, but it was a syhren that took you, so it was to Melodias you went.'

Lamorna swallowed. 'I don't remember,' she said in a small voice. Her hands were shaking and there was music in her ears. Had she really been with the God of the Seas? No, it wasn't possible. He wasn't real. None of them were real.

The baker shrugged. 'It's probably better if you don't. Some say his realm is beautiful, but then, who's to know they're speaking true, because those who go there never return.' He paused, his eyes crawling over her again. 'You're the only one I've ever heard to come back. Did you—'

'That's enough,' Bryn ordered, stepping forward and putting his hand on Lamorna's shoulder; his palm was so large his fingers spread down her upper arm and brushed her clavicle. She shivered. 'I'll take her home.'

Without consultation, the baker nodded, gesturing towards the rear of the shop and Lamorna suddenly understood. She hurried past him into the back room, past the giant ovens and the suffocating heat of the bakery, shoving the back door open and gulping at the fresh air.

Bryn walked her home. They didn't speak as they made their way along an unfamiliar path, ducking between cottages and skirting the edge of the town, and Lamorna wondered how often Jenyfer had walked this same route, and whether she'd been alone or if Bryn had been with her. At the cottage, Bryn took her basket, and didn't say another word

28

until they had left the food with Tamora and were sitting at the far end of the garden on the soft grass.

'Thank you,' Lamorna said softly.

He shrugged. 'I would have done the same for Jenyfer, so …'

Silence fell between them, until Lamorna cleared her throat and spoke out of turn.

'Where is Arthur Tregarthen?' she asked. 'Aunt Tamora says he left.'

'He ran away,' Bryn said simply. 'After he attacked his father, our Chif, and the Witchfinder. He ran away and no one knows where he is. The Chif is furious. You've seen his face?'—Bryn pointed at his own face— 'Arthur did that.'

'How?' Lamorna whispered.

Bryn's eyes tightened. 'He's a Magic Wielder. He used his sorcery against his father. He's a coward – you know he wanted me to free Jen?' When Lamorna frowned, Bryn shook his head. 'You don't know? They locked her up after you were taken beneath the waves. The Witchfinder was going to take her to Malist. Maybe Arthur helped her escape, I don't know. All I do know is she's not the person I thought she was.' There was an odd weight to his words that caused Lamorna's stomach to clench.

'I saw her in Port Leore, not long before you came back. I'd travelled there to help spread the Word and I saw her with …' He stopped and turned his face away.

'You saw her?' Lamorna pressed. Excitement rushed through her. Bryn mumbled something, then sighed and rubbed at his face, avoiding his nose, which she was certain had been broken. Lamorna's heart was thundering painfully. She waited, impatience crawling through her and was almost bouncing with nerves by the time Bryn spoke.

'Yes I saw her,' he said, his voice low, pained. 'And her new boyfriend rearranged my face.'

'Oh,' Lamorna said softly. Then, 'Wait, boyfriend? Are you sure?'

'From the way they were practically pulling each other's clothes off in the street – yes, Lamorna, I'm sure,' Bryn said crudely. His voice was bitter. 'I know she didn't want to marry me, but I thought she might have cared for me enough to not …'

Lamorna didn't know what to say, so she said nothing.

'And then, she … did something. To Alric. She made him stab himself, and now he's dead,' Bryn added.

Lamorna gasped, her hands flying to cover her mouth.

He shot her a look. 'Jenyfer's a Magic Wielder,' he stated bluntly.

'I know,' she whispered, dropping her eyes, studying her hands. Her nails were chipped. She frowned, running the tip of one finger over the jagged edges.

'You know?' Bryn said, his voice rising. Lamorna looked up – his face was folded into a frown and fear pierced her. 'And you didn't tell anyone?'

'She's my sister,' Lamorna whispered. 'What was I supposed to do? Send her to her death? It doesn't matter what she is. She's your friend – your wife.'

'Was,' he corrected harshly. 'She made it very clear that anything we had is gone.'

'She saved my life,' Lamorna said, so softly she wasn't sure Bryn had heard her, but when she glanced at him again, he was watching her in a way that made her stomach tighten once more. Her memories of that moment on the beach were hazy, but she knew, instinctively, that whatever had happened was because of her sister and her magic. 'You won't tell the Chif, will you? That I knew?'

Bryn said nothing for a long moment; by the time he spoke, Lamorna's insides had almost dissolved in panic. 'No, I won't.' He glanced over his shoulder at the cottage, at Tamora sitting in the shade of the house, the Decalogue open in her lap, though Lamorna knew she was not reading a word of it. 'I was about to come looking for you before you appeared outside the bakery. I've got a message to deliver.'

Lamorna waited patiently, even though her stomach was twisted.

'The Chif and the Konsel wish to see you. Tomorrow, after dawn. They wish to question you about where you were, about what you learnt,'

Bryn said. 'You could have important knowledge, Lamorna. You must tell them everything you know.'

'But I don't know anything!' Lamorna began wildly, before she remembered her place, remembered to remain civil when speaking with a man, no matter how afraid she was.

Bryn gave her a brief smile. 'I'm sure you do. You just don't know it.'

She nodded, not daring to point out that what he said contradicted itself, and he stood. They walked back to the cottage together, Lamorna remembering to stay behind him, to let him walk ahead of her, as was expected. He nodded to Tamora, who rose from her seat and inclined her head in his direction, and then he left. Lamorna watched him until he had vanished down the path towards the town.

'The Konsel want to question me,' she said softly.

Tamora looked at her in alarm. 'When?'

'Tomorrow. But I don't know anything!' Lamorna exclaimed, that panic rising up in her chest again, her chest tight with anxiety. She wrung her hands, then took a deep breath and pulled calm over herself. 'I shall recite the Word this evening. The One God will make the answers clear to me.'

The look her aunt gave her – pitying, slightly irritated – stayed with her long after she had gone inside to her room, long after she had knelt for hours on the hard floor, her hands clasped together, the Word spilling from her lips until her voice had fled and she tumbled into bed, exhausted, her sister's absence an ache in her blood.

Tamora escorted her to the Chif's house the following morning after dawn, as Lamorna had been instructed. They were met by one of the Konsel, a man whose name Lamorna did not know, and reminded herself she had no need to know.

He sent Tamora away, ignoring her softly-voiced protests, leaving Lamorna to follow him through the cold, dark house and into the main room alone. She did not look at the paintings on the walls, or the tapestries, or anything. Fear had given way to blind terror and, by the time they reached the main Hall, a strange numbness had taken hold of her body.

Waiting for her, standing before the altar, was the Chif, the cross of the One God looking down on them from the wall behind his head, and two other Konsel men. Ulrian smiled, a brief curling of his lips, coming forward to grasp her hands and draw her into the room. There were no lanterns lit – sunlight poured through the windows, cutting through the gloom in snatches of bright light.

'It is time, Lamorna,' the Chif said softly, 'for you to tell us what you know.'

'I don't know anything,' she said in return, keeping her eyes lowered, noting how large his hands were, how small hers were in comparison. She swallowed. 'I've thought and thought, and I've recited the Word and asked Him for guidance, but there is nothing. Just blackness and music—'

'Music?' One of the Konsel cut in.

Lamorna nodded, lifting her head in time to see the man exchange a glance with the Chif. Encouraged, she went on. 'There was music. Not any music I have ever heard before,' she added. 'It was dark and sinful music.'

'Did the music make you do anything?' the Chif asked.

Lamorna frowned. 'I don't know. I can't remember.'

'I need to ask,' the Chif began gently. 'Your sister is a Magic Wielder, as I'm aware you know by now. We are not interested in whether you knew or not – family is complicated,' he said, reaching up to touch the ruined skin of his cheek. He cleared his throat. 'We are interested in knowing if *you* have any magic, Lamorna.'

'Me?' she gasped, then shook her head. 'No. By the Word, no. I am no Magic Wielder.'

'Do you see faeries?' one of the Konsel demanded. Lamorna shook her head. 'Have you ever heard the voice of the Beast?' She shook her head again. 'Have you ever dreamt something that came true?'

'No, no,' Lamorna whispered. 'I have done none of those things.'

'I'm sorry to question you,' the Chif said, 'But these abominations often run through family lines. What about your aunt?'

Lamorna's breath hitched. She looked the Chif in the eyes, and lied. 'No. I have seen nothing to make me believe my aunt is a Magic Wielder.'

She was certain they could hear her heart, that they could smell the lies dripping from her. She kept herself still, her hands clasped tightly. She kept her face smooth, and ignored the wickedness she could feel twisting her insides.

Eventually, the Chif nodded. But she didn't dare show any sign of relief.

The Konsel exchanged more glances, and then one of the men peeled away from the rest. Lamorna watched, curious, as he went behind the altar of the One God and returned with a ceramic jar. She had no idea what could be inside, her frown deepening as the man bent and scattered what looked like crystals on the stones before the altar.

'You will kneel, Lamorna,' the Chif said softly. Someone nudged her in the back; she moved forward a step, then halted, horrified. It was not crystals. It was broken glass. The shards glittered in the light spilling into the room. The hand in her back pushed, and she stumbled forward. 'Pain,' the Chif continued, still in that soft, sepulchral tone, 'Can be a great motivator for the truth.'

'But I have told you everything I remember!' Lamorna cried. The men frowned and she dropped her eyes. She had spoken out of turn and she had raised her voice to them. Her palms had grown sweaty and she wanted to wipe them on her dress but she didn't. She remained still, her back straight, muscles rigid.

'Kneel, Lamorna,' the Chif commanded.

With a sob, she stepped forward. 'It will hurt,' she whimpered.

'Yes, it will. You will suffer, as the One God suffered for our sins,' Ulrian said reverently. He touched her cheek gently, smoothed his hand over her head. 'Lift your skirts above your knees and kneel, Lamorna.'

'For how long?' she whispered, her cheeks reddening at the idea of showing these men her flesh. She swallowed her tears, thinking of what her sister would say, what Jenyfer would do in her place.

But Lamorna was not brave. She was not defiant or wicked.

'Until the One God is satisfied,' the Chif said simply.

Lamorna shifted her eyes from the Chif's ruined face, lifted her skirts, and knelt.

CHAPTER 5

Arthur followed Melhala into the forest, Nimus Arbores
disappearing amongst the trees behind them. It was late
afternoon and the light was slinking away. Arthur glanced up;
branches criss-crossed above them, slices of a sky bleeding to indigo
visible through them. The air was warm, but a chill lingered beneath it, a
reminder that the season was turning. It would still be warm in Kernou,
the air humid, the breeze carried to them from the ocean damp and salt-
drenched.

'Keep up.' Melhala had been assigned as Arthur's magic tutor by the
High Priestess, and Arthur was glad. At least she was not a complete
stranger, even though he knew nothing about her. They hadn't had more
than a passing conversation since he and Jalen had arrived, but she had
been friendly.

Most people treated him with the type of reverence his father would
deem the One God worthy of. After that first night, with the High
Priestess on her knees before him, Arthur had wanted to run into the trees

and never come out. He had barely had a moment to process anything that had happened to him, anything that he had learnt since fleeing Kernou – now, he was following a Cruithean Magic Wielder through the forest to learn how to use a magic he could not even think about without feeling sick.

Katarin had told him to take the time to learn, to practise, while in Avalon, but he hadn't been able to even try and reach the thing that had lived for years beneath his skin, lurking there and not making itself known. Jalen had told him his magic had lain dormant on purpose. Arthur didn't know what to think about that. And then there was the prophecy, all those words that stole whatever future he might have made for himself. Another thing on his growing list of things he did not understand, that caused his belly to twist uncomfortably.

At least in Kernou he knew his place.

Here, he had no idea. A door inside him had been thrown wide open, but he was still too scared to step through it – in case he was not what everyone imagined him to be. In case he let them all down.

In case he failed.

Failure, he knew, had to be punished. His father's voice reminded him of that.

Up ahead, Melhala had stopped. She put her hands on her hips and nodded to herself, satisfied with something. They were in a clearing, the trees arching over the space, branches like a cage. Leaves littered the ground, which sloped gently, the clearing resembling a shallow dish. Birds chittered above Arthur's head, settling down for the night while, in the distance, an owl hooted, the sound soft, mournful.

'I wanted to come earlier, but I had students,' Melhala said apologetically, removing a flint stone from the belt at her waist. She spoke as she gathered leaves into a pile, adding small sticks and lighting a fire with a deft flick of her wrist. 'That's what I do – I teach others to use their magic. It doesn't matter which element it is. All magic comes from the same place.' She removed her dark brown cloak, folding it carefully before setting it on the ground. She unhooked the waterskin from her belt, removed her weapons, the blades of the daggers catching the slowly growing flames of her fire, and rested them beside the cloak. Then she straightened, turning to face Arthur.

'Coat off,' she ordered. 'You want freedom of movement. Your hands, Arthur, are about to become your new tools.'

He held out his hands, studying them. Scholar's hands, Jalen called them. Pale and slender. Arthur flexed his fingers, feeling what he now knew was magic shifting beneath his skin.

A fractured piece of memory floated behind his eyes. Golden light pouring from his hands, a whirlwind of dreadful power. His father, face down and bleeding. The Witchfinder, slammed into the wall.

Melhala came to stand before him, oblivious to his inner turmoil. She held out both hands, palms up, and instructed him to do the same. 'Imagine your magic as something alive, a seed, and your hands are the soil that feeds it. You're going to let that seed grow, Arthur. Like this.'

As he watched, a trickle of silvery-blue light emerged from the centre of Melhala's palms, like a sprouting bean searching for the sun. Reaching further, Melhala's magic grew, until it was as thick as the rope the fishermen used in Kernou, wrapping around her wrists and curling its way up her arms until it rested around her shoulders like some sort of pet. Arthur swallowed. His magic tingled in anticipation, as if it had a mind of its own.

'It will feel strange at first,' the Magic Wielder was saying. 'But you will get used to it. It is part of you and, while it can never run out, you can use too much too quickly. So I want to concentrate on teaching you to summon it when needed.'

'And if it isn't needed?' Arthur asked quickly.

A frown pressed against Melhala's brown face. 'Your magic is not something you can ignore, Arthur. I know what happened with the Witchfinder and your father,' she added before he could argue with her. 'But think of it this way – it's inside you. It is woven through your blood, your bones, the very core of your body. Yes, you could keep it trapped, but if you did that, you would eventually fall ill.'

'I would?'

She nodded. 'I have seen it before, with a man who had lost his wits. He lost the capacity to reach his magic, and … well, he died. His magic had lain dormant for too long.'

Arthur bit his lip. 'Alright,' he said softly.

'Then let's begin.'

For the next hour, he tried to reach his magic, to do what Melhala instructed, but every time he called it to the surface, it would go no further, wallowing beneath the confines of his skin, warm and soft. He could not coax it out. He could not force it out. His seedling magic would not take root.

Defeated, he dropped his hands. 'I can't.'

'You can. You're just afraid to,' the Cruithean said. She strode away from him to add some more sticks to the fire and collect the waterskin from the ground, taking a long drink before jamming the cap on and returning to Arthur. With a sigh, she sat, folding her long legs up so her knees could rest under her chin. 'Do you know why I'm a teacher?' she asked. 'Because I believe there is potential in everyone, that all anyone needs is the right person to believe in them so they can believe in themselves.' She paused and glanced at him. 'I believe in what you are going to do.'

Arthur's knees gave out and he dropped wearily to the ground, her kindly-meant words adding to the heaviness of the weight pressing down on him.

'You know about the missing Magic Wielders?' Melhala asked, passing over the waterskin. Arthur took a small drink, before passing it back and wiping his mouth with the back of his hand.

'Katarin mentioned it,' he said.

'It's been happening for years. Just a few people at first, and we didn't find out about it until Morgause's spies returned before winter.' Melhala's eyebrows lifted at the surprised look Arthur gave her. 'You didn't believe the High Priestess of Cruithea allowed herself and her people to be blind to what was going on in the rest of Teyath, did you?'

Arthur blushed. 'No, of course not.'

Melhala rubbed at her cheek. 'While the news was worrying, it was something that was happening a long way from here. The High Priestess' duty is to her people first, and we were safe. Who in their right mind would steal a Magic Wielder from under the noses of the Inborn?' She shook her head. 'But soon, people went missing from Cruithea as well. Children, at first, defenceless and unaware. They were taught not to wander, to stay together. For the first time in living memory, the forests were not safe for us. People were frightened, and Cruitheans are never frightened. It wasn't until the Inborn managed to capture a Witchfinder that we began to understand the scale of the disappearances.'

Arthur frowned. A memory tugged at him, a conversation heard from behind a closed door, his ear pressed against the timber. His father and the Konsel talking long into the night. Something about the Sacellum. He swallowed. 'They were being taken to Malist,' he said.

Melhala's eyes widened. 'Are you sure?'

'I only heard part of a conversation, but it makes sense, doesn't it?' Arthur thought of the Witchfinder they had left behind in Avalon. The man had crammed his lips closed the moment he was brought onboard *The Night Queen* and had not spoken a word, even when faced with the Goddess of Magic, who stared at him for a long time, before she snapped her fingers and he fell into a sleep he did not wake from. He had been cared for by the Priestesses after that. That had surprised Arthur. He had thought the Witchfinder would be killed on arrival, or tortured for information, and had been ashamed of himself for his thoughts.

But Cruithea was not Avalon.

'What will the High Priestess do?' he asked.

Melhala chewed on her bottom lip. 'I don't know. The Sacellum's power is growing, their influence is spreading. The voice of the One God slithers like a serpent, and is difficult to pin down or refute. I didn't know how we were supposed to fight that,' she said softly, then turned to him, her expression fierce, 'until you.'

The look she gave him was sympathetic. 'Your fears are normal. Fear is something we have learnt to live with here. But the Myrddin's prophecies are true, and *you* will see this world changed.'

Arthur took an unsteady breath. 'And if I can't do what everyone thinks I can?'

'You will,' Melhala assured him. 'But you have to get a handle on your magic first. So, let's try again.'

For another hour more, the Cruithean drove Arthur relentlessly through the same set of drills they had already practised and, by the end, he could manage to conjure a ball of golden light and hold it in his palm. Standing there beneath the trees, the sounds of the forest surrounding them, and his magic held in his hands, Arthur began to think that maybe, just maybe, he could do this.

Melhala slapped him on the shoulder; the golden light vanished. 'That's enough for now. We will continue tomorrow.'

He nodded. She extinguished the fire and they walked back to the village together without speaking, but Arthur didn't mind. Ethinne was waiting for them at the first of the kibitkas. She was dressed in her Priestess' dark green robes, her hair unbound and flowing over her shoulders. Melhala squeezed Arthur's arm and hurried to Ethinne's side. They embraced, Melhala's fingers curling around Ethinne's cheek gently before she leaned in and pressed a kiss to the other woman's mouth. They headed toward the square, not looking back to check if he was following. Arthur watched them go a moment, his heart warming at the sight.

The more time he spent in Cruithea, the more he relaxed, that part of him that he had been hiding for so many years overjoyed at the knowledge that there was no crime in loving Jalen here. There was no need to hide. Smiling, Arthur wandered between the tents, heading for the main square, wondering where Jalen might be. A few children joined him for a section of the walk, dancing around him, showing him little tricks with their magic. It was so natural for them that he felt a pang of remorse for what he had potentially lost. Had he grown up here, so free, maybe he would be different.

Melhala and Ethinne had already joined the crowd gathered in the square. It was evening meal time and the cooking fires were lit, the smell of stew floating through the air. Arthur was about to join them when a group of men arrived at the other side of the square. Arthur was unable to look away from them. The man who he supposed was their leader walked at the head of the group, striding confidently into the gathering. A few people came to speak with him before melting away again.

The man was tall, his bare arms decorated with swirling tattoos that flowed over the curl and swell of muscle. He wore his long, dusk-coloured hair in intricate braids, and they were bundled on top of his head, making him appear taller than he already was. He let his eyes move over the people assembled there, pausing when he came to Melhala. The look he gave her told Arthur there was bad blood between the two, leaving Arthur frowning. Melhala had been nothing but welcoming to him, and so incredibly patient that Arthur could not imagine anyone finding fault with her. She laughed often, and her smile was warm; she had a way of making him feel less of a failure and more of a novice, another of her students.

Arthur caught the arm of one of the children bouncing around his feet. 'Who are they?' he asked, indicating the group of men as subtly as he could.

The child, a boy around ten with hair like fire, looked at him like he was mad. 'That's the Inborn,' he whispered in awe. 'They've been away for ages,' he added, then raced off, straight towards the group of Cruithean warriors, who, Arthur realised, were all armed – axes, spears, daggers, and bows and arrows. The leader of the group snatched the child into his arms as he darted towards him, spinning him around before setting him down again with a laugh. The child gestured, and the warrior dropped to one knee, his face impassive as the child whispered to him, before he ran away with his friends.

Slowly, the man stood, looking across the square and meeting Arthur's eyes. He passed the quiver of arrows and the bow he was carrying to one of his men, then made his way towards Arthur, his stride long, dripping with the type of confidence Arthur could only dream of. The man stopped a few feet from Arthur, and it was like a strange sort of silence fell across the square. Arthur was being studied, and it made him squirm. Since his arrival in Cruithea, most people had looked at him with a strange sort of awe, with expectation. But this man looked at him like he was something he had stepped in with his very large feet and he hadn't decided if he needed to wash it off or not.

Arthur cleared his throat. 'I'm—'

'I know who you are,' the man said, his voice low, tinged with distrust. 'Are you your father's son, Arthur Tregarthen? Have you come to spread disunity and dissent?'

Arthur's heart paused, then surged so quickly it left an ache spearing through his chest. 'I'm nothing like my father,' he managed. His tongue was thick in his mouth, his throat dry.

'That will remain to be seen,' the man said simply. His eyes roamed Arthur's face, as if he was trying to see inside him. 'My mother thinks you're here to save us all, that you're part of some great prophecy.'

'Your mother?' Arthur stammered. His head was spinning. He could *feel* the power, the magic, rolling off the leader of the Inborn in waves. How did this man know the Chif of Kernou?

'The High Priestess.'

Arthur swallowed. 'Then, you're my family.'

'Am I?' the man mused. 'Family or not, you have to earn my trust, Arthur, son of Ulrian. I'm not like my mother.' He took a step closer. 'You will have to prove yourself to me. Igraine was my aunt and I loved her dearly. She was with child when she left us – carrying you.'

'I didn't know that,' Arthur murmured.

'I wonder what else you don't know,' the warrior said quietly. 'And Morgaine? She's still alive, I hear. Still risking herself out there on the water.'

'She is.'

The man nodded. 'And now, she risks herself for you.' He lowered his voice even more. 'Do you regret your birth, Arthur? After all, if not for you, Igraine would be alive. If not for your father and his poison, she would never have left.'

'I ...'

The man turned and left abruptly.

'That walking thundercloud is Mordred. He leads the Inborn, unfortunately for all of us,' Ethinne said, appearing at Arthur's side. She passed him a bowl of stew; he took it, even though his appetite had fled and his fingers were trembling. She frowned, taking in Arthur's blood-drained face. 'What did he say to you?'

'It doesn't matter,' Arthur muttered.

'Ignore him,' Melhala said, joining them. She scowled in Mordred's direction. 'He hates everyone and everything.'

'Unless you have something he wants, and then he'll do everything in his power – literally – to woo you to his side.' Ethinne's face darkened.

'Woo?' Melhala laughed. 'That's one way to put it, I suppose'

As the women argued playfully about Mordred, Arthur felt something jab into his head. He glanced up in time to watch Mordred, the Magic Wielding warrior, leader of Cruithea's Inborn, Arthur's cousin, as he stalked away from the cooking fires. Before he disappeared between two tents, he glanced over his shoulder. His eyes met Arthur's – a slow smile pulled at his lips, and then he was gone.

That evening, lying in Jalen's arms, Arthur could not sleep. He was twitchy, his skin prickling with unease as his magic squirmed inside him, as if now it had had a tiny taste of freedom and wanted out. But he still wasn't sure he should let it. His father's sternest expression was pressed behind his eyelids even as Melhala's dire warning about what happened if a wielder's magic was suppressed for too long.

Untangling himself from Jalen, Arthur sat up, rubbing at his face. The darkness was interrupted by the soft glow from their fire, and the kibitka was warm and cosy. It made Arthur's cheeks heat to think of the size of the kibitka he had been given – he had tried to refuse, but the High Priestess would not hear it; and so here he was, a nobody, sharing a tent with a demi-god in the wilderness of Cruithea, while the people around him believed he was their saviour.

Having such a thing tossed onto his shoulders was bad enough, but to be revered for something he hadn't even done yet? That was worse, and most mornings he wanted to bury himself under his blankets and never come out. Cruithea was where he had always longed to go, but to seek family, connection, that belonging that he had so sorely craved his whole life. He hadn't wanted *this* – whatever it was.

Careful not to wake Jalen, Arthur eased himself out of bed, padding across the floor – timber, not packed earth – to hold out his hands to the fire. A habit he had developed years ago, a way to hide his nerves, and his face, from his father when Ulrian's questions had ventured into places Arthur did not want to visit. Ulrian had hated it, not being able to see his son's face, and so Arthur had never stood facing the flames for long. The heat of his father's glare was worse than the burn from any fire.

That heat had been replaced by the stares of the Cruitheans.

Sometimes, he wasn't sure what was worse.

'Arthur?'

'Here,' Arthur murmured, listening as Jalen threw back the blankets and, moments later, joined him by the fire. He held out his hands like Arthur was doing, and Arthur smiled. 'Do demi-gods get cold?'

'No,' Jalen answered, leaning over to plant a kiss on Arthur's cheek. 'Come back to bed.'

'I can't sleep.' Arthur withdrew his hands from the warmth of the fire with a deep sigh. He could feel Jalen's eyes on him and normally, when he would cherish it, he wished Jalen wouldn't look at him.

'Arthur—'

'How can you have such faith in me?' Arthur blurted. 'How can you be so sure I can do what everyone thinks I can? Maybe they've all got it wrong. Maybe the Myrddin, whoever he is, is wrong.'

'Are we going to go over this whenever you can't do something perfectly the first time?' Jalen said softly. 'Magic takes work, Arthur. It takes years of practice and yes, you're being asked to learn something that many people spend a lifetime mastering, and you've been thrust into this new world without any warning. I wish I could have given you some.'

'Why didn't you?' Arthur demanded, suddenly angry. He was still rattled by his conversation with Mordred, the other man's words swimming around his head, burrowing beneath his skin and making him feel sick. 'You lied to me, Jalen.'

'I didn't lie,' the demi-god murmured. 'Not intentionally, anyway.'

Arthur laughed – a dark, horrible sound he had never heard leave his lips. 'If you have such faith in me, in what I'm supposed to become, you should have placed enough trust in me to tell me who and what you really were.'

'You think I didn't tell you because I didn't trust you?' Jalen asked incredulously.

Arthur nodded sullenly.

Jalen sighed, an exasperated sound that Arthur hated to hear, especially when he knew he was the cause of it. 'It has nothing to do with trust and everything to do with *time*. And everything has happened a lot faster than we intended,' he added, turning from the fire to sit on the end of the bed. 'I was supposed to have time to prepare you for this, but when Jenyfer summoned that syhren and was set to die … that wasn't supposed to happen.'

'Wait …' Arthur began. 'What does that have to do with anything?'

Jalen smiled. 'You saw her in your dreams for a reason, Arthur.'

'The prophecy,' Arthur gasped. 'She's one of the two, isn't she? A foot in the sea?'

Jalen said nothing, and that was all the confirmation Arthur needed. He didn't know Jenyfer well – they had spent time together as children, crammed into the prayer circle like everyone else, until Ulrian had decided Arthur should learn from him and not the Konsel; a pattern that was to repeat itself throughout Arthur's life. His father had kept him caged, kept him from making friends, from forming a connection with anyone other than the One God.

Jenyfer, Arthur remembered, had sat sullenly throughout the prayer circle, arms folded, or fingers tugging on a loose thread on her dress. He had always sensed that beneath the scowl was fear, so deep and dark it threatened to drown her. He knew this, because that fear had been his only friend, his companion through the long, dark hours imprisoned in his father's house.

And now, she was caught up in something outside of her control, as he was. He wondered if she knew, what she was feeling, and if she felt as lost as he did.

CHAPTER 6

The tavern in Carinya was dark and warm, clean, and mostly empty. It was mid-afternoon and most of the fishing boats were still out on the water, so it was also quiet. Only a few older men crowded the bar. They'd barely raised a bushy eyebrow when Katarin had dramatically flung open the main doors, waltzing inside with Jenyfer and Tahnet in tow.

Jenyfer and Tahnet sat at a table close to the door while Katarin casually made her way to the bar, one hand caressing the hilt of her cutlass as she went. Jenyfer noted the swagger, the sway in the Captain's hips that wasn't there on the ship. Katarin's face was different here as well, Jenyfer realised. Her expression was harder, fiercer, her eyes sparkling with a promise of violence if anyone crossed her.

A mask.

The Captain was a lot kinder than her reputation would have anyone believe. Kat cared about her crew. She always made sure everyone was fed and warm, and although she made them work hard, she gave the women on the ship a purpose, a sense of self. And Jenyfer knew they respected Katarin – she could see it in the way they looked at her, the way they spoke about their Captain when she wasn't around.

The women on *The Night Queen* were a family, and Katarin was the glue that kept them together. Jenyfer snuck a glance at Tahnet. She was one of the only humans among the crew. Most of the women Katarin rescued from around the continent would find refuge in places like Cruithea, or often on Avalon, where Jenyfer had heard they lived with the Priestesses.

Tahnet was a Magic Wielder, and Jenyfer had assumed she'd been pulled from a stake like the others, but something told her that wasn't the case. 'Tahnet,' she began. 'Can I ask you something?'

The blonde woman turned to her, smiling. 'Sure, Tidbit.'

'What happened for you to end up sailing with Katarin?' Jenyfer asked quietly. Then, when Tahnet's face closed, she hastened to add, 'Forget I asked.'

'It's fine,' Tahnet said, her voice low, sad. 'I was a healer and midwife to my village. A small place near Kunis, not even big enough to make it onto the maps. There was a man who beat his wife for not giving him children. I tended to her injuries and then, when I suggested that maybe the problem was not his wife but him, he ...' She paused, took a deep breath, and Jenyfer felt the blood drain from her face. 'He told my husband I had seduced him with my magic, and my husband, fool that he was, tried to murder me. He tossed my body into the water and Katarin found me, almost dead.'

'I'm sorry,' Jenyfer whispered, aghast.

Tahnet sighed. 'For a long time afterwards, I hated my magic. Because without it I'd have not been a healer, and I'd have never been in the position to open my mouth and almost die for it.'

'But it wasn't your fault,' Jenyfer said.

'No, but it didn't change how I felt.' Tahnet gave Jenyfer a curious look. 'Your magic is something else, though, Jenyfer. I can work herbs and heal and sometimes my intuition guides me to things that others can't find or see, but you?' She shook her head. 'Your power is so much more than that.'

Jenyfer fidgeted, dropping her eyes. 'It's a burden.'

'How so?' Tahnet asked gently.

Water beaded on Jenyfer's skin. 'I never knew what I was. All I knew was that there was something different about me. I could feel it, my magic, beneath my skin, pushing and pushing at me. I was always edgy. Unsettled. Sometimes irrational. Angry for no reason. My sister used to tell me to be calm.' She stopped, took a deep breath, her eyes flickering to Katarin, who was still at the bar. Jenyfer didn't want the Captain to know these things about her; she did not want Katarin to think she was weak in any way. 'Not long after I met Ordes, I asked him to teach me how to hide my magic so it would not ruin my life. He told me he couldn't, that it was part of me. I didn't understand what he meant, but I think I'm starting to.'

Even though she still had little idea what she was doing, since her swim from *The Excalibur* to *The Night Queen*, Jenyfer felt calmer, like that journey through the water had soothed something inside her, something she didn't know needed soothing. She was more aware of herself than ever before, more conscious of the thoughts and feelings that swirled through her. It didn't make them any easier to deal with, but at least she knew why she'd been so moody and quick to boil over with emotion her whole life – her magic had been trying to escape the cage her aunt had built around it.

She'd built herself a new cage, she knew that as well. The map on her skin tingled and she rubbed at her arms, pushing the feeling away. It was getting easier to do that as well – control what she was feeling – but sometimes she could not control the images that flashed into her mind without warning. The one that replayed itself more than the others was the way Ordes had looked as he lay sleeping the night she left. Peaceful. Content. *Happy*.

She'd shattered that peace. She knew it, instinctively.

Katarin returned to the table, plonking into a seat and crossing one leg over the other, tapping the toe of her boot against the table leg rhythmically. She didn't speak, watching the room, not hiding her scrutiny of the tavern and its occupants.

A girl bearing a wooden tray and three mugs appeared at Katarin's side. She placed each mug on the table and when she had gone Katarin picked up her drink.

Resting below it was a folded scrap of paper. Jenyfer's mouth shifted; Tahnet nudged her and shook her head, waiting as Katarin read the note, then slipped it into her pocket.

'The Sea Caves,' the Captain said simply. 'We'll go just before sunset.'

Tahnet nodded as Jenyfer picked up her mug with trembling fingers.

Katarin noticed. 'Scared, Little Morsel?'

'No,' Jenyfer said. 'Excited.' And she was. She loved being on the ship, but she needed something different, something else to shift her focus and keep her mind busy. She had been surprised when Katarin had asked her to come and help search for the Treasure. She'd argued against it, saying what was the point if she couldn't reach her magic? But, she'd also learnt there was no point in arguing with Katarin when she had made up her mind.

Katarin sat her mug down. 'Do you know anything about the Treasures of the Gods?'

'Just childhood stories,' Jenyfer admitted quietly.

'One of the Treasures is rumoured to be in one of the Sea Caves of Carinya, no doubt right at the back buried under a tonne of sand,' Katarin added with a sigh.

Jenyfer fiddled with her mug. 'And Niniane wants them?'

'They're necessary for Arthur's quest,' the Captain answered. 'He won't be able to find the Grail until the other Treasures are in his possession.'

Jenyfer had wondered how Katarin communicated with the Witch of the Mists, but hadn't asked her; she'd asked Tahnet instead, who revealed

Katarin and Niniane used a magic mirror. Jenyfer ached to see it. If something like that could reach across the realms, surely it might be able to show her Lamorna. At the moment, Jenyfer would settle for knowing Lamorna was safe, or even just alive.

They stayed in the tavern until it was nearing sunset. Katarin drained her second mug, pushed her chair back, and stood. Jenyfer and Tahnet did the same, Jenyfer noting that a lot of the tables were now occupied with fishermen and, she realised with a smile, women.

The Sea Caves of Carinya weren't far from the village and by the time they reached the far end of the beach the sun was hovering over the ocean, painting the ocean a burnished orange.

'The Caves are in the headland,' Katarin explained. 'I've been there a few times. They're actually rather beautiful. But we will need to be quick. We can't get caught in the Caves when the tide comes in. We can't all breathe underwater,' she added, and Jenyfer felt her cheeks heat.

She wasn't embarrassed by what she was, but she was embarrassed by her lack of understanding about her magic, even though she knew it was not her fault. She followed Katarin and Tahnet along the beach, the headland growing larger the closer they came, until it filled the space around them. They had to climb over a stack of rocks, slippery with sea spray and algae.

'Niniane thinks the Treasure is really here?' Tahnet asked Katarin as Jenyfer jumped from the rocks to join them on a stretch of pale sand. The Captain of *The Night Queen* put her hands on her hips, leaning forward to stretch her back.

'Yes,' she said, straightening. 'But she couldn't say exactly where, only that we should go to Carinya. And Aelle sensed we should be here as well. Come on.'

Kat led the way along the beach, the rocks scattered about haphazardly until the sand vanished and there was nothing but water-worn stone beneath their feet. The cliff towered above them, secluding the beach. Down here, with the water smashing against the rocks, the beach felt like a wild place, untouched by people. The water was a deep aquamarine, flecked orange with the sun, and as clear as a bed of crystals.

Katarin led the way to the first of the caves, the entrance nothing more than a slit in the side of the cliff. 'We won't have long,' she said. 'We need to be out—'

'Before the tide comes in, yes,' said a musical, male voice. Jenyfer spun around so quickly she almost lost her footing as Ordes and *The Excalibur's* boatswain, Iouen, hopped over the rocks and headed towards them. Iouen was grinning; Ordes' face was smooth, his expression carefully controlled.

'What are you doing here?' Kat shoved her hands on her hips. Jenyfer's breath caught and her stomach tightened, her heart pounding painfully. Part of her had forgotten how beautiful Ordes was and now, lit up by the setting sun, he glowed. She swallowed. Ordes' eyes flickered to hers, holding her gaze long enough for her belly to start burning and her lungs to tighten, before he shifted his attention to Katarin.

His lips curled in a challenging smirk. 'Sightseeing, obviously.'

Katarin narrowed her eyes. 'Treasure hunting?'

'Maybe.'

'What does Tymis want with them?' Kat demanded.

'Nothing. He thought my mother might like them, considering one of them is hers,' Ordes said casually, then, at Kat's quizzical look, 'Niniane. I think you've met.'

Katarin's jaw dropped. 'She's your *mother*? And you never told me!'

Ordes ran a hand over his face. 'I didn't know. Let's get this done, Kat, and then we can go our separate ways,' he added, avoiding Jenyfer's eyes this time. She didn't know what to say, what to do, what to think. A million words jumped to her tongue and away again. Now was not the time, she reasoned, so she put her back to him and followed Katarin into the cave, Tahnet close behind her. Sandwiched between the two women, with their weapons and their magic and their fierce strength, Jenyfer felt a bit better.

But nothing could protect her from the ferocity of her heart beat and the memory of what it felt like to touch him, to be touched by him. It was a set-back, nothing more. She had made the right decision. After this, she wouldn't have to see him again and she could get back to learning to move forward, like Aelle said.

Jenyfer's inner song moaned in protest. She rubbed at her chest.

It was dark inside the cave, but Katarin clicked her fingers and a sphere of light appeared above their heads. As Jenyfer's eyes adjusted, she saw that the waves had created patterns in the rocks – lines of green, and brown, and white, and black wove through the stone around them. Further in, the rocks changed, becoming deep pink and apricot hued.

Jenyfer tried not to gape, but she couldn't stop her mouth from dropping open. It was beautiful. She was vaguely aware of the others as she turned in circles, taking it all in. The mouth of the cave was a jagged slit behind them, the final rays of the sun poking through before they vanished. The roof of the cave was as high as the tallest tree Jenyfer had ever seen, and it glittered with tiny lights.

'What are they?' she asked no one in particular.

It was Iouen who answered. 'Insects. I have no idea why they glow like that.'

'They're beautiful,' Jenyfer whispered.

Iouen shrugged, then moved past her, heading deeper into the cave, following Katarin's magic light. Jenyfer swallowed and hurried after the rest of the group. She had no idea how big the cave was and didn't fancy being lost.

Katarin and Tahnet had reached the back of the cave and were looking around when Jenyfer caught up to them. The Captain ran her hands over the cave walls; her finger shimmered as she used her magic to try and locate the lost Treasure.

'Nothing,' she said. 'Let's try the next.'

The second cave was smaller than the first, but just as spectacular. The ceiling was lower and covered with the same glowing creatures. Jenyfer thought she could touch them, so she reached up her hand.

'Don't.' Ordes grabbed her wrist, pulling her hand away. 'They bite.'

'Oh.'

He released her, turning to the nearest pile of pink and cream rocks, running his hands, and his magic, over them. Jenyfer rubbed her wrist. He hadn't hurt her, but her flesh was burning where he had touched her.

'Nothing,' Katarin called, her voice rising from the darkness. 'Let's go.'

They followed Katarin back onto the beach. Tahnet gestured at the water.

'The tide is turning,' she announced.

'Okay, the last cave is the biggest,' Katarin said. 'We'll have to split up and be quick about it,' she added, eying the waves pushing eagerly at the sand and sliding over the rocks.

The final cave consisted of a large, cavernous space with several tunnels leading from it.

'Pick one,' Ordes ordered, heading for the closest one. The others nodded, hurrying off towards different tunnels. Jenyfer suddenly found herself alone. Taking a deep breath, she took the last tunnel. It was narrow and dripping with darkness, the walls close. Just as she felt panic begin to wrap around her, the tunnel ended, the sandy floor sloping upwards before opening into another cave.

Ordes was standing near the far wall, hands on his hips, a ball of silver light hanging over his head. Jenyfer cleared her throat; he spun around, his face freezing when he saw her. She ignored the way his eyes glowed with silver fire; she ignored the sweep of his shoulders and the length of hair that had escaped its binding to brush against his cheek; she ignored the fluid grace in his stance and the way his lips lifted gently at one corner.

Just like she ignored the realisation she saw flash across his face before the barely-there smile fell and he turned from her. Something hot and claw-like dug into Jenyfer's belly. She ignored that as well, not knowing what name to give the feeling and not liking the way it sat there like a hunched, accusing thing.

She dug at the sand with the toe of her boot.

'Did you find anything?' she asked quietly.

'Nothing.' He still wouldn't look at her.

She could hear the sea pushing against the rocks. Her magic tingled. She clenched and unclenched her fists as her stomach turned over.

Ordes' voice was firm in the darkness. 'We should go.'

She nodded, hurrying towards her tunnel, but his voice cut through the darkness.

'When did you know? That you were going to leave?'

Jenyfer froze, but did not turn around. She couldn't look at him. It would be so easy to lie to him, but something made her be honest instead. 'Not long after we returned from The Vale.'

When he spoke, his voice was low and angry. 'You knew for that long?'

'I'm sorry,' she whispered, aware how pitiful it sounded, how those two little words undid nothing. 'I tried to tell you, I did. I asked you to come with me, remember?'

Ordes scoffed. 'For a whole month, you let me believe you cared about me.'

'I did care – *do* care,' Jenyfer corrected, turning to face him. 'Ordes—'

He stared at her, face hard, eyes burning.

'I …' she faltered, took a deep breath, feeling her bottom lip tremble and suddenly everything she was feeling, everything she had felt, was clawing at her, sharp and vicious, and she knew she hadn't managed to push any of it away, hadn't moved forward one step. She was still in his cabin on *The Excalibur*, wrapped in his arms, her head against his chest. 'I didn't know if any of it was real!'

'Of course it was real!' Ordes shouted, making her wince and take a step back.

'How can you be sure? I'm not in control of my magic. How can you know what you felt for me was real and not a result of who I am – a fucking syhren who can't control herself?' Jenyfer was shouting as well, her song surging beneath her skin. It wasn't happy, her magic swirling around furiously, making her feel sick.

'Because I felt it – feel it,' Ordes said.

'I can't be what you want,' she managed, rubbing her eyes. She took a deep breath, then hurried into the darkness, her magic swirling, blood burning. She was ankle-deep in water before she realised it. 'Ordes,' she called, backing up quickly. 'The tide is coming in.' She indicated the water, which was rising swiftly.

'This way,' he said, pointing towards the tunnel he must have followed. Jenyfer ran across the sandy floor, only to hear him curse and step back, running into her and knocking her off balance. He reached out a hand to steady her as water rushed into the cave, closing over their ankles.

His sphere of light went out, plunging them into darkness.

'Ordes—'

'It's okay. It's just water.'

'It's rising fast.'

'You're a syhren, Jenyfer. It's not like you can drown.' His tone was biting.

'You said you can't drown, so what are you worried about?' she shot back as the water crept up their legs; he still had hold of her arm and her skin was on fire, the lines of the map flames on her flesh, her magic pulsing beneath the surface. She swallowed and pulled her arm free. 'Is there another way out?'

'No.'

Ordes held out his hands; silver light danced over his knuckles as the water around them pulled back a fraction. Jenyfer held her breath, waiting.

The water continued to rise, foaming white curling around their legs.

'Help me!' he snapped.

'How?' she cried.

'Use your magic, Jen.'

She threw up her hands uselessly. 'I don't know how!' Her voice bounced off the walls of the cave as the sea licked at their chests. 'Can't you do something? I was there with you, remember, when *The Excalibur* was attacked that day. I saw what you did!'

Ordes lowered his hands, the silver light fading. 'I can't hold back the tide, Jen.'

The ocean swirled and rushed around them; Jenyfer felt her feet leave the ground. Her song was purring away as salt water brushed against her flesh, teasing something to life. Ordes wasn't far from her, treading water.

Their eyes met.

'I can't get you out of my head,' he said quietly. 'I can't stop thinking about you. I can't eat, can't sleep. You're under my skin, and I can't dig you out. I'm not sure I want to. I'm not sure I can.'

Before Jenyfer could speak, the ocean surged up and swallowed them.

The moment she was submerged, her pulse jumped and instinct roared into life. She moved her hands, and the water responded, swirling around her. Something was tugging at her insides, the same way it had when she dove from *The Excalibur* and into the sea. She hung, suspended in the water, as something inside her urged her to take a breath, to fill her lungs with the magic of the sea, magic she knew, instinctively, was hers to use. She opened her mouth, and pulled the sea inside, feeling her lungs fill and expand. Her vision was crystal clear. There were scales on her fingers and forearms. Jenyfer examined them in her underwater world before realising Ordes was nowhere to be seen.

Panicked, she spun around, but there was nothing.

She closed her eyes, trying desperately to sense him, to lock onto his heartbeat.

Nothing.

Water foamed around her as she pushed herself to the surface, the roof of the cave inches from her head. Still no sign of Ordes. Jenyfer dove, scanning the darkness of the water, but all she could see was shifting sand and chopped sea-foam. She let the current move her and kicked her legs, shooting into the tunnel so quickly everything around her was a blur. She moved on instinct, ducking and weaving around rocks as the tunnel led her through the main cave, past the sharp teeth of rocks, and into the ocean. Jenyfer could hear music, could hear the song of the sea calling to her.

The power of the sea was in her fingertips, in her lungs, in the blood and bone of her as she sped like an arrow through the water, turning for the beach, rolling in with the waves to rise from the breakers. Katarin, Tahnet, and Iouen were on the sand, all dripping with water, their hair plastered to their scalps. They stared at her – Iouen's mouth dropped open.

'Where's Ordes?' Katarin asked frantically.

Without a word, Jenyfer turned and flung herself into the waves.

CHAPTER 7

O rdes was going to drown. Maybe. He'd been underwater for much longer than he ever had been and he hadn't died yet. Maybe his father was right.

Or maybe not. Spots began to dance in the corners of his eyes and his lungs felt like they were about to explode. His chest was burning. He fought the desperate desire, the instinct, to open his mouth and breathe. His shoulder stung, the burn of saltwater into an open wound. He'd hit the rocks when he was swept from the cave and into the ocean like a piece of debris, his magic useless against the true power of the ocean.

His vision started to fade, and his head spun. Blackness began her descent, death trailing her. Ordes' mouth opened, unable to deny his lungs what they wanted anymore.

Something shot towards him, moving much faster than anything natural. Ordes blinked, trying to see what it was, but his eyelids drooped as the sea rushed eagerly to fill his insides. A flash of silver, a head of dark hair, glimmering scales, and he was grabbed around the middle and pulled at an incredible speed through the water until he was lying on his back on the sand, gulping down air and blinking at the night sky, his shoulder and lungs screaming.

Someone rolled him onto his side, smashed their fist between his shoulder blades, and he vomited until his throat was burning and his eyes streaming. He tried to speak, but couldn't, his tongue thick, his mouth gritty with sand and salt. He was hauled to his feet; the tide was still creeping up the beach. Someone said something about a fire, and then Ordes was being dragged along the sand in the darkness.

'Jenyfer,' he managed to mumble.

'She's fine.' Katarin's voice. She was tucked against his side, his arm slung around her shoulders. He blinked; Iouen was on the other side.

'What—'

'The syhren saved your life,' Iouen said simply.

In the distance, further up the beach, the soft orange glow of a fire beckoned. Ordes' vision held out long enough for him to keep his eyes on the flames as he was lowered to the ground. The last thing he heard was Katarin saying they'd sleep the night on the beach, before he fell into blackness.

Ordes woke before dawn, rolling onto his side, blinking and rubbing at his face. The fire was out. On one side of the smoking coals lay Katarin and Tahnet, Iouen sprawled on the sand not far from them. Ordes sat up slowly, licking lips dry with salt. He patted his chest – he was dry, and covered in sand.

Jenyfer wasn't with them.

Groaning, he climbed to his feet, stretching aching and stiff muscles. Someone had dressed the wound on his shoulder; he touched it gingerly, wincing, then walked towards the ocean, watching the waves roll in, gentle and calm. He stopped where the waves left lacey foam on the shore, and just looked.

He'd nearly drowned.

His whole life on the water and the sea almost claimed him.

'Thinking of going for a swim?'

Jenyfer was perched on the nearest rock, bare-foot, her hair tumbling over her shoulders to be tugged by the wind. She wasn't looking at him; her attention was on the waves. Her skin shone in the grey-light of pre-dawn. Ordes could see the scales on her forearms.

'Seems I don't need to teach you to swim anymore. Have you been sitting here all night?'

'Just a few hours. How are you feeling?' she asked quietly.

'Like I've swallowed the ocean. My throat is on fire,' Ordes responded. He didn't draw closer to her, keeping a safe stretch of wet sand between them. The sea reached out to caress his bare toes.

Jenyfer glanced at him, and away again. 'Hot water and honey,' she said softly. 'My aunt was a healer, before she wasn't allowed to be. How's the shoulder?'

'It stings.' Water brushed against Ordes' ankles. He stepped back. 'You pulled me from the sea.'

'You sound surprised.'

'I am.'

Jenyfer snorted and shook her head.

'Can you blame me?' Ordes asked quietly. 'I don't know what you're feeling, Jenyfer.'

She spun around to face him, her eyes furious, and he took a hasty step back at the rage on her face. 'I'm angry, Ordes, and I'm allowed to be angry. I'm angry because I don't understand myself! My whole life has been a lie. Everyday something happens to remind me how little I know about the world, how unimportant I am. When you were asleep, everyone was talking about the Treasures and the Grail and magic and prophecies and places I've never heard of, let alone visited, and I ... that's why I'm here and not sleeping. Because I feel like a child who thinks they know something, only to realise they haven't got a clue.'

He was silent for a moment, then climbed onto the rocks to sit beside her, ignoring her glare. 'It's not your fault, Jen, for not knowing about the world.'

'I know,' she said. 'But I'm still angry about it.'

'And you're not unimportant, not to me,' he said. She didn't respond for a long moment, and he held his breath while watching the water lap at the rocks. 'Jen—'

'I don't want to hear it,' she said. 'Whatever you're about to say, I can't hear it. I don't want to talk about what happened between us, or anything really.'

'Alright,' he said. 'Am I allowed to say thank you? For saving me?'

'Call us even,' Jenyfer said, and he nodded. Slowly, light crept into the world, climbing over the land behind them, over the forest and the town, to slide across the sand and paint the world with colour. The ocean sparkled in those first rays, sunlight dancing off the tips of waves as a breeze tickled Ordes' cheeks.

Jenyfer sighed; a tight, almost painful sound. 'Ordes—'

Then Katarin was calling it was time to go, and Jenyfer's face closed up tight. She stood, giving him a guarded look before jumping from the rocks to land lightly on the sand. He watched her jog up the beach to where Kat and Tahnet were waiting. Katarin gave him a wave.

'Ordes,' she called. 'Glad you're not dead.'

He snorted, then turned back to watch the waves.

CHAPTER 8

Leaves trickled down in bursts, as if they had made a simultaneous decision to be free of the branch that held them. Arthur watched them fall, wishing his life could be as simple as that – live, die, start again, for the leaves would decay on the earth and become food for whatever came next.

Only he knew nothing was as simple as that.

In his hands he held a wooden practice sword. It was time for him to discover his warrior's heart, apparently. Apart from the moment with his father, Arthur had never hurt a thing in his life. He had never raised his fist in anger, or even his voice, until leaving Kernou. It had never been necessary. His life, his privilege, meant he had wanted for nothing.

Except his freedom.

Halymere stood a few feet away, a wooden sword similar to the one Arthur held between his large hands, where it looked like an absurd children's toy. The High Priestess had given Halymere this job. Halymere was one of the Inborn; Arthur wondered if he wished he was somewhere else right now, not standing in the forest with a man who wished *he* was somewhere else.

'Now,' Halymere began in his deep voice. 'You will learn how to hold the sword.'

An image flashed into Arthur's mind – the sword he had held in his dream with the Fisher Queen. He glanced down at his hands, adjusting his grip instinctively. The dream Arthur knew what he was doing, so maybe the real Arthur would know as well.

'Have you held a sword before?' Halymere asked, eyebrows lifted.

'Only in my sleep,' Arthur muttered, then, at the Cruithean's curious look. 'I have dreamt about a sword. And a battle on a barren, burning wasteland.'

Halymere nodded, as if such dreams were common things, and maybe they were, Arthur thought. The world of magic was quickly expanding, but Arthur's understanding of that world was struggling to keep up. Sometimes he wanted to rush through it, learn everything he could as quickly as he could, cram everything he needed to know into his brain and hope it all fell into place somehow. He knew, though, that he couldn't. If there was one thing he could take from his father, it was that patience was required to truly learn and absorb everything; only, Arthur had a feeling there wasn't time for patience.

'Then we shall begin,' the Cruithean said. 'No magic, just the sword.'

Arthur adjusted his grip again, copying Halymere, bringing the sword up and in front of him.

'Wrists loose,' Halymere instructed. 'Or you'll break them when I strike you.'

Arthur relaxed his grip, then his stance, on Halymere's order. When the Cruithean was satisfied Arthur was standing correctly, and his hold on the wooden sword was sufficient, he began guiding Arthur through a series of movements, slowly at first, then faster, until Arthur was sweating as he parried and thrust, dodged and side-stepped the Cruithean's strikes.

Halymere went slowly, gently, his tone one someone might use on a child learning to fight. Arthur blocked a blow, the force of it rattling his bones, making him wonder how he'd keep his feet in a real battle, how he'd have the strength to wield a real sword. Gritting his teeth, Arthur saw an opening and took it, lunging forward, only for his feet to be swept from beneath him, leaving him lying on his back blinking at the branches above him. Halymere offered his hand and Arthur let the man lift him to his feet, dusting off his backside and looking anywhere other than at the Cruithean.

'Again,' Halymere simply said, and they resumed their stances, working through movements and Arthur began to see a pattern to the other man's actions. Spotting another opportunity, he leapt on it, but when he slammed his sword against Halymere's, all his strength behind the blow, the Cruithean barely batted an eyelid. His arms did not shift and the force of the blow vibrated along the wooden sword and back into Arthur's own hands, travelling along his arms and into the muscles of his shoulders.

With a sigh, he let his sword drop.

'I can see we will have to work on building up those muscles of yours,' Halymere commented neutrally.

Arthur screwed his face up, then sighed, because Halymere was right – he was weak. He'd never done any physical work in his life. His hands were not warrior's hands. They were the hands of a man who could scribe the entirety of the day. They were the hands of a man who had spent his life in comfort.

But it was important that he could do this, if everyone was to be believed. If his dreams were to be believed. He glanced again at his hands, seeing not the hilt of a wooden practice weapon, but the decorative hilt and pommel of the dragon sword he held in his vision. He saw the burning wasteland again, smelt the smoke, and could feel a sense of dreadful urgency creeping up on him.

65

Melhala appeared in the corner of Arthur's vision. Arthur blushed, wondering how long she had been there. She shot Halymere a look; the man held up his hands and stepped away, and Melhala turned to Arthur.

'You will get better,' she assured him, reading his failure in his face. 'Just like you will learn to reach your magic.'

'Somehow, I don't believe you,' Arthur said, digging at the ground with the point of his sword, before he tossed the wooden weapon onto the leaves in disgust. He had been avoiding Melhala since the fourth failed magic lesson.

Another failure. It didn't matter how often he experienced the bitterness of defeat, it always left a sour taste on his tongue and his father's voice taunting him.

'If there is one thing I have noticed about people, it's this: we are too ready and willing to accept fault with ourselves,' Melhala said simply. She bent and scooped the wooden practice sword from the ground, weighing it in both hands, as if testing its reliability as a weapon. She flipped it in one hand, wrist moving like water, the blade of the wooden sword slicing the air with a dull hiss, before she smiled and held it out for him.

Arthur reached for it but, before Melhala released the sword to his grip, she looked Arthur in the eye. 'Do you believe you are the man your father always said you were?'

'I don't know,' he whispered. 'Sometimes.'

'That would be normal,' she said, keeping her voice low. 'But let me tell you something – no one determines a man's worth, except for the man himself. What you believe you are worth will be what you are worth, Arthur.'

Arthur stared at the sword in his hands. Around them, the forest was silent, as if it was waiting, listening, wondering what his response would be, wondering if he should say anything at all. Melhala was watching him, her shrewd brown eyes pinned to his face. Halymere waited at the edge of the clearing, allowing them their conversation.

A breeze skimmed the tops of the trees, shaking loose more leaves. A shower of red and gold and orange rained down around them for a moment, each leaf slowly pulled towards the earth, each battling with gravity until it couldn't any longer.

Arthur watched one come to rest on the ground near his boot. He swallowed. 'And what if you don't know how to be anything other than what you've been told?' he asked quietly.

Melhala shrugged. 'If everyone accepted what was said about them, there would be no heroes, no one doing great deeds in our world. You have two choices, Arthur – cling to your self-doubt, your fear, like the leaves on the branch, not letting go even though it is time to. Or, let yourself fall, let yourself be drawn into the next phase of your life, and be what you are supposed to be.'

Arthur licked his lips. He took a deep breath, fingers curling around the edges of the wooden sword. Slowly, he lifted his eyes, first to Melhala, then to Halymere, who was leaning against the trunk of a tree, his expression smooth. Both of these people wanted nothing more than to help Arthur achieve his potential, fulfil the role he was prophesied to fulfil, and unlock whatever cages he still had inside him. Arthur stood up a little straighter. He squared his shoulders, his eyes falling briefly to the leaves at his feet. In order to become what he was supposed to be, he needed to let go of what he was.

'Let's go again.'

That evening, Arthur was invited to dine with the High Priestess in her kibitka. When he entered, it was to find Mordred sitting at the table. His eyebrows lifted when he noticed Arthur lingering in the doorway.

'Since when did you feed strays, Mother?' he drawled.

Morgause narrowed her eyes. 'Enough. Arthur is—'

'I know what he is,' Mordred said simply. 'Or, I know what he is supposed to be. Does he look like the saviour of magic to you?'

'Looks can be deceiving, Mordred, you know this as well as anybody,' Morgause said firmly. 'Besides,' she said, her voice softening, 'Arthur is your cousin, and you will treat him with respect.'

Mordred turned his dark gaze on Arthur. He chuckled, then returned to his meal. 'Will I? My respect has to be earned. I will respect my *cousin* when he shows me he deserves it.'

'And what would you have him do to earn the high praises of Mordred?' his mother said sharply. She shook her head, turning to Arthur. 'Are you going to stand there, or are you going to join us?'

'I ...'

Mordred laughed, giving his mother a look, as if to say, '*See, what did I tell you?*'

Arthur cleared his throat and stepped into the kibitka, approaching the table, his courage faltering with every step. But he kept his chin lifted and his spine straight, reminding himself that he had been invited here by the High Priestess, not her son, who had not spared Arthur another glance.

'Thank you, High Priestess,' Arthur said, sitting down at the table. Morgause smiled.

'This is not a formal occasion, Arthur. You can call me Morgause,' she said. 'Or aunt, if it pleases you.'

Mordred dropped the chunk of meat he had been chewing, the bone clattering against the plate. 'I think I've lost my appetite,' he said, standing, but his mother slammed her hand on the table, making Arthur jump.

'Sit down,' she hissed at her son, who sighed but did as he was told. 'Whether you like it or not, Mordred, we are family. Arthur is family. We will not have this conversation again.'

'Whatever you say,' Mordred said, picking up his meat and resuming his meal.

Arthur shifted uncomfortably on his seat. There was a plate already prepared for him, full of roasted meat and vegetables, but like Mordred, Arthur had lost his appetite. His stomach was twisted into knots, and his muscles were so stiff he wondered when he'd snap and fall to the floor in a puddle of flesh and bone.

He snuck a glance at his cousin.

No. He wouldn't, Arthur decided. He would be strong.

'Thank you, aunt,' he said.

Morgause's lips twitched, but she said nothing. They finished their meal in silence and afterwards the High Priestess led him outside to sit by her fire. 'You will stay,' she demanded of her son; Mordred begrudgingly plonked himself on a short wooden stool across the flames from Arthur. 'You need to be part of this conversation, Mordred.'

'Do I?' he replied sullenly.

'You're my son, our warrior general, and the leader of our Inborn so yes, you need to stay, because what we need to discuss concerns you as well – you can sulk later,' Morgause said simply. She did not sit, choosing to stand close to the fire, her hands held out. At first, Arthur thought she was merely warming herself, but at her nod, he focused his gaze on the flames. Slowly, shapes began to form within the orange and yellow tongues.

A face.

Arthur swallowed.

His father.

'It looks good on him,' Mordred commented, and Arthur realised Morgause had not only rendered a vision of Ulrian, but she had included the terrible scar left on his face from Arthur's magic, which meant ...

'Is this real? Are we really seeing him as he is now?' Arthur asked.

She nodded, and when she waved her hand, the vision expanded, and they were watching Ulrian in his study, in the room where he had forced Arthur to open the flesh on his back in punishment. Arthur's eyes moved to where he knew the cabinet containing the whip lay, off to the side of Morgause's magical vision. Ulrian was sitting at his desk, a stack of papers in front of him. As they watched, Ulrian picked up the papers and shuffled through them, setting some aside.

Mordred was frowning. 'What is he doing?'

The question was directed at Arthur. 'I don't know. He had only begun teaching me about being Chif, but there was a lot he kept to himself,' he said. 'He has records of all the people he and the Konsel have ever accused of being Magic Wielders, and records of all the people they have gifted to the sea, or burnt. Katarin – Morgaine's – name is on one of the lists.'

Mordred ground his teeth.

'What about the Witchfinder?' Morgause asked.

'When I left he was still there but ... I don't know,' Arthur replied.

'The one Morgaine captured will be brought here,' Morgause announced. 'We can ask all our questions then.'

Mordred ran a large, tattooed hand over his face. 'You mean I shall ask him questions.'

Morgause nodded.

'And does the High Priestess of Cruithea wish for me to kill him?'

Arthur sucked in a breath at the casual mention of a man's death. Mordred's gaze slid to him. 'You didn't think we sat them down and had a polite chat, did you?'

'No,' Arthur said quietly.

'Does the idea of his death bother you?' Mordred asked. Arthur glanced at him, his cousin's face was painted with flickering flames and shadows. 'Would you like to know how many Sheletari I've killed, cousin?'

Before Arthur could respond, Morgause rested her hand on his shoulder. His father's face vanished from the flames. 'Do not regret their deaths, Arthur, for these are the same men who would see you, or any of us here, burn for their god. They would kill us simply for being what we are.'

'I hate irony,' Mordred muttered.

'I find it difficult to understand why they go against what they are,' the High Priestess mused.

'I don't,' Arthur replied quietly. Both Mordred and his mother looked at him curiously. 'Faith,' Arthur said. 'You do not know what belief in the One God does to a person. I have seen men I have known my whole life become something different, all for their faith. I have seen people turn on each other, accuse each other of being Magic Wielders, to gain favour with my father and therefore, the One God. Don't underestimate what someone is willing to do for a little power,' he added.

'Power is only as strong as the one who wields it,' Mordred said, flexing his fingers. Waves of deep golden light sprang to life on his knuckles, dancing up the length of his arm as the air around him swelled with magic.

'We have people across the continent, Arthur. Spies, if you want to call them so. We have only recently learnt that the Sheletari take those they capture to the Sacellum, and those people are never seen again,' Morgause said. She suddenly sounded much older and wearier than she appeared.

'They are,' Mordred cut in. His mother looked at him in surprise. 'You have your spies – I have my own,' he added with a shrug. Morgause looked like she would argue, but instead, she lifted her chin.

'And what do your spies have to tell you, son?'

Mordred's eyes glowed in the firelight. 'You would not recognise a single one of our people taken if you saw them again, for when they emerge from the Sacellum they are much changed,' he said. His gaze shifted to Arthur, then back to his mother. 'You want to know where all the Witchfinders are coming from? There is your answer.'

Morgause paled. 'It is confirmed then? They are using our own against us.'

'They are,' Mordred said. He met Arthur's gaze again. 'Perhaps when I see our people next, I shall ask them.'

'Ask them what?' Arthur said.

'What they're willing to do for a little power.'

CHAPTER 9

'It's *The Queen*!'

Panicked feet raced across the deck. Ordes rushed out of the galley, leaving his dinner and arriving on deck as *The Night Queen* surfaced from beneath the waves, water streaming from her hull. The sphere of magic that surrounded the ship dissolved as Tymis leant casually against the railing.

'Evening, Kat,' he sang as Ordes hurried to his father's side.

Katarin's eyes touched his briefly, before she turned her attention to his father. 'Permission to come aboard, Captain,' she called. Ordes snorted, then almost choked on it when Tymis straightened, and *smiled* at her.

'Permission granted.'

He could only watch in mute disbelief as Katarin returned the smile and climbed onto the railing. She lifted her arms and, much like Ordes did at times, stepped off, a wave rising to meet her and curl around her body. He did not take his eyes from her face as the water carried her across the narrow gap between the ships, depositing her over the side. She landed lightly and sketched Tymis a mock bow.

'So,' she said, hands on her hips as she cast her eyes around the ship; the crew were staring at her, eyes wide. 'This is how the other half live.'

Tymis motioned dramatically towards his cabin. 'Rum?'

'Yes please.'

Before Ordes could say anything, before any of the crew could say anything, another set of feet landed on the deck. Ordes knew who it was without having to look. He felt it in his blood, in the very marrow of him. He could almost smell her.

Tymis frowned. 'I'm not sure—'

Kat was smiling. 'Scared?'

Tymis folded his arms. 'I'm assuming you know what she is?'

'I know, and she'll behave herself, won't you, Little Morsel?' Kat threw over her shoulder.

Jenyfer nodded. She was dripping wet, hair plastered to her scalp and clothes clinging to every part of her. She squeezed the water out of her hair, keeping her eyes on Tymis. Ordes wasn't convinced Tymis had nothing to do with Jenyfer's decision to leave, so he watched, holding his breath, waiting for something, anything, to show on his father's face. Muttering, Tymis strode towards his cabin, barking at the crew to get back to work.

Katarin peeled away to follow him, tossing Ordes a wink. He swallowed and followed them. At the door, Kat turned, casually leaning against the doorway, a silent challenge in her eyes.

'What are you doing on my ship?' he demanded.

She raised her eyebrows. 'Your ship?' When he said nothing, she laughed softly. 'It seems *your ship* is happy for me to be here. She must know something you don't.' Kat smiled a slow smile and leant forward, lowering her voice to a whisper. 'Daddy dearest wants to see little old me.'

Ordes went to push past her, but she put her hand on his chest.

'Not you. This is for the Captain's ears only,' she added, then leant forward until her lips were almost touching the skin below his ear and her breath tickled the side of his neck. 'Do something about Jenyfer, will you? I'm tired of her moping.'

Katarin disappeared inside Tymis' cabin, slamming the door behind her as silence rang out across the deck and the last sliver of the sun dropped below the horizon, plunging the world into darkness.

Bare feet padded across the deck. Ordes could feel Jenyfer watching him, reading him, but he kept his eyes on his father's door. He could hear voices, but couldn't make out what Tymis and Katarin were talking about. 'What does she really want?'

Jenyfer said nothing.

Ordes bit his lip. That anger he'd felt for months was still there, begging to be let out, a swirling storm living beneath his skin. Even though she'd saved his life, Jenyfer had made it clear she didn't want him. 'Why are you here?'

She hesitated, and then decided to answer his first question instead. 'Katarin's passing on a message from Niniane.'

'What message?'

Jenyfer's sea-storm eyes walked his face. 'I don't know, Ordes. She doesn't tell me anything.' She shook her head, pushing past him, moving towards the ladder, the one that led below deck — to his cabin. Some of the crew scuttled out of her way. 'I need something to drink.'

Ordes followed her down into the lantern-lit passageway. 'Bad idea, bad, bad idea,' he said under his breath as she pushed open the door to his cabin and disappeared inside. He took a deep breath and went in, finding her perched on his bed.

'Where's the rum?' she asked.

'I haven't got any.'

'Oh. Sorry about getting your bed all wet,' she said.

Ordes bit his lip in utter frustration, then snapped his fingers and lit the lanterns, not wanting to be in the dark with her. He could feel Jenyfer's magic, could sense the power of it, swirling through the air around them, flowing over him like a wave, dark and beautiful and alive.

It swelled around her, shifting as she breathed, a cloud of silver mist that he could actually see.

A memory flashed into his mind – silvery-pale skin and scales, water. Jenyfer lifted her eyes to his while all he could hear was his heartbeat and the thundering of his blood in his ears. Ordes fidgeted, dropping his eyes, running his fingers over his tattooed knuckles. Jenyfer was still watching him so he made himself look at her.

'Did you really not know Niniane was your mother?' she asked.

'Yes. Tymis kept it from me.'

'Why?'

'Something to do with the bloody prophecy. My father is full of shit so I don't even know if that's true.' Ordes wanted to tell her what else he'd learnt about his father but didn't. That revelation was something he was struggling to deal with himself.

'If your mother is a goddess,' Jenyfer said softly, 'what does that make you?'

Ordes dragged his hand through his hair. 'I don't know,' he replied, like he didn't know how he was going to lay down in that bed and sleep later. Like he didn't know what the morning was going to bring, knowing he'd be waking alone.

After Tymis' revelation about the bow, going to Carinya had given Ordes a purpose; but that purpose had fractured around him the moment he and Iouen had climbed over those rocks and found Jenyfer staring at them, that curtain of dark hair billowing around her like it was alive. Ordes had barely been able to concentrate on what they were looking for, all thoughts of the bow or any Treasures washing out of his brain.

He'd wondered for days what Jenyfer was going to say to him when they were sitting side by side watching the ocean – before Kat called her away.

Jenyfer cleared her throat, hesitating for a moment before something he couldn't name flashed across her face. 'I've got to go.' She jumped up and headed for the door.

Ordes stepped in front of her, his body moving before his brain. Her breath caught, her features freezing. His fingers flexed and he couldn't help it any longer – he had to touch her. He trailed his fingers over the curve of her jaw and down her throat. He wondered if, for just a fraction of a moment, a heartbeat of one, she was remembering the last time they'd been in this cabin together.

'Do you regret it?'

'Every moment,' she replied.

Four syllables, two words, and everything melted away like it had never existed, all the anger, the pain, the layers of self-doubt and loathing. Jenyfer's eyes moved over his face, searching for something, some answer to a question she hadn't asked, as if she was trying to decide if it was worth asking.

'Jen,' he began.

She placed her hand on his chest, over his heart; her throat shifted as she swallowed but she didn't take her eyes off his face. Slowly, he stepped closer, her hand still on his chest. She could push him away if she wanted, but she didn't. She let her hand drop, let him slide his arms around her, the warm damp of her sinking through his clothing to brand his skin, one hand cupping the nape of her neck, the other on her lower back, pulling her into his body. He rested his forehead against hers, breathing her in, his insides a twisted, tormented mess, heat and longing raging through him with all the ferocity of an approaching storm.

'I miss you,' he found himself saying. Jenyfer pushed herself onto her tiptoes. Their mouths grazed against one another lightly. 'Do you have any idea what goes through my mind, all those times when I can't sleep?'

Jenyfer's breathing became short and sharp. 'What?'

Ordes shook his head. 'Not until I know what you're thinking right now.'

'I'm thinking I wish I could turn back time, take us back to the last moment we spent together.' Her voice was low, rough.

'And if we could turn back time?'

'But we can't, Ordes,' Jenyfer whispered, running the tip of her nose along his throat, her breath on his skin. He needed every layer between them to be ripped away. Needed to feel her fingers on his flesh until his body was boneless and torn to pieces.

'Why not?' he managed, throat tight. 'My bed is right there.' Colour danced across her cheeks at his words, and her chest heaved with the force of her breath. He brushed his lips against hers again, his fingers curling against her hip. 'I need to touch you.' Desperate words, but he didn't care. A tremble rippled through her.

'Then touch. Please.'

'Is that really what you want?' he asked, his fingers inching slowly over her ribs until he could brush the underside of her breast.

She pushed herself into his hand in response.

He ran his thumb over her nipple, felt it harden beneath his touch as goosebumps sprang to life along the back of his neck and his belly flooded with warmth. He could taste nothing but the saltwater of her skin. His blood boiled and he thought he'd burn until he was nothing but ash.

'Fingers or tongue, Jenyfer?'

Her eyes dropped closed. 'Both.' It was a breath, filling the space between them. Ordes fisted his hand in her hair and kissed her, his whole body sighing in relief at the touch of her lips, his other hand dropping between her legs as she rolled her hips against his fingers and pulled at his shirt; he broke away, stripped the shirt off, then claimed her mouth again, going under, drowning in her as she undid the buttons on his trousers and eased them down his hips.

Music floated through his brain as he slipped a hand beneath her shirt, closing his palm over her breast; she gasped and tipped her head back, exposing the column of her throat to his mouth. Ordes ran his tongue along her neck before closing his teeth over her earlobe. She shuddered, fingernails digging into his arse as she pulled him closer.

Someone pounded on the door; Jenyfer jumped. Her nails sliced his skin.

'We're leaving.' Katarin's voice smashed into the room. 'Sorry, Ordes,' she added cheekily, 'I'm sure you can finish things off yourself.'

Jenyfer cleared her throat, pushing him away gently. She fixed her clothes and ran her fingers over her face, smoothing her expression. 'I can't ... we can't do that again.'

'Jen—'

'No,' she said forcefully. Her eyes blazed, her mouth set in a thin line, her cheeks flushed. 'I shouldn't have done that. I can't risk hurting you, or any of the others. After what happened in Port Leore ...'

'Jenyfer, you were defending yourself,' Ordes argued.

'No, defending myself would have been punching him in the face. I made him *stab himself* in the gut,' she said fiercely. 'My magic doesn't work on Kat or the crew of *The Queen*. I'm not a danger there,' she added, flinging open the door and vanishing.

Ordes found his father in his cabin, sitting with leather-clad boots on the desk, a glass of rum dangling lazily from one tattooed hand. Ordes cast his eyes around the cabin, looking for evidence of ... what, he wasn't sure.

'You look dreadful.' Tymis poured a second glass of rum and slid it in Ordes' direction.

'Of course I look dreadful. My brain is going to explode. I'm part of your fucking prophecy, there's a bow somewhere in Teyath with my name on it, I wouldn't know Arthur Tregarthen if I fell over him, and Jenyfer—' He stopped abruptly, sinking into the seat opposite his father. Ordes snatched the glass from the table, tipping his head back and pouring it down his throat in one long gulp. He barely tasted it. Tymis was watching him closely.

'More rum?'

'Please.' Ordes held out his glass for another.

Tymis gave him an interested look. 'You like her, and I don't mean the way you like Katarin. Liked, I mean. Sorry, it's all very confusing, Ordes.'

'Fuck you,' Ordes said. 'This is all your fault.'

'Listen,' Tymis said firmly. 'Kat came bearing an invitation from Niniane. Your mother has invited you to Avalon. Katarin had no idea who you were to her mistress until someone recently opened their mouth.'

'I didn't realise it was such a secret. Or maybe it was, considering you never told me.' Ordes swirled his rum around the glass, watching the amber liquid shift like the tide. 'Should I go? I mean, is this because she wants to meet me, or is this something else?' He watched his father carefully, looking for the tiniest sign, but Tymis' face remained closed.

With a sigh, Ordes reached across the table for the bottle of rum, but his father did not release it from his tattooed fingers.

Their eyes met. 'When a goddess invites you to dinner, you don't refuse.'

'That isn't an answer,' Ordes shot back. He tugged on the bottle.

Tymis' face softened and he released the rum. 'Go and see your mother. Tell her …'

When his father didn't continue, Ordes prompted, 'Tell her what?'

'Nothing.'

CHAPTER 10

Jenyfer was sitting on a pile of cushions. Katarin was lounging beside her, casually examining her fingernails, legs crossed, one booted foot dangling in the air. Across from them sat the Goddess of Magic. Niniane's dark hair breathed with life about her shoulders and a faint glow came from her skin. Her eyes were as blue as the clearest summer sky and her lips as red as cherries. She was one of the most beautiful people Jenyfer had ever seen, like something from a dream.

The legendary island of Avalon didn't seem real, either; from the water surrounding it, which sparkled like jewels in the sunlight, to the fields of golden grass and the vibrant greens of the trees that grew right up to the edges of the castle. The courtyard they were in had grey stone columns, wound with ivy from floor to ceiling, and opened onto a sweeping balcony. Purple-peaked mountains were visible in the distance and, even though she couldn't see it, Jenyfer could smell the sea. She glanced at the scales on her wrists; if they didn't fade, the next time she went ashore she'd have to hide them beneath her sleeves.

Since Tamora's binding spell had been released, Jenyfer had felt nothing but a lack of total control. She wanted to be normal. Although, she had no idea what normal felt like, or what it looked like, not when Kernou had been her home. Whenever she was on the water her song pulled at her insides, and if she wasn't on the water, or near it, her magic swirled sullenly in her veins. Even now, on a magical island with water all around them, Jenyfer's song was crooning unhappily.

Niniane was watching her. There was nothing of Ordes in her face, except perhaps the shape of her eyes, and Jenyfer's thoughts shifted. Letting Ordes touch her had been a mistake, but being in his cabin where so much had happened between them, she'd been pulled towards him, like she had in Carinya, like she had ever since she met him. He was angry with her but he had still kissed her and told her he missed her. The truth was that she missed him as well.

Katarin was talking about the sea caves and their fruitless search. When she got to the part about Ordes' almost drowning and rescue, Niniane's bright blue eyes swung to Jenyfer.

'Leave us,' Niniane said quietly, cutting Katarin off mid-sentence. 'Please, Katarin, dear. I would like to speak with Jenyfer alone.'

Jenyfer cast the Captain an imploring look, but Katarin rose to her feet and dusted off her clothes. 'I'll find myself something to do then,' she said, and left without a backwards glance, her footsteps echoing off the glittering stone.

'You have many questions,' Niniane declared softly.

For a moment, Jenyfer's song flared to life, as if challenging her to ask what she already knew, as if challenging her to deny it. 'How do I use it? My magic?'

'Syhren magic is complicated. It isn't like mine, or my son's, or your aunt's. It's also very dangerous. Without someone to teach you how to use it …'

Jenyfer could guess what the Queen of the Isle left unsaid. 'Can you teach me?'

'I can't,' Niniane said softly. 'I know that's what you want, Jenyfer, but I can't help you.'

'What do you mean?' Jenyfer asked. A chill settled over her. 'You're the Queen of the Isle,' she added desperately. 'You're an Old One.'

'So is your father.'

'My father? My father was a fisherman.'

'No.'

Jenyfer felt her mouth run dry, and then flood with moisture; her heart stuttered and her palms grew sweaty as music suddenly tore through her body, so loud and powerful she could barely hear the next words Niniane spoke.

'Your father is the King of Lyonesse. The Master of Songs and Death, he who guards the passage to the Otherworld. The God of the Seas.'

Jenyfer opened her mouth, but nothing came out.

'Melodias fell in love with a human woman, and you are the product of that union,' Niniane went on. 'Your aunt's magic did more than keep yours contained – it kept you hidden from him; it must have been a powerful spell, to last so long,' Niniane added. 'But, she did the right thing. Melodias is fickle and selfish, and you are his only true offspring. Your aunt would have known he wouldn't have allowed you to remain in the human world with your mother, even though you are partly human.'

Jenyfer sucked in a breath. 'My father—'

Niniane's words were sharp. 'He cannot be trusted. The Old Ones cannot lie, but Melodias is skilled at bending the truth to suit himself. He is an expert manipulator. He will want your power, Jenyfer.'

'My power?' Jenyfer's laugh was shaky and she could feel hysteria bubbling up inside her. Her father was a god? She shook her head, her chuckle dying as inside, her song flared to life, an acknowledgement that what Niniane said was the truth.

'You know of the prophecy,' Niniane said, her tone soft. 'It was foretold that one with a foot on the land, one with a foot in the sea and one with a foot in both worlds would wield the Grail and reshape the world. Only then can the Once and Future King take his place and build the world anew.'

Jenyfer stared at her. 'Yes, but what has this got to do with me?'

Niniane's eyes locked with Jenyfer's. '*You* are part of the prophecy.'

Jenyfer automatically shook her head. 'You're wrong. You must be wrong. Things like this don't happen to people like me!'

Niniane's smile was amused. 'People like you? There aren't many people like you. You're the daughter of a God. Your power will help heal the land and shape the future.'

Jenyfer stared at her, aghast. 'I don't want this, whatever this is.'

'No one usually does,' Niniane said. 'But, it is as it should be.'

Jenyfer's fists clenched, a reflex action she didn't even think about. 'What do I do then? Just sit around and wait?'

'No, you learn, you grow. Come.' Niniane stood, indicating Jenyfer was to do the same.

'I need to know if my sister is alive,' Jenyfer said quickly. 'Ordes thought she'd been taken to Lyonesse. But I don't know where that is or where to start looking.'

Niniane moved towards a large circular structure covered with a cloth. It was a mirror, its surface reflecting nothing – the mirror the Goddess used to communicate with Kat, Jenyfer realised. She drifted nearer, the surface of the mirror swirled like mist and slowly, something took shape.

Lamorna, sitting at the kitchen table in the cottage in Kernou, a cup of tea between her fingers. Tamora appeared, placing her hand on Lamorna's shoulder, before moving away again.

'She's alive!' Jenyfer breathed. A weight lifted free of her shoulders. 'She's alive. I didn't send her to her death.'

'Your magic saved her, even when you had no idea what you were doing,' Niniane said softly. The vision of Lamorna faded as Niniane returned the cloth to the mirror.

'It doesn't make it any less terrifying,' Jenyfer said.

'I feel fear is an old friend of yours,' Niniane said softly. She glanced at Jenyfer over her shoulder.

Jenyfer could not argue; Kernou had taught her about fear, and anger and hatred, a worry so strong it was woven into her bones.

'You cannot hope to master your magic if you remain afraid of it,' Niniane continued.

'I don't know how to not be afraid of it,' Jenyfer replied. 'It has been a target on my back my whole life, enough to see me burn. They were going to burn me, or take me to Malist, until Ordes …'

'Pulled you from one life and into another. Do you wish he hadn't?'

'No,' Jenyfer answered. 'I don't.'

Niniane nodded and told Jenyfer to follow her. Jenyfer was led through a door with leaves and flowers engraved in the timber, and the hallway beyond was dark and cool, the air crisp and slightly sweet. More tapestries lined the walls but Jenyfer didn't look at them, keeping her eyes on the waterfall of Niniane's dark hair.

She chewed her fingernails as they walked. 'Katarin said Arthur needs the Treasures of the Gods. How do we find them? We've been looking but—'

'We will discuss these things later,' the Goddess said. 'Keep up. Avalon has its own rules. This castle can change shape, if it wishes. It is easy to get lost, but you will find the castle always leads you to where you need to be, eventually.'

Jenyfer quickened her pace. Niniane paused at the end of the hall, before another carved door. She pushed it open, gesturing for Jenyfer to enter. It was a lavish bedroom, and Jenyfer barely had time to look at anything before Niniane's voice echoed through the room.

'This will be your room while you are here, and you are welcome here, Jenyfer,' Niniane said. 'The Treasures need to be found before the Grail. One for Arthur, one for Ordes, and one for you.'

'Ordes?'

'Yes.'

'Does he know this?'

'Perhaps,' Niniane answered.

'You've never met him, have you?' she asked, watching Niniane's face carefully. She wasn't sure why, but she needed to know how this woman felt about the child she had been apart from his whole life.

'No. Tell me what he's like,' the Goddess asked, though it sounded more like a commandment. She wandered out onto the balcony, the hem of her white gown trailing along the ground behind her.

Jenyfer did not join her, choosing instead to lean in the doorway. In the distance, mountains scraped the clouds. 'He's ...' she paused, trying to think of the right words. Her thoughts tumbled over each other furiously. 'He's a good person,' she said eventually; Niniane glanced at her over her slim shoulder. 'He's kind and he cares about people,' Jenyfer added. *And I ran away from him.*

'Thank you,' Niniane told her. 'I'm glad to know that. It was not easy to let him go.'

'Why did you?' Jenyfer blurted.

Niniane came back into the room, pausing for a moment to lay her hand on Jenyfer's arm. 'He was better off with his father,' she said. 'Everything I've told you is a lot to take in, Jenyfer, but you have time to come to terms with it. This is an island – we are surrounded by water. There is no safer place for you to explore your magic. The magic that ties you to the natural world, the type of power all Magic Wielders have – is intuitive. Trust it. Let it guide you.'

All Jenyfer could do was nod numbly.

It was too much.

Her father was a *god*.

Her brain, usually so active, so brimming with thoughts, felt oddly empty. She couldn't find the words, any words. Her whole body felt hollowed out and brittle, and she was so tired all of a sudden. Niniane told her to rest, and then left. Jenyfer stared out at the mountains, watching black birds swoop through the clouds. She wrapped her arms around herself as any control she thought she had over her life was swept away from her – again.

CHAPTER 11

Everyone was gathered in the main square. Lamorna stood with her aunt. She had wanted to be at the front of the crowd, where she would usually have stood, but something in her stomach had twisted at the idea, so she found herself lingering towards the back. It did not stop people from turning to glance at her over their shoulders, even though it had been … weeks? Months? She could not remember how long it had been since she'd washed up on the beach like a piece of driftwood. She swallowed, but did not drop her eyes.

No one knew what the meeting was for. A wooden stage had been constructed in the middle of the square, directly beneath the cross of the One God. On the stage stood the Konsel, the men stern and severe in their dark cloaks, the gold chains around their necks gleaming in the bright sunlight. The sky was free of clouds and behind them the sea pushed against the sand, gentle and calm today. Lamorna closed her ears to the swell and breath of the water and focused on the Konsel as the Chif, wearing a deep red coat, strode onto the stage.

Ulrian Tregarthen turned his ruined face to the assembled crowd. He raised his hands, and the murmurs fell silent.

'My friends. We need to root out the evil that is heresy. We need to ensure our town, indeed all of Teyath, is safe from the deceptive hold of magic. This is the task the One God has set for us. He sees Kernou and He hears your prayers, and He has chosen us for this task.' Ulrian paused, his eyes sweeping over the faithful of Kernou. 'I have had word from the Sacellum in Malist – we have been granted permission to establish an arm of the Red Hand of God here in Kernou.'

Beside her, Lamorna sensed her aunt stiffen. She kept her attention on the Chif.

'The brave men of the Red Hand will be who you turn to in the darkest hours, and there will be darkness to come, friends. The heathen practices of the Old Ways have been slow to die. We, the Konsel, know this. We know there are those who still believe in the deep darkness of the pagan faith. But now, with the Sacellum behind us and the blessing of the One God, whose work we do here, we shall prevail. Light shall banish the Darkness.'

A cheer rippled through the crowd. Lamorna's back was aching but she did not shift her weight, nor did she reach up to wipe the sweat from the back of her neck as the sun beat down on her head. She stared straight ahead, as the Chif began to announce those privileged enough to be chosen by the Konsel for the Red Hand of God.

Her head jerked as Bryn's name was called, and she watched with a strange feeling in her stomach as he approached the Chif, his head lifted proudly. She watched as he was helped into a red coat, as deep as blood, then was handed a shining dagger and a fresh copy of the Decalogue, beautifully bound in the best leather.

Lamorna thought about her battered copy, resting on her bedside table.

Bryn's face was shining with pride, caught up in the glory of what he'd been given; he met Lamorna's gaze. Colour washed over his cheeks briefly, and then vanished as the Chif clapped a large hand on his shoulder.

'The Red Hand shall protect our town from the evil of magic. They will be trained to hunt and dispose of those who wield magic, those who refuse to hear the Word of the One God. They are an extension of the Warriors of the Light, that noble arm of the Sacellum. Perhaps, some of them shall leave here and join the Warriors in their great work,' the Chif said loudly.

Lamorna watched Bryn, wondering what he was thinking.

Was he thinking about Jenyfer, like Lamorna was? Her sister's face pressed into her mind. She swallowed.

Jenyfer was a Magic Wielder. The enemy. And Bryn had been given permission to hunt down her kind and drag them into the Light to face the One God's judgement. Lamorna listened as the Chif explained anyone accused of wielding magic would be given the opportunity to atone, to pledge themselves to the One God, to undergo a series of trials to prove their faithfulness.

Lamorna's knees ached, the scars screaming. The glass in her mind glittered with nasty promises.

Bryn was one of five men, all young, all strong. Did he have it in him? She wondered suddenly. Could he really put the torch to the pyre? Could he stand back and watch a person Burn for what they were? Make them kneel for hours on shattered glass while their knees wept blood?

In the sunlight, Bryn's eyes glowed.

Yes, Lamorna realised, recalling the look on his face when he last spoke about Jenyfer.

He could.

'It's despicable,' Tamora raged when she and Lamorna were in the safety of the cottage and the front door was firmly shut. 'The Red Hand, here. What is happening to this place?'

Lamorna rested her hands on the back of a chair to steady herself. Her head was spinning. 'Will they find her?'

'Who?' her aunt asked sharply.

'Jenyfer,' Lamorna replied, her voice nothing but a whisper.

Tamora sank into a chair with a sigh. 'No.'

'Where is she?'

Tamora glanced out the window. 'Far away from here. I hope,' she added quietly.

'Where?' Lamorna pressed. 'Bryn says he saw her in Port Leore.'

'What?' Tamora's eyes were wide. 'When?'

'She killed Alric,' Lamorna said simply. Her aunt paled. 'She did something, with her magic, and she made him stab himself and now he's dead. How could she do that?'

Tamora shook her head. 'You weren't there, so don't judge,' she said.

'But—'

'You can't know what things were like for her, Lamorna,' Tamora said softly. 'It's different for me – don't look at me like that, please, you know what I am – because my magic is not the same as hers.'

'How?' Lamorna asked. She pulled her chair away from the table and sat down slowly, keeping her eyes on her aunt, who was watching her with suspicion. Lamorna felt the sting of it, and then pushed it away. 'I want to understand.'

Tamora drummed her fingers on the tabletop and sighed. 'Jenyfer is your sister,' she began. 'But Jenyfer is …'

'What?' Lamorna asked. 'What is she?'

Tamora's face became guarded and her lips pressed together. 'It doesn't matter. She's your sister, and that's all you need to know. Despite what disagreements you may have had, she loves you and only wanted to protect you – and she could not hide what she was any longer.'

'I wish I could have seen her,' Lamorna said. She dropped her gaze to her hands, clasped tightly on the tabletop, as if she was praying. Her aunt said nothing, though Lamorna could feel Tamora's eyes on her. 'I don't know what to feel,' she said. 'Or think.'

'What about?' Tamora's voice was gentle.

'Jenyfer.' Lamorna sighed, unclasping her hands and rubbing her eyes so hard her vision blurred. 'She's a Magic Wielder, an enemy of the One God, but she's my sister and I do love her.' She looked at her aunt; Tamora's face was carefully composed. 'I'm glad she isn't dead. Bryn told me the Witchfinder was going to take her away. I'm glad she escaped.'

Tamora's eyes crawled over her face. 'You are?'

'Yes.' Lamorna swallowed. 'Yes, I am.'

Firm knocking on the front door made both women jump. Lamorna wiped at her face while her aunt rose to greet whoever was at their door. Tamora returned with Bryn. Lamorna looked at him curiously, then at her aunt. The lurid red of Bryn's coat sucked all the light into it, so the material glowed and it appeared, for a moment, that his head was haloed in gold. Lamorna bit her lip, not wanting to think about what it meant. It was a trick of the light, she told herself. It didn't mean anything else.

She rose, inclining her head in Bryn's direction.

'I looked for you after the meeting,' he said. 'I had hoped you would be there to congratulate me, Lamorna.'

'I …'

'Lamorna was not feeling well,' Tamora cut in smoothly. 'So I took her home. I hope that was alright. I believed the ceremony was finished.'

Bryn's smile was tight. 'It was, yes. There is no sin, Ms Rosevear, rest assured.'

Lamorna frowned, and then rearranged her face before he could see. Bryn had never, as far as she knew, called her aunt by such a formal title. He had been coming to their cottage since he was a small child, when he and Jenyfer would run off into the world and leave Lamorna at home, the little sister who was not old enough to join in their games.

The Bryn who stood before them now had definitely grown out of childhood games. His expression was proud, carefully schooled, like the faces of the Konsel whenever they stood behind the Chif during an announcement, or the way they stood at the back of the room during prayer circle, eyes and ears everywhere.

Lamorna made herself smile. 'I'm sorry, Bryn,' she said. 'I should have stayed and congratulated you. Are you pleased?'

'It doesn't matter if I am pleased or not,' he said importantly. 'It only matters that this is what the One God has chosen for me.'

'He sees your worth,' Lamorna said, resuming her seat, her knees suddenly unable to hold her upright. A spasm crossed Bryn's face. He had not given her leave to sit, but he was still unsure of himself, unsure of this new role he inhabited. Lamorna knew the rules better than he did. She smiled again. 'I get tired easily, ever since …' She swallowed dramatically, and looked away. Inside, her heart was pounding with the words she had shared with her aunt and she had some terrible notion that Bryn could read those words on her face. 'I'm sorry.'

Bryn took a seat opposite her, while Tamora offered tea and biscuits. He began to shake his head and then changed his mind, as if just realising what this new position gave him – privilege, and more than he had before. Jenyfer used to complain that Bryn couldn't see the privilege he had simply for being born a man in this place.

But looking at him now, at his expression, at the way he sat back and let Tamora wait on him, Lamorna knew that this Bryn, the Bryn of the Red Hand, was very aware of his privilege and she suspected he had been for a lot longer than Jenyfer knew. What Jenyfer and Bryn had not known was that Lamorna watched them and, while she was no expert of how things were between men and women, she knew from the look on Bryn's face whenever he was around Jenyfer that he liked her. That he wanted more. And Jenyfer had not realised it.

Lamorna had not given herself leave to think about the role she had played in what had happened to Jenyfer. She had thought that she was doing the right thing, that it was what her sister did want, deep down – a man to love and protect her, a house to care for, and, later, children. She thought that was what Jenyfer had wanted because deep down, she knew it was what she wanted.

Becoming a Sister was a way to avoid the truth that no one would ever look at her the way Bryn had looked at Jenyfer.

Lamorna was not likeable, she knew that as well. There had been a lot of time to think when she was ... wherever she was, surrounded by music and darkness and water. There had been a lot of time for her to consider things.

They did not speak while Bryn ate his biscuits and drank his tea, and when he stood Lamorna stood also, walked with him to the door, but she did not go any further. Bryn gave her a little smile, then smoothed his face clear of emotion, running his hands over his new red coat gently.

'Don't forget the prayer circle,' he said sternly, and Lamorna wanted to remind him that she never forgot and ask why he felt he needed to mention it, but she only nodded and kept her eyes lowered. When she heard him close the gate, she hurried inside and locked the door.

Tamora was waiting for her in the kitchen. 'What did he really want?'

'I don't know,' Lamorna said.

'He's been coming here a lot, Lamorna,' her aunt said, a hint of worry in her voice. Lamorna looked at her, forcing herself to ignore the squirming in her belly. Tamora sighed, running a pale hand over her face. 'Either he has some interest in you, now that Jenyfer is gone, or ...'

Lamorna swallowed, fear leaving her unable to speak; that evening, she pretended to be ill and did not attend the prayer circle.

Chapter 12

The water was licked with mist, the waves rolling gently against the sand. Jenyfer let the water brush over her toes, her song flaring to life, music floating through her brain. She stripped off her clothes and dumped them on the sand, then took a deep breath and walked out into the ocean, the mountains of Avalon rising behind her.

She shivered as her skin tingled and scales flecked her arms and thighs. How had her mother, an ordinary girl from a fishing town, even met a god, let alone bore one a child? It had to be a mistake. Surely if her father was a god he'd know of her existence, but Niniane had said Tamora's spell kept Jenyfer hidden.

Until it didn't anymore.

Jenyfer thought about the syhren she had met in The Vale, the one who had tried to drown her. But what if that hadn't been the syhrens intent? There had been something in the sea faery's eyes that night, and Jenyfer had sung with her, her voice drawn from her throat without consent, without thought.

Jenyfer waded deeper, until the water was curled around her chest. It was early morning, not long after dawn. The water should have been cold, but to her, it was blood-warm and soothing. She took another deep breath, and slipped beneath the surface.

Like when she was underwater in the sea caves, her mouth opened and her lungs filled with liquid. There was a moment where she froze in terror, but then it was gone, and she was weightless, free, part of the water. Jenyfer swam slowly; without the urgency of her last underwater moment, she had the chance to truly see what lay beneath.

Everything was diffused light, blue and green and golden. Rocks on the ocean floor were dark silhouettes. Jenyfer swooped towards them, startling a school of brightly coloured fish. Some shot away, but others were slower, lazy in their escape, and she marvelled at their scales and tiny fins, their ease of movement through the water. There were corals, so intricate and delicate in their design that they did not look real. Each section was completely unlike the other. An octopus peeked out from between two rocks, slinking away as she swam by. A forest of kelp rose in ribbons of browns and greens. Swimming between them Jenyfer found seahorses, and beyond the kelp, the open ocean.

Weak sunlight left the ocean bed glittering like jewels, reflecting off the shells and fragments of crystals that were scattered over the sand. Something curled itself around Jenyfer's ankle as she let her feet touch the sand. Another octopus, this one not frightened of her. The creature crawled its way up her leg, making her laugh, bubbles exploding from her lips. Gently, she prised it free of her skin and it shot off, moving faster than she had imagined it could.

Further out, something moved. Curious, Jenyfer walked along the ocean floor as easily as she could walk on land. Seals, three of them. She stopped, not wanting to scare them, watching as they twirled and spun through the water. There was a simple joy in their movements that made her heart soar.

It was like a dream world beneath the water, one she wasn't sure she wanted to leave, but she didn't know how long she could stay under without air. Using the seafloor as a springboard, Jenyfer shot for the glimmering light above her, surfacing without a splash. She took a breath, felt her lungs expand with air, then headed for the shore.

Katarin was waiting on the sand. She didn't say anything as Jenyfer squeezed the water from her hair and pulled her clothes on. Once Jenyfer was dressed, Katarin tossed something at her.

It was a dagger; the blade embedded itself in the sand at Jenyfer's feet. A second one landed near the first. Katarin stood, dusting her backside free of sand, and drew the blade at her hip.

'Ummm,' Jenyfer began.

Kat nodded at the daggers. 'Pick them up. I'm going to teach you how to use these things. Yes, I know someone would have probably tried already, but the thing about Ordes is he can't do two things at once; not very well anyway.'

Jenyfer pulled the dagger free of the sand. 'What do you mean?'

'I'm sure he showed you how to stab things, but I'm going to teach you how to use your magic *and* a dagger, together,' Katarin announced. She flipped the dagger she was holding; it tumbled over itself, heading towards the ground, when a stream of water suddenly snapped across the beach and curled itself around the handle. Slowly, the dagger was lifted up, until it was level with Katarin's hip, the blade pointing towards the sky.

Jenyfer's jaw dropped. 'No, he did not show me that.'

Kat's answering grin was smug. 'Sometimes, you need more than two hands, Jenyfer.'

'Before we start,' Jenyfer said quickly. 'You should probably know, I managed to stab Ordes. Not on purpose,' she added, as Katarin burst out laughing.

Kat wiped her eyes. The stream of water wielding the dagger was still waiting patiently. 'Do what I did – call the water to you and shape it into something you can use. Think of a hand maybe, or a rope, anything that can grip the hilt of your blade.'

Jenyfer nodded. There was no asking how this time. She did what Niniane had told her to do – used her instincts. A stream of water coiled from the ocean and crept across the sand towards her. It rose and hovered near her ankles, but she needed it higher. *Climb*, she thought. The water leapt upwards; Jenyfer held out her arm and it wove its way around her like a snake, the same way she had seen Ordes do it on *The Excalibur*. She grinned.

'Let it go and do it again,' Katarin commanded, and Jenyfer repeated the action, positioning her stream of water at different heights, Kat barking orders at her. When she was satisfied, Katarin told her to offer the water her dagger.

'Holding it is one thing – using it is another,' she said.

'You're going to make me fight you, aren't you?' Jenyfer guessed.

'Of course.'

Like Katarin had done, Jenyfer tossed one of her daggers into the air, watching it tumble blade over hilt towards the sand. At her thought, the water shot forward and snatched the dagger from the air, curling around the hilt like a hand. She realised she could feel it. The water was an extension of her. Her fingers flexed and the water tightened its grip on the dagger as she tightened her grip on the other.

'Good,' Kat murmured, moving one hand in the air in front of her. A shield of water appeared there. She held it there, and with her other hand, pulled a second dagger from her belt. 'Now, let's see what Ordes managed to teach you before you stabbed him.'

'Where is everyone?' Jenyfer asked. She and Kat were sitting facing the ocean. Four daggers lay on the sand before them. Jenyfer had a slight headache and her blood was buzzing, but her magic felt strong, capable, for the first time ever. She had done more with it this session with Kat than she ever had before.

'On the ship,' Katarin answered. She passed Jenyfer the waterskin she had brought. 'The island makes them nervous. Niniane makes them nervous.'

'I can understand that,' Jenyfer mumbled, taking a sip and passing the water back.

'What did she say to you yesterday?' Katarin asked.

Jenyfer chewed her lip, wondering how much she should reveal. She decided quickly that the information about Melodias would remain locked away, for now, until she could work out what it meant. 'It's almost too crazy to be true,' she said. 'She told me I'm part of this prophecy – Arthur's prophecy – and one of the Treasures of the gods is mine to find.'

Kat was silent for a while, her eyes on the water. 'Did she say which Treasure?'

'No,' Jenyfer answered. 'You believe it's true?'

'If Niniane said it, then it's true, Jenyfer.'

Jenyfer rubbed at the scales on her wrist. Waves lapped gently at the shoreline, sunlight bouncing off their peaks.

'The third person?' Kat asked.

'Ordes.'

Kat sighed. 'Of course it is.'

'You truly believe Arthur is going to be a king? He's so ... shy and quiet. He never did the wrong thing,' Jenyfer said, thinking back to the last moments she had seen Arthur Tregarthen. He had been walking across the town square while she'd been locked in that cage. Arthur had stopped, caught her eyes, then turned away. She had no idea where he went after that, and she never saw him, or anyone, after that night.

'He did,' Katarin replied. 'Just no one knew about it.'

The whip marks on Bryn's back flashed into Jenyfer's mind, and with it, a renewed hatred for Ulrian Tregarthen. 'So, what do we do now?'

'We can stay here a bit longer,' Kat answered. Then, 'You learn fast.'

'But I've got lots to learn, right?' Jenyfer quipped, a smile pulling at her mouth.

'We've all got lots to learn,' Kat said. 'The Priestesses here – they never stop learning. They are always studying, gathering knowledge and practising magic. They believe that the moment you think you've mastered something is the moment you realise you know nothing.'

'I wish someone could teach me about syhren magic,' Jenyfer said quietly.

Katarin stood, scooping the daggers from the sand. 'Come on. I'll take you to the library.'

'There's a library?'

Kat laughed. 'Of course. Have you never seen a library?'

Jenyfer climbed to her feet, brushing sand from her clothes. 'No. We didn't have one. We didn't even have books, except for the Decalogue.'

'Well,' Kat said, 'you're in for a treat.'

Jenyfer followed Katarin back to the castle in silence, but it was a companionable one. This was the most time she had spent with the Captain without anyone else present. Katarin still frightened her, but not as much as before. She was different in Avalon – quieter, softer, the mask gone. Jenyfer felt she was seeing the real Katarin Le Fey, and she liked her. Kat's care for Arthur, the brother she had never known, was proof there was much more to the notorious pirate than anyone realised. Jenyfer knew the story – Tahnet had told her one night – and Katarin could have easily hated Arthur, but she didn't. She supported him, and she had faith in the person he was meant to become.

They passed a few of Avalon's Priestesses on the way to the library, which was at the top of a flight of never-ending stairs in the southern tower of the castle. Katarin led her down a wide hall decorated with more lifelike tapestries, these ones depicting forest scenes, before pushing open a heavy timber door with a dramatic flourish.

Rows upon rows of books greeted them. The shelves stretched high above Jenyfer's head and the library was lit by orbs of softly glowing light, floating above their heads. One followed them as they made their way into the room. There were chairs and tables amongst the rows, but there was no one sitting at them. Jenyfer trailed her fingers over the books as she went. Each aged leather spine she touched shimmered beneath her fingers – the ink etched into those leaves of paper contained the knowledge of Teyath.

'The books aren't arranged in any order,' Katarin explained as they walked. 'You want a book on something, just ask for it.' She held out her hand and moments later, a book pulled itself free of a shelf and floated to her hand. Jen peeked at the title of the book.

'Cruithea?'

Katarin sighed, setting the book on a nearby table. 'Being here always makes me think about home, about where I belong. Cruithea was my home, then Kernou, Avalon, and now, *The Queen*, I guess.'

'What if you don't know where you belong?' Jenyfer mused. She reached out and touched more books, fingers tracing the spines gently. She could sense Katarin watching her.

'You'll work it out, Little Morsel. I'll leave you to it.'

Jenyfer nodded, and when she was sure she was alone, she turned to the library of Avalon with one thought in her mind. In hardly any time at all, a book landed in her outstretched hands.

Faery Creatures of the Sea.

CHAPTER 13

Arthur rolled his aching shoulders. Halymere had put him through his paces that morning, pushing him harder than their previous lessons, but Arthur had begun to improve. His timing had gotten better, and he was swifter on his feet; the Cruithean had reminded him it had been two days since Arthur had landed on his arse, which Arthur took as a compliment.

It was cool beneath the trees, and Arthur was enjoying a rare moment alone. In Kernou, he was often alone and, while loneliness had been a constant companion that he despised, here in Cruithea he yearned for a quiet space where he could clear his head.

He loved the energy of the forest, the calming presence of the trees, and came here as often as he could, although most times, he was being shadowed by one of the Inborn set by the High Priestess to guard him, or Jalen was with him. Arthur enjoyed those walks, which often ended with them on the forest floor. That was another thing Arthur was still adjusting to – the freedom to be who he was, to be with Jalen without having to look over his shoulder. In Cruithea relationships between men were common, but Arthur still experienced a brief moment of panic whenever Jalen closed his arms around him, or put his lips on Arthur's skin.

But while he was progressing at sword fighting and searching for his warriors heart, magic still eluded him. Arthur liked the way it felt in his veins – like sunshine and light, so warm and golden, but the idea of letting it free after what it had done to his father … He shook his head and pushed on through the trees. The thought that his magic would hurt someone else, someone he cared about, terrified him. What if he couldn't control it? He glanced down at his hands, pausing in his walk, and concentrated.

A trickle of golden light emerged from his skin. It crawled over his knuckles, reaching around to pool in his palms. He turned his hands over, watching that golden light form itself into two small spheres that hovered above his skin. It was warm, like a fire, and he smiled, then took a deep breath.

He couldn't hurt anyone out here, so he closed his eyes and let his magic spread, let it grow until it curled around his hands and up his arms, tickling the skin on the back of his neck. He opened his eyes, casting his gaze around until he found what he was looking for. A shrub, its white flowers barely clinging to life, the petals curled and browning at the edges. He reached out with his magic, watched it wrap itself around one of the flowers. Slowly, the petals unfurled, and the brown faded away.

Smiling, he directed his magic to the leaves at his feet. The crunchy brown slowly morphed into a deep green, the curled edges unfolding until they were smooth. Arthur withdrew his magic, tucking it away, and bent to collect a leaf.

It was perfect, the veins thick and pulsing with life; he could feel it leaching into his fingertips. The Cruitheans believed there was magic in the living world – intrinsic, natural magic – which Arthur had not understood, until now.

He had never walked the shoreline in Kernou for the simple act of appreciating the waves and the way they tumbled over one another, or the wind that was on some days fierce enough to tear the skin, and on others as soft and gentle as a kiss. Since being in Cruithea, he had come to understand the complexity of the natural world. For Cruitheans, Inanna was part of nature and the natural world was sacred. They did not take more than they needed and they lived without impacting the forest. Cruitheans recognised Inanna's influence in the cycles of the world around them, the turning of the seasons like the turning of a great wheel, never faltering.

It was a cycle of life, death, and rebirth. Death, he had come to learn, was not something the Cruitheans feared. There was no Pit of fire ready to consume sinners – even the concept of sin was unheard of here. As far as Arthur could gather, as long as one lived their life as best they could, that was all that mattered.

He turned the leaf over in his palm, running the tip of his finger down the central vein, before he bent and gently placed it back on the ground. As he watched, the leaf shifted from vibrant green back to brown, folding back in on itself as the life-giving moisture was sucked from it.

'The Wheel turns for everything – not even magic can change that.'

The voice made Arthur whirl around in fright, his magic leaping to life in his palms again, startling him. This time, it did not feel like soft sunshine. He held a raging flame in his hands.

The voice chuckled.

'Who's there?' Arthur demanded.

The air shimmered, and the sounds of the forest – the gentle chirping of birds in the branches and the breeze that rustled the leaves – fell away. Arthur held his breath, his magic at the ready, as from the very air around him a body began to take shape.

A man, tall and slender, dressed in brown. Bark-coloured hair tumbled over his shoulders, and from his head rose a set of glorious antlers. His face was smooth of lines, but hair crept along his throat to tickle the line of his jaw.

An Old One.

Arthur let his magic fade.

'You are learning, that is good,' the Old One mused. He swept his golden eyes over Arthur critically and Arthur had the sense the god was seeing inside him, his gaze piercing the cage of flesh until it traced the shape of Arthur's bones. 'Yes, there is much work to do but, in time, you will be what we have seen.'

'You're …'

The Old One inclined his head. 'I am the God of the Earth, Arthur Tregarthen. Some call me the Green Knight. You, like others, may call me Gawain.'

Arthur's knees shook as the Green Knight's voice washed over him. With Niniane, he could feel her power – he could feel magic and mysterious things he knew nothing about. But with the Green Knight, Arthur could sense the age of the world, the beginning of the mountains and the rivers, the strength of the trees and the life-giving richness of the soil.

'I know you're scared, that the weight of your task feels like it could crush you,' the God said softly. Arthur made a little noise and looked at the ground. 'You think there's a mistake?'

'Yes,' Arthur said.

'We have known you since before you existed, Arthur Tregarthen, and we have been waiting a long time,' Gawain added.

Jalen has said something similar. 'I still don't …'

'You don't have to walk this path alone. You already have people who will walk beside you. Why do you fight it?' the Old One asked him. There was no scorn, no reproach. Just gentleness.

'I don't know,' Arthur said.

The Green Knight smiled. 'You do, but you don't want to admit it. Soon, the Myrddin will come and he shall show you what you are capable of.'

'Can you tell me who he is?'

'He is not of this world, not like you are, yet he is not like I am either. The Myrddin has seen one of many possible futures,' the Green Knight said.

Arthur frowned. 'One of many?'

'The future's not set in stone, Arthur. Think of it as a wave, shifting and changing, but always there. What the Myrddin has seen is a possibility, nothing more. It will be up to you to make the future a reality,' the Green Knight said. 'But ask your question, the one you wanted to ask my sister on Avalon but did not. The one that has plagued your sleep. Ask and I shall answer.'

Arthur licked his lips. 'How do I find the Grail? I know the Treasures have to come first, and then they will show the way, but how? How do I do this?'

'The Grail can only be found once the Fisher Queen shows you the way,' the Green Knight said. 'And she will not show you anything unless you can prove you are pure of heart.'

'No man is pure of heart,' Arthur argued. 'Such a person does not exist.'

'I think it very much depends on what you consider purity to mean,' the Old One said. 'For example – a man who does not seek power over others, who only chooses to act in the greater good, could be considered pure of heart. Or, a man who does not wish to see the suffering of others, who acts not for himself but for the benefit of all people, could be considered pure. There cannot be purity without darkness, Arthur, remember that.'

'What do you mean?'

The God of the Earth began to fade, the edges of him beginning to blur and shift. 'For one to be pure, he has to cast out the darkness that lives inside him. You need to find your darkness – and destroy it.'

Arthur looked at his feet and when he lifted his head, questions – doubts – bursting to life on his tongue, the Green Knight was gone and he was standing beneath the trees, the sunlight filtering through the branches to capture him in a beam of golden warmth.

The sun had set and the kibitka was lit by lantern light. Arthur knew he should get up and go to dinner, but even though he was hungry, his mind was too busy for food.

He had met an Old One, and now he was pouring out everything in his head onto the pages of the book he had quietly asked Melhala about acquiring. There was something about the process of writing everything down that he found cathartic. Perhaps it was the hours of his life he had already devoted to the act, the hours spent scribing the Word in a neat hand.

His letters now were not neat. His father would not be pleased, but Arthur was too busy writing down everything that had happened since he left Kernou to be worried about whether his letters were perfectly formed.

The prophecy called him the Once and Future King. Arthur had thought that meant the future that he was to build had already been decided, though now he had been told it was up to him. He hadn't wanted to believe that such a decision would be his to make. The weight of it threatened to crush his skull, like the weight of the crown in his dreams.

With a sigh, he closed the book, setting it to the side, and was about to make his way to the communal cooking area when Jalen entered, his hands full – a bowl in one, a plate in the other – a delicious smell accompanying him.

'What's all this?' Arthur asked. He went to get up from the table, but Jalen shook his blonde head.

'Dinner.'

'Did you cook this? You can actually cook?' Arthur asked.

'I did, and yes, I can.'

Arthur smiled. 'I just assumed you used magic.'

'No!' Jalen's face was a mockery of outrage. He grinned sheepishly, coming to set the plates down in front of Arthur. 'Well, I might have ducked down south for the spices. And possibly to Avalon for the apples, because I know you love them. And maybe to Carinya for the cheese.'

Arthur ran his eyes over the food. Vegetables covered with some sort of glaze – honey, Jalen told him – goats' cheese was sprinkled over them, all soft and starting to melt; there was roasted meat and gravy, the smell so rich that Arthur's stomach let out a loud rumble; bread, steam still rising from it, and, in the bowl, spiced apples.

Food in Kernou was plain and simple, as the One God decreed it should be. There were no spices or sweets, and definitely no gravy.

'Is it against the demi-god rules to use your magic like this?' he asked.

'Maybe, but I don't care,' Jalen answered.

Arthur swallowed, his eyes on the food. 'No one has ever done anything like this for me before,' he confessed quietly. Jalen joined him on the other side of the table, dragging a chair around so he could sit close and take Arthur's hands, running his thumbs over Arthur's knuckles.

'I know, which is one of the reasons why I did this. If something as simple as a meal prepared for you helps you see your worth, then I'll continue to do it. Every day if I must.' He leant over and pressed his lips to Arthur's cheek. 'Now, enjoy your feast.'

'Where's yours?' Arthur asked, suddenly realising there was only enough food for one. Demi-gods, he was pretty certain, did not really need food, but Jalen enjoyed a good meal like any normal man.

'I thought we could share,' Jalen said.

Arthur smiled, and slid the plate over so it sat between them. There was no cutlery in Cruithea, so they used the bread to soak up the gravy and their fingers to eat everything else, then, when they had almost licked the plates clean and Arthur sat back with a contented sigh, Jalen's fingers found their way to his cheek.

'You've got food …' he said, voice low.

'Do I?' Arthur murmured, lifting his fingers to his lips, but Jalen caught them, pulled them away gently.

'I think I'll get that for you,' Jalen said, then pressed his lips to the corner of Arthur's mouth, so lightly it was nothing more than a whisper. He kissed the other side of Arthur's mouth next, his touch still feather-soft and teasing.

'I don't really have food on my lips, do I?' Arthur managed.

Jalen's hands wound through Arthur's curls. 'No. I wanted an excuse to kiss you.'

'You don't need an excuse,' Arthur breathed. Jalen smiled and kissed him again, then stood, holding out his hand.

'Walk with me,' he invited.

'Where?'

'Does it matter?'

Arthur rubbed his belly. 'I'm about to burst, I'm so full.'

'Come on,' Jalen insisted. 'It's a lovely night out there.'

Arthur placed his hand in Jalen's and let himself be pulled to his feet. They left the dirty plates on the table and headed out into the night. The sky was a blanket of stars and thin clouds, their undersides tickled by moonlight. Arthur had meant to tell Jalen about the Green Knight and the things the Old One had said, but Jalen tugged on his hand, leading him away from the kibitka and towards the heart of the village.

Arthur's steps faltered.

'What is it?'

Swallowing, Arthur paused, listening to the beating of his heart, feeling the warmth of his magic flowing beneath his skin. Jalen's hand was curled around his firmly, protectively, and Arthur realised suddenly that something was different. He waited, muscles beginning to tighten, but then, it didn't come.

The fear, usually so hot and potent, so dripping with the promise of punishment, did not arrive this time. There was no fear of discovery. No anxiety, no fear of the whip that lay in the dark confines of a cupboard in his father's study. No fear of his father's face. As Jalen stepped closer, his eyes concerned, Arthur smiled and shook his head.

'It's nothing, not anymore,' he murmured. Warmth rippled to life in his chest, then burst through him, swimming through the network of veins until it settled in his bones. The smile that broke across Arthur's face was broad. He turned to Jalen, kissing him gently on the mouth, making him smile in return and place his spare hand over Arthur's heart.

'I can feel your heart,' Jalen told him. 'And do you know what else I can feel?'

'What?'

'Everything you are yet to be, Arthur. Everything I know you are and more.'

That night, Arthur dreamt of the Grail. He dreamt of the burning barren wasteland. He dreamt of fire and blood and a sword that sang when he held it, the hilt decorated with a dragon, the blade inscribed with words written in a language he did not understand and had never seen before. He couldn't recall if the words were there in any previous dreams. He woke early, heart hammering, hands stiff, as if they'd been clutching a sword for hours. Jalen wasn't sleeping beside him; worry shot through Arthur, so he scrambled out of bed and threw on some clothes hastily. It was still dark. The fire in the kibitka had gone out.

Arthur crammed his boots on and pulled his hand through his hair, rubbing the sleep from his eyes, before heading out into the world.

It was not yet dawn, but he could sense the coming of the light, the sensation pulling his eyes to the east. It was cool in the village, and Arthur rubbed his arms to coax some warmth into his skin, wandering through the kibitkas, moving towards the communal meeting and cooking space, hoping that maybe Jalen was there, preparing breakfast.

The demi-god liked to cook. It made Arthur smile.

But Jalen was nowhere to be found.

There was only Mordred, crouched near the fire. Arthur watched him wave his hand and the flames spring to life. Fire, that was Mordred's main element. No one had told him, but the glyph on his cousins' brow and the tattoos that decorated his body indicated his skill. Arthur cleared his throat.

Mordred did not turn around. His arms were bare, the swirling black inked across them somehow darker in the wane light. As Arthur watched, Mordred put his hand close to the fire, and a ball of flame leapt obediently into his palm. He stood, and slowly turned around.

Eyes glowing with reflected fire, Mordred's lips curled. 'What's the future king of the world doing out of bed at this hour?'

Arthur blushed. 'I was looking for—'

Mordred gestured over his shoulder. 'Off doing storm demon things I imagine. Are you worried he won't come back?'

'No,' Arthur said automatically.

Mordred chuckled, the ball of fire dancing across his knuckles now, before he moved it to his other hand. Arthur watched, fascinated. Mordred's eyes drifted to his again.

'Have you worked out what your element is?'

'No,' Arthur admitted, scuffing at the ground with the toe of his boot. 'I'm not very good at this magic thing.' He didn't know why he was admitting such a thing to his cousin, who didn't like him and who always managed to make Arthur feel small and insignificant, but Mordred was family, and Arthur knew he would keep trying to reach him, to form some sort of connection with the leader of Cruithea's Inborn warriors, even if it took years. He needed someone like Mordred on his side, although Melhala would argue he didn't.

Mordred sighed, and the ball of flame vanished. He ran a large, tattooed hand over the braids of his dark hair, his expression half-way between conflicted and amused. 'Why do you always do that?'

'Do what?'

'Play the victim.'

'I'm not,' Arthur protested, shoving his hands in his pockets. He could feel his magic waking up, could feel it shaking itself off like a wet dog and shifting through his veins. The sensation still took him by surprise whenever it happened.

'Whatever you say.' Mordred stretched and Arthur couldn't help but envy the muscled physique. 'You'll make a terrible king with your shitty attitude,' he said.

Arthur held his gaze. The sun had risen and pale golden light was making its way through the trees, creeping across the forest floor and kissing the undersides of the leaves with gold. Arthur could hear the village waking up and wanted to get the words out before they were interrupted. 'Probably.'

'You don't want it?' Mordred mused. 'Interesting. Most men take whatever scraps of power they are offered, but you aren't interested. You aren't interested in the power my mother is offering you either, and *that* makes me curious. Most people do not refuse the High Priestess of Cruithea.'

'You don't like that she cares for me, do you?' Arthur asked.

Mordred's eyebrows lifted. 'If that is what you believe. But know this, *cousin* – my mother is very good at making someone feel special, at making them believe they are worth something. She is skilled at twisting words and telling people what they want to hear. But, she is also persistent. She will wear you down, if for no other reason than you and the Myrddin's prophecies fit into her world view.'

Something cold skittered down Arthur's spine. 'Are you telling me not to trust your mother?'

Mordred shrugged. 'You don't know her, but I'll let you make your own assessment.'

Arthur considered the other man, studying the way he stood. Mordred appeared calm, relaxed and casual, but his fists were clenched and Arthur could see the tightness in the muscles of his neck. Mordred carried a dagger at each hip, and a quiver of arrows were slung over his shoulder, a bow resting against a stump not far from him.

'Are you offering to help me?'

Mordred laughed openly. 'No. Continue your games with Melhala and continue playing with your wooden sword. When you're ready, cousin, perhaps you'd like to spend the day doing what I do, seeing what it actually takes to lead. Seeing what it is like to have people's lives between your fingers. I'd like to see if you could hold onto it, or if you'd turn tail and run like the coward I suspect you are. After all, you're good at running, aren't you?'

Arthur went to reply, to defend himself, to say *something*, anything that wouldn't leave him standing there like a fool, but a whirlwind suddenly ripped through the trees and Jalen was standing beside him, blonde hair ruffled, cheeks rosy. His eyes moved between Arthur and Mordred and he frowned.

Mordred gave Jalen a mock bow, then turned to greet the Inborn warriors who were striding towards him. Arthur could not hear what was said between them, but as Mordred collected the bow, several sets of eyes swung in Arthur's direction. The group headed off into the trees.

'What do they even do out there?' Arthur asked. Mordred's words had stung more than he liked to admit, even if they were true. He had run. From his father, from the challenges of his old life, only to be thrust into a new set of challenges.

'You can't trust a thing Mordred says, Arthur,' Jalen replied. 'He's jealous of you.'

Arthur burst out laughing, shaking his head in disbelief. 'Him? Jealous of me?'

'You are all the things Mordred is not – yes, you're still learning how to use your magic but you're so much more than that. You're calm, measured, and considerate of others. You have a good heart,' Jalen said, kissing Arthur softly on the cheek before asking what he wanted for breakfast.

After seeing the way the Inborn looked up to Mordred, Arthur wasn't so sure that being everything Mordred was not was really what made a leader.

CHAPTER 14

Ordes was taken by rowboat to the edge of the mists that cloaked Avalon. *The Excalibur* was already lost to the fog, the world around them silent and still, waiting. Carbrey's strong arms pulled the oars to rest. The mist was so close Ordes could reach out and touch it; it was warm, not cold like he was expecting. He pulled his hand back and examined his fingers. They were dry.

Carbrey's silence was heavy.

Ordes gave the old man a quick look. 'Thank you.'

The sailor grunted. 'Now what?'

Ordes turned to face the island. His magic felt stronger this close to the place of his birth, like all the pieces of him had solidified. He felt calm and soothed. He flexed his fingers and the air around them shimmered. He'd barely had to think about it and a sphere of water appeared in his palm. 'Now, I think I'll get out.'

'Into what?' Carbrey exclaimed.

Ordes peered over the edge of the boat.

'Don't be stupid, boy.' There was a note of fear in Carbrey's voice. 'There'd be all manner of fey things in there.'

'I'm a fey thing, remember?' The longer Ordes stared at the water, the clearer it became. Below them, he could see the ocean floor, the smooth pebbles and colourful fish that darted there, tufts of green seagrass bursting from the sandy bed.

'Why come here?' Carbrey asked. 'When your father has spent years keeping you from this place and she who rules it.'

'She's my mother,' Ordes confessed; he didn't miss Carbrey's intake of breath.

'Some questions don't need answers, Ordes,' Carbrey warned.

'Maybe not, but how do I know which answers are wrong, or which questions are right?' The boat rocked gently as Ordes stood, the water around them shifting into ripples that vanished almost as soon as they appeared. He pushed a sharp breath from his lungs. He could feel Carbrey's eyes on him as he lifted his hands, holding them out in front of him.

I need to get to Avalon, he thought.

Slowly, he moved both hands in a circular motion – the mist swirled in response. Instinctively, he dropped his hands, and the mist parted like a curtain.

Carbrey made a noise, but Ordes didn't look at the old man. From the ocean rose stepping stones, pulling clear of the water until they floated on its surface.

'You shouldn't go,' Carbrey said sharply.

'I have to,' Ordes replied. He could feel it, beneath the terror that gripped him, an instinctual calling he had never felt before. He could hear music and smell apples; the island was tugging at him as his magic danced and pushed and pushed against his skin. He stepped from the boat onto the first stone. He moved to the next, then the next, glancing back to watch the stones sink beneath the water.

He lifted his hand in a wave to Carbrey, whose eyes were wide, his skin bloodless beneath his tan, then turned to face Avalon.

With each step closer, each smooth, grey stone he placed his foot on, Ordes could *feel* the island, feel its heartbeat slipping inside him, the magic of the place flowing through him. By the time he reached the beach, the mist had closed behind him and Carbrey and the boat were hidden from his sight. The pebbles that lined the beach glistened with water, crystals of various colours and shapes buried between the pebbles and speckled through them. They crunched beneath his feet as he took another step.

'Now where do I go?' he asked the air.

The answer came swiftly: footprints – that didn't belong to anything he could see – appeared in front of him, one after the other, leading away from the beach. Ordes took a deep breath and followed them. The beach gave way gently to grass, green as jewels and as high as his knees. It parted for him as he walked and he soon found himself in a field of flowers, the colours so bright they hurt the eyes. Names he knew but shouldn't have jumped into his mind as he recognised bluebells and snowdrops, foxglove and heather and liverwort.

Faery creatures appeared as he walked, things he instinctively knew but couldn't name. They followed him along behind him and by the time he reached the glittering castle rising from the landscape, its towers draped in mist, there were dozens, trailing him like he was at the head of a great parade.

A tiny thing with wings darted ahead of him, flying excitedly around the entrance to the castle. Ordes took the steps one at a time, slowly, even though his body was buzzing and his head was filled with white noise.

Inside the castle, he could feel her.

As ancient and powerful as the land around him.

His mother.

He followed the winged faery through a wide hall with walls covered in tapestries, each scene so vibrant, so alive, that Ordes wanted to touch them. He swore the images shifted slightly, like the figures were trying to see who he was. The little faery grabbed a length of his hair and tugged, a signal to keep moving, to hurry up. Ordes barely noticed the mossy carpet beneath his feet, or registered that he was now alone, all the faeries having vanished – except the small winged one, who fluttered around his head, chittering in a language he didn't understand. She perched on his shoulder, her shrill voice in his ear, and when she realised he didn't know what she was saying, she flitted off again, hovering impatiently near a wide archway at the end of the hall.

Ordes quickened his steps. All around him, magic swelled and breathed and the air shimmered like a glossy curtain. On the other side of the stone archway was a wide, open space with a cathedral-like ceiling. Stone columns covered in ivy lined the edges of the room, the greenery slowly growing and climbing and winding itself around everything in its path, only to pause, as if on a sigh, and pull back again. The breeze that blew through the sheer white curtains was warm and smelt like apples and sunshine and all the things he had missed but had never known.

The Queen of the Isle was sitting on a throne of mahogany timber on a dais at the far end of the room. She was beautiful, her dark hair a waterfall that swept its way over her shoulders and curled in her lap. Eyes the colour of a summer sky stared back at him; the air around her shimmered with silver light when she shot to her feet.

'Ordes.' It was a whisper, but her voice filled his ears as if she stood beside him, her mouth close to his skin. He could feel her breath on his neck and he wanted to close his eyes and sink to the floor, curl up in a ball and let himself be swept away. He stood tall instead, squared his shoulders, and looked at her.

'Mother.'

Niniane was tiny. He wasn't sure what he'd expected of a Goddess, but it wasn't this woman who looked like she'd blow away like mist on a breeze. She took another step towards him, the hem of her white gown trailing along the ground behind her. There were tiny white flowers caught in the length of her hair; they sparkled like jewels and he wanted to touch one.

This woman was mighty and powerful, and yet, she had never come to claim him.

Did she not want him?

Niniane smiled. 'You look like your father.'

'Is that a bad thing?' Ordes still hadn't moved. He wasn't sure he could.

'You sound like him as well.' When she spoke again, her voice was soft.

There were no words, not anymore. Everything Ordes had ever wanted to say if he ever met his mother vanished. He swallowed and let his eyes move around the room, but they quickly swung back to her, to the power he could sense radiating from her.

'I've watched you grow,' she said fondly.

He took a step towards her. 'How?'

Niniane moved towards an object covered in a white cloth so thick Ordes could not guess what was beneath it. She gave him a quick look, then tugged on one side of the cloth. It fell away to reveal a mirror. He expected to see his reflection, but the surface swirled and danced, shimmering with light. He drifted closer to it.

'Is Tymis what and who he says he is?'

Niniane's voice was soft. 'He finally told you? Yes, he is what and who he says he is. Tymis, *Merlin*, isn't some pirate I took pity on because he washed up on the shores of Avalon. He is the beginning and the end.'

'What does that mean?' Ordes couldn't take his eyes off the mirror. Things were taking shape there, things with wings, great scaled wings that stretched to cover the sky. Red, and white. A bow, its limbs curved like a smile. The feathered tip of an arrow. He shook his head and the visions faded into swirling silver smoke, only to begin to form again almost instantly.

'It means he can see between the worlds. It means he knows what has been, what is and what will be. The question is – did you inherit his gifts, or only mine?' Niniane mused.

The mirror whispered, tugging at Ordes' mind. There were voices, layers and layers of them, tumbling over one another until they were so jumbled he could not decipher a single thing. 'Can you cover that thing up, please?'

'As you wish,' his mother replied. When he next looked the mirror was hidden and with it the assault on his senses. 'Your father kept the truth from you to protect you.'

'Protect me?' Ordes snorted.

'Too much knowledge can be a burden,' Niniane said. She finally, finally, moved closer to him, but made no move to touch him; he was glad and saddened by it at the same time.

'I want to know who he is,' Ordes said. 'Not what he is, but *who*.'

She hesitated, and then sighed lightly. 'I don't know. I cannot give a name to it. He was born of a mortal woman and was a normal child – happy, if perhaps a little melancholy with a flair for the dramatic—'

Ordes chuckled.

'—but a normal, human child. Until he wasn't. Until the things he dreamt about began to come true. A plague of locusts on the harvest. A dry spell, where no rain tumbled from the sky to quench the earth. He knew who in the village would die, could predict the birth of children before they were even conceived. Even though people believed in the Old Ones and still made shrines to us in the forest, Merlin was viewed with suspicion, because power like that was something a normal boy, Magic Wielder or not, shouldn't possess. His mother took him from the village and hid him in the forest. She told them he had drowned, though she would continue to visit him until the day she died.'

Ordes closed his eyes, seeing everything Niniane told him clearly, like a series of brightly coloured moving pictures in his head. 'And then?'

'Now a man, he wandered the world for many, many years. I don't know everything that happened to him, Ordes, but eventually he found a boat. He rowed out as far as he could, tossed the oars into the water, lay back and waited to die,' Niniane said. 'He washed up on the beach of Avalon instead. You know the rest of the story.'

'Yes,' Ordes whispered.

'But what you won't know is that every Old One came here to see him, to hear him speak.'

Ordes frowned. 'Why?'

'Because they knew who he was. They felt it, as I did. They felt his power, and when he spoke his prophecies, they knew the world would change,' Niniane replied.

'How did he lose his magic?'

'Avalon punished him for leaving. This island is mine, I am tied to it. So, perhaps the magic of this place felt my anguish, my sorrow, and took from him the thing that made him, him. It was not what I wanted and I did not know it would happen,' Niniane said.

'Will he get it back?' Ordes asked; his skin prickled at the idea of it, of seeing the person his mother spoke of, of getting to know that man.

'Yes,' Niniane said. 'But you are not here for me.'

'Why am I here then?'

'That second heartbeat.'

Ordes didn't ask how she knew. He pushed a breath from his lungs and concentrated on the beating in his chest. There, beneath the rhythm of his thundering heart, was Jenyfer's. He placed his fingers on his chest.

'It's part of who you are,' Niniane told him. Then, 'Come.'

She led him deep into the castle; silvery light danced along the back of his hands, his magic pulled from his body. His mother walked beside him, her eyes falling to his hands, but she said nothing, practically floating through the castle as one hallway became another, then another, the last opening up to a wide archway, and beyond, a world of water.

Pale rocks covered in ivy and soft pink flowers bordered a great lake. Stone stairs swept downwards, continuing into the water, which glittered like crystals in the sunlight and lapped gently against the rocks. A woman's head emerged from the lake, dark hair moulded to the shape of her. She ducked back under then surfaced again, her hair falling over one shoulder, exposing her naked back and the black lines that were inked there.

Ordes took a step towards the lake without thinking.

Jenyfer turned to face them; she gave him a startled look, then smiled broadly, her whole face lighting up. Delicate silver and blue scales decorated her forearms and temples, licking the sides of her neck. Ordes walked the rest of the way down the steps in a daze, until he was standing at the edge of the lake. Water lilies the size of dinner plates floated near his feet.

Spheres of water danced around Jenyfer's head. She flicked one at him. It stopped before it crashed into his face, making him smile and nudge it out of the way with his magic. Jenyfer beckoned, urging him to get in.

'I'm not dressed for swimming,' he said, crouching where the water lapped the steps.

She rolled her eyes and ducked beneath the surface of the water. He watched her swim along the bottom, stayed where he was as she swam up the steps and emerged between the lilies, her hair plastered to her scalp. 'Get in,' she demanded.

There was no way he could refuse her, so he stood, slipping his boots and shirt off, aware his mother was watching them. He glanced at her over his shoulder.

Niniane's smile was wistful. 'You were born on the edge of this lake. Not far from where you're standing now.'

Ordes swallowed, turning back to the lake of Avalon, and Jenyfer.

She smiled again and, without another thought, he stepped into the water.

Niniane led them along a wide corridor with a vaulted ceiling. Jenyfer's face was blissful, a serene smile on her lips. That last moment they had seen each other on *The Excalibur* had lived in Ordes' head ever since, as had all the things he wished he'd been able to do or say before Katarin knocked on the door and broke whatever spell had been woven between them.

Now, she was here, squeezing the water from her hair as they followed Niniane through the castle. They didn't speak as they walked; he had his boots tucked under his arm and his shirt slung over his shoulder. Water dripped from his hair to trickle down his back and chest. Jenyfer was dressed in a white gown that floated around her legs like it was alive, her hair a dark streak down her back. They turned left into another corridor, then right, stopping at a door, the timber carved in intricate patterns of leaves and flowers.

A sumptuous room lay beyond the door. Wide windows were dressed in billowing white, the breeze neither too cold nor too warm. A large four-poster bed, also dripping with white curtains, took up the majority of the space and a luscious, woven rug decorated the pale grey stone floor. There was an ornate wooden table, big enough for four people; an armchair covered in pale fabric; a timber wardrobe and dressing table with a stool; and a forest of potted plants, greenery climbing the walls and twining itself around the decorative cornices. Each cornice was a wizened face that reminded Ordes of piskies.

Jenyfer had grabbed a towel and gone out onto the balcony. She was drying her hair, humming to herself happily. Ordes dropped his boots on the floor and stepped onto the balcony. Mountains rose in the distance, their tops draped in clouds that flowed over and around them like waves, the sky a dazzling cerulean. Directly below them were fields of flowers and golden grass that shifted in the breeze. A smaller stone building sat between the castle and the fields, a manicured garden taking up space between each building. The House of the Priestesses, Ordes guessed.

Niniane cleared her throat. 'Once you've dried off, I need you both in the main courtyard.'

Ordes didn't turn from the view. 'Why?'

'We need to talk about your father,' his mother said.

'What's he done now?' Jenyfer mumbled, bundling her hair in the towel.

'Tymis is up to his eyeballs in a whole pile of stuff he hadn't seen fit to mention,' Ordes told her quietly, then to his mother, 'We'll be there soon.'

'Of course.' Niniane nodded, then vanished. She didn't open the door and leave – she disappeared. Ordes wished he could freeze time, give himself a moment to catch up. He'd come here for answers and now he had more questions, the first one being why Jenyfer was here in the first place. Left alone with her, he found himself unable to find the words he needed to tell her how he hadn't been able to think without her, how he couldn't think *with* her, and how he wanted to crush her to his chest, lay her out on that massive bed and bury his face—

'How long have you been here?' The map on his flesh was tingling.

She shrugged. 'I'm not sure. Time moves differently here. Tymis?'

'He's the Myrddin, Jen,' Ordes said. 'The prophet of the gods. My father is hundreds of years old. Remember how I told you about the stories he'd tell me as a child? He was telling me about himself, and all of it was true.'

Jenyfer's mouth dropped open; something crossed her face, some sort of understanding, and Ordes' skin prickled as she shook her head. 'You had no idea?'

'I thought he was nothing more than a pirate who stole a ship from a goddess and lost his magic in the process.' He pushed a hand through his damp hair. 'I could never have imagined this.'

'Well,' Jenyfer said with a sigh, unwinding the towel from her head and draping it over her shoulder. 'Let's go and see what earth-shattering thing your other parent has to tell us. Can't be anything heavier than she's already told me.'

'What's she said?' Ordes asked.

'Oh, nothing important. Only that I'm part of this prophecy of your *father's* and one of the Treasures of the Gods is mine to find,' Jenyfer quipped. Her fingers drummed rhythmically on the balcony railing. 'It's why you were told to rescue me from Kernou, right?'

'I was going to rescue you anyway,' Ordes said, resting his hands on the railing next to hers, feeling her look at their hands for a moment before she lifted her eyes to the mountains in the distance.

Jenyfer, Arthur Tregarthen, and him.

'Do you ever wish none of this was happening?'

'All the time,' he answered. 'Jen—'

'Can we be friends again? Like we were?' she asked quickly.

His fingers tightened on the balcony railing as she moved hers away. 'I don't know if I can do that.'

'Please,' Jenyfer said, her voice no more than a whisper. 'There is so much noise in my head I can't think straight at the moment. I need a friend right now.'

'What about Kat?'

'It's not the same,' Jenyfer said. 'I feel like you understand me even when I don't fully understand myself. I've spent my life looking over my shoulder, always on the edge, never truly calm unless I was on the sand with the sea washing over my toes. I never thought I would know anything else, any other life, but then you changed that.'

Ordes shifted his weight. He couldn't take his eyes off their hands, so close, yet not close enough. Jenyfer glanced at him; their eyes locked together for a heartbeat, before she lowered her gaze and sighed deeply.

'I know friendship isn't what you want,' she continued, her voice rough around the edges, strained. 'And I'm sorry. It isn't that I don't care for you – I do – but I—'

'I understand, Jen,' he said. A fire was burning in his chest, the same fire that had been burning there since he'd seen her in Carinya. 'If a friend is what you need, then that is what you'll get.'

Jenyfer was silent for a long moment, then, 'Thank you.'

There was a long table laden with food in the courtyard when Jenyfer entered, Ordes not far behind her. Niniane was sitting at one end, Katarin to her left. Kat's expression was irritated and her eyes widened at the sight of Ordes. He took the seat opposite her and she narrowed her eyes at him as she reached for the nearest bowl, serving herself. 'What are you doing in my space?'

'Your space?' he shot back.

Jenyfer seated herself next to Katarin as the Captain continued to bicker, then realised almost immediately it was a mistake. Whenever she looked up, she met Ordes' eyes across the table. She had already decided she wasn't going to tell him that Melodias was her father. Not until she worked out what it meant. Being a syhren was one thing – being the daughter of the Master of Songs and Death quite another. But the weight of the things left unsaid between them was there in his gaze.

Niniane cleared her throat gently. 'Merlin's prophecies have begun to unfold. You all know by now that Arthur Tregarthen is the Once and Future King. However, before he can claim that title the Treasures of the Gods must be recovered.'

'Do you know where they are?' Ordes asked. His eyes shot to Kat, then Jenyfer – a message that she understood. Kat wasn't to know about Tymis. Jenyfer wasn't sure why Ordes wanted to hide it, but it wasn't so different to her wanting to keep the truth of her father from everyone, so she nodded as subtly as she could.

'Only those who are destined to find them will uncover their whereabouts. Remember, the Treasures are yours to find, Ordes – yours, hers'—Niniane nodded in Jenyfer's direction— 'and Arthur's. Once you find the Treasures, you will find the Grail.'

Katarin was muttering under her breath. Jenyfer knew what she was thinking – the Myrddin couldn't have picked three less prepared people.

'The Treasures have already picked you. They will find you, each of you. They are magical artefacts, and like calls to like. Each Treasure has a song that can only be heard by those who created them – and those who are destined to find them,' Niniane explained.

'A song?' Jenyfer asked sharply. Her palms grew sweaty as anxiety twisted in her belly. 'Who owned them before they went missing?'

'They didn't go missing – they were stolen,' Kat cut in.

Jenyfer was very still as Niniane spoke of the Old One who had betrayed them. She could barely breathe, waiting for Niniane to name her father as the culprit; but she didn't. Sitting back in her chair, her face sorrowful, Niniane said, 'She fooled us all.'

'She?' Ordes asked.

'The Red One,' Niniane said. 'Ereshki. The Dark One. She betrayed us for her own selfish gains, to be worshipped exclusively and above all. It is only the Grail we can hear, now, but it's a useless song – we cannot use it, or even find it, without the other Treasures. So it continues to sing to us, tormenting us, as it has for hundreds of years.'

Silence dropped into the room. Ordes chewed on his lip, his eyes on his mother. Her expression was smooth, a hint of sadness in the way her mouth was twisted.

'Why us?'

'I cannot say,' Niniane replied.

'Can't, or won't?' Ordes shot back, and Jenyfer could feel his anger from where she sat, could almost see it threaded through the air around him, which swelled and shifted as he breathed.

Niniane pursed her lips. 'I understand you're angry, Ordes—'

'I'm entitled to be angry,' Ordes cut in. '*We* are entitled to be angry,' he added, glancing at Jenyfer.

'You're not entitled to be an arse,' Kat said.

Ordes leant his elbows on the table. 'Remember that time I called you her bloodhound?'

'Will you two stop?' Jenyfer said. She rubbed at her temples wearily. 'Seriously. If all of this is true, if we are meant to find the Treasures, shouldn't we all go to Cruithea, collect Arthur and get on with it?'

Niniane shook her head. 'Not yet. There is much you all need to learn about who you are,' she said, 'and much you need to understand. Arthur's time in Cruithea will be invaluable to him. That land will begin to shape who he is to be. When it is time, you will all be together.'

Jenyfer dropped her eyes to her plate as the weight of fate, or whatever they wanted to call it, draped itself over her shoulders.

CHAPTER 15

Jenyfer lingered in the doorway of the dining room. Ordes hadn't noticed her yet, his eyes on the piece of paper between his hands. His face was creased, but with frustration or confusion, Jenyfer could not tell.

Something sparked in her chest. She'd woken up with the feeling that there was a fire smouldering beneath her skin. She rubbed at it, willing the burning to go away.

Sensing her, Ordes glanced up. His hair was loose around his shoulders, and he was dressed in a fitted grey shirt and dark pants. He stared at her, then smiled and indicated the seat opposite him.

'You've missed breakfast,' he told her as she sat.

'Not hungry.'

His eyes moved over her, taking in her appearance. 'No dress today?'

Jenyfer had woken to a note from Kat. They were training today, so she'd pulled on pants, her boots, and a fitted shirt. 'You're not wearing a dress either,' she told Ordes, and he laughed. 'What's that?' she asked, nodding at the paper.

Wordlessly, he passed it over.

It was Merlin's prophecies, written in Ordes' neat hand. It was strange to see it written down, like those words frozen on the page somehow made them more real. Jenyfer swallowed the lump that suddenly formed in her throat.

'You believe this is true?' Jenyfer asked, not lifting her eyes from the page.

'I honestly don't know,' he said softly. 'Once, I believed every word that came out of his mouth. I was a child who idolised his father.'

'And now?'

When he didn't answer, Jenyfer looked up. Ordes was examining the tattoos on his knuckles, his expression thoughtful. 'Does it matter, Ordes?' she asked. 'Does it truly matter who or what he is. He's still your father. I don't think he kept it from you because he was trying to deceive you.'

Ordes met her eyes.

'That day with the Witchfinder's ship – you didn't see his face when you collapsed, but I did. I saw a man worried about his son.'

'Worried about his son, or worried about his great prophecy?' Ordes mused.

'You don't actually believe that, do you?' Jenyfer asked.

Ordes sighed. 'No, no I don't.' He nodded at the paper, still clutched between Jenyfer's fingers. 'What do you think it means? Tymis isn't here to help, so we may as well start trying to figure it out. He told me about it, but he never actually explained any of it.'

'Helpful,' Jenyfer murmured. She ran her eyes over the words again. 'The Once and Future King is Arthur, and the three sets of hands refers to all of us, I guess. What's the stone?'

'The Grail,' Ordes answered.

'One set of hands to pass alone,' Jenyfer mumbled. 'What does that mean?'

Ordes shrugged.

'Your mother said something else to me, the day she informed me of my destiny,' Jenyfer said, unable to keep the bitterness from her voice. 'She said something about "one with a foot on the land, one with a foot in the sea, and one with a foot in both worlds" would wield the Grail. Let's assume Arthur is the foot on the land.'

'You're obviously the sea,' Ordes replied.

'That could be you,' she argued.

He shook his head. 'Tymis told me I was born between the worlds. Niniane told me I was born on the edge of the lake, the one you were swimming in when I arrived. We could consider that between the worlds I guess – the land, and the water,' Ordes said. 'Or it could be something to do with my parents – an Old One and a human.'

Jenyfer's belly twisted but she pushed it aside. 'Okay, but what about this bit? "The one who stands between the worlds shall bear the weight of them both" – that sounds ominous.'

'Worried about me, Jen?' Ordes asked, giving her a wink.

'No.'

'Liar.'

'Maybe the Treasures are heavy?' she guessed.

'Maybe.'

Jenyfer nodded. 'What about the other lines? Camlann Field—'

'East of Kernou, over the mountains. It's a wasteland, the home of the former rulers of Teyath from hundreds of years ago,' Ordes supplied.

'Dragons are mentioned twice – do you think that means actual dragons?' Jenyfer asked.

'There haven't been dragons for centuries,' Ordes told her. 'My father told me they were hunted to extinction – by people, of course. Things like that make me wish I wasn't human at all,' he added. 'I know what people can do, to each other, to the land, but still I'm somehow always surprised.'

'Because you want to see the good in everyone,' Jenyfer said without thinking. She looked up, met his eyes, and felt her cheeks heat.

His lips curled into a smile. 'Was that a compliment?'

'No,' she replied. She knew what he was doing – exactly as she'd asked him. He was showing her the man she first met. It was what she had asked for, but it didn't feel right when she knew he hadn't truly put anything between them aside. He was playing the game, for her, giving her what she wanted, like he always did. She hadn't put it aside either. Everything that had happened between them, every moment they had shared, was still there, simmering away beneath the surface of her. She hadn't lied to him; she did need time, and his friendship.

But she missed him. That was also the truth.

'This is you,' Ordes said, tapping a finger on the paper. 'A song. It has to be you because I can't sing.'

'Great. My magic that I don't know how to use is part of a prophecy we don't understand,' Jenyfer replied.

'Sarcasm doesn't suit you.'

She rolled her eyes. 'Who are the Red Ones? And what's the House of Bone?'

'It rings a bell, but again, I'm not sure. I listened to Tymis' stories with a kid's attention – I was more interested in the idea of dragons and magic than what any of it actually meant.' He glanced at her, then said casually, 'Have you checked the library? I know that's where you've been hiding since I got here.'

'I haven't been hiding, exactly,' Jenyfer argued. 'Just … reading.'

'I know – you like books. I remember.'

Before Jenyfer could respond, Katarin burst into the room, Aelle on her heels, both of them dressed for training. They were both armed as well. 'There you are! Right, up, Jenyfer, it's training time. And you,' she said, pointing at Ordes, 'need your arse kicked.'

He sat back in his chair, a smirk crawling across his lips. 'Oh, I do, do I?'

'Come on,' Katarin said impatiently. 'I'm bored and I want something to do.'

'We're fine here,' Ordes said, but his eyebrows lifted when Jenyfer stood. 'Or not.'

'You don't have to come,' she said quickly. Part of her didn't want him to see what she had learnt to do, but the other part wanted to show off with a desperation that surprised her. Without waiting for his response, Jenyfer snatched up the paper with the prophecy and tucked it into her pocket, then followed Kat and Aelle out into the bright sunshine.

Thanks to Katarin, Jenyfer was much better at using her water magic; not perfect, but she could at least manipulate the water with much more ease than before. She hadn't mastered using both magic and a dagger, but her fighting skills had started to improve as well. She was never in any danger of hitting Katarin with her blade, and that made her feel better. Kat pushed her, a lot harder than Ordes had, and Jenyfer appreciated Katarin's conviction that she could do it. Kat didn't treat her like she might break. Ordes hadn't, either, but Jenyfer knew he had made it easy for her in their short lessons. She understood now that was not because he didn't think she could do it – it was just who he was. If he could make something easier for someone, he did it.

Like agreeing to be her friend.

Eventually, footsteps echoed along the stone path behind them and Jenyfer slowed her steps a little, letting Ordes catch up with her. They didn't speak. Kat didn't lead them to the beach this time, but beneath timber arches dripping with flowers and fruit. As they entered an orchard, Ordes plucked an apple free as he passed one of the trees, its trunk gnarled and ancient, juggling the fruit between his hands before biting into it.

Katarin stopped at a clearing in the middle of the orchard, hands on her hips as she surveyed their surroundings.

'This will do,' she announced.

Ordes continued to munch his fruit, his expression amused. In the distance, the mountains stretched into the sky, clouds wrapped around their peaks like skeins of wool, and the breeze was soft and warm.

Katarin's eyes moved over each of them slowly. Her gaze fell on Ordes and she smiled. 'You're first.'

Ordes tossed his apple core away. 'Of course I am.'

Kat nodded, shedding her coat and tossing it onto the ground. She made a show of swiftly plaiting her long red hair and flicking it over her shoulder, rolling the muscles in her neck and stretching her arms. When Ordes didn't copy her movement, she narrowed her eyes at him.

'Are you going to get ready?'

'I was born ready, Kat,' he said.

She scoffed and continued warming up her muscles, then her magic; silvery-blue light curled from her palms, creeping up her arms to slither around her neck and back down again.

'My brother will need you two to be on your game,' she replied, her gaze shifting from Ordes to Jenyfer. 'We have no idea what is going to happen, but one thing I have learnt about humans is that they don't like to give up their power, and they don't like things to change. I can't imagine Arthur will plonk a crown on his head and announce he's a king and everyone will drop to their knees in front of him.'

'You expect a fight then?' Jenyfer said.

'It's better to be prepared for one, don't you think?' Kat challenged. She withdrew a dagger from her hip and tossed it in Ordes' direction. The blade embedded itself in the ground at his feet. 'Pick it up.'

He sighed, but did what he was told.

'Come on, Ordes,' Kat ordered, twirling a dagger between her fingers with ease. 'We're in Avalon. She's your mother. If my magic is stronger here, so is yours. Dig into it and actually use it for once.'

Ordes pursed his lips. 'Fine. How do you want to do this?'

In answer, Katarin shifted into a fighter's stance, resting her weight in her thighs, feet shoulder width apart, fists raised; she gripped a dagger in one hand and her expression was deadly.

'Like that, then. Okay,' Ordes mumbled as she moved towards him.

She struck first, a sharp jab that he blocked. Kat was fast, managing to lay a series of punches along his ribcage, each strike making Jenyfer wince and Aelle chuckle. Cursing, Ordes sidestepped her next attack, hooking his foot behind hers and sweeping her off her feet. She hit the ground with a huff, flipping quickly upright, daggers clenched between her fists. She stared at them, then smiled, and tossed one of them into the air.

There was no water here, so it was a vine that crawled across the ground, shooting into the air to take hold of the dagger.

'Don't hold back, Ordes,' Kat ordered.

He eyed the dagger-wielding vine. 'I don't want to hurt you.'

Katarin glared at him and Jenyfer bit her lip. 'Because I'm a woman?'

'No, because—'

Katarin shot forward. Ordes managed to block the fist she threw at his nose, catching her wrist and swinging her off-balance. She righted herself almost instantly, dancing away as Ordes moved towards her, making her duck and weave to avoid his hands. Katarin slipped out of reach, then beckoned to him, a signal to go again.

Jenyfer held her breath, her stomach tight and her mouth dry.

Ordes threw himself at Katarin, fists flying. She blocked his attacks, narrowly avoiding the blade he drove in her direction. Katarin was fast, but so was he. The way they both moved, had Jenyfer bouncing on the balls of her feet, swept away by the fluidity as they dodged each other's blows, avoiding shining silver blades and magical vines, until Ordes managed to slip beneath Kat's arms. His fist connected with her stomach.

The air went out of her and she folded in half, hands on her knees, back heaving.

'Shit, Kat,' Ordes gasped. 'I'm—'

She blasted him off his feet with a wave of magic. He hit the ground, and, with a groan, rolled over to blink at the sky as Aelle laughed.

Jenyfer turned to Kat, hands on her hips. 'Was that necessary?'

Three faces turned in her direction and Katarin raised an eyebrow. Jenyfer's cheeks burned. She hadn't meant to say that – Ordes was capable of taking care of himself – but the words had shot free of her before she had even thought them. Her chest felt as hot as her face.

'Are we done, Kat?' Ordes asked, getting to his feet.

She shook her head. 'Magic, Ordes. You've got it. Use it.'

Green light poured from Katarin's palms. As it stretched across the ground, it twisted itself into more vines.

Jenyfer wasn't sure what Ordes was going to do. She had only ever seen him manipulate water, but they were standing in an orchard with trees all around them. He moved away from Kat's vines, and she could almost see his mind whirling, trying to come up with something. A vine curled around his ankle, and he slashed at it with the dagger.

'Magic, Ordes,' Katarin shouted.

Ordes grit his teeth and, suddenly, mist was swirling around his feet as silver light exploded from his hands like ropes. The mist thickened and raced across the ground towards Katarin. Aelle sucked in a breath as Katarin moved, darting through the mist, blue-tinged light cupped in her palms. She drew her hands together at her chest and flung her arms out, sending that light in Ordes' direction.

Almost lazily, his hands lifted and there, in the air in front of him, was a shield made of silver light.

Katarin's magic slammed into it and Ordes rocked back on his heels a little, but his magic held. Mist curled around his body like a pet seeking his approval. He frowned, reaching up to rub at the back of his neck. His magic failed and the shield dissolved, the mist slinking back through the trees.

No one spoke until Kat's face split into a grin. 'Not totally useless, then,' she said.

Ordes didn't smile back.

Katarin's smile dropped. 'What's wrong?'

'I don't know,' he mumbled.

Jenyfer opened her mouth, but Katarin spoke instead. 'Right. Jen, you're up.'

'There's no water here,' Jenyfer commented; she was still watching Ordes, who was frowning at his hands. 'How am I supposed to use my magic?'

'There is water here,' Kat said. 'You just can't see it. It's in the earth beneath your feet.'

'It's in your body as well,' Aelle cut in. 'If you wanted, you could pull the blood from someone's veins.'

Jenyfer was aghast. 'I don't want to do that.'

Aelle shrugged. 'You could, though, is all I'm saying.'

Katarin's vines had disappeared. 'Then maybe I can teach you how to use your fists instead, Little Morsel. Let's go.'

CHAPTER 16

Lamorna woke with a start, rolling over and sitting up, her dreams spinning around her head – music and water, darkness and endless cold. Always the same, and always unclear. The music faded the moment she opened her eyes. She had tried to hold it within her, tried to remember, to sing a few bars, but it was like the sound wanted to remain elusive, existing only as a thing to taunt her, to remind her that she could not remember what she had been through.

She opened her mouth, then stopped, her eyes finding what she knew but had forgotten.

Jenyfer's bed was empty.

Swallowing her rolling stomach, Lamorna swung her legs out of bed. She'd ask her aunt to make her tea, like the ones Tamora used to make for Jenyfer when she was feeling ill. That had settled her before, when she first came back.

There were voices in the kitchen, floating down the hall and into the room. Lamorna froze while dressing. Her aunt's voice, low and rushed, and another, one Lamorna had heard before but couldn't place.

Lamorna hurried over to the window, climbing onto Jenyfer's bed so she could pull back the curtains. Dawn was a thin, pale light creeping over the hills in the east and gently kissing the tops of the buildings in the village below her. Letting the curtain fall, Lamorna crept out into the hall, edging closer to the kitchen doorway, keeping her feet as silent as she could, wondering who was visiting at such an early hour.

'We can't—' Tamora's voice.

'We have too.' Keraine, that was her name, Lamorna remembered. She was one of her aunt's prayer circle friends. Lamorna didn't like Keraine – she thought she was proud and arrogant – and Keraine didn't like Lamorna. She'd endured the other woman's glares enough to know it was true, and whenever Keraine spoke to Lamorna she did nothing to hide the disapproval in her tone.

Tamora's voice was soft when she spoke again, with a tenderness to it Lamorna wasn't familiar with. It was different to how she spoke to either of the girls. 'Keraine, we have to be careful, now more than ever. With Jenyfer gone, and Lamorna … I'm worried about her, the way they watch her. I'm worried about what she has been asked to do. Although she has told me nothing, I think … I think she is starting to reassess things.'

Lamorna felt a quick spike of guilt, but pushed it away.

'I'm sick of being careful,' Keraine replied.

Lamorna moved closer to the door as Tamora's voice dropped. 'We have to be. After what they did to Shayana … I can still see her, Keraine. She is in my dreams, and my nightmares. She is warning us from the Otherworld to be careful, or it will be us up there burning. It will be us led into the darkness and tortured for information we don't know and answers we don't have.'

Since the Red Hand, things had been different. Lamorna could not argue with that. Two women in the space of two weeks had been accused of witchcraft, questioned by the Konsel, then tied to the pyre and burnt. The whole town had been made to watch. Lamorna had gone home afterwards and vomited until her stomach was tight with pain.

Shayana had been her aunt's friend, one of the women who came to read the Word with Tamora. Lamorna had waited for the Konsel, for Bryn or one of the others, to march up the hill and take her aunt away for questioning, but it had not happened. Yet.

Lamorna had not wanted to go into town after the burning. A thin layer of smoke hung over Kernou, and not even the fiercest ocean winds could wash it away.

'We need to leave,' Keraine was saying. 'Tamora—'

'I can't but ... I don't know how much longer I can pretend to believe,' Tamora said quickly. 'I don't see the Small Folk anymore. They have fled this place. I fear the noose is tightening around our necks and—'

'I know, love. I know.'

Love? Lamorna frowned. She stuck her head around the doorway in time to watch Keraine place both hands on Tamora's cheeks, then lean in and press her lips against Tamora's.

Lamorna's hand flew to cover her mouth. It wasn't quick enough – a choking sound escaped her and she quickly pulled her head back as Keraine asked, 'What was that?'

Tamora mumbled something in return, and then sighed. 'You're right. We will have to leave, but I don't want to leave Lamorna here alone.'

'I'm sure she'll be perfectly fine,' Keraine replied bitterly. Lamorna clenched her fists and grit her teeth. Their voices moved away, and moments later, Lamorna heard the front door click shut. She pushed herself off the wall, hurriedly tying her hair into a knot at the base of her skull, and ran her fingers over her face, schooling her expression before stepping into the kitchen, a smile planted on her lips.

Her aunt was standing near the stove, the kettle coming to the boil, but Tamora did not move.

'It's boiling,' Lamorna pointed out, marching into the room, grabbing a cloth and removing the kettle from the heat, setting it on the bench. Steam billowed into the chill of the morning air as Lamorna found two mugs and the teapot. 'Did you sleep alright, Aunt Tamora?'

'I know you heard,' Tamora said simply, moving away. She sighed and pulled out a seat, sitting heavily and resting her chin in her hand. Her sharp eyes appraised Lamorna, who pretended she didn't hear her aunt's words, humming a prayer song to herself while scooping herbs into the teapot. 'Lamorna, answer me.'

Lamorna pursed her lips, turning from the bench and putting her hands on her hips. 'Yes, I heard.'

'Does the One God allow you to listen at doorways now, does He?'

'I …'

Tamora frowned. 'You heard me say it, so I'll say it again – I'm worried for you, in this place.'

'There is no—'

'They tortured you!' Tamora snapped. 'Don't think I don't know. Don't think I didn't notice how you were walking stiffly, how your eyes were filled with pain. Don't think I didn't notice the calendula salve missing from my supplies. Show me,' she demanded, pushing back her chair and standing. 'Lift your skirt and show me what they did.'

Lamorna wrung her hands, then lifted her chin proudly. 'They did nothing. I accepted the One God's methods without complaint,' she added, trying desperately to keep the waver from her voice as she recalled the sharp, slicing pain of the broken glass, how she had hidden away in her room and removed the pieces of it from her flesh, wrapping them in a cloth and burying them in the yard while her aunt was out. She had wanted to vomit at the brightness of her blood against the milky tone of her skin, at the smell of it and the slick feel of it against her fingers, but she held her stomach and, therefore, her resolve.

Tamora came around to stand in front of her. 'Sit down and lift your skirt, Lamorna.'

Lamorna sighed. A part of her was glad someone else was going to see the horrid red welts left behind on her knees, but another part of her was terrified at what Tamora would do. She swallowed. Jenyfer, if she knew, would probably march herself down the hillside, into the town and scream at the Chif.

Lamorna choked back a sob. She missed Jenyfer.

Slowly, with her sister's face planted in her mind, Lamorna sat and lifted her skirt over her knees, allowing her aunt to see. She watched Tamora's face, but when her aunt's eyes, full of horror and pity, snapped to hers, Lamorna looked away.

Silence dropped into the room, deep and heavy.

'We're leaving this place,' Tamora announced finally, standing and wiping her hands on her skirt. 'Keraine and I. And you are coming with us.'

'No, I—'

Tamora bent so she could stare into Lamorna's eyes. 'If you think I am leaving you here to be butchered by those men, you are mistaken. You come of your own free will, Lamorna, or ...'

'Or what? You'll use your magic to make me?' Lamorna shot back. Anger was growing inside her again – anger at her aunt's magic, at Jenyfer's, at Keraine and that kiss she had witnessed. 'Or will you and your sinful lover simply tie me up and drag me out of here?'

Tamora stepped away from her. Her face was hard and her eyes glittered. 'You don't understand anything,' she said, her voice low and angry.

'I understand that you're a blasphemer,' Lamorna said, pulling her skirt over her knees and standing up. 'And I understand that you will burn in the Pit for all eternity. It's a sin.'

'You understand nothing,' Tamora hissed, 'nothing at all. We leave in two days. You will carry your own things, so pack light. Take bedding and sturdy clothes. The season is turning and it will grow colder the further north we go. Two days, Lamorna. Tell no one.'

Tamora turned and strode from the room, vanishing down the hallway. Lamorna heard her bedroom door close. She made tea, drank it while it was still hot enough to scald her throat, then hurried into the town.

'She wants me to leave with her,' Lamorna said softly. The Chif placed a cup of tea before her. He hadn't said a word while Lamorna had told him what had happened that morning. Her stomach churned as she thought about the two details she had left out – her aunt's magic, and Tamora's relationship with Keraine. The scars on her knees throbbed with guilt. She had not thought about what she was doing until she was sitting in the Chif's house, and it was too late to turn around and go home. She had just wanted to punish her aunt's wickedness.

'And so you should,' the Chif said simply, taking a seat across the table from her. They were sitting in his formal room, the heat from the fire making Lamorna feel woozy. It was always so hot in this house, she thought. She was alone with the Chif. Something screamed in the back of her mind that this was not proper, not what the One God would want, but he was the Chif, the One God's representative, the One God's voice. Surely, if this was not allowed, He would say.

Jenyfer's voice told her not to be an idiot, to get up and leave, make an excuse. Lie.

'I don't want to leave Kernou,' she said instead. She heard the tremble in her voice.

'It doesn't have to be forever, Lamorna,' the Chif said gently. 'You will be most welcome on your return, once you complete your mission.'

'What mission?' she asked.

'This is an opportunity,' Ulrian said smoothly. 'For you to spread the Word. I have no doubts your aunt will flee to Cruithea. The people there have not yet heard the Word of the One God. They are Magic Wielders, heathens and sinners – all of them. Do you understand?'

'You want me to convert them? To spread the Word?'

'*I* do not want this. It is the One God who wants you to do this, Lamorna,' the Chif replied. 'You will go with your aunt, bring the people of Cruithea into the Light, and you will send me reports of your progress. Can you do this?'

She nodded. Pride filled her but she swallowed it away, only for it to be quickly replaced with fear. But the Chif was watching her, so she lifted her chin and said, 'I can.'

As she left the Chif's house, one weight fell clear of her shoulders while another fell heavy onto them. She would no longer have to suffer the glances and reverence of the people of Kernou, but she would be crossing into enemy territory, into a wild world of hedonism and sin.

She hoped she was strong enough.

The One God would not have chosen her for this task if He had doubts.

She risked a look over her shoulder. The Chif was standing in his doorway, the house dark behind him, watching her. Lamorna swallowed and turned her face back to the path.

CHAPTER 17

Arthur was alone in the forest. Ethinne had walked with him part of the way, before she left him with no instruction except to wait.

Wait for what, he wasn't sure.

The previous evening, the High Priestess had come to his kibitka and told him he would make his way to the World's Door at dawn. When he'd asked why, her response was simple: to learn. Morgause had offered nothing more than that, leaving him staring after her, his head spinning. He knew from the books he had read in Avalon that deep in the forest, in an undisclosed location, was the Temple, the World's Door. It was here that the Priestesses of Cruithea would eventually spend their lives in devotion to Inanna, the Goddess they served. Since his arrival, Arthur had seen no effigies or idols of the Goddess of fertility and war. He had heard no prayers, nor noticed any outward sign of worship.

It was Ethinne who explained that, for a Cruithean, worship was not a practice as much as a way of life. 'The Goddess is in everything. She is everywhere. She is the trees and the soil and the air we breathe. A walk through the forest is worship, taking a moment to breathe deep and listen to the trees is worship.'

'But you will give yourself to the Temple?' he'd asked her.

'I will give myself to Inanna,' she'd corrected him.

Arthur did not know what to expect from the Temple, nor the Priestess he would soon meet. Jalen would tell him nothing, only to keep his mind open and listen to what she would tell him.

The forest was still and silent around him, the sun having risen moments ago. The light wove its way through branches and trunks and kissed the grass with golden lips. Anticipation was a burn on Arthur's flesh. The skin on the back of his neck prickled as a voice rose from the trees, a whisper that reminded him of the wind through the leaves.

Come deeper.

Swallowing, Arthur moved further into the forest. The more he walked, the more the trees closed their arms around him. The air grew chilled and crisp, like the first breath of winter at the turning of the season, the sunlight swallowed so suddenly it made him rub at his arms.

Deeper.

Arthur sucked in a breath and continued, not sure where he was going, letting instinct guide him, doing as Jalen had told him and keeping his mind open. He could feel his magic stirring as the trees became taller, their trunks thicker, the leaves a deep green. He blinked. The trees closer to the village were painted in autumn colours, but these trees were rich and vibrant, as if it was the heart of summer.

The deeper he went, the darker it became, no light breaking through the dense canopy. Small things rustled through the undergrowth and Arthur could feel them watching him, could sense their curiosity, and he wondered did they know about the prophecy, or were the words spoken by the Myrddin for human ears only? Did the creatures of the world, fey or other, have any expectations for what was supposed to happen?

The trees suddenly gave way to a clearing, the ground carpeted in flowers that twinkled like tiny lights. Magic rippled through the air. Arthur could see it, a bending and shifting of silver light.

'Hello?' he called.

Movement in the corner of his eye made him jump and spin around, heart hammering. He had not brought a weapon – not that he really knew how to use one, anyway.

Standing at the treeline was a woman with silver hair that fell to her waist. She was dressed in dove-grey robes, like the ones he had seen Ethinne and the other Priestesses wearing. The woman lifted her arm, placing a finger on her lips. Vines wove their way up her arm, disappearing beneath the sleeve of her robe.

Arthur did not move as she approached him and he was startled to see she was not an elderly woman, as he first suspected. Her face was young and fresh, her cheeks round. She studied him for a long time, amber eyes moving over his face, until she nodded.

'What—'

She placed a finger on his lips and stepped away from him, reaching into her pocket to remove a stone. She held it out for him to see and then turned her back on him, bending to place the stone on the earth. He could not understand the words she spoke and he had no idea what was happening, but the ground beneath his feet began to tremble. He took a step back as the woman stood; when she turned to him her face was old and withered with time, deep lines puckering the skin around her mouth and eyes.

She smiled as the earth heaved and, suddenly, in the space behind her a granite monolith shot from the earth, followed by another and another. Arthur stumbled back in shock. His magic curled around his hands, warm and golden, as the monoliths shifted and blurred, their boundaries dissolving, only to reform and shift again, until a building of lichen-encrusted stone now sat where before there had been nothing. It was almost as tall as the trees surrounding it. Arthur watched as those trees bent their branches until they formed a cage around the stones and vines as thick as Arthur's wrist wound their way up the sides of the building, moulding tight to the stones.

Gaping, he looked at the silver-haired woman.

'She will see you now,' the woman told him, stepping aside to reveal a door slowly unfolding from the stone. Beyond it was a dark space that called to him.

Arthur took a shaky breath. 'Who will?'

The woman only smiled and gestured to the door.

He took a step towards that mysterious building, then another, his magic dancing beneath his skin, filling his body with warmth. Another step. The dark mouth opened wider as he neared it. Arthur turned back to the silver-haired woman, but she was gone.

He closed his eyes, forcing his breathing to steady, wishing Jalen was there with him. Wishing anyone was there with him.

'Courage cannot be given, Arthur,' came a voice that resonated with power. 'It can only be unearthed, like a treasure you didn't ever expect to find.'

Arthur's eyes snapped open.

'Come,' the voice called.

Arthur glanced over his shoulder again. He could feel the eyes of the trees watching him, could feel the soil beneath his feet holding its breath, and the very air around him was pulsing.

He reached inside for a sliver of courage, then stepped through the World's Door.

The darkness was thick, so thick and heavy Arthur had no idea where he was going. He put one foot in front of the other, trying to call on the part of him that had run for days, that had crawled on board a pirate ship and faced the legendary Katarin Le Fey. The part of him that had given him the courage to take Jalen's face in his hands and kiss him the first time, defying his father and eventually turning his back on the only life he knew.

'You will find,' said the voice, 'that courage, once used, is not forgotten.'

'Who are you?' Arthur asked the darkness.

A lantern on the wall next to his head burst into life and Arthur jumped. Golden light smoothed out the darkness, spreading slowly and the belly of the Temple was revealed.

Stone walls, a ceiling that vanished into the darkness above his head. More lanterns jumped into existence along the walls, and he saw he was in a wide hallway. As his eyes adjusted, a figure moved at the end of that hallway.

'Come,' she said.

The lanterns nearest Arthur's head went out, so he hurried towards the end of the hall. The woman turned and walked away from him, her robes whispering over the stones below them as she walked. No matter how quickly he moved he could never seem to catch up with her, until eventually the hall opened into a wide chamber. He paused, looking around. The chamber was empty, except for the lanterns lining the walls, casting halos of gold on the dark stones.

His eyes finally fell on the woman, who was now sitting in the middle of the chamber. Arthur peered at her, trying to see her face, but she was wearing the hood of her robe over her hair, her features hidden by the shadows. 'Sit,' she told him.

He did, crossing his legs, the stones hard and chilled beneath him.

'I am Goerika,' the woman said, reaching up to remove her hood. 'The Priestess of the World's Door. And you are the King of prophecy.'

She shifted in and out of focus, her features dissolving and reforming until she was both old and young at the same time, cheeks plump and then shrunken, lips red and then colourless, the skin around her eyes smooth and then wrinkled. Only her eyes remained the same – blue and piercing, they stabbed straight through the magical barriers he could not construct.

Her magic was warm, like fire, as light as air, and cool as a winter rain. He could smell soil and the decaying scent of leaves.

The elements?

'Yes,' she murmured.

'What are you?' he asked.

A slight smile. 'He wouldn't tell you anything, would he?' At Arthur's confused look, she chuckled. 'The storm-demon.'

'You're a demi-god?' Arthur breathed.

'We are the last, he and I, bound to different masters ... and different fates,' she added, her voice dropping. 'I serve the earth, and he serves the seas. Well, he did. Now, he serves you.'

Arthur leant forward. 'What does that mean?'

Goerika's eyes moved over his face. 'I cannot answer that question – only you can. But, I would ask a question of you: what do you know of the history of this land?'

Arthur shifted uncomfortably. 'Probably not enough. I only know what my father wanted me to know, and what I was able to learn before leaving Avalon.'

The Priestess waved her hand through the air. 'This land was once a world of magic, faeries, wonder and mystery, of druids and witches, dragons ...'

'Dragons,' Arthur whispered in awe; in the space between them, the shadowy shape of a giant winged beast formed. He watched it beat leathery wings, almost able to hear the sound they made, before it vanished.

'Yes. And the Old Ones and the demi-gods were many. Teyath was ruled by a brother and sister, Enyon and Eseld—' Goerika paused. 'But you know this story already.'

Arthur nodded. 'Katarin told me.'

'Did she? Did she tell you that Enyon and Eseld worshipped the One God?'

Arthur's heart faltered. 'What?' he stammered.

'The One God is much older than anyone thinks, Arthur, and goes by many names: the Deceiver, the Tempter, the One with Many Faces. But what many don't know is that the One God is female,' the Priestess said.

Something clicked into place in Arthur's mind, words from a conversation on an island shrouded in mist. 'She stole the Treasures of the Gods?'

Goerika nodded. 'Some say she appeared as a red serpent, who whispered poison into the ears of Enyon and Eseld. They say she convinced Enyon to kill his sister. Corrupted by the idea of power, Enyon wounded Eseld in the thigh with a poisoned blade and, when she died, the land around Dinas Emrys also died. The Old Ones banished the Red Serpent and punished Enyon with wandering the world until his death, where Ankou sent him into the abyss, a pit of everlasting fire. Eventually, there was nothing left alive at Dinas Emrys – the earth was cursed, dead and barren through the spilling of familial blood.'

Arthur started.

'You know this as well?' Goerika asked sharply.

'I have seen this place. In my dreams.'

'Eseld was instructed not to hand the Grail to anyone except he who does not seek it. The Grail symbolises a union with the Old Ones and, therefore, with magic.'

'But the One God—'

'Her true name is Ereshki, the Red One. She has gained much power over the years – the power of an idea, Arthur, is as strong as the thing itself. And that idea, that power, is spreading,' Goerika explained softly. 'But, I suspect, things have not turned out as Ereshki had wished. She was ever blind to those that she loved the most.'

'Who?'

'Humans.'

'Are you telling me that Ereshki, the One God ... I'm sorry, I can't make sense of this. Niniane said Ereshki betrayed them,' Arthur said, frowning.

'Betrayal is a strong word,' Goerika mumbled. Her eyes found his, held his gaze. 'You must understand – history is written by those who hold power over others, Arthur. The stories that have shaped this world are just that - stories. Truth,' she said, her voice dropping, 'truth can change depending on who is telling the story.' She glanced at him, those blue eyes burning in the lantern light.

Arthur swallowed. 'Are you telling me the Old Ones lied?'

'I'm telling you that truth is subjective. Your truth, Arthur, is something you are yet to discover,' the demi-god said.

'So what am I supposed to do?' he asked wildly. 'I thought … the prophecy says—'

'That the Grail will reshape the future of this world? Yes, it will, but what you seem unable to understand is *you* and the choices you make will be what crafts the new world. The Sword of the White Dragon – the sword made for your hands – will spill blood on the cursed earth and Camlann will thrive once more,' the Priestess said simply.

Arthur swallowed, his head spinning, words tumbling over one another until they existed in a storm of confusion. 'I have to kill someone?'

'Perhaps.'

'Enyon killed his sister. Does that mean I have to kill mine? Because I won't.'

'The spilling of familial blood will break the curse.'

'So, my father?' Arthur felt sick.

'Perhaps, and perhaps not,' the Priestess said.

Arthur rubbed at his face. 'I can't do this,' he said. 'I can't be what they all think I will be. I don't have the power everyone thinks I should have.'

'What if I was to tell you your power has nothing to do with what flows through your veins?' Goerika said. 'What if I was to tell you that your power lies not with your magic, but with who you shall become? The man that waits inside you. The man whose compassion, whose lack of judgement, whose morality, will be the thing to unite people?'

Arthur was silent and, then, he felt it again, that spark, the warmth in his chest. It uncurled like the petals of a flower reaching for the sun. He reached up and rubbed at his chest.

'Be that man, Arthur. Be that man, and Teyath shall have the king it deserves. But,' Goerika said, her voice falling until it was nothing but a whisper, 'heed this, King Who Shall Be: darkness and blood will come for you before the end, when the battle is waged in the skies, in the seas and on the land, darkness and blood will come for you.'

Arthur swallowed tightly. A remnant of his dream flashed into his mind. His fingers twitched and he felt the weight of a sword in his hand, and the weight of a crown pressing down on his head. 'I regret it,' he said. 'What I did to my father. He's not a good person, but that doesn't make what happened right.'

'No,' Goerika said. 'You will see your father again, Arthur. When you do, there are things you must ask him. There are things he knows, things that have been put in motion by something other than the words of prophecy.'

'How will I know what to ask him?' Arthur said. The thought of seeing his father again was terrifying but, deep inside, he needed it. He needed some sort of closure. Ulrian's face still appeared in Arthur's mind occasionally, a reminder, perhaps, of punishments already had and punishment yet to come. Arthur didn't know, and didn't like to think about his father and what he had left behind; so he avoided it, shoving Ulrian's stern face away whenever it presented itself. He could not begin to imagine what they would have to say to one another, not anymore.

Part of Arthur was worried that maybe he wasn't as strong as he thought he was. That maybe one word from Ulrian would be all it took for him to crawl back into his shell and bend his knee to his father's will.

'You will ask him the questions you need to ask.' Goerika reached up to pull her hood over her hair once more. The lanterns on the walls went out. 'Trust your instincts, because even when you think you don't know what the right path is, the man inside of you – the one who is yet to be brought into the light – he knows.'

CHAPTER 18

There were insects scurrying beneath his skin – at least that was how it felt.

Ordes grimaced and rubbed at the back of his neck. Ever since he'd done whatever he'd done with Katarin, his magic had not stopped swirling and pushing at the cage of his body. Every part of him felt strange, even his bones ached ferociously with an energy that threatened to splinter them.

But it was the burning, tearing, *itching* that was driving him mad.

He'd gone looking for his mother, hoping she would have some answer – about the unsettling feeling inside him, but also about what he had done.

Water was his element. Did that explain the mist? Perhaps, but it didn't explain that shield of light he had made. It didn't explain the feeling that had coursed through him as the light of his magic had left his body and shaped itself into the air without a thought. The only thing Ordes had been thinking at that moment was stopping Katarin from stabbing him with one of those daggers, or smashing him in the face again. His nose hurt.

Niniane was nowhere to be seen. The courtyard was empty. The dining room was empty, nothing but billowing white curtains shifting in the wind-kissed darkness. Ordes knew he should find Kat – she knew more about magic than he did, had much better control over herself, and could possibly offer him something. But he found himself scratching at the back of his neck and banging on Jenyfer's door urgently.

She flung the door open; her eyes widened when she saw him. 'Ordes! What—'

'I need you to check something for me,' he said. He wasn't sure what his expression was like, what she saw in his face, but she nodded and stepped aside to let him in without a word. Ordes hurried into the room, tugging his shirt over his head as he went.

'Umm …'

'My back,' he said quickly, turning to put his back to her. 'Is there anything on my back?'

'Skin?' Jenyfer said.

'Jen, please.' His voice was strained and tight.

'Alright,' she said quietly. He stood still as she approached him, feeling like he was about to burst. He could feel her eyes trailing over him – the itching increased. He swallowed and tried to shove it away, but it persisted.

'There's nothing there,' she said eventually.

'Look with your hands,' he bit out.

She hesitated, but the moment she touched him the terrible itching stopped and his magic felt calmer. Jenyfer ran her palms lightly over him, sweeping her hands from one shoulder to the other, along the length of his spine. He felt his skin pucker into gooseflesh as she trailed her fingers back up his spine to feel along the back of his neck.

'What am I looking for?' she asked.

'I don't know.'

She didn't take her hands off him. 'What's going on? You're terrified,' she added.

'Nothing.' Ordes turned around swiftly, taking her by surprise. She sucked in a breath. Her hands rested against his chest and she was so close to him he could feel the heat from her body, see each freckle and—

'Your hair is wet,' he commented. Without thinking, he reached out and picked up the length of hair that was dangling over her shoulder.

'I had a bath,' she answered.

'Oh.'

Jenyfer frowned and slowly lowered her hands. 'What happened today?'

Ordes dragged his hand through his hair irritably. 'Kat has known me for a long time. She knows I don't really use my magic.'

'But you do.'

'Not like she does. Kat knows her power,' Ordes explained. 'She knows what she can do and she isn't afraid of it. I don't know the true extent of my power because I've never found the bottom of it.'

Jenyfer pulled her lip between her teeth. 'That day on *The Excalibur*, you fainted,' she reminded him. 'You called it burn out.'

'That's probably not the right word,' Ordes said. They were still standing close. A droplet of water from her wet hair trailed its way down the side of her face, over her cheek and towards her jaw. She reached up and brushed it away. 'Because I don't usually use a lot of my magic at the one time, when I do sometimes it overwhelms me. It's like overworking a muscle you don't exercise enough. You know it's strong, but it's untrained. It's like that.'

'And today?' Jenyfer asked.

He sighed and moved away from her, perching on the edge of her bed. 'That didn't happen. Maybe Kat was right – maybe it's being here.' He glanced at Jenyfer, who hadn't moved. There was a towel hanging over one shoulder, he realised. 'When you tell me you're scared of your magic, I know what you mean, because I'm scared of mine as well. I don't know where it comes from, not anymore. Not with my parents being who and what they are.'

Jenyfer took a small step towards him. Someone knocked on the door; she jumped, then hurried to answer it. Ordes rubbed at the back of his neck absently – there was no itching anymore, just a slight burning between his shoulder blades.

When Jenyfer came back, she had a tray between her hands. It was laden with food.

'I'll let you eat,' Ordes said, standing.

'I can't eat all this,' she said. She kept her eyes on him, and a small smile played on her lips. She indicated the tray with a nod.

'You want to have dinner with me?'

Her cheeks flushed. 'Only if you want to – it's okay if you don't.'

He thought for a moment about saying no, but then thought again. He'd long stopped pretending he could do anything other than what she wanted, so he nodded. 'Sure.'

Jenyfer's smile was bright. She set the tray on the table, and pointed him to a seat as she inspected the food – fruit, cheese, freshly baked bread slathered in butter, roasted almonds, sliced meats, and a bottle of wine and two glasses.

She took a seat opposite him. 'If there is one thing about this place I love, it's the food. And you can't tell me you're not hungry. You're always hungry.'

He supposed this was what friends did. Shared a meal. Chatted. As they ate, Jenyfer kept sneaking glances at him, her expression deeply curious.

'What?' he asked.

Jenyfer pulled her lip between her teeth, tapping her fingers gently on the edge of her plate. 'I wasn't going to tell you, but … your father said things to me before I left the ship. He told me I would help find the Treasures of the Gods but I didn't believe him.'

Ordes' heart skipped a beat. 'Did he tell you to leave?'

Jenyfer shook her head. 'He gave me a choice, Ordes. He told me my magic was influencing the ship, that that was why we were becalmed. He also said … he thought you were under a spell – my spell. And I thought he was right. I didn't tell you I was leaving because I didn't want you to follow me or do something stupid.'

'Why didn't you say, when we were in the sea caves?'

'You were really angry and I didn't expect you to listen to me,' she said simply.

They stared at one another; he could feel her heart beating alongside his, steady and calm.

'Well, let's not let this go to waste,' Jenyfer said with false brightness, reaching for the bottle of wine. The moment she popped the cork, the smell of it hit Ordes in the face – elderberry, cloves and sugar, pears, apples and vanilla. Faery wine. He knew what it was because Katarin had plied him with it once. He remembered the way it tasted – like liquid starlight and fire, flooding his veins and trying to mess with his head. Katarin hadn't realised the wine of Avalon didn't work on him – neither had he.

'You shouldn't drink that,' Ordes warned, but Jenyfer took a small sip, then, as the taste of it hit her, a bigger one, until she had drained the glass. He sighed, grabbed a handful of grapes, and sat back to wait. It took less than five minutes for the wine to take effect.

First, Jenyfer giggled soundlessly, then she cried, and then, she pushed her chair back and stood, stumbling around the table to plonk herself in his lap. She grabbed hold of his face with both hands and rested her forehead against his. Her breathing was heavy and deep.

Ordes gently removed her hands. 'It's the faery wine, Jen.'

She climbed off him, waving her hands through the air, before she started moving, her body swaying. 'Can't you hear it?'

'Hear what?' Ordes asked, biting his lip to stop from laughing.

'The music!'

He managed to shove some cheese in his mouth before she tried to pull him to his feet, giving up quickly, spinning around in circles instead. Her hair was like streamers, her arms flung out as she danced to her unheard music, humming and swaying and spinning.

She beckoned to him mid-spin. 'Dance with me.'

'Fine.' Ordes stood, catching hold of Jenyfer's arm as she spun past him, pulling her into his body. 'Since I can't hear the music, you're in charge.'

She nodded, face serious.

He couldn't help smiling. There was something so joyous in her face – something that he knew wasn't real, just an effect of the wine, but it was nice to see it. They danced like they had on *The Excalibur*; he spun her effortlessly around the room, her head flung back, mouth wide in a smile.

She stopped suddenly, pulling out of his arms and stepping away, removing her dress and tossing it carelessly over her shoulder, standing naked before him. Her skin was burnished gold from the lantern light, the breeze blowing in from the balcony casting flickering shadows on her flesh. He could see the sweat glistening on her skin, beaded across her forehead and down her neck like tiny jewels. Her chest rose and fell sharply with her breath.

Ordes kept his eyes on her face as she stared back at him. Two steps. That was all it would take to close his arms around her, but he didn't move. He wasn't sure he could. He wasn't sure he should. Something crossed her face, too quickly for him to read, and it was she who came to him. She wound her arms around his neck and pushed herself onto her toes so she could brush her mouth against his.

She tasted like faery wine, like lost inhibitions and carelessness. He trailed his fingers along her bare arms, over the faint fleck of scales. His fingers inched over her shoulders. More scales, soft and delicate, decorated her throat. His fingers curled over her ears and moved into her hair.

Jenyfer pressed her mouth to his again, urgent this time. Music slid into Ordes' mind and he felt her magic rushing through him, pouring into him, winding itself around his insides as one of her hands slid down his chest.

'Jenyfer, you need to go to bed,' Ordes murmured against her mouth.

He untangled her arms and hands from his body, then guided her around to the side of the bed, reaching down to pull back the bedcovers. She clung to him, her intention clear.

He was getting in that bed with her.

She had about five more minutes before she passed out, so he swept her into his arms, cradling her against his chest for a moment, enjoying the warmth of her, before lowering her to the mattress. A frown crossed her face.

'Alright,' he said, taking a deep breath. 'Move over then.'

Jenyfer shuffled sideways, never taking her eyes off his face. When he was lying beside her, she curled herself against him, and kissed him again, her hand, her *nails*, digging at his flesh, before she sighed – and fell asleep.

Jenyfer was using an arm as a pillow. A bare, muscled arm with a very familiar map inked on it. She blinked as the room spun into focus. Ordes shifted behind her, then his fingers were in her hair, smoothing the tangled mane back from her face.

'Morning,' he said. His voice was too loud, burrowing into her skull and digging into her brain. Jenyfer closed her eyes against the light pouring into the room. Slowly, she rolled over to face him, her heart stuttering at how close they were, how naturally they fit together.

Her memory of the night before was a blank space, nothing but blackness.

'What happened?' she managed.

'You drank the wine.' Ordes chuckled. 'I did try to warn you, but, like usual, you decided not to listen to me.'

She shoved him; he eased his arm out from under her and climbed out of bed.

'I'll get you some water.'

The remains of their dinner had vanished, and there was a jug of water and a glass – one – waiting. Jenyfer scowled. Ordes looked like he usually did. He did not look like he'd been run over by a thousand horses. She rubbed her eyes. 'Why don't you look like death?'

'Faery wine doesn't work on me,' he told her.

'Of course it doesn't.' Jenyfer scowled again, then swallowed the sand in her mouth as he pressed the glass into her hand, taking it from her when she was done. She lifted the sheet and gazed down at her body. She was naked. Alarmed, her eyes found his.

'You pulled your clothes off and tried your absolute best to seduce me,' Ordes said simply. There were scratch marks on his chest and across his lower belly. She gestured at them. 'You've got sharp nails.'

'I did that?'

'You did.'

'Oh. Sorry.' Jenyfer stared at him, heart pounding, her brain searching, searching for the truth of the night before, but there was nothing.

'Nothing happened,' Ordes said softly. 'You weren't yourself.'

Throat tight, she nodded, then winced, the movement making her head pound. She held out her empty glass. He came and took it from her. Their fingers brushed and a jolt shot through her blood. If he felt it, he didn't react. As he turned away from her, Jenyfer's chest was burning. She rubbed at the space between her breasts, frowning.

It felt like her heart was on fire.

CHAPTER 19

The sun cut through the curtain of mist that covered Avalon. Gold and grey fought a quick battle, before the mist sighed and fell back, allowing the dawn to swoop across the hills and orchards, the smell of apples floating through the air.

Jenyfer rested her hands on the balcony railing, watching the world come to life. It felt like there were parts of her spread across the continent, broken pieces scattered to the winds, all fighting to come back together. As the sun rose further and the island was bathed in golden light, she was unable to stop her thoughts from churning and turning in on themselves. Her sister, Bryn … everything that had happened since Ordes broke the lock on her cage. Had it all been leading to this moment? She felt caught in the middle of something so much larger than herself, with no way out of it.

Sometimes she wished she'd never left Kernou, that she'd been left to her fate.

Fate had different ideas, and there appeared no way to get off the path that had been laid out before her. She would search for the Treasures of the Gods and one of them, according to Niniane, would be hers. Jenyfer wanted to laugh; if she didn't, she thought she might cry.

Had Tamora known? Jenyfer recalled her aunt's words, her warning, to stay away from the Master of Songs and Death. And her mother. Jenyfer desperately wanted to *know* how a mortal woman had ended up birthing the child of a god.

What did that make Jenyfer? What did it make Ordes? They were both children of gods. Was that why they were caught up in prophecies made long ago?

She wasn't hungry, so she changed from her nightgown and headed towards the library. Her favourite table was tucked away in a corner of the spacious room. Sunlight filtered through the window beside her, bathing her book in golden light. There was no dust in Avalon, no specks stirring into the air as she turned the pages of the book. She had read it more than once already, but could not help returning to it.

Faery Creatures of the Sea. There was no author attributed to the book. It was the same with each book Jenyfer had removed from the shelves. No one claiming ownership of the words and ideas that filled the pages. Whoever had penned *Faery Creatures of the Sea* had a neat hand; the script was small and delicate. A woman, Jenyfer thought, wondering had the Goddess of Magic herself written the volume. It was more likely one of her priestesses or their apprentices did - she knew from Lamorna that the copies of the Decalogue that made their way around Kernou were meticulously scribed by lesser members of the Konsel.

Turning back to the book, Jenyfer skipped through the pages on kelpies and waterhorses. She skipped the part about mermaids, resisting the urge to rip through the book until she found what she was looking for. The pages were thin, old, and she was being careful not to tear them, even though a storm of words lifted from these very pages rested inside her. Biting her lip, she kept turning, slowly and gently, until she found what she was looking for.

Syhrens.

On one page was an illustration of a woman with silver hair and almost translucent skin. The artist had rendered the syhren's scales in great detail - they littered her temples, jaw line, the sides of her neck, travelling down her body, over her bare breasts until they reached her hips, where, instead of legs, she had a tail.

Jenyfer glanced down at her legs. Had she had a tail when she swam from the *Excalibur* to Newlyn? She couldn't recall one, and no tail had appeared whenever she was in the waters of Avalon.

But it wasn't tails Jenyfer was interested in. She scanned the first few pages of the chapter, her eyes flying across the paper, until she paused.

Syhrens were created by the Master of Songs and Death, Melodias, the God of the Seas. Consequently, they possess his magic, his power over the waves and the water, and the power of music; which, for a syhren, resides in their song. Although beautiful, syhrens are known for their deadly nature, more likely to sing a man to his death than rescue one from drowning.

Her song was buffeting away at her insides, less than pleased with her. Her thoughts shifted again to Alric and what had happened in Port Leore before she pushed the image away quickly and kept reading.

Human men are particularly prone to enchantments. Syhrens are by nature vicious and cruel. They delight in the misfortune their song can cause. Like the Old One who made them, they are master manipulators who enjoy toying with those they choose to slay.

Jenyfer re-read the passage, and was reading it again when Oides found her. She didn't lift her eyes from the page, although her skin prickled. She hadn't seen much of him since she'd woken curled against his body, faery wine still swimming around her brain.

'Anything interesting?' he asked her.

She shoved the book at him.

His eyebrows lifted. 'You want me to read this? This page?'

Jenyfer nodded, and did not move as he pulled the book towards himself. She gazed out the window, at the clear blue sky, and gnawed on her bottom lip, then her fingernails as he read. Eventually, Ordes set the book to the side.

'It's just a book,' he told her.

'I'm dangerous.'

'It's just a book, Jen,' he repeated softly.

'How do you know it's not true?' she challenged.

'I don't believe you would willingly hurt anyone,' Ordes said.

'What about Alric?'

'He deserved that.' When she stayed silent, he asked, 'Did you want to hurt him?'

She shook her head.

'Did you want him to hurt himself?' Another shake of her head. 'There you go then,' he said. 'You did what you did to protect yourself, to protect me,' he added. 'It's human nature to want to survive, Jen. That you acted out of that instinct and not out of malice proves, to me, that you are not what this book says you are.'

She sighed, pushing the book away and shifting her gaze out the window.

There were no images of Melodias in any of the books Jenyfer had found, as if the God of the Seas did not want her to know what he looked like.

Morgause had summoned Arthur to her kibitka after the evening meal. Belly full of roasted meat, he was smiling as he pushed aside the flap of the kibitka and entered. That smile fell as soon as he saw his cousin standing behind the table. Mordred's eyes found Arthur's, and Arthur waited for the biting remark, but none came.

'You're here, good,' Morgause said, striding into the kibitka after him. She shed her cloak, revealing muscled arms covered in the swirling tattoos of the Inborn. While her arms were not as thickly decorated as her son's, Arthur understood what they meant – Morgause was one of the Inborn before becoming the High Priestess. The tattoos meant she had been, and possibly still was, a fierce warrior.

Morgause moved towards the table, indicating Arthur was to follow her.

Spread before Mordred was a map, one that was familiar. Arthur frowned, leaning over to study it. 'I've seen this map before.'

'Morgaine drew it for us,' Morgause told him simply.

Arthur felt Mordred looking at him and he lifted his eyes to his cousin's. Mordred's braids were tied at the base of his neck, some dangling over his shoulder like chestnut snakes.

'You're as pale as a serpent's belly,' Mordred commented. 'Nothing of your mother's colouring.'

'Mordred,' Morgause scolded, but when she glanced at Arthur a slight frown rested between her brows. 'You've spent a life indoors, Arthur,' she said, 'which isn't your fault. But it's now time to learn about the world, about this continent that you will one day rule over.'

Mordred made a noise, but said nothing. He gestured to the map. 'Tell me what you know.'

'Of Teyath?' Arthur asked, and Mordred nodded. Arthur cleared his throat. 'I don't know much,' he admitted. 'Only that Malist is the seat of the One God's power, the home of the Sacellum. It is the centre of trade and commerce.' He let his eyes move around the map. 'Arcdon and Port Leore are trading ports, visited by merchant ships. Skulls Rest is a known pirate town, and they grow spice somewhere in the south, don't they?'

'They grow them in the plantations just outside Skulls Rest,' Mordred said. 'Along with coconuts and dates and some other useless fruit. What else?'

'The Vale ... jewellery and cloth,' Arthur said. He lifted his eyes again. 'But this isn't about cloves and coconuts, is it?'

Morgause shook her head. 'No, it isn't. Yes, those things will be important, but before then, an understanding of what makes this world work is what you need, Arthur.'

'Politics,' he murmured.

'Politics and religion,' Mordred said. 'At the moment, the continent is divided. The southern towns have fallen to the One God, while in the north we remain true to the Old Ones. Kunis is devoted to the Red One, as they have always been, although I have heard a rumour that things are changing there,' he added, glancing at his mother, who pursed her lips. 'Carinya and Newlyn are with us – they show no preference to one particular Old One, but they stay true to the Old Ways. Their shrines have not fallen.' Mordred tapped the map. 'Port Leore and Arcdon are close to Kernou, and these were the first places to fall. Skulls Rest remains loyal to her pirate population, and follows no gods that I know of. They trade with the rest of the continent because they need something to fill the gaps when merchant ships are thin on the water.'

'The Vale?' Arthur asked.

'Gold is their only god,' Mordred stated. 'They will support whoever buys their shiny things, and at the moment that is the good people of Malist. Supply ships run the coast between the two towns.'

Arthur stared at his cousin in awe. 'How do you know all this?'

'I have eyes and ears everywhere,' he said. 'It's my job, Arthur, to know who are Cruithea's allies, and who are her enemies.'

Nodding, Arthur returned his gaze to the map. 'The Teeth,' he murmured. 'What's there?'

'Things you don't need to meet,' Morgause told him.

'Faeries,' Mordred supplied. 'Trapped there for a long time.'

'Trapped by whom? And why?' Arthur asked, his eyes moving over the jagged assortment of rocky isles that made up The Teeth.

'The Myrddin,' Morgause said. 'Not all faeries have good intentions. Not all are as placid as the piskies you've seen around here, or the nymphs you would have seen in Avalon. There are many dark things in this world, Arthur, and dark things have an uncanny ability to draw other dark things to them. Medb and her ilk in The Teeth had ambitions far greater than the world could handle. So Merlin trapped them there. It was a mercy,' she added, her voice lowering. 'He could have wiped them from existence.'

'If they are so bad, why didn't he?' Arthur asked.

It was Mordred who answered. 'Because it is not his job to determine who lives and who dies, or who has a right to be. And as for the idea of good and evil – the line between those two things is constantly shifting and blurring. Nothing is either one or the other. We all carry the potential for great good, and great harm.'

Arthur could understand that. He had seen it, in Kernou, in men he thought were good and just people. He had seen their capacity for wrong, and their affinity to blame it on the belief they were doing right.

There was one place on the map Mordred had not mentioned. Dinas Emrys and the wasteland of Camlann Plain. Arthur's eyes lingered on that place, nothing more than black lines on parchment; but in his mind he could see more than that.

He saw smoke rising from a battlefield and, for a moment, felt the weight of a sword in his hands and a crown on his head.

CHAPTER 20

Lamorna was on her knees, the Decalogue opened before her. She did not need to read it, she knew the Word by heart, but not opening the book was a sacrilege in itself. She was finding it difficult to focus today. The Word left her lips, her voice low and smooth, but while she spoke about sin and temptation and the need to purify her mind, her thoughts were shifting like water.

Water and music flowed over her.

The long, cold dark.

A man with black hair and piercing blue eyes.

His fingertips were black, she remembered suddenly, pausing in her recitation.

Horrified, she started again, but her lips stumbled, and the hot rush of tears took her by surprise. Lamorna never cried. It was a weakness, and the One God did not abide weakness in any of His children.

With a little sigh, Lamorna opened her eyes. The light slanting into her room was bright today and a quick glance out the window revealed a sky free of clouds. The sun had risen hours ago. She could not remember how long she had been kneeling by her bed.

Tamora was in the kitchen. Lamorna could hear her aunt moving about, trying to be quiet, not wanting to interrupt Lamorna's prayers. She closed the Decalogue and left it waiting on her simple nightstand before standing on stiff knees.

Knees that still hurt. She shot a quick glance at the door, then sat on the bed, lifting her skirt, exposing her ruined flesh to her eyes. Gently, she traced the angry pink lines with the tip of her finger. It had been right for this to happen, she thought. An angry voice rushed into her head.

No, it wasn't. Jenyfer's voice.

Lamorna hurriedly dropped her skirt, arranged her face, made sure her hair was tucked securely beneath her cap, and went into the kitchen to find a cup of tea waiting for her. She looked at her aunt; guilt raced in to swallow her, but Lamorna pushed it away.

There was a bag on the table. It was open, so Lamorna peered inside.

Food, and some blankets, rolled tight.

Tamora caught her looking.

'When do we leave?' Lamorna asked quietly.

Her aunt studied her face for a long moment before speaking. 'Tomorrow. Keraine is making the arrangements. We will go at night, Lamorna, so make sure you rest during the day.'

'I cannot,' Lamorna said softly, sitting down and curling her hands around her cup of tea, allowing its warmth to sink inside her. 'I have to …'

'Have to do what?' Tamora's voice was sharp.

Lamorna shook her head. 'It doesn't matter. Nothing matters anymore, I suppose. We won't come back, will we?'

'We won't.'

Lamorna nodded and sipped her tea. She had wanted to see the Chif, to ask again if he was certain this was what the One God wanted. If he said she was not to go, she would find some way to stay here. But she recalled his face when she told him of her aunt's plans, how pleased he looked, as if he'd been expecting it. Other people had already left, Lamorna had heard people talking about it. She wondered absently where they had gone, but did not think about it for long.

'I'm going to go into town,' she announced. 'Are there things we need for the journey?'

'Lamorna—'

'We don't want anyone to suspect anything,' Lamorna said quickly. 'I should keep up my normal routine, shouldn't I?'

Tamora narrowed her eyes for a brief moment, then relaxed her face. 'Yes, you should.'

Lamorna nodded. 'Then I will go and pretend to shop.'

Bryn was the first person she saw when she entered the market square. His cloak was alarmingly red against the cobblestones and the soft blue of the sky. He was standing at the edge of the square, his eyes moving over everything and everybody, his chin lifted in a proud manner. Lamorna swallowed, checked her hair was covered, and strode into the square.

Knowing she was leaving made her confident, all the worries and the anxiety she'd been feeling since returning to Kernou sliding away from her, shed like a skin.

Bryn saw her and nodded. He had cut his hair again, she noted. It was shorn close to his head, the sandy-blonde mop she was accustomed to gone. His face was different as well, she realised. Bryn had always worn a half-smile, his eyes always soft, but now the smile was gone, like the hair, and his eyes were hard and watchful.

He inclined his head in her direction as she approached.

She stopped, unsure if she should speak to him. A little frown pulled at his face. He nodded at her basket.

'Your aunt was already here this morning,' he told her.

Lamorna's heart sped up. 'Oh? She must have come while I was still at prayer. She was in the garden when I left. I should have checked with her.'

Bryn was pleased with her answer.

'Do you miss the water?' Lamorna asked him, the words leaving her mouth before she could stop them. Bryn had spent his life in his boat. Jenyfer said that was all he ever talked about – fish, fishing, and the sea. There was nothing of the fisherman left, Lamorna thought, as his expression shifted again. 'I'm sorry,' she said in a rush. 'Forgive my rudeness. It must be such a change for you, that's all I meant by it.'

He nodded, and some of the tension left her shoulders. 'It is, but I am doing what the One God demands of me. It is an honour to serve Him in this way.'

'Yes,' Lamorna agreed. She was starting to feel twitchy. There was something about the way Bryn was looking at her that made her want to run home and never leave the cottage again. But she could not leave, not until he gave her permission to do so. It was not her place to decide if the conversation was over, as it had not been her place to start one at all.

Bullshit, Jenyfer's voice said fiercely. *It's all bullshit, Lamorna.*

She cleared her throat gently, hoping it did not come across as rude. Jenyfer would just walk away, she thought, wondering what her sister would say to this new Bryn, who was all sharp lines and tightness. Who carried a dagger instead of a fishing knife, whose red cloak hurt the eyes.

Bryn waved her away. Grateful, Lamorna inclined her head and hurried off. She could feel his eyes on her back and was suddenly glad she would not be here to watch him continue to become someone he was not, even if it was on the One God's orders.

CHAPTER 21

The curtains danced in the warm breeze. The scent of apple blossom, rich earth, and wildflowers floated into the room with each breath of the wind. Ordes rolled over and stared at the ceiling. Even though the bed was the most comfortable thing he had ever laid on, he could not sleep. His brain was in overdrive and his magic was restless, making him irritated and edgy, and the insect-feeling between his shoulder blades was back.

Ever since that morning with Katarin and her dagger-wielding magical vines, her insistence that he use what was inside him, Ordes hadn't felt like himself. Jenyfer had told him there was nothing on his back, nothing crawling free of his skin, but he couldn't shake the sensation that there was something wrong with him.

He wanted to curl into a ball, bury himself beneath the covers and never come out.

He also wanted to get up and throw himself into the ocean.

There was no escaping it – he knew that – but it didn't stop the flash of burning hate he felt for his father and his prophecy. But it wasn't Tymis' fault, either. Ordes knew that as well, which made it harder, because there really was no one to blame.

The future that the prophecy was leading to was only one future, one possible moment, in all the possibilities of the world. Ordes rubbed at his eyes, groaning. The future would also never happen if they did nothing. There was no time to wait for their future selves to show up and solve this problem, do the hard work and then let them all sit back and enjoy the spoils.

His mother had said the Old Ones could not find the Treasures, which Ordes understood to mean they could not interfere. This quest, or mission, or whatever anyone wanted to call it, truly was up to Arthur, Jenyfer, and him.

If his father was here, Tymis would tell him to grow up, to step up.

But he wasn't here.

Ordes climbed out of bed, the twitching in his muscles making it impossible to lie there and let his brain continue to churn, to overthink every aspect of the prophecy and what might or what might not be. He didn't bother with a shirt or shoes, pulling on some pants and wandering out into the dark hall.

The stones were cool beneath his feet. He walked, not thinking about where he was going, just needing to move, to try and calm some of the restless energy inside him. Pausing, Ordes glanced at his hands. He had tried, alone in his room, to conjure that shield of silver light, or to conjure mist again like he had in the orchard, but he couldn't do it.

He walked through the empty courtyard. Moonlight slanted through the arches, and this time, it wasn't apples he could smell in the air. It was water. He followed the scent down a hall, not stopping until he found himself at the top of the sweeping flight of stairs that led to Avalon's Lake.

Ordes took a deep breath, and was halfway down the steps when he realised he wasn't alone. Jenyfer was sitting on the bottom step, water washing over her toes. Her hair looked like it had been tossed about in a storm.

She turned to look at him and a faint smile lit her face.

'Can't sleep either?'

'No. My head is …'

'Full?' she supplied. 'Mine too.'

Ordes sat beside her, doing as she did and letting the water lap at his feet. They sat in silence until Jenyfer sighed.

'I miss the water,' she said softly. 'The sea. I miss it. The sounds of the waves on the shore, the smell of salt and seaweed. The sand between my toes.'

'Me too,' Ordes admitted.

She glanced at him, giving him another small smile, then turned back to the lake.

'How do you feel, being here?' she asked. 'And I don't mean the prophecy or anything to do with it. I mean here, Avalon, where you were born. That must mean something.'

'For years, I wondered about this place,' he replied. 'Whenever I'd wake at dawn and stand on deck to watch the sunrise, the world would be cloaked in mist and I'd wonder – where was it? Where did Avalon lie? Sometimes, I could smell apples in the air,' he added. 'Before I knew what this place was to me, I wondered. And then when you asked me to take you here …' His voice trailed off, regret leaping up to swallow him. He should have shut up, but he didn't, unable to stop himself, tired of stopping himself from saying what was truly on his mind. 'Should I have done as you asked? Maybe if I did, you wouldn't have left.'

Jenyfer opened her mouth, and closed it again, shaking her head, a frown creasing her brow. She cleared her throat and stood swiftly. 'I've got to go.'

'Jen—'

When she looked down at him, her eyes were glistening. 'You saw what your mother's books said about syhrens. In one book, it said syhrens were unable to be trusted. In another, it said we should never have existed, that Melodias broke the rules when he created us. And in another—'

'I don't care what some book says,' Ordes shouted, then sighed. 'I'm sorry. I'm sorry. I'm trying. I'm trying to do as you asked and be your friend but every part of me is screaming in objection.'

Her expression was tight, pained. She put her back to him, her shoulders lifting as she took a deep breath. 'I can't.' Her voice was low and rough, watery, and she was at the top of the steps before he spoke again.

'I miss the sea, but I miss you more, Jen. I miss what we had. I want it back. I want you back – I feel like I'm dangling on the edge of a cliff, and I don't know whether to throw myself off or cling on with my fingernails,' he said.

Slowly, she turned to face him. Her breath hitched, and that ragged movement of her chest had him taking the steps two at a time so he could close his arms around her. He wanted to hold her, just for a moment, and he wasn't sure if she'd let him. But she sighed, folding against him like a piece of a puzzle. She tucked her face against his neck, her breathing ragged.

Ordes closed his eyes. He could smell the sea, feel the sun on his face, feel the water against his flesh and the sand between his toes. Every part where she touched him was melting and his heart felt like it was on fire; music roared in his brain and Ordes knew at that moment he'd do anything she ever asked. He'd crawl on his hands and knees over burning coals for her. He'd give up his magic, cut off his hands, never set foot on the deck of a ship again – *anything* she wanted.

Step away. Step away step away step away.

Jenyfer's voice. It was a whisper, rushed, panicked almost.

And it was in his head.

Slowly, Ordes pulled away from her.

Their eyes met.

'You're frowning,' she said.

'Am I?'

'Ordes, what is it?'

'Nothing,' he breathed, resting his forehead against hers. 'It's nothing.'

They stood that way, pressed against one another, the heat from her body beneath his skin, until she shifted away. He caught the tiniest hint of a smile before she turned away, leaving him to watch her disappear down the hall.

When his mother found him, Ordes was sitting cross-legged on the edge of the pool, staring unseeing into the depths of the water, Jenyfer's face imprinted on the back of his eyes.

Niniane eased herself to the floor beside him. She lent over and trailed her fingers through the water – shapes formed in their wake, and then dissolved just as quickly. 'We call it the heartfire.'

'What are you talking about?' Ordes mumbled. His chest was still burning, and his insides felt tender, like he'd held himself too close to a flame.

'That feeling in your chest,' Niniane said softly. 'That burning in your blood.'

She gave him a gentle smile.

'Soulmates, Ordes, that's what you are – you and Jenyfer. You could hear her voice in your head, if you wanted. She could hear you, if she wanted.'

The words echoed through him, beating against the confines of his skin. 'I already did. Just now. I thought I was imagining it.'

'I sensed the heartfire the moment I saw you together. I suspect you already knew, or at least guessed,' Niniane continued.

'Yes,' Ordes whispered. It all made sense now – that empty feeling he'd carried his whole life, that empty space inside him. The yearning for something he couldn't quite name. He'd thought it was his lack of understanding about his magic, about where he came from, but he knew now it wasn't true. 'What does it mean exactly?'

'It means you will never love another, not because you don't want to, but because you can't. Whatever you do, you will always be drawn back to her, and she to you. She is your other half,' Niniane explained. 'Even now, you can sense everything about her – from her breathing to the rhythm of her heart. You can't tell the difference between your heartbeat and hers, between your breath and hers, your skin and hers.' She paused, giving him a knowing look. 'Your fate was bound from the moment you met.'

Ordes frowned. 'But—'

Niniane sighed. 'You don't believe me? Tell me this – why do you think you could never love Katarin? Yes, I know about that. There isn't much she doesn't tell me.'

'Oh, good. I hope she spared you the details,' Ordes muttered, feeling his cheeks heat.

Niniane chuckled, then, 'You couldn't love Katarin because you were waiting for *her*, Ordes. Because something inside you knew that, even if you couldn't give it words.'

'Can't there be one thing in my life that doesn't have to do with magic?' he said.

'You're a magical being, son, and so is she,' Niniane answered gently.

'This isn't magic,' he argued. 'These are my feelings. And hers. And you're telling me we don't have any control over them?'

'You do,' Niniane answered quietly. 'You don't have to love her.'

'It's too late for that,' Ordes admitted, knowing it was the truth. He kept his gaze on his hands, his eyes tracing the tattoos on his knuckles, stopping on the symbol for love. 'I can't tell her about this.'

'Ordes,' Niniane warned.

'She wants to make her own choices. It was one of the first things she ever shared with me, and if I tell her this – that this choice has been taken from her – she'll resent me for it,' he said.

'If you don't tell her, she'll resent you even more when she finds out you knew and kept the truth from her,' Niniane said sharply. 'Nothing good ever comes from lying to the person you love, Ordes.'

'She doesn't love me back,' he said.

His mother sighed, then stood, surprising him by dropping a kiss on the top of his head. 'I wish I could have been there for you,' she said. 'There is so much you've missed, so much I've missed, because of it. But, your father did what he thought was right.'

Ordes swallowed. 'Did he though? Do what was right?'

Niniane's hand dropped to his shoulder. 'Yes. You are the man you are because of him. Remember that, in the end, Ordes. He loved you enough to take you away from here, and give you a life as removed from what is going to come as was possible. He isn't perfect, but he doesn't try to be. Remember that as well.' Niniane's smile was sad. 'Call it love or magic or whatever you want, but you care about Jenyfer, possibly more than you should.'

Something cold skittered down Ordes' spine, quenching the burning ache inside of him instantly. 'What is that supposed to mean?'

'It means things may not end the way you want them to,' Niniane answered, her beautiful face suddenly grave; the coldness dancing along Ordes' spine increased.

'You have my magic inside you, and I exist out of time, but you also carry your father's magic. Jenyfer is half-human. You ... are something else entirely.' Then Niniane was gone, leaving him sitting alone in the great cavern of the room, the magic of Avalon swelling with each unsteady breath he took.

Chapter 22

It was dark beneath the trees, but Arthur was not cold. Someone walked beside him.

The Fisher Queen was with him. She held her fishing rod, but the hook was bare – no bait squirmed there. She didn't speak, didn't even look at him, so Arthur simply strolled along beside her, wondering where this moment was going to take them. Eseld was barefoot and her toes were corpse-pale, like the rest of her, and she was wearing her chipped crown of coral and her ragged dress.

The trees thinned suddenly and Arthur and Eseld were standing at the edge of the barren wasteland. Smoke rose from the earth, creeping towards a blood-red sky, before it was snatched by the wind and pulled away.

'Where are we?' Arthur asked.

'Camlann.'

It was not Eseld who spoke to him, but another.

Mordred.

Arthur's cousin stood beside him now, muscular arms bare, his warriors' tattoos curling over his shoulders. Mordred did not look at Arthur. He nodded at the wasteland that was the Camlann Plain. 'Look.'

Arthur looked. In the distance, a castle unfolded itself from the ground, a monolith of black stone. Its spires twisted towards the sky, its windows gaping at them like empty mouths. Something large and winged circled the highest spire as an ear-splitting roar ripped across the world.

Arthur clapped his hands over his ears. 'What is that?'

'Destiny,' Mordred answered.

The beast gave another almighty roar, and the world fractured around the edges, sending Arthur into darkness that dripped with the scent of blood.

Arthur was alone when he woke late in the morning. He used to wake before dawn. In those moments before sunrise, he would always lie in his bed and breathe, wondering how the day would unfold, if anything would be different. It never was though.

Jalen was not in the kibitka. Arthur sat up, rubbing at the skin on his arms. The air was chilled – the fire had gone out. He lay back, pulling the blankets up around his throat. He was pretty certain Jalen didn't need to sleep, and there had been many times when Arthur had woken at night and found Jalen staring at the roof of the kibitka. The fact he stayed there, tucked up next to Arthur when he didn't need to be, caused Arthur's belly to flop. They fit together, bodies curled against one another. Jalen was a piece of a puzzle Arthur always knew was missing but one he had never expected to find.

Happiness was a feeling he wasn't familiar with, but he was getting used to it, the way it felt. Contentment was as warm as sunshine on his face. And joy. Arthur had no words to describe what joy felt like, and he wasn't even sure what he was feeling was joy, but it seemed to fit.

He looked forward to waking each day, even if it was to find Halymere outside the kibitka with a serious expression that only the Cruithean Inborn was capable of so early in the day.

Arthur linked his arms behind his head, thinking of what he had learnt about this country he found himself so immersed in. The High Priestess' role was usually an inherited one but, with no daughter, Morgause would have to wait until the Priestesses received a vision from Inanna to appoint a successor. Arthur experienced a pang of remorse for his cousin. Mordred was a leader. He was strong and capable, yet he would never truly lead these people because their customs would not allow it.

Arthur had spent a moment watching the Inborn train, watching the way his cousin commanded those men and women. He had admired the strength of their bodies, the way they worked as one. Skilled with both weapons and magic, the Inborn were what Arthur wished he could be – confident and strong in body and mind. He admired their discipline, their devotion to their role.

He frowned. Discipline and devotion had been the song of his life. If he had been able to pretend to devote himself to something he didn't care for, what would happen – what would change – if he turned true devotion towards something he thought was important?

He could devote himself to the Grail and the Treasures, to the prophecies and his role in them. He could devote himself to the people here, for now at least. Or he could do neither of those things, until he understood who he was and what he wanted with more clarity.

Arthur threw back the blankets and rubbed the last of the night from his eyes, reaching over the edge of the bed for his clothes. While dressing, he thought about the rest of the people in Cruithea. If not a member of the Inborn, there were several other groups people could belong to – cabals, the Cruitheans called them. There were farmers and craftspeople, the Priestesses, who he had heard referred to as the Archeion cabal, and those who hunted the game that moved with the seasons.

The biggest difference between Cruithea and Kernou was not the way people looked. It was not the use of magic, or the goddess they chose to believe in. It was the way everyone, regardless of gender, of age, or physical capabilities was respected. It was the way everyone worked together, and how no one, even the High Priestess, was considered better than anyone else. Morgause was respected for who she was, not for what she was.

As he pulled on his boots, Arthur's thoughts shifted to his father.

Ulrian had been in this place. He had been part of this world, of this society and the people here. He had loved a Cruithean woman. Igraine. Arthur's mother. Morgause had shared her memories with him, as she had promised, and he'd learnt his mother was a powerful Magic Wielder, like Kat had said. She healed those who were sick. She set bones and delivered babies to the world with skilled hands. She helped those too ill to be saved pass peacefully to Ankou's realm. She was loved and cherished.

And then she gave up everything, her life, her family, for Ulrian Tregarthen.

Arthur frowned. What power did his father have over a woman like that? Had he been able to sway her with his words? Or was it simpler than that? Had she simply loved him? Perhaps he had been a different man then. Katarin said he had not yet turned towards the One God when he arrived in Cruithea, ill and almost dead from his journey from … where? Where had Ulrian been? From what Arthur could see of Cruithea, it wasn't the sort of place someone stumbled into.

Arthur wished he could know his father as he was then, as the young man who had found himself in this place of trees and fierce beauty. He realised sadly he could not recall his father's smile.

Expecting to see Halymere waiting for him, or Melhala, Arthur was startled to find Mordred outside his kibitka. His cousin was leaning with casual grace against the trunk of the nearest tree. Arthur's heart sped up when he noticed Mordred was twirling one of his daggers between dexterous fingers.

'You were in my dream,' Arthur blurted, then blushed, looking at the ground.

'Was I?' Mordred mused. 'Did I do anything interesting?'

'Not really,' Arthur answered, lifting his head. Mordred's expression was calm, still. There was none of the anger Arthur saw there last time they spoke. Encouraged, Arthur went on. 'We were standing at the edge of Camlann Plain.'

Mordred's eyebrows rose. 'The wasteland? Why?'

'I don't know,' Arthur said with a shrug. 'There was a castle there.'

'It's a ruin,' Mordred said.

'It wasn't a ruin in my dream,' Arthur answered. 'You've seen it? You've been there?'

Mordred nodded. 'Not for a long time.'

Arthur drifted closer, tucking in his shirt as he went and running his hand through his unruly hair. Mordred watched his every move, his scrutiny making Arthur nervous. 'Why did you go there?' Something from the dream was pulling at him.

For a moment, he didn't think his cousin would respond.

Mordred fingered his chin, his dark eyes on Arthur's face.

'Destiny,' was all he said, before he turned and walked away.

CHAPTER 23

Mist cloaked the world. It was early morning, but sunlight was yet to push through and stroke the shores of Avalon. As beautiful as the island was, Ordes missed *The Excalibur* and her crew. He even missed Tymis.

Merlin, he reminded himself. His father's name was Merlin.

'You're brooding.'

Ordes nearly jumped out of his skin at the unexpected sound. Katarin was standing beside him, arms folded. She didn't look at him, watching the mist swirl and dance over the surface of the water. She waved a hand casually and the mist washed away, revealing brilliant turquoise water that sparkled in the morning sun. *The Night Queen* was moored in the distance, sails catching the morning sun.

'I'm not brooding.'

Kat chuckled. 'When you brood, you have this way of standing – feet wider than your shoulders, arms folded, fists clenched, face folded into a frown as you try and solve whatever problem is swimming around your pretty little head. So,' she said, turning to him, her hair blood red and shining, eyes dancing with mischief. 'What is churning around that head?'

'Nothing.'

'Are you cross that I called you pretty?' Kat quipped. When he didn't respond, her face shifted. 'What's going on Ordes? You've been different since I kicked your arse.'

'I don't know,' he mumbled. 'Maybe you're right – maybe it is being here that makes me feel different.'

She flashed a quick smile. 'That shield was impressive. Can you do it again?'

'No idea,' he said. Then, 'Please don't attack me. I'm really not in the mood.'

'No,' Kat agreed. 'You're not. Spit it out.'

'What do you know about the heartfire?'

'Ah,' Katarin said. 'I see. I thought you'd be happy about it.'

'It's not like it matters what I want, or feel,' he argued.

'I'm guessing Jenyfer doesn't know?' Katarin asked.

He shook his head.

Katarin sighed, then grabbed him by the shirt, pulling him close to her. 'You're an idiot, Ordes. If you think keeping something like this from her is a good idea, you'll deserve it when she rips your head off. You asked me once, years ago, why I did what I do – why I target idiot men? This is why – because men seem to think they have the right to decide what women can and cannot know. Men seem to think they have the power to make choices for women, without consulting them.'

'It's not a choice though, is it?' Ordes snapped, wrapping his hands around Katarin's and trying to pull himself free. She shook him hard enough to rattle his brain around in his skull, and he could feel her magic wrapped around him as the mist closed around them again.

'Don't make me toss you off this jetty and drown you,' she hissed. 'I care about that girl. And, believe it or not, she cares about you, Ordes.'

'She doesn't want me,' he said.

Kat rolled her eyes. 'Do you truly not get it? She's scared of being hurt.'

'I won't—'

'She doesn't know that. Jenyfer is protecting herself in the only way she knows how and she doesn't deserve to be lied to, especially not by the man who claims to—' Katarin let him go abruptly and stepped back as a ship suddenly emerged from the grey that blanketed the world.

The Excalibur.

Katarin snorted, turning and walking away, her footfall sharp and purposeful along the jetty. Ordes felt his heart lift at the sight of the ship, and of Iouen, leaning over the railing as *The Excalibur* eased alongside the jetty.

'Had enough?' he called.

'Yep,' Ordes called back, unable to stop from smiling when Carbrey's weathered face appeared. The old man eyed the mist suspiciously. A tiny faery darted out of nowhere to zoom around Iouen and Carbrey's faces; Carbrey stumbled back, scowling, before his eyes fell on Ordes again.

'Nothing to do but gawk at the faery in his own habitat?' Ordes teased the old sailor, who laughed, then stepped aside as another face appeared.

Tymis Merlyni looked at his son for a long moment, then he ordered the gangplank to be lowered. Ordes waited, not taking his eyes from his father as the Captain made his way from the ship to the jetty, long coat streaming behind him. His dark hair was unbound, brushing his shoulders gently, and each step was filled with purpose.

'Staying a while?' Ordes commented, watching as the anchor was dropped.

'It depends,' Tymis replied.

'On?'

But his father was no longer looking at him. His gaze had shifted to what lay behind Ordes – Avalon, the tops of the mountains rising from the mist.

'She told me what you really are. What do I call you?' Ordes asked, tossing Iouen a wave and falling into step beside Tymis as he headed towards land.

Tymis shot him a quick look, then, softly, 'Father will do.'

Ordes smiled. 'I thought you might like "great and powerful one",' he suggested.

'I don't know whether to be pleased you still have your shitty sense of humour or be pissed off,' Tymis mused, but a smile tugged at his lips. 'Your mother?'

'Personally, I think she's a little insane. She's missed you apparently,' Ordes joked as they stepped from the jetty onto the carpet of grass that would lead them to the castle. The mist vanished with a wave of Ordes' hand; he sensed his father look at him but didn't acknowledge it and they walked in silence. Ordes was aware of the fey creatures of the island, just as he was the first morning he had arrived, darting about the trees and the flowering shrubs. He could see the tall grass to their left shifting as something passed, invisible, through it.

Tymis quickened his pace as they approached the castle, but at the doors he paused.

'Never has anywhere felt more like home to me than here,' he said softly. 'Not even *The Excalibur* comes close,' he added. Before he stepped through the doors, Ordes caught his arm.

'I've missed you as well.'

Tymis' eyebrows lifted and Ordes waited for the cheek, but his father smiled. 'Come on. Let's see if the Witch of the Mists is as happy to see me as you think she will be.'

'Should we leave?' Ordes asked loudly. His parent's reunion after thirty years apart was something he wished he could wipe from memory. Jenyfer and Katarin were on the far side of the room, both of them looking pointedly out at the purple-tinged mountains in the distance. Katarin glanced over her shoulder, rolling her eyes, before she turned and put her hands on her hips.

'Can we get on with things?' she demanded. 'I have places to be.'

'Don't let us stop you from leaving, Katarin,' Tymis rejoined, slinging his arm around Niniane's waist. She hit him playfully, but did not pull away from him.

Katarin stomped across the floor and flopped onto the pile of cushions, withdrawing her dagger and running her fingertip over the blade, her eyes shifting to Ordes before moving to his father. 'I don't take orders from you,' she said. 'Care to tell me what the fuck you're doing here?'

Tymis' face hardened. 'You might be Niniane's pet, but you don't make demands of me.'

'Enough,' Niniane commanded. 'He'll tell you.'

Tymis ground his teeth. 'He will?'

Niniane ignored him. 'You deserve to know, Katarin.' She and Tymis shared a look, and he nodded gently. 'I'd like you to meet the Myrddin – Merlin.'

Katarin laughed. 'Bullshit. Him?'

'Kat,' Ordes said quietly. Her gaze fell on him, before it shifted to Jenyfer, and slowly, the amusement faded from her face, replaced by shock and then anger.

'Why the fuck did no one tell me this?' she said, her voice rising. 'The prophet of the gods is a bloody *pirate*? Why? Why hide what you are?' she demanded of Tymis.

'The same reason you hide who you really are, Katarin,' Tymis said. 'Sometimes, it's easier to be someone else. Yes,' he said softly. 'I know who you are, where you come from and—'

'Stop,' Katarin commanded. She waved her dagger around in a menacing fashion, glaring at Tymis as Ordes wondered what his father was about to say; whatever it was, Kat looked like she would fly across the room and rip his tongue from his head. Her face was hard, jaw set. She was angry, and likely to be for some time, Ordes figured. He didn't blame her.

No one spoke for a long moment, until Kat tucked her dagger away purposefully. '*The Queen* will set sail tomorrow. We'll go south and continue the search for the Treasures,' she announced.

Tymis shook his head. 'No. You'll go to Cruithea,' he said firmly. 'All of you.'

'We will?' Ordes asked. His mother nodded.

Kat scowled. 'Fine. We leave at dawn, Jenyfer.'

Jenyfer nodded. A smile pulled at her mouth. She met Ordes' eyes briefly, and he smiled at the excitement he could see there. He was unable to stop feeling something similar. He turned to his father. 'North for us then?'

'For you, you mean,' Tymis answered. He shared a quick look with Niniane, then, softly, 'The ship is yours, Ordes.'

'What?'

'I won't be coming with you,' his father replied.

'Good, that's settled,' Katarin said, leaping to her feet and sweeping from the room, Jenyfer following her.

Ordes couldn't take his eyes from his father's.

'Lovey-dovey bullshit, remember?' Tymis said.

Ordes caught up to Jenyfer in the hall. Katarin was nowhere to be seen, and he realised she'd been waiting for him. She cleared her throat. 'So, you get to be the Captain?'

'You could always come with me,' he said.

She looked at her hands. 'No. I'm no closer to understanding how to use my magic than I was before. The magic in my voice, I mean. All I have to guide me are the pages in your mother's books, pages that might not even be telling the whole truth. You can say it all you like, but I'm worried that I'm a danger to you, to the crew – your crew now,' Jenyfer added. 'And you can't protect them from me, no matter how much you try. You know that as well.'

'*The Queen* will take the lead, Ordes.' Katarin's voice echoed down the hallway. She was leaning against the wall a little further down the hall, arms folded and inspecting her fingernails. 'You get to sail consort.'

Ordes scowled. 'Katarin—' he began.

She stalked off down the hall. With an apologetic smile, Jenyfer followed her.

Ordes was waiting at the end of the jetty, *The Excalibur* on one side, *The Night Queen* on the other. Katarin strode towards him, long coat flapping in an invisible breeze, Jenyfer flowing along in her wake, her soft gowns exchanged for pants and a linen shirt. She was barefoot, and carried a dagger at her hip. The Captain didn't spare Ordes a glance, striding past him towards her ship. The gangplank was already lowered and she marched up it, not looking back.

Ordes caught Jenyfer's arm. 'She's really pissed, isn't she?' he murmured.

'That's an understatement,' Jenyfer replied. Her skin was burning beneath his fingers. He watched the movement of her throat as she swallowed, and he hated it, hated that the choice had been taken from her, again, even if she didn't know it yet. His insides tightened, his mother's words, her warning, squirming inside him. He pushed it away as Jenyfer slipped her hand in his and squeezed.

'Jen, I need to tell you something,' Ordes said, but Katarin called out impatiently.

'Come on, Little Morsel.'

'See you in Cruithea.' Jenyfer gave him a smile, then pulled away and hurried down the jetty. She didn't look back as she skipped along the gangplank and vanished onto the deck of the ship, and Ordes had never felt so helpless in his entire life. Katarin met his eyes briefly, before she turned away and disappeared from sight. He could hear her shouting orders to her crew.

The Queen's sails opened in a flourish of bone-coloured cloth, immediately filling with wind. Ordes closed his eyes, and when he opened them, his mother was standing beside him, long dark hair shifting around her face. Her white gown sparkled in the early morning light.

'Where's Tymis?' he asked.

'He doesn't like goodbyes.'

'Right.'

Niniane placed her palm over Ordes' chest before he could object. The moment her hand touched him, he could feel her power. Something hard and warm formed beneath her palm. Ordes felt it sink into his flesh and when his mother removed her hand, he tore open the front of his shirt and rubbed at his skin.

'What was that?'

'A charm. It'll protect you – from her,' his mother said.

'One moment you're telling me she's my heartfire, and the next ...' He shook his head.

Niniane ignored the bite in his tone. 'Loving her for *who* she is, is different than loving her for *what* she is.' She patted his chest. 'This will allow you to keep your head clear when you're around her, and you'll need a clear head. You need to find Arthur, and find the Treasures.'

Before Ordes could stop her, Niniane reached up to tuck his hair behind his ear. 'Don't hide them,' she said, her fingers trailing over the pointed tip.

He scowled. 'I have to go.'

Niniane's smile dropped. 'Ordes, you need to understand the heartfire. You need to understand its potency. Apart from loving her, you will do anything to protect her, for no other reason than you *have to*. Do you understand?'

The Night Queen had pulled away from the jetty; Iouen was calling to him from *The Excalibur*.

'Go.' Niniane stood on tiptoe and pressed a kiss to his cheek.

CHAPTER 24

Water tugged at her dress, pulling with wet fingers, the soft grey material turned dark and foreboding. Hands bound, the child clung to the wooden stake as much as her tiny, numb fingers would allow. A splinter sliced her skin. The stake was newly wedged between the rocks on the beach, the timber roughly cut. Sand curled over her toes, carried in with the rising tide. A wave broke nearby; salt spray coated her face. She licked her lips, took a deep breath, and screamed until her throat was raw.

The waves embraced her, closing around her chest, surging higher, until they licked at her throat. The girl crammed her lips shut, but the water wanted to come in. It tickled the corners of her mouth and, if she wasn't so scared, she would have laughed.

The sky was blanketed with clouds, their undersides painted purple and blue. Bruised and broken, like she was. She strained her neck, tried to look back at the town, tried to find the house where her mother lay, her belly swollen, her breathing laboured.

The beach was empty. No one was coming.

The girl did not bother to scream again.

She closed her eyes. 'Inanna take me,' she whispered.

The water rose over her head and then it pulled back; she was left dripping and gasping, her toes clinging to the slippery rocks beneath her feet.

The ropes fell away from her hands.

Bright light flashed into her eyes and then, nothing.

Katarin opened her eyes with a groan. She blinked, letting her senses come to life, her ears filling with the gentle lapping of the water, the tongue of the ocean slow and sensual, a rhythm pulled from the heart of eternity.

She experienced a moment of panic, sitting up quickly as the world rocked beneath her.

The ship. She was on a ship. She let out a sigh of relief.

She rubbed at her eyes, forcing the dream away. It had been a long time since that moment had haunted her with such clarity. Katarin glanced at the nightstand, where her potion sat, the cork still in the small copper-coloured bottle. She had forgotten.

No one knew about the dreams, except Aelle. It had been Aelle who had brewed the potion for her – a draught to keep those past memories at bay. She wasn't fond of sharing the nightmare of her past with anyone. It was why she had always kicked Ordes out of her bed before he could get too comfortable. It was only Aelle who had seen, Aelle who had held her as she thrashed about in sweat-soaked sheets, Aelle whose hand had smoothed back the tangled mass of her hair. But Kat hadn't been able to let that continue either. Part of her had broken a long time ago. She couldn't give a heart that was missing pieces to anyone. It was easier to be what she was now – tough and fierce, a strength to others.

She was glad she hadn't been the one to take Arthur to Cruithea, even though she would have if he'd asked. It meant she didn't have to go back there – yet. Her path would lead her to the forest of her birth eventually. Seeing her aunt was always painful and there were too many memories in that place, both past and recent ones.

Part of her thought she was crazy, living this life on top of the thing that almost took her from the world. No, Katarin reminded herself. It was not the sea that tried to kill her. It was a man, someone she thought she could trust. Someone she had begun to look at as a father.

She hadn't even been there when Arthur had been born. Ulrian had already tied her to that stake, his dark eyes not looking at her as she cried and begged and asked him why. Her last memory of Ulrian Tregarthen was as he walked away from her, his ears, and his heart, closed to the terrified screams of a child.

She was still in bed when Aelle entered, carrying a steaming cup of tea. The other woman took one look at her, saw the unopened potion bottle and made an exasperated sound.

'*The Excalibur* still keeping up?' Kat asked, forestalling the lecture she knew was coming. Aelle closed the door behind her with her foot, coming over to the bed to press the mug of tea into Kat's hands. Cruithea was at least a week away at the pace they were making; if they didn't have to wait for Ordes, *The Queen* would slip beneath the waves and they could be there in moments. Katarin didn't mind the wait, though – it gave her time to organise her thoughts.

Aelle nodded. 'Yes, and our syhren does nothing but watch that bloody ship.'

'The lovesick fool,' Katarin answered, shaking her head.

'You were a lovesick fool once,' Aelle reminded her.

Kat ignored her, sipping her tea. 'You make the best tea.'

'Don't avoid the subject,' Aelle said sternly, but a smile played at her mouth. 'Do you trust her?'

'It doesn't matter if I do or not,' Kat said quietly. 'She's part of the prophecy, part of Arthur's destiny. It's our job to help her and Ordes.'

'Alright,' Aelle concurred, sitting on the edge of the bed. 'And then what?'

'What do you mean?'

'You've spent the better part of your life helping everyone else, Kat. When will you let someone help you?' Aelle asked gently.

'The last person to ask me that got a black eye for his troubles,' Kat snapped, and then sighed, pushing away another memory, another reason to avoid Cruithea. 'I'm sorry. You're not him.'

'No, but I still care. We all do.'

Katarin was silent. She turned her attention to the tea, realising with a start that the cup was empty. She couldn't remember drinking it.

'The dream?' Aelle asked.

'Just water, I think,' Kat whispered. 'No flames.'

'What happened in Malist was not your fault,' Aelle said softly. 'I know I wasn't there that day, but I know you well enough to say it wasn't your fault.'

Kat closed her eyes against the memory. 'I didn't save her.'

'But you've saved so many others, myself included. That means something, Kat,' Aelle argued.

Kat said nothing. She didn't like mornings. She didn't like conversations like these, so heartfelt and raw, especially not before she'd had a chance to properly wake up. Aelle knew it as well. She didn't say anything else, reaching over and taking the cup from Katarin's stiff fingers.

When she left, Kat was still staring at nothing. In her mind, water washed over her ankles. Snarling, she threw back the covers and climbed from the bed, dressing quickly and pulling on her boots before heading out into the brightness of the day. Aelle was at the helm; Kat felt her eyes on her face but didn't look at her, turning instead to Erin, who was mending a sail, a great swathe of canvas sprawled over her lap. Tahnet was inspecting a list of something, while Isla and Ewella worked the rigging. Clem and Loren were swabbing the deck with more enthusiasm than the task deserved. Keren was perched on top of a barrel, her eyes on a map. She had only started learning how to read them, and was not seen without one recently. Tamsin and Merryn were arguing good-naturedly about something.

Kat knew the names of every single woman on board her ship. She knew their stories, where they had come from, what had led them to the pyre. She never asked questions, never pressed for their tales unless they wanted to tell them.

Aelle was right. Katarin had spent half her life helping others, and she wasn't so unaware that she didn't know why – her nine-year old self demanded nothing less. She hadn't been able to save herself then, but she could save others now, and each woman they rescued was one more *fuck you* to men like Ulrian Tregarthen, who thought they knew what was best, who thought they had the right to take away a person's choice.

Kat looked out across the wide expanse of ocean. They were far off the west coast of Teyath, moving slowly north. Jenyfer was leaning against the railing, staring out to sea. *The Excalibur* was behind them. Since leaving Avalon, Jenyfer had been quieter than usual, her face more often than not pulled into a frown.

It was more than Ordes swimming around her head.

Niniane had told Kat about Melodias being Jenyfer's father.

Ordes had told her about the heartfire.

Jenyfer had told her nothing.

CHAPTER 25

O rdes stretched out his legs, putting his feet on the desk like he'd seen his father do a million times. He closed his eyes, linked his hands behind his head and stretched until his back cracked. They were following *The Queen*, as instructed, bound for Cruithea. He had no idea what would happen once they dropped anchor in The Moon's Bite and stepped into the world beneath the trees. He'd never been there. There had never been a reason to. The Cruitheans kept to themselves mainly, not trading with anyone, but he had heard enough over the years to be curious about what they would find there.

What sort of man was Arthur Tregarthen? Was he feeling as lost as Ordes was, as swept away with everything that was unfolding outside of their control? Was it possible to ignore fate, he wondered, and make his own path, or would fate always find him, stripping away all his choices?

Ordes rubbed at his face, pressing the heels of his hands against his eyes. Since the moment he'd set foot in Kernou and then followed a wild-haired Magic Wielder into the hills, his world had been shaken into pieces and hastily put back together.

Except, his mother would say it was fate.

Jenyfer. The Grail. A man he'd never met. The Treasures of the Gods. A prophecy he wished he had no part in. They all swirled around his head.

Ordes gazed at the bed. He probably shouldn't bother. He couldn't sleep.

The heartfire was burning in his chest. He rubbed at it, frowning.

With a groan, he made himself stand and walk across the Captain's cabin that was now his, plonking on the edge of the bed to take his boots off, followed by his shirt. He glanced down, catching sight of the dark ink of the map. The one that would supposedly lead them to the Grail; except no one, not even his mother, recognised a single landmark etched across his skin or Jenyfer's. So far, they had sailed north from Avalon. Newlyn lay to the east of them, her lights not visible this far out into the Eastern Sea. Ordes wandered back to the desk, leaning over to stare at the map of the known lands. They were halfway between Teyath and the southern tip of Aileryan, a place he had never been. What would he find there if he ordered the ship north-west instead of north-east?

Snapping his fingers, Ordes extinguished the lantern and threw the cabin into darkness but, no matter how much he tried, sleep would not come. His chest burnt. His back itched. With a sigh, he gave up, heading out onto the deck. The moon was hidden and clouds streaked the sky. The crew were below deck; Ordes could hear their chatter, hear them playing cards and the clink of glasses. He considered joining them, like he used to, but was that his role now? Did the Captain drink and gamble with the crew?

Iouen was on watch and Ordes joined him on the quarter deck. The ocean was a black slick surrounding them, but it was calm. Up ahead, visible to his faery eyes, was *The Queen*.

'Don't know why we couldn't take the lead,' Iouen grumbled. 'Consort, Ordes?'

Ordes smiled. 'Let her have her moment, Iouen.'

His friend sighed. One hand was resting on the wheel, but he didn't need to steer the ship. 'Are you going to talk about it?' Iouen asked eventually.

'Where would you like me to start?' Ordes said. 'With the fact that my mother is a goddess, my father is the Myrddin and Jenyfer is bound to me for the rest of our lives because of some fey thing that I haven't told her of yet? Oh, and apparently I have to find one of the Treasures of the Gods, because it's mine.'

Iouen gave a low whistle. 'I was actually referring to you being Captain now, but sure, start with all those things I guess.'

Ordes bit his lip, and then it all came pouring out, everything he was feeling about his mother, his father, the prophecy – all his worries, his doubts, his fear at what he was being asked to do, what they were all being asked to do, and the uncertainty of it all.

'He never told me, and I'm always going to wonder why,' Ordes finished. 'Wouldn't it have been better for me to know in advance what was going to happen?'

'Maybe he didn't want to burden you with it? Who knows? Family is complicated,' Iouen said. He drummed his fingers against the wheel. 'Did I ever tell you about my family?'

'I don't think so, no,' Ordes answered.

'I grew up in Kunis – my father's family had been wealthy landowners, and my father inherited everything from his father and so on, this grand estate passed down through the generations,' Iouen said, shaking his head. 'My father's name was Krien, and my mother was Sennara. I had a sister – Olwen. My twin.'

Ordes realised quickly that Iouen was talking about his family in the past tense. His friend was watching the ocean, his face tight.

'After our mother died of a long illness and our father turned to drink, Olwen and I only had each other. It was enough. But then, he sent her away.'

'Why?'

'Olwen was a Magic Wielder,' Iouen explained.

Ordes frowned. 'And your father didn't like that?'

'Oh no, he loved it. A daughter with magic was a valuable asset. Ever the businessman, he sold her,' Iouen said, his voice dark with bitterness.

'Sold her? To whom?'

'To the Ossuary,' Iouen replied. 'To the Red Sisters. My father was a devout believer, see.'

'In the One God?' Ordes asked.

Iouen shook his head. 'No. The Red One. Ereshki.'

'Ereshki?' Ordes said sharply. 'The Old One who stole the Treasures of the Gods?'

'Stole isn't the word my father would use,' Iouen mumbled. He caught Ordes' shocked look. 'I know about the Treasures, and I know about the prophecy. I've always known. I just didn't know if it was true or not and I didn't know who you were, or your father ... he's the fucking Myrddin, Ordes. I honestly can't believe it.'

'I don't know what to say,' Ordes said eventually. 'I thought I knew you.'

A muscle feathered in Iouen's jaw. 'You do. When my sister was whisked away, I took off. I left my home, the land that I would one day inherit, the wealth – without Olwen, there was nothing there for me. My father didn't come after me, Ordes. He didn't care. He had delivered a Magic Wielding daughter to the House of Bone—'

'The *what? Forever entombed in the House of Bone* ...'

Iouen took a deep breath. 'The House of Bone, the Ossuary, lies in the Dead Woods between Cruithea and Kunis. I don't even know if Olwen is still there, or if she's alive. Once a woman is given to the House of Bone she does not leave. Her life belongs to the Red One.'

Ordes' head was spinning.

Iouen kept talking, to fill the silence perhaps, or because he had to. 'I made my way to Malist, kicked about there for a while, living on the streets, getting my arse handed to me. I was a poor little rich boy in a world that was ready to chew me up and swallow me. I had to get tough, and smart, and I needed a job, so ...'

'So you joined the crew of *The Georgiana*,' Ordes finished.

'You know the rest,' Iouen said with a shrug.

Ordes frowned, pulling his bottom lip between his teeth and chewing on it. The only sound was the gentle snap of the sails as they caught the wind, and the lapping of the water against the hull of the ship. The men below deck were silent, curled into their hammocks for the night.

'Does my revelation mean we've broken up, Ordes?' Iouen joked, but his eyes were worried and the hand that gripped the wheel was tight, the skin around his knuckles white.

'No,' Ordes said with a shake of his head. 'You just took me by surprise.'

'Upset I stole your thunder? I mean, yes, with your parents being who they are and everything I can see why you don't want to be upstaged by your quartermaster. But while your story is interesting and awe-inspiring and all that, mine is much more tragic, don't you think?' Iouen said, grinning. It was his usual grin but, for the first time, Ordes was aware of what was hidden behind it.

He rested his hand on Iouen's shoulder. He had questions, so many of them. They were crammed against the outside of his brain, but he shoved them away. There would be time to ask later, starting with what Iouen knew about the House of Bone and the Red Ones.

A song will sing the Red Ones home, forever entombed in the House of Bone.

CHAPTER 26

Night was falling and the storm that had been approaching for hours was upon them. Lightning flickered like veins, like the lines on the map inked across Jenyfer's skin. The wind increased, tugging at her hair, ripping pieces free of the braid that snaked down her back, shoving them in her face. Jenyfer pushed the hair away and huffed a breath, shifting her weight from one foot to the other, gripping the railing tightly. Anticipation sat like a stone in her belly.

The Excalibur was somewhere behind them, probably being tossed about like they were. Aelle had ordered the sails shortened, and everyone else was below deck, where Jenyfer should be. Tahnet had come and tried to drag her away, muttering to herself in frustration when Jenyfer had refused. She needed to be up here, with the wind in her hair and rain kissing her skin, and she didn't know why. Her blood was burning, a terrible itching in her veins, her magic churning like the water that threw itself against the hull of the ship.

The storm was getting worse. Everything was grey. Jenyfer narrowed her eyes against the wind and adjusted her grip on the railing as *The*

Queen crested a wave, the ship crashing down roughly. Water sloshed over the sides, soaking Jenyfer's feet.

Suddenly, she could hear music; her inner song responded with what sounded like laughter, triumphant and deep, throbbing in her ears, in the core of her body. It was happy, excited, swimming through her like a river of sound and water and melody.

Something shifted on the horizon.

A silvery head broke the surface of the ocean, then vanished so quickly she thought she imagined it. Jenyfer's inner song was so loud it drowned out the clash of thunder that she knew followed on the heels of the lightning now shooting across the sky, one dazzling bolt after another.

The waves grew mountain-large.

Another silver head appeared, a blink of light in the dark water.

Vanished again.

Jenyfer turned from the railing, flinging herself across the pitching deck to pound on the door to Katarin's cabin.

A cranky Captain answered, rubbing at her eyes. 'Have a bad dream, Little Morsel?'

Jenyfer shook her head. She grabbed Kat by the wrist, ignoring the other woman's protest, and hauled her out onto the deck, gesturing wildly to the storm bearing down on them. The clouds swirled in front of them, a mass of grey shot through with silver. The stars were devoured. The only light came from the flashes of white that split the sky. Rain lashed the ship.

'It's just—' Katarin froze. 'Music,' she whispered, eyes wide.

'You can hear it?' Jenyfer whispered back.

Katarin's face shifted suddenly, some conclusion Jenyfer had not come to flashing through her eyes. 'Wake the others,' she demanded, racing back into her cabin as Jenyfer nodded, throwing herself down the ladder, stumbling through the dark world below deck, shouting at the others to get up.

The ship pitched violently to cries of objection.

Not waiting to see if the crew listened, Jenyfer hurried back onto the deck.

Music exploded all around her.

The magic in her blood rushed to the surface and she couldn't hold it – her lips opened and her song filled the air, blending with the others that drenched the night as a wave spilled over the side of the ship. The moment the saltwater touched her skin, Jenyfer's song surged; a prickling broke out over her arms and chest. Her scales. Jenyfer kept singing, caught up in the music that swelled and breathed with the pounding of the waves.

Someone grabbed her arm.

Someone slapped her face, hard enough to make her gasp, her song dying.

She blinked, cheek stinging. 'What—'

'They're attacking my ship,' Katarin snarled, giving Jenyfer a violent shake. 'Syhrens,' she spat. 'Your kin are trying to bring down *The Queen*, so either help me or throw yourself overboard.' Katarin gripped Jenyfer's chin and forced her head around to face the water.

Syhrens.

Dozens of them, silvery heads clear of the water as they sang, their voices growing louder, washing over the world. Another wave crashed into the ship, then another, the strength, the power, of the sea, of the syhrens magic, flinging *The Queen* around like she was nothing but a child's toy.

Jenyfer swallowed, fear gripping her. She was frozen, unable to move as the ship tipped dangerously and someone screamed; a body went overboard and vanished beneath the violent waves.

Where was *The Excalibur?* Where was Ordes?

Katarin had gone, lost somewhere in the chaos. Jenyfer looked around frantically, choking on a scream as the main mast groaned and slowly, slowly, toppled towards the water.

Lightning flashed, blinding them. Jenyfer covered her eyes – she could feel magic in the air but she didn't know whose. The world around her was breaking into a million pieces, shattered by music and the sea. The wind pulled at her, tugging her towards the railing, gripping her in claws of ice.

The music continued, layers and layers of sound tumbling over each other.

With the next crack of lightning, *The Night Queen*, the magical ship, fractured down the middle, and Jenyfer was flung into the welcoming embrace of the sea.

Ordes, arms folded and eyes narrowed, was at the helm of *The Excalibur*. Beside him, Kayrus had both hands gripping the wheel. The ship rocked dangerously, the waves lifting her up then letting her crash back down. Mist and sea-spray billowed around them.

Up ahead, the clouds were shot through with black, the ocean like chopped soup.

And they were sailing right for it.

The Queen had already been swallowed by the storm.

'It's a ship killer, Ordes,' Iouen shouted from the main deck; Carbrey stood behind him, jaw set. 'We need to turn around!'

'Kat's ship is in there somewhere,' Ordes shouted back, gesturing at the swirling clouds.

'Let's hope *The Queen*, and us, hold then,' Iouen yelled.

'Tell the men to secure everything, including themselves.' Ordes turned to face Kayrus as Iouen and Carbrey hurried away. 'Can you hold her?' he asked the helmsman.

'As much as I can. We need to shorten those sails before it hits,' Kayrus added, gesturing at the sails fluttering in the shrieking wind. 'I know she's a magic ship, but if we lose the mast …'

'I know,' Ordes said. 'Secure yourself, Kayrus.' He raced down the ladder and hurried to the main mast, snatching a rope from the deck. He had almost finished tying himself to the mast when Iouen was back.

'What the fuck are you doing?'

'What I can,' Ordes shouted, lifting his voice over the roar of the whine and the waves. 'I can't hold the ship, but I should be able to hold the mast with my magic. It'll help.'

'Ordes—'

'You can't help me do this, Iouen.' Another wave washed over the ship, almost knocking Iouen off his feet. Water sloshed angrily around their ankles. Ordes nodded towards Kayrus, the man's hair and clothes drenched. 'Help him.'

Iouen nodded and hurried away.

The Excalibur was pulled at unnatural speed towards the swirling mass of clouds that blocked out the stars and painted the sky grey. The waves rose and fell around them, the ship tugged closer to the storm. Ordes grit his teeth as a wall of water crashed over the ship, sweeping his feet from beneath him – the rope cut into his middle but held him to the mast. Magic shot through his veins as he clenched and unclenched his hands, silver light bleeding across his knuckles. He poured everything into his hands, not daring to close his eyes as the ship rocked violently, trying to pull up something like the magic he had unleashed that day in Avalon. He could feel it, lurking beneath his skin.

Ordes drew his hands together at his chest. Jenyfer was in the middle of that storm somewhere. At the thought, the heartfire surged and burned, carving its way through Ordes' insides as his magic reacted. Silvery light exploded out of him, stretching across the ocean like a giant hand and plunging its way through the clouds, searching for any trace of her.

He could suddenly hear music over the din of the wind and the raging of the water. His breath hitched as comprehension dawned. He had no idea if any of the crew could hear him, but he had to warn them. 'Block your ears!' Ordes shouted, as *The Excalibur* was sucked into the belly of the storm.

The world turned dark with water, bright with flashes of lightning, and the music swelled and filled his ears. The charm in Ordes' chest throbbed as he gripped the main mast, the deck a slick of water and swirling white foam. He could hear nothing but music now, the wind ripping at his clothes, his hair, as if trying to pull him from the ship and into the sea.

Until it was over.

The music stopped, the wind vanished, the clouds peeled back like the skin of a ripe fruit and then slipped away, the sky dotted with stars once more, the wane light of the moon returning to light the night.

Ordes blinked, hastily untying himself and rubbing at his stinging belly.

'Captain,' Kayrus called, his voice shaking, 'look.'

Strewn across the water all around them was the wreckage of a ship.

The Night Queen.

Ordes opened his mouth, but nothing came out as he stared at the debris bobbing gently on the waves. He heard someone order the boats to be lowered, ordered the men to search the wreckage for Kat's crew.

'Ordes.' Iouen shook him. His face was pale, hair plastered to his forehead. He dragged Ordes over to the railing. 'Snap out of it. Katarin needs you.'

Ordes swallowed and scanned the water, dread pooling in his belly. He spotted Kat clinging to a barrel, the water around her steady as she used her magic to keep those of her crew close to her afloat. As the last woman was hauled, lifeless and limp, into one of *The Excalibur's* small boats, Katarin let go of the barrel, and slipped beneath the waves.

Ordes didn't think twice. He flung himself overboard, the waves rising to meet him. He cut through the water as sharp as a knife, opening his fey sight – the world beneath the waves was a thick soup of debris, sand, and—his heart lurched.

Bodies. So many. He could tell by their glassy eyes that they were already dead, so he pushed himself past them, seeking Katarin.

A flash of red hair cut through the gloom. He could hear her heartbeat – she was alive, but she was fading. Ordes kicked out, shooting towards her, hooking his arm around her middle and making for the surface. When he broke through, Carbrey was waiting, the old man's eyes frantically scanning the water. He reached over the edge of the boat to take Katarin's weight, hauling her up and over the edge as Ordes climbed in after her.

'Is she dead?' the sailor asked.

Ordes shook his head, dropping to his knees, cradling Katarin's head between his hands. She was as pale as milk, her skin blue around the lips, but her chest rose and fell with jagged breaths. Her eyelids fluttered, then flew open. She sat up swiftly.

Ordes wrapped both arms around her, pulling her back into his chest.

'Ordes?' she breathed.

'You're safe, Kat,' he said softly. 'Where's Jen?'

Katarin spoke through her chattering teeth. 'Syhrens,' she whispered, before she collapsed against his chest and fell into darkness.

They saved twelve women. They were spread out across the deck, tucked up in blankets, some sitting up, sipping at warm tea. If anyone had any issues about having so many women on board, they didn't voice it. Ordes ran his hand through his damp hair and glanced out to sea. The water was calm, the sky clear, no sign of the storm that had caused so much destruction. Dawn was coming, a thin light creeping into the world. Everything around them was grey.

Jenyfer was not one of those pulled from the water, and Ordes' heart was racing, his palms sweaty, muscles bunched as tight and firm as steel. The taste of fear was bitter in his mouth, coating his tongue and creeping down his throat. He could feel her heartbeat, so he knew she wasn't dead, but where was she?

Leaving Iouen to manage the deck, Ordes returned to his cabin, where he'd put Katarin. She was sitting up when he went in, her knees pulled up to her chest, her face haunted. She didn't even look at him, just tucked the blankets close to her throat and rested her cheek on her knees. He didn't speak either. He had no idea what to say. His belly was still twisted with the death of *The Queen's* magic, but he knew it would be nothing to what Katarin would be feeling.

Slowly, she lifted her head, turning to face him. 'How many did you save?' she asked, her voice salt-water raw.

'Twelve,' he answered softly.

Kat closed her eyes. 'Twelve. Out of thirty. I sent them to their deaths.'

'You gave them their freedom, Katarin,' Ordes corrected gently.

'The Bag Noz will be full tonight. Have you seen it?'

He nodded. He'd seen the Night Boat a few hours earlier, hung low in the water, the helmsman staring straight ahead, face hidden beneath the dark hooded cloak.

Katarin swallowed tightly. 'Aelle?'

'I'm sorry, Kat.'

Ordes was used to Katarin's strength, her swagger, the arrogant tilt of her mouth. Watching her close her eyes, watching the single tear slip down her cheek, was not so much a surprise but a reminder of the things about her she let no one see. He didn't comment on it as she furiously wiped at her eyes. Her lips shifted as the sorrow became fierce anger and her mouth set in a grim line.

'The Master of Songs and Death targeted my ship,' Katarin said.

'What?' Ordes managed. He swallowed. 'Jen?'

Katarin's eyes flickered to Ordes' before she looked away. 'I don't know.' She sighed and rubbed roughly at her eyes. 'There was nothing I could do. My magic can't compete with syhren magic. No one's magic can, not out here, not on the water. The music … it didn't stop, getting louder and louder, until the ship …' She swallowed, looking at her hands. 'I felt her die, Ordes. I feel like part of me went down with her.' She raised her eyes to his again. 'Thank you.'

He nodded, throat tight. 'You didn't see—'

'She sang with them when they attacked.'

'Are you saying she *helped* them?'

Kat shook her head. 'I don't think she meant to. I don't think she had any control over what was happening, but her voice … there is such power in it.' She paused, then, 'Melodias is her father.'

Ordes gripped the edge of the desk for support.

'She doesn't know I know. Niniane told her, but I'm guessing by the look on your face, Jenyfer didn't tell you,' Katarin said. There was no scorn, no smugness to her voice, just a heavy weariness. She stared at him. 'You're going to do something stupid, aren't you, Ordes?'

'If Melodias has her—' Ordes began.

'You don't know—'

'There is only one way to find out.'

'Well,' Kat said simply, tossing back the blankets and stretching her legs out in front of her. 'I'm coming with you.'

'No, you're not. You nearly drowned, Katarin.'

She glared at him, then sighed. 'Arthur needs her. And, believe what you will, but I actually like the little shit, so I'm going to help you rescue her.'

CHAPTER 27

Since his return from the Temple, Arthur had spent a lot of time alone, trying desperately to sort through the things tumbling through his mind. Goerika had told him it was not his magic that would make him a king, but who he was. Arthur looked at his hands, turning them over in the fading afternoon light. He had not told anyone what the Priestess of the Temple had said to him. He couldn't. Doubt was an old friend of Arthur's but, this time, instead of doubting himself he was doubting the stories he'd been told. Goerika's words had made a permanent home in his head and had him questioning everything anyone had told him about the prophecy, the Treasures, his role in the whole thing …

Arthur didn't like to think anyone had willingly lied to him. He didn't want to think Jalen had lied to him. Goerika had said truth was subjective, and that was something Arthur had personally experienced in Kernou – but, even now, if he weighed his truth against his father's, who was to say which one of them was ultimately correct?

Did it even matter?

The One God was *real*.

Arthur could not stop the laugh that crept up his throat. Real, and *female*. His father would pitch a fit. He thought then of what Goerika had said about things not working out as Ereshki had wished, wondering what she meant by that. What had the Red One hoped to achieve by reinventing herself?

His head hurt.

He laughed again, and found he couldn't stop, the sound erupting out of him until his belly was hurting and he was bent double, his hands braced against his thighs.

The snapping of a twig caused him to straighten, his laughter dying.

His cousin was leaning casually against a tree on the other side of the clearing. 'Where's your pet demi-god?'

'Not here. I wanted to practise my magic,' Arthur lied. He could only imagine how hard Mordred would laugh if he told him what he was really doing out here – brooding.

'So you're alone? Is that wise? Do you know what lurks out here?' Mordred asked.

Arthur said nothing, watching the way his cousin stalked along the treeline, as if trying to make up his mind about something, before he stepped into the clearing, not taking his eyes from Arthur's. Arthur tensed - his magic stirred into life again, slithering around beneath his skin.

'I've heard stories about you my whole life,' Mordred said in a quiet voice. 'Stories about the King of Prophecy, the man who would save magic. I always hoped I'd be still living when you appeared.' He paused, ran his eyes over Arthur. 'Never meet your heroes, they say.'

'Sorry I haven't lived up to your expectations,' Arthur said sourly.

'It's not my expectations you should be worried about. It's the expectations of every Magic Wielder on this continent, Arthur. Every Magic Wielder who is waiting for *you* to deliver them, to free them from oppression, even the ones who don't know it yet. Have you ever been to Malist?' Mordred said fiercely.

'No,' Arthur admitted in a quiet voice.

'There is not a tree or blade of grass in that place of man. Nothing of the world the Old Ones created remains there. And that poison, the poison of men, will spread, and I'm not talking about that god of your father's. They will cut down the forests of the Green Knight's realm. They will plunder the riches of the earth, block out the sun with the smoke from their industry, and eventually they will strip Melodias' realm and fill the waterways with corruption.' Mordred's face was hard, his jaw tight.

'How ... how do you know this?' Arthur asked faintly.

'You think you are the only one to see things in your dreams? I have seen this future, I have been shown it in a vision, and I am prepared to do whatever is necessary to stop it from happening. But the question is – are you?' Mordred snapped his fingers and fire leapt to life in his palm. Before Arthur could say anything, a fireball shot across the clearing. Straight for his head.

His movement was instinctual, as was the golden shield he conjured around himself. He was as surprised as Mordred, who chuckled.

'I do like a challenge,' he said.

'Wait—'

Mordred flexed his fingers; vines erupted from the earth, curling around Arthur's ankles. Cursing, he stumbled back, ripping his feet free. Another vine shot from the ground to grasp at his wrist. He slashed at it with his hand; golden light, razor sharp, sliced through the vine.

Another fireball, deflected by the magic shield. Mordred advanced on Arthur, who dodged fire and vine, moving faster than he thought he could, the golden shield solidifying the longer he was under attack.

'Why are you doing this?' Arthur gasped.

'You need to be prepared – you're supposed to be a king. All I can see is a weakling without conviction,' Mordred snarled. Another fireball was launched in Arthur's direction. It crashed against the golden shield and

Arthur felt his magic begin to slip as his knees trembled. 'Be the man magic needs, or get out of the way and let someone else—'

Through the flames that littered the ground and the smoke swirling around them, Arthur stared at his cousin as something slid into place. 'You think you should be the one?'

His cousin said nothing.

Arthur sighed, letting his magical shield dissolve. 'We're on the same side, Mordred.'

'Are we?' Flames danced in Mordred's palms, but he did not strike.

'Yes. I want the same things you do. I want a new world, for all of us,' Arthur said softly. 'What that world will look like, I don't know. But, you can help me build it.' He swallowed and took a step forward. 'Will you help me?'

His cousin's face was hard. 'We shall see.' Before he left, Mordred clicked his fingers – all the little fires decorating the ground, all the smoke that had crept down Arthur's throat and burnt his eyes, vanished.

Arthur was washing the sweat and smoke from his skin when Jalen found him. Without a word, the demi-god stripped and climbed into the tub; the water rose dangerously near the edge.

'You look worried,' Jalen said with a frown. 'And you smell like a wildfire.'

'I had a run-in with Mordred.'

Jalen stood up, water streaming from his skin. 'What? Do you want me to—'

'Sit down,' Arthur mumbled, grabbing Jalen's hand and pulling him back into the tub. 'How am I ever supposed to find my strength if every time someone challenges me, you leap to my defence?'

'Arthur—'

Arthur leant forward and kissed Jalen on the mouth. 'I like it, don't worry – you being all protective and demi-godly – but I need to fight my own fights.'

Jalen nodded, although he was still frowning. 'Was he trying to hurt you?'

'No. I think if he wanted to hurt me he would have. I think he was trying to scare me, but he actually ended up helping me, which I'm certain was not his intention,' Arthur answered. 'I was able to defend myself against his magic, so maybe I have a warrior's heart after all,' he added, smiling.

Jalen was not smiling. 'Be careful. I know he is your cousin and I know you have this dream that you will finally get the family you have always wanted, but Mordred ... there is a darkness hanging over him, Arthur. I can sense it.'

Arthur didn't dispute that. 'He's angry, but I don't want to talk about Mordred anymore,' he said, flicking water at Jalen playfully. Droplets hit Jalen's cheeks and caught in his hair, glistening in the lantern light like tiny golden jewels.

'That's brave of you,' Jalen said, a smile replacing the frown. 'Tossing *water* at a storm demon.'

Arthur did it again; Jalen laughed and held up his hands.

'Alright, no more talk of Mordred. What would you like to talk about instead?'

Arthur's smile dropped as Goerika's words rushed back to him. 'You didn't tell me there was a demi-god here.'

Jalen was watching Arthur closely. 'What did you think of her?'

Arthur made himself shrug, made sure his voice was light. 'She's a little strange.'

Jalen laughed. 'Yes, she is. What did she tell you?'

Arthur swallowed, then shifted closer to Jalen, closing his arms around Jalen's neck, fingers moving into his hair. 'I'm not sure I want to talk about Goerika – or my cousin,' he murmured. He was rewarded with a slow smile, the sort of smile that made his belly tighten and his breath thicken.

Jalen raised his eyebrows. 'Alright, don't tell me,' he said, a smile still tugging at the corners of his mouth. His fingers trailed down the side of Arthur's face, his touch pulling butterflies to life in Arthur's belly. It didn't matter how often Jalen touched him – each time was like energy shooting through him, warm and heady, making him feel drunk.

Making him feel alive. He was comfortable here, in Cruithea. He was comfortable with Jalen; he felt he could tell Jalen anything and everything without any fear of judgement. Kat had asked Arthur if he loved Jalen. The word love danced around the cavern of Arthur's mouth. It sat on the tip of his tongue, waiting behind his teeth, waiting desperately to come out into the light, but Arthur didn't say it.

He wasn't sure if what he felt was love. Was the fluttering in his belly whenever Jalen looked at him love? Was the warmth in his blood, the burning in his lungs, the breathlessness – was that love? Or was love simpler than that? Was it that feeling Arthur experienced each morning when he opened his eyes to find Jalen beside him? Maybe it was that first kiss good morning, or the last of the evening, or maybe it was the simple brush of Jalen's fingers on the back of Arthur's hand, or the back of his neck.

Arthur couldn't recall the last time anyone had told him they loved him, and those words, three simple words, were words that he had been made to reserve for the One God. Love that he had been told he had to give. Love that was supposed to give him love in return, but the love the One God had given was a fierce love, a frightening love that left Arthur trembling.

Three little words. Maybe, Arthur thought, catching Jalen's smile, there were different sorts of love. And, just maybe, he deserved it.

CHAPTER 28

The sound of waves lapping against a shore burrowed beneath Jenyfer's skin, shifting in time with her heartbeat. She rested her hand on her chest, concentrating on keeping sleep wrapped around her; she didn't want it to leave. But it was a losing battle. Groaning, she sat up, blinking as her surroundings swam into focus.

A room … with a window, the curtains open wide. No breeze sauntered in and the sky outside was a deep blue, shot through with flecks of silver. Jenyfer frowned. She was on *The Night Queen* – wasn't she? But she was not in her hammock below deck, the sounds of the other women sleeping rising all around her.

She was in bed – a very soft bed with sheets that felt like silk beneath her fingers. She went to scramble out, and then froze as memories filled her, rushing into her head so fast they knocked the breath from her lungs.

A storm, fierce and unrelenting. Music coming from all around her. The splintering of timber. Screams and shouts. Waves of magic flowing into the night and water, so deep and cold. Hands grabbing at her.

The Queen had been attacked.

Jenyfer gasped, clutching at her chest.

'Take deep breaths,' a soothing male voice murmured. 'I believe humans, even part-humans, need to breathe.'

In the semi-darkness of the room sat a man on an armchair, long legs crossed in front of him. Jenyfer could not see his face, but the air around him shimmered silver with magic.

'Who are you? Where am I?' she rasped, her throat tight, raw, like she'd swallowed the ocean.

When he unfolded his black-clad legs and stood she shuffled backwards, until she could go no further. The wall was cool against the exposed skin of her back. She glanced down, relieved to find she was dressed, but what was she wearing? Black silk? She lifted her eyes, watching as the man stepped from the shadows into the pale blue light that draped itself around the room.

He was tall and slender, with hair the colour of the deepest night. An angular face with high cheekbones and a perfectly straight nose, eyebrows like two black slashes on his forehead. Full lips and eyes ... eyes the colour of the sea beneath a raging storm, a mix of cerulean and grey.

The man she had never been fully able to see in her dreams.

He came towards her, stopping short of the edge of the bed, every movement of his limbs like liquid grace.

Jenyfer swallowed. Music wove through the air and, as she breathed, the notes settled in her lungs and spread through her blood. 'Who are you?' she repeated, clutching the bedclothes in trembling fingers, though she was beginning to suspect.

He cocked an eyebrow. 'Don't you know?'

'Melodias,' she whispered.

Those eyes, so like hers, twinkled with pleasure as he sketched a bow.

'Welcome home, daughter.'

The Master of Songs and Death was sitting on a throne of bones when Jenyfer was brought to him that evening.

Lyonesse.

She was in Lyonesse.

A syhren had been waiting for her. Despite Jenyfer's questions, her pleas for answers, the faery did not speak to her, simply ushered her out of bed and into a steaming bath, then made her dress in a gown of sparkling silver that left too much of her flesh exposed. The dark lines of the map were fully visible and she'd begged for a coat or a shawl, something to cover them, but the syhren had simply shaken her silvery head and gestured for Jenyfer to follow her.

Every winding, snake-like hallway looked the same in this place, whatever it was. No artwork decorated the stone walls and the floor was scattered with silver sand. As Jenyfer walked, every now and then a flash of white appeared in the dark stone. Curious, she paused and moved closer to the glowing white, then recoiled when she realised what it was.

Bones. This place was made of stone and bone.

Each doorway she passed was decorated with shells and pearls, opalescent scales and carved stone scenes featuring octopuses, sea horses, sea dragons, mermaid tails and corals, all in muted blues, greens, white and greys: the colours of the ocean.

Music floated through every pocket of air. The syhren led her down a sweeping flight of slippery steps and through a stone archway curved like a wave, where Jenyfer found herself in a cavernous space with a high ceiling. Braziers sitting atop black stone pillars lit the space, evenly spaced on each side of a long stretch of black carpet.

At the end of that carpet, the floor dropped away to reveal a pool of water, the surface so dark and still it was like a mirror that reflected nothing. On the other side of that pool of water, on a dais of stone shot through with pieces of bone, was Melodias on his throne.

Jenyfer had a million things she wanted to say but could not get a single word to leave her lips as she stared at him, at that face that was so like hers. At his cold beauty and the power that she could see rising from his body. He was wearing a crown of bones and she started, stepping backwards as she recognised it as the one from her dreams.

Melodias reached a long-fingered hand to touch the crown. His fingers were covered in black scales. Scales also licked the sides of his neck, sweeping upwards to curl over his jaw and vanish into the dark of his hair.

'You know this, don't you?' he asked simply, that voice so rich and musical Jenyfer wanted to fall to her knees and weep. He removed the crown from his head and held it out to her. 'It's yours.'

'Mine?' she managed.

He nodded.

Jenyfer didn't move. 'Am I in Lyonesse?'

'Well, technically, you're beneath the island,' he answered

'Is this the Otherworld?'

'No. But the river that leads to the Otherworld is here. You can see it later,' he said casually, as if he expected her to stay.

'I don't want to see anything,' she said. 'I want to leave.'

He raised his eyebrows. 'Without getting any of your answers?' A chuckle. 'I don't think so. You're too curious. You want to *know* what you are. You want to know what you can do, don't you?' He rested the crown in his lap. 'Come closer. I won't harm you.'

'What did you do to my friends?'

'Ah. The ship? It sank.' There was no sympathy, no sorrow or apology, in his voice.

Jenyfer clenched her fists. 'They're dead?'

He shrugged.

She swallowed, forcing herself to breathe and made her way around the edge of the black lake, avoiding looking into its strange surface. She could sense things moving beneath the water and faint music, distorted by its depths, swirled through her ears. Melodias did not move, simply watching her approach, a smile playing on his lips.

'Your sister was here, if you're interested.'

'What did you do to her?' Jenyfer demanded.

'Do? Nothing. I had no use for her,' Melodias said. 'She has no magic, or anything really, and all she talked about was her god. It was actually rather boring. She isn't smart enough – none of them are smart enough – to realise the One God is nothing but a deception, created for fools who wish to change the world, who think they have the power and the right to do so.'

Jenyfer frowned. 'What do you mean?'

'The thing about gods, daughter, is we are only as strong as the belief in us. When enough people believe – that is true power. The One God will never walk the earth the way I can, not anymore, but the very idea could be enough to undo us. I doubt she factored that into her plans.'

Jenyfer frowned. 'She?'

'Yes, *she*.' Melodias chuckled.

A chill walked Jenyfer's spine. The One God was *real*! And *female*! 'I still don't understand.'

'Our power exists because belief in us exists. If the people cease believing in the Old Ways ... we won't disappear, but we won't *be* anymore.' He paused and ran a black-fingered hand through the length of his hair. 'Even Lyonesse will fade away.'

Jenyfer swallowed.

'I've tried to call you home many times before now, so you could take your place beside me and help me fight this, but you've been ignoring me – so I had to take drastic measures. I am sorry for the loss of your friends up there.'

'The dead fishermen in Kernou? That was you?' Jenyfer guessed. She had forgotten about those men, about poor Will Sanderson. 'Why?'

'Why? Because humans are a plague on this earth. They rape the seas, plunder the ground, tear down forests for their towns and it will only get worse. I don't know how the others can stand to have anything to do with them.' He stopped and ran his eyes over the marks on Jenyfer's skin. 'That was a stroke of genius on her behalf, I will admit.'

Melodias clicked his fingers and they were suddenly no longer in the cavernous room with the lake, but a dining room, with a long table draped in black cloth. The table was set for two. The King of Lyonesse stood behind a chair at the head of the table. He gestured to the other place setting to his right. 'Sit. You need to eat. We can discuss everything later.'

Jenyfer sat, not sure her legs would hold her any longer. She didn't look at Melodias when she spoke, keeping her eyes on her empty plate, her head spinning so fast it hurt. The One God was not only real, he was a *she*, and if Melodias was to be believed, she was an Old One.

'Who is she? The One God?'

'Her true name is Ereshki.'

'What—'

'I said we will discuss it later,' Melodias said, irritation flashing across his face.

Jenyfer licked her lips. 'If Niniane is the Goddess of Magic, what exactly are you?'

Melodias swept his chair out and sat. His eyes bored into the side of Jenyfer's face. She made herself look at him again, to take in that unnaturally handsome face. 'I am the God of the Seas, the Master of Songs and Death. I command the water and the creatures of the ocean. Lyonesse is the portal to the Otherworld – souls pass through here on the Bag Noz – and that portal is mine to guard. Always a rather mournful sight, the Bag Noz. So,' he said cheerfully. 'Shall we eat?'

Jenyfer did not pick up her fork. 'What do you know about the prophecy?'

Melodias' eyebrows lifted. 'I'm not sure you're in any position to make demands.' He nodded at her plate. 'Eat.'

This time she could not refuse the power in his voice, in the simple command. She tried, but it was like her body moved without her consent, her fingers picking up the fork, her mouth opening, her jaw shifting as she chewed and swallowed.

Jenyfer kept her eyes on her plate, blinking back tears as she thought of Kat and the crew of *The Queen*. Of her sister and her aunt, of Ordes.

All of them were so far away.

CHAPTER 29

Lamorna struggled to keep pace with Tamora and Keraine, who moved much faster than women their age should be able. She wondered on many occasions if it was witchcraft that kept them going. They never said it out loud, but Lamorna knew they were using magic to disguise their passage through the forest. She had no idea where they were and could not remember which direction they had travelled from.

Tired and sweaty, Lamorna was in desperate need of a proper wash. Splashing a bit of water from a stream onto her face and hands was all she could do. They slept on the ground each night, a fire crackling between them, disguised with magic. Tamora and Keraine had kept their distance from one another to begin with, but as the days passed the two women were rarely apart, walking close together and sleeping side by side, curled under the same blanket. Each morning Lamorna would avert her eyes, not wanting to see, not wanting to think about it. And each morning she would feel Keraine's eyes on her.

Her aunt's lover didn't trust her. Lamorna had overheard her, the first night away from Kernou, when the older woman thought she was asleep.

'She's not here out of concern for your welfare,' Keraine had said quietly.

'Hush,' Tamora scolded, but an uneasy silence hung around her. Eventually, she sighed. 'Lamorna needs guidance and our help, not our suspicion. The girl is still deep in Ulrian's pockets and still too brainwashed to see the truth of things. We will have to be gentle with her.'

Brainwashed! Lamorna thought, seething, as she clenched her fists. She forced away her anger and bit her lip. She would have to try and make them believe she had turned from the One God.

Tamora was gentle with her, but Keraine was not.

'You think I can't tell?' Keraine lowered her voice one evening, keeping her eyes on Tamora's back as she spoke. 'You might have your aunt fooled, but it's only because she loves you that you're here. If it were up to me, you'd have stayed behind to rot with the Chif and everyone else.' She spat on the ground at Lamorna's feet.

Lamorna held the other woman's eyes, remembering why she was here. The Chif trusted her, and had faith in her. She lifted her chin. 'I am here for Tamora. For my family, who has suffered enough.'

Keraine put her face close to Lamorna's. 'I see through you. I know why you're here, Lamorna Astolat. And it isn't for your family.'

Lamorna swallowed the now-familiar feeling of panic that surged through her – the same feeling that had risen every time she had gone into the village since returning from the sea. 'I don't know what else to say,' she said, keeping her voice calm and her expression contrite. 'I have renounced the One God and all he stands for. The Chif is wrong. Why would I continue to support a god who tried to kill me? Who tried to kill my sister?' She shook her head, and rubbed at her eyes with the heel of her hand. 'I wish you wouldn't think ill of me.'

Tamora turned to them as Lamorna's voice rose. She frowned, leaving the fire she was bringing to life and coming over. Lamorna sniffed and stepped away from Keraine, leaning into her aunt.

'Is everything alright?' Tamora asked.

'I'm just tired,' Lamorna answered, forcing some weariness into her tone. 'I'd like to rest.'

'Of course,' Tamora said, smoothing her hand over Lamorna's hair. At the touch of her aunt's hand, she froze, then remembered she didn't wear the linen cap anymore, instead her hair was loose and wild around her shoulders. She hadn't packed a brush in their haste to leave and knew she must look dreadful, like a beastly, wicked thing in this savage landscape.

She turned away from Tamora and took her time rolling out her blankets, bundling herself into them like a hibernating animal. Lamorna pulled the blanket over her head, her lips moving soundlessly as she recited the Word.

The following morning, Tamora approached her gently. 'We will be in Cruithea soon. You cannot take the book with you.'

Lamorna's stomach twisted. 'What book?'

Her aunt's face was kind. 'I know you have the Decalogue stashed away in your bag, Lamorna. You cannot bring it.'

'But—'

Tamora gestured to the fire. 'You need to burn it.'

Lamorna snatched up her bag and held it close to her chest. 'No. You can't make me.'

'Do you think the Cruitheans will understand?' Tamora asked, keeping her eyes on Lamorna's. 'We will be asking them to take us in, to care for us and provide for us until we work out what to do next. You cannot take the Decalogue into Cruithea, Lamorna.' She gestured again at the fire.

Lamorna looked around wildly. Keraine was watching her from the other side of their crude camp and Lamorna thought she saw a flash of triumph in the other woman's eyes.

Swallowing, she dropped her bag. Kneeling beside it with tears in her eyes, she dug to the bottom of her bag, pushing aside the few clothes she'd been allowed to bring. Her fingers closed around her copy of the Decalogue and she drew it out, choking on a sob. She looked up at her aunt. 'Please don't make me,' she pleaded, not caring how she sounded, not caring that tears were starting to make their way down her cheeks. 'Please.'

'I'm sorry,' Tamora said softly. 'In the fire, Lamorna.'

Shaking, Lamorna stood and made her way to the smouldering coals, jumping back in fright when the fire roared into life. She glanced up to see Keraine lower her hand.

'It's fitting,' she said. 'Magic being the thing to devour that hateful book.'

'Keraine,' Tamora warned, but Lamorna shook her head and lifted her chin.

It's just a book, she told herself fiercely. *It doesn't mean I love the One God any less. I will succeed in my mission. I will be rewarded.*

With a final, proud look at Keraine, Lamorna tossed the Decalogue into the flames; as the bright orange tongues curled around the pages of the book, she wondered what her reward would look like.

They journeyed over a rise of small hills, until they entered an almost-hidden path through the Nemhain Mountains. Lamorna did not like the mountains, the way they stretched into the sky and caged her in. She did not like the strange silence that followed them as they laboured over the rough track. It was cold in the granite belly of the continent, and when they emerged after three days and freezing nights, they were facing a barren plain.

'What is this place?' Lamorna asked crossly. She was hungry and tired and wanted to go back to Kernou, but she didn't dare voice it. She had barely spoken since being made to burn the Decalogue.

'Camlann,' her aunt replied.

'Why is it dead here?'

'It is cursed,' Tamora said, and Lamorna shuddered. She didn't ask who cursed the place or why. She wanted to hurry; she didn't like the brown, lifeless earth that stretched on forever. To her dismay, her aunt and Keraine led the way into another mountain path, but this one was easier, the mountains not as high, and it wasn't long before they entered another forest – The Hunter's Forest, Tamora said it was called.

As they drew closer to Cruithea, Tamora and Keraine grew excited, their chattering louder and more animated. Anticipation and fear burnt a hole through Lamorna's belly when they did not stop and make camp, but continued into the growing dark. The shadows of this forest were long, twisted things, stretching further and deeper than shadows should. Lamorna hung back, not wanting to step beneath the trees for fear of being caught in the snared embrace of those shadows. She did not want to know what it would feel like to be touched by the cruel dark.

Her aunt and Keraine continued without pause, yet Lamorna did not follow.

'What is it?' Tamora called back to her.

Lamorna could not see her aunt's face from the shadows. She shivered, lifting her eyes to the trees and the absence of light beneath them.

'Lamorna?'

'I don't want to go!'

Tamora's face softened. 'They're just trees.'

Lamorna could not explain it. She had no words for what she could feel coming from the trees. Something whispered in her mind, telling her that if she kept going, everything would change.

Nearby, an owl screeched and took flight from a branch, floating like a ghost through the shadows. It came towards her, great white wings spread, and Lamorna stifled a cry, racing to her aunt's side.

The shadows reached for her. She sniffed, trying not to tremble, trying to be brave, to be the soldier the One God had declared she was.

She forced herself to breathe, to take in the scent of the forest. A wild, feral smell saturated the air – wood rot, fungi, smoke, and animals, so dreadfully unfamiliar. Then, it was the temperature, the air chilled beneath the trees. Lamorna's skin prickled. The forest floor was a mix of dead leaves, twigs and small white flowers, so bright in the darkness. She bent to collect one—

'Don't!' Tamora warned, her voice sharp. 'They're poisonous.'

Lamorna pulled her hand back, looking around wildly, fear a sharp tang in her throat. The trees grew in no form of order, no harmony to their growth. Trunks exploded from the earth wherever they wished, and stretched high above them, branches interlinked, caging them in. The moon pushed through the spindly, clawlike branches, pale and glowing. Arthritic roots emerged from the ground to trip her, and the shadows were filled with whispers and secret things.

They walked for what felt like hours – time moved strangely beneath the trees, the eerie sameness of their surroundings and the pale darkness making it difficult for Lamorna to know how long they'd been in the forest.

Thick cobwebs hung, lace-like, from the lower branches of the trees. Lamorna shrank from them and what manner of beast they may contain and quickened her pace, catching up with her aunt and clinging to her arm, like she used to when she was a small child.

'Lamorna,' Tamora said gently. 'It's fine. We're safe here.'

'Are we almost there?' Lamorna whispered.

'Yes.'

Lamorna thought she could hear a tormented whisper in the air. She gulped as the sound of a snapping twig echoed behind them. The hair stood up on the back of her neck but she held her breath, determined not to look back this time, not wanting to know what horror haunted their footsteps.

The trees were alive with nocturnal creatures. Another owl took flight from one, great wings soaring into the blackness. Moments later, an eerie, pained shriek filled the night and Lamorna jumped. The forest swelled with malignant energy, with something unnatural and eldritch, slow and seeping through the air, the rocks, and the soil like a poison.

Unseen things moved around them. There was no evidence of human life anywhere and Lamorna was certain they were lost. As she opened her mouth to ask the dreaded question, she stumbled, falling face-first on a bed of spongy grass that smelt of something dead. She blinked, nose scrunching up at the smell, before it hit her – an animal, its body withered and decayed, rested not far from her face.

With a cry of horror, she scrambled backwards, unable to take her eyes from that deflated slice of death resting on the forest floor. Tamora rushed to her side and helped her to stand while Lamorna gulped air into trembling lungs, regretting it immediately.

'I hate this place!' she wailed. The taste of death coated her tongue.

'Death is part of life, Lamorna,' her aunt said softly. 'It doesn't have to be feared.'

Lamorna shook her head. She did not believe that – the Word told her death was to be feared, because it was after death that a soul could be sent to the Pit for all eternity.

'Something has been following us,' she blurted.

Tamora nodded. 'Yes. Piskies mainly, and some sprites. They're curious.'

'Faeries,' Lamorna spat, unable to keep the acid from her tone.

Her aunt frowned. 'They won't hurt you.'

'Or maybe they will,' Keraine called from where she had paused up ahead. 'If you fail to show them the respect they deserve. There are worse things than piskies out here, girl.'

'Don't scare her anymore than she already is,' Tamora scolded gently.

Keraine shrugged, and Lamorna felt deep hatred burn through her.

'It's true,' came another voice.

A man stepped from the trees. Lamorna jumped and grasped at her aunt's arm. As he approached them, he was joined by another man, both appearing as if they'd stepped from the very air around them. Lamorna swallowed – both men carried weapons and their faces were hidden by the shadows of the forest, but she could feel their eyes crawling like insects over her body.

Tamora inclined her head. 'We wish to see the High Priestess, Morgause. We are seeking sanctuary.'

There was a flash of teeth in the darkness as one of the men smiled. 'Come with us – she has been expecting you, Tamora Rosevear.'

At that moment, a swirling wind rushed through the trees. Lamorna gasped and covered her eyes; when it had stopped, she rubbed at her face and looked around in fright. Standing across the clearing from them were two more people. One was tall with hair the colour of sand, and he had his hand resting on the shoulder of the other man, who made a little noise in the back of his throat and reached up to remove the hood of his cloak.

'Lamorna? You're supposed to be dead!'

Lamorna forgot her fear, hurrying across the clearing to grasp his hands. 'Arthur! Thank the Word! Everything will be alright now.'

His smile was tight. 'How are you here?' He shook his head. 'Never mind – you can share your story later. First, you need to meet Morgause. Come.'

'You know the High Priestess?' Lamorna asked.

Arthur glanced at her, and then away again. 'She is my aunt.'

Lamorna dropped his hands and didn't say another word, letting herself be swept along the path, the trees towering over them, until they thinned and she was standing at the edge of a village unlike anything she had ever seen before.

She stood and stared, her eyes running over the strangeness of the houses, which were not houses at all, not like her cottage in Kernou was. A wave of helplessness washed through her and she must have made a little noise in the back of her throat because her aunt turned to look at her, and then Arthur was there, his expression sympathetic.

'It's different,' he said softly. 'But it doesn't matter where or how someone lives, does it? It does not make them bad people,' he added. The man with the sand-coloured hair was there as well, close to Arthur, a lot closer than Lamorna had seen men standing together in Kernou. Arthur and this man, whoever he was, stood as close to one another as Tamora and Keraine did, and Lamorna had to cover her mouth to hide her gasp.

Did the Chif know?

Arthur's eyes slid to her face and away again, but he did not introduce the man, simply clearing his throat and rubbing at the back of his neck nervously. That was a gesture she was familiar with – the small hope she'd harboured that Arthur would be her ally in Cruithea shrivelled and died. Lamorna squared her shoulders and made her way to her aunt's side.

She would not falter.

CHAPTER 30

'Sail, ho! Two ships!'

The call came after dusk. The ocean was painted with gold in the west, the approaching vessel a silhouette against the dying of the day. *The Excalibur* was off the western coast of Teyath, close to Carinya. The mood onboard was a sombre one. Ordes' crew hadn't known Kat's people well, but no sailor could ignore the stark reminder of the watery grave that awaited them all, perhaps just beyond the next swell.

Ordes gripped the railing, his mind racing, eyes on the approaching vessels. He and Katarin would leave for Melodias' realm as soon as she was fit for travel – which she insisted was now, but she was yet to regain full strength of her magic, so Ordes had won the argument.

Beside him, Iouen lowered his spyglass. 'They're too far away. Can you see their banner?'

Ordes nodded grimly. 'It's Marsh and Booth.'

'Wonder what they want?' Iouen said. 'Should I ready the cannons?'

'Do it,' Ordes said, even as something inside him protested. He would not let his crew be caught out, especially not now they had Kat and her crew on board. Iouen started shouting orders. 'But we'll let them in range,' Ordes added.

Iouen stopped mid-command and raised his eyebrows. 'We will?'

Ordes nodded, glancing at the sails. 'Keep us ready to run, just in case.'

'We could take them,' Iouen pointed out.

'And take a lot of damage in the process,' Ordes reminded him, refraining from reminding Iouen that the personal scores he needed to settle with Marsh would have to wait for another day. Iouen nodded and Ordes returned to check on Katarin. Katarin scowled when she learnt *The Crimson Shadow* and *The Black Rose* were headed their way.

'Are you sure you don't want to fight?' she demanded.

'I'm sure,' Ordes said. 'What purpose would it serve? If either ship opens her gun ports, we'll open ours, but I'm not doing anything until I have a better understanding of the situation. We'll be ready, Kat.'

'They were tracking you before, remember?' Katarin reminded him.

'I know, and they didn't engage us then. They're still tracking us so, whatever they want, it must be important enough to not want to risk damaging their ship – or mine,' Ordes said, rubbing his cheek wearily. He knew what the other Captains wanted as surely as Kat did, but neither of them said it out loud.

Katarin nodded. 'Tell the bastards I said hi.'

Ordes chuckled. 'I said I don't want them to fire on us, Kat.'

The two hours it took for Marsh and Booth to draw close to them crawled by, and the sun was gone by the time *The Black Rose* came to a stop beside *The Excalibur*. *The Crimson Shadow* waited a little way back, ready to swoop in if needed. Iouen had the gun crews at the ready, as Ordes was sure Marsh did as well. Shots from such close range would rip both ships to pieces, so he was counting on the Captain of *The Black Rose* wanting to avoid that situation.

Ordes leant against the main mast and waited. The moon was full, giving them plenty of light, the water a black sheet flecked with silver.

Marsh had managed to remain Captain for years, surviving multiple rumoured mutinies. He was the sort of pirate mothers would tell their children to stay away from, a notorious brute with an appetite for blood and battle. Ordes had heard that he had once keel-hauled two of his own men when his quartermaster at the time had failed to dish out what he considered adequate punishment.

Marsh was feared, and he was smart, and most people had a healthy respect for both, which was why Iouen was mumbling under his breath and the crew were nervous. How would his father have dealt with this? Ordes thought, going over in his head the last conversation he had witnessed between Tymis and Marsh, wondering if he could pull up enough of his father's swagger and confidence to be believable.

And he *was* curious. Marsh kept his gun ports closed, which only made Ordes more interested

No one spoke as the Captain of *The Black Rose* approached the railing. Marsh was a beefy man, with broad shoulders and unruly dark hair that fell half-way down his back. He wore a black long-coat and a dagger at one hip, a cutlass at the other. His large hands caressed the pistol tucked into his belt as his eyes moved over *The Excalibur's* crew.

'Where's the Captain?'

'That would be me,' Ordes announced, striding towards the railing, Iouen trailing him.

Marsh threw back his head and laughed. 'Tymis left his brat in charge?' He addressed the crew. 'And how do you lot feel about taking orders from a kid?'

'What do you want?' Ordes asked, folding his arms.

'*The Queen* went down a few nights ago,' Marsh said. 'Wreckage all over the place. Must have been one tempest to destroy a ship like that.'

'We were there,' Ordes told him.

'And your ship survived? Without a scratch, it seems?' Marsh tapped his chin thoughtfully. 'Le Fey and her crew? They alive?'

'Mostly.' Ordes flexed his fingers, light dancing over his knuckles.

Marsh grunted at the display of magic.

'What do you really want, Marsh?' Ordes asked. 'Because I don't think you're overly concerned about the fate of Kat and her people.'

Marsh had not removed his hand from his pistol. 'I want the syhren.'

Ordes' blood ran cold. 'She isn't here.'

'Mind if my men step over there and take a look?'

Iouen cocked his pistol.

Marsh sighed. 'If she isn't here, then where is she?'

'I don't know,' Ordes said simply.

The Captain of *The Black Rose* fingered his stubbled chin. 'That's the most transparent lie I've heard in a long time, but it doesn't matter. I'll find her eventually. Me, or one of the others. Word has spread – people talk, Ordes. I've heard other interesting things as well. Would you like to know what they are?'

Ordes said nothing, keeping his expression as calm as possible, his breathing steady, hoping his raging heartbeat was not evident in any part of his body.

'I heard you're looking for the Treasures of the Gods,' Marsh said smoothly. 'You and Le Fey, and if Katarin is involved, I bet she isn't looking because she likes shiny things. She'd be acting on the orders of that bitch goddess she follows. But you? What's in it for you?'

Ordes said nothing, but he let his magic out a little more, the threads of silver increasing their strength. Marsh's smile faltered a fraction, but then the man shrugged, nonplussed.

'Are you looking for the Treasures of the Gods, Ordes?' he asked.

'Why would we tell you?' Iouen shot back.

'You wouldn't, which is answer enough,' Marsh said. 'Well then, children. Until next time. Say hello to your father for me, *Captain*. Where is he, by the way?'

Ordes didn't answer.

Marsh scoffed. 'I can't imagine he got sick of the life. I've known Tymis Merlyni for a long time – we were at this game before you were old enough to wipe your own arse. So, again, where is he?'

'Again, not your business,' Ordes replied. Marsh laughed, calling out to his men, and the crew of *The Excalibur* did not stand down until *The Black Rose* and *The Crimson Shadow* pulled anchors and started drifting away.

'The sooner I find Jenyfer, the better,' Ordes mumbled.

'You're not seriously going to Lyonesse?' Iouen said, keeping his voice low. 'That is a suicide mission if ever I heard of one. What would your father say?'

'My father would shut his mouth,' Ordes said fiercely, 'and so will you. We need to alter course, turn around and get further south. Kat and I leave tomorrow. Her crew will remain here, and you will stand in my place while I'm gone.'

'Me?'

'Yes, unless you want the men to vote for a new quartermaster before I go?'

Iouen shook his head and sighed. 'Where should we wait for you?'

'Halfway between Teyath and Lyonesse. Remain below the horizon on either side, so you'll be out of sight,' Ordes said.

'I'm fairly confident the Master of Songs and Death will know where we are,' Iouen pointed out. 'And if you don't come back?'

Ordes glanced out to sea, in the direction he now knew, instinctively, that Avalon lay. Mist was rolling across the water. 'You sail for the Isle and find my father.'

CHAPTER 31

Lamorna hated Cruithea. She hated the village. There was no order here, just chaos, people everywhere, laughing and talking too loudly. Children ran wild, in various states of dress. Lamorna had been horrified to see some of the younger ones were completely *naked*.

'I want to go home,' she announced, aware she sounded childish and feeble, but she didn't care.

Tamora sighed lightly, turning from tending the fire in the stove that sat in the middle of the tent they had been given for their stay. A chimney poked through a hole in the roof of the tent. Kibitka, Lamorna silently corrected herself. It was called a kibitka. The whole village was made up of them. They were round, some larger than others, and made of canvas and animal hide, which, she noted unpleasantly, still smelt like the animal it had belonged to. Most people ate their meals outside in the communal cooking area, where a fire pit burned day and night with several large cooking pots suspended above it.

Tamora wrung her hands, her face tired. 'We can't go back.'

'You mean *you* can't,' Lamorna shot back, stamping her foot as sharp anger speared through her. 'I can't stand this place.'

'You will get used to it,' her aunt told her, in that tone Lamorna knew meant she was not to argue, but she opened her mouth, words and wickedness bristling on her tongue.

'I won't,' she snapped. 'These people are heathens. They are uncouth and wild. They are not proper.'

'They are different, that is all,' Tamora said quietly. 'And lower your voice. Someone will hear you.'

'I don't care,' Lamorna raged.

Across the room, Keraine folded her arms. 'Watch your tongue,' she scolded.

Lamorna turned her anger on the other woman. 'You don't tell me what to do. You're a sinner. You both are.' She swung back to Tamora. 'You lied to me. You and Jenyfer both lied to me.'

'You knew your sister was a Magic Wielder,' Tamora said sharply.

'I didn't know she was a faery!' Lamorna shouted, resisting the urge to clamp her hand over her mouth. She never shouted.

'Where did you hear that?' Tamora demanded.

'I heard you,' Lamorna snapped. 'And her,' she added, gesturing at Keraine. 'You thought I was asleep, but I wasn't. You lied to me,' she added again. 'It's one thing for Jenyfer to have magic, but it's another for her to be ... *that*!'

Her aunt's face hardened. 'You will mind how you speak and you will be grateful to the people of this country for taking us in. You will work while you are here. You will earn your place in this community. And you will not speak ill of magic, or your sister. Do you understand me?'

Lamorna tossed her head. She turned away, stomping across the kibitka to flop onto her bed, where she rolled over and faced the canvas wall. She shut her eyes, willing herself not to cry as, in the background, Tamora and Keraine argued softly and the sound of the wind in the trees slowly lulled Lamorna to sleep.

It was evening meal time. Lamorna glanced up at the slice of night sky visible through the interwoven branches of the trees. She still felt like a caged beast, but after some time – days, maybe, she couldn't exactly tell – in Cruithea, she was growing used to the way the light beneath the trees never shifted. It was like a permanent twilight, filled with bark and leaves and the scent of the soil.

Sparks from the fire shot upwards, flecks of gold against the darkness. What lurked outside the sphere of light cast by the fire, Lamorna didn't want to think about. She'd heard tales of the unnatural terrors that stalked the wilds of Cruithea, had brushed the stories aside as nothing but fancy at the time, but now that she was here her muscles were tight, her tongue thick and heavy in her mouth.

She did not belong here. She'd barely left her aunt's side since they'd arrived, completely terrified. While Tamora knew it, she never mentioned it, and for that Lamorna was grateful. Despite their argument the other day, Tamora was looking out for her, Lamorna knew that.

She had not spoken to Arthur again and had avoided him as much as possible, but it was difficult when the people here believed he was some sort of saviour. Out of everything she had been told since arriving, Lamorna found that the hardest to swallow. Arthur Tregarthen was a devout believer in the One God, as she was, but now … Lamorna wasn't sure that was true. She caught sight of him across the camp, where he sat with the High Priestess and the man who was glued to his side. Arthur was at ease here, if a bit nervous. He smiled more, and she realised she had never really seen him smile before.

And Bryn had told her Arthur was a Magic Wielder. She did not understand how someone like him, his veins full of wickedness, could have ever truly believed in the One God. Lamorna sighed, rubbing at her eyes in irritation at all the things she did not understand.

They had been given extra clothing and shoes. Lamorna fingered the coat she was wearing. It was too big for her, and smelt like an animal, but it was chilly beneath the trees, the weather not as temperate as Kernou.

She had managed to smuggle one of her linen caps to Cruithea, but had not been allowed to put it on. That, too, had been tossed into the fire by an irritated Keraine on their second night when Lamorna had tried to wear it to dinner. She felt naked without it, and when she said so, Keraine had shrugged and told her she could go completely naked here if she wished and no one would care.

The food was different. Her shoes were different. *Everything* was different and she hated it. To hide her rising dismay, she sipped at the tea she'd been given, allowing the warmth of the liquid to settle in her belly. Tea was familiar, even if it didn't taste exactly like the ones she brewed. Another different thing in this alien world.

Lamorna watched her aunt and Keraine as they talked with one of the men who had found them in the forest. Lamorna didn't know his name, but he was the biggest person she had ever seen, with long, dark hair and tattoos inked on his flesh. She reminded herself once again of her task – the task the Chif, and the One God, had set for her. But, looking at these people, taking note of the wildness of them, her will faltered, the wrongness of this place taunting her, as malicious as a sickness.

All Cruitheans had darker skin than anyone Lamorna had ever seen, and both the men and women wore their hair long, in intricate braids decorated with beads and feathers. The women wore ankle-length dresses in a simple style, the colour of pale bark, with a bodice embroidered with brown thread, like the one Lamorna was wearing now. She had seen some women wearing trousers like a man, fit close to the curves of their bodies. She couldn't look at them, averting her eyes at their indecency, but not before she noticed they were armed with daggers and axes and other weapons she did not have a name for.

The men wore their pants as close-fitting and as indecent as the women. Lamorna had seen some with sleeveless shirts, some without shirts at all (the shame!) and had not failed to notice the swirling tattoos that decorated their flesh.

Tamora came to sit by her, touching her knee gently. The heat of the fire was welcome in this dark, cold place, and Lamorna had barely moved for hours. She'd not spoken to anyone and her aunt passed her a bowl of stew. Lamorna set her tea aside and balanced the bowl on her knees.

'Who are they?' Lamorna heard herself ask.

Her aunt followed her gaze to two of the tattooed men standing on the edge of the circle of light. 'They're Cruithea's warrior class – Magic Wielders, known as Inborn here, but highly skilled with their weapons. They train from a very young age. The tattoos tell the stories of their victories. The more tattoos, the more skilled the warrior.'

As Tamora spoke, a third man joined the other two warriors.

Lamorna had never seen a man who looked like he did. She tried not to stare, knowing it wasn't proper, but her eyes kept returning to his face – the firelight accentuated his sharp jaw and high cheekbones, straight nose and wide forehead. He wore his chestnut-coloured hair in braids bundled in a knot on top of his head, making him seem taller than he already was. The sides of his head were shaven. She couldn't see the colour of his eyes from where she sat, but the light from the fire made it appear like tiny flames were captured there. She watched his mouth as he talked with one of the other men – his top lip was thin, the bottom plump. He was wearing a short-sleeved tunic beneath a dark leather vest, the skin on his arms covered with swirling black tattoos, the inky lines following the curve and swell of muscle.

At that moment, he looked across the fire, pausing mid-conversation and catching her eye. She held his gaze, until she remembered she shouldn't and lowered her eyes, but she could feel him observing her.

'Are you going to eat, Lamorna?'

'I'm not hungry,' Lamorna managed. The man was still watching her.

Tamora stood and stretched, taking the stew. 'Come then. You should sleep.'

Lamorna let herself be led away from the warmth of the fire. She could still feel the warrior's eyes on her back long after she had fallen asleep.

His name, she later learnt, was Mordred.

He was the son of the High Priestess Morgause. In her land, that would make him important, someone who was to be respected simply for being who he was, but here, she knew it was different. Mordred had had to prove himself, as any warrior did. One of the things that had surprised Lamorna the most about Cruithea was the structure of their society, which was organised into four cabals, or groups: the warrior class, the Inborn; the guilden and tradespeople; the hunters; and the Priestesses of the Temple.

Here in the wilds, it was women who held power. Women who ruled, as the High Priestess Morgause did. Lamorna wondered how Mordred and the other men felt about that. The next High Priestess, her aunt had told her, would be chosen by the Goddess in a ceremony – titles were not passed through family lines in Cruithea.

The High Priestess did not like Lamorna. The proud woman didn't have to say anything – Lamorna could tell by the way her eyes remained on her face longer than was necessary, and the way Morgause looked through Lamorna when she spoke to her on their arrival. The High Priestess did nothing to hide her suspicion and Lamorna was glad her aunt had made her burn the Decalogue. She had no doubt the High Priestess would have thrown her out of the camp and left her to the wilderness if she knew Lamorna carried the One God's Word in her bag.

They had been made welcome; Lamorna could not argue with that, but what intrigued her was the realisation that Tamora and Keraine knew the High Priestess. They had greeted each other like old friends, and Lamorna knew it was that friendship that saw her with a warm place to sleep and food, however strange, in her belly.

As the days passed, Lamorna couldn't deny it any longer – as heathen as they may be, the sense of community in Cruithea was strong. She'd observed people in harmony, in tune with each other. Everyone had a role, regardless of their position or their gender.

And that sat ill in her belly.

CHAPTER 32

Early morning saw a slow warmth creep through the forest and over the village. Arthur had eaten and was on the way to wash his bowl and return it to the large stack that sat near the cooking fires when he halted.

Lamorna was walking across the communal area, her eyes on the ground, long blonde hair loose around her shoulders. Arthur stared at her. He had never, in all the years he had known her, seen her hair like that. Lit up by the growing dawn, she glowed, like some avenging goddess from one of the story books he had read in Avalon's library. For a moment, he could see a sword in her hand and droplets of blood painted across her cheek as a great plume of smoke rose behind her.

He blinked, shaking the vision, or whatever it was, from his head.

Lamorna came towards him, not looking where she was going. She was muttering to herself, her tone displeased about something. She almost barrelled into him, stopping just in time, lifting her eyes.

She gasped, and looked away.

'Lamorna—' he began.

'I've got to go,' she mumbled, stepping around him.

'Tell me what's been happening in Kernou,' Arthur said quickly, closing his hand over her forearm, stalling her steps. Lamorna shook him off and spun around to look at him. It was one of the only times Arthur could recall her actually *looking* at him. He thought she might need time to choose her words, to decide what was the proper thing to say, but she came at him like a fireball and the venom in her tone made him take a small step backwards.

'Why do you care? You left.'

'I ...'

Lamorna tossed her head, eyes flashing. She folded her arms across her chest, defiance in every line of her body. 'I expected better from you, Arthur,' she said haughtily, and Arthur jolted as anger, so hot, so potent, rushed through him.

'Did you expect better of my father when he put a whip in my hands and made me open the skin on my back?' he challenged in a low voice. Lamorna's face twitched but she said nothing, holding his gaze. He watched a muscle feather in her jaw, and went on. 'Did you expect better of the Konsel, who did nothing whenever my father ordered a young woman bound to that wretched stake – someone like *you*, Lamorna, innocent of the crimes she'd been accused of. Did you expect better of my father when he—'

'There is an arm of the Red Hand in Kernou now,' Lamorna cut in. There was no pleasure in her tone. She was still milk-pale, eyes wide and glistening.

Arthur felt sick. It had been something his father had wished for, something Ulrian had spoken about with relish, but Arthur had never imagined it would actually happen. For the Sacellum to allow such a thing meant something had changed.

'What else?' he asked.

'Burnings. Two before we left. Many people have left,' Lamorna added quietly.

'And you? Why did you leave?' He made his tone gentle, sorry for his anger. It was not Lamorna's fault. He knew, better than anyone, how blind faith could make a person, how it could twist someone's morality, their commonsense, their empathy. The scars on his back twinged in memory.

Lamorna glanced over her shoulder, back in the direction she had come from. 'My aunt. I did this for her. I didn't want her to be alone, not with Jenyfer … gone.'

Arthur swallowed. 'Family is important,' he said. 'Especially now. Especially for us, so far from everything we've ever known.'

'I heard you attacked your father. Is it true?' Lamorna asked, her pale blue eyes pinned to his again.

'I didn't intend for that to happen,' Arthur said quietly. 'It was an accident, and if I could change it, I would.'

Lamorna lowered her voice. 'The One God will forgive you, Arthur, if you ask Him.'

Arthur managed a weak smile. 'Maybe.'

'Lamorna!'

Lamorna spun around. Her aunt was coming towards her, a bundle of clothing in her arms.

'Here you are. Arthur, it's good to see you,' Tamora Rosevear said warmly. 'I can only assume how strange it all must be for you, but Morgause will look after you.' She turned to Lamorna, thrusting the bundle of clothing at her. 'Come. You're going to learn how to do the laundry, Cruithean style.'

'Must I?' Lamorna mumbled.

Arthur laughed. He couldn't help it. He had never heard Lamorna Astolat complain about a task set by her elders. It was against the One God's rules. Perhaps, he thought as he watched the two women walk away, Lamorna almost buried under the mountain of clothing, he was not the only one to have changed since leaving Kernou.

It was not Halymere or Melhala Arthur sought out that day. It was Ethinne. He had questions that he suspected no one else could answer.

It took a lot of asking before he found the acolyte. Unlike in Kernou, there was no prayer room, no cross or symbol of Inanna for people to worship at. Ethinne had told him the goddess was in everything, that she was everywhere, so therefore, they could worship where and when they chose. It did not matter to Inanna how often one worshipped, or even how, only that they did. There were no punishments, no threat of everburning fire for them to be banished to after they died, and no rules, save one – if it harms none, do as you will.

Arthur found Ethinne by a thin, winding stream east of the village. She was seated on the ground, a circle scratched into the dirt around her. Arthur did not want to disturb her, so he waited beneath the trees, watching as a vine crawled free of the earth and wrapped itself around Ethinne's wrist, coiling up her arm. She held out her other hand and slowly, a feather floated into the air, hovering a few centimetres above her palm. Arthur jumped as a ring of fire shot into life around her, only to be quenched by a burst of rain that came from nowhere.

The feather dropped, and the vine eased back into the ground.

'That was—' Arthur began, then clapped his hand over his mouth.

Ethinne glanced at him over her shoulder, then gestured to the space in front of her, an invitation to sit. He did so, sheepishly rubbing the back of his neck.

'I didn't mean to interrupt,' he said.

'I'm finished for now,' she said. 'There is only so much magic I can work at once. I'm still learning. It is getting easier. Managing all four elements at once is challenging.'

'I can't even manage one,' Arthur commented.

She smiled, reaching up to push a long dark braid over her shoulder. The sleeves of her gown fell back, revealing a chaotic storm of black ink, barely visible against the darker tone of her skin. Ethinne pulled her sleeve higher so he could see.

'Inanna's marks,' she told him softly. 'Each time we master an element, we make a mark on our skin.'

'But there are only four elements. Why so many marks?' Arthur asked. Ethinne's skin was covered with dozens of glyphs. She ran her finger over them gently.

'You do not master an element only once, Arthur,' she said, letting her sleeve fall. 'But you are not here to talk about the elements, are you? There are other things you wish to know.'

He nodded. 'What can you tell me about Ereshki?'

Ethinne frowned. 'We are not supposed to speak of her.'

'Please,' Arthur began. 'Goerika told me who she is, who she has remade herself to be. The question is – why? Why would a goddess pretend to be a god?'

'Why does anyone do anything, Old One or not?' Ethinne asked in return. 'She would have her reasons I am sure, but what they are, I do not know. The Red Sisters would know.' She stopped, bit her lip, and gave him a stern look. 'But you are not to speak with them, Arthur. No one speaks with them. It is forbidden.'

'I won't,' he assured her. 'Ethinne, can I ask you something else?'

'Of course.'

'Do you believe I am the one in the prophecy?'

Ethinne plucked at the end of her sleeve, fingers searching for a loose thread to vandalise. Arthur knew the gesture – it was something he used to do when he was nervous. 'What do you believe? In your heart, Arthur. What do you believe to be true?' When he said nothing, she went on. 'We believe that, if you want something and you are not sure if you truly want it, or if you are deserving of it, that you should ask Inanna. She will show you the way if she decides you are worthy of what you seek.'

He frowned. 'If I ask her, how will I know her answer?'

'It will depend on what you ask, Arthur.' Ethinne climbed to her feet; Arthur followed, and they walked back towards the village in silence. As the first of the kibitkas came into view, Ethinne lay her hand on his arm.

'Sometimes though, it is Inanna's way to give you not what you ask for, but what *she* determines you need.' She smiled. 'But you do not need Inanna, Arthur.'

'I don't?'

'You need faith. In yourself. Only then will everything become clear to you.'

CHAPTER 33

Lyonesse was a world of water. The weight of the ocean above was held back with a sheen of silver magic, and a multitude of creeks and streams wound through the landscape to pour into the dark river that sliced Melodias' realm in two.

'I want to know everything about my magic,' Jenyfer announced.

'That's a rather strong demand to make during breakfast,' Melodias drawled. They were sitting at a small table on a balcony, the dining room behind them, the blue and aquamarine-hued mountains and rivers spread out before them. Jenyfer had been in Lyonesse, in this underwater place that tugged at her, for three days. She didn't want to get comfortable here, or let the music and the silvery-blue light inside her in case it changed her.

Jenyfer kept her eyes on Melodias, until he sighed.

'I'll entertain you, daughter – why do you want to know?'

'Why? Because I have this … thing … inside me that I do not understand and cannot control,' Jenyfer said fiercely. Fear made her angry, and possibly reckless. She didn't know a thing about the Master of Songs and Death. She didn't know how far she could push, what she could get away with. Common sense told her to behave, to remember her place, but another part of her raged at the very thought of being subservient to a man who had stolen her from her friends – who had *drowned* her friends. She stabbed at her food with her fork, pushing aside thoughts of *The Queen* and her crew. 'What is this anyway?'

'Raw fish. And that *thing*, as you so basely put it, is called power,' Melodias replied. He sat back in his seat, crossing long legs over each other. Jenyfer couldn't help looking at him. She knew she looked like him – same eyes, same hair, same shape to their face – but she wondered what else he had given her.

Since arriving, she had barely slept, her nights filled with dreams of water and bones, and of the music that never stopped, that dripped from the very air.

'Did you take the time to ask Niniane anything useful?' Melodias asked, then laughed at the look on Jenyfer's face. 'Darling, I have spies all over the place. I've been keeping tabs on you since you left that horrible town.'

Jenyfer stared at him. 'So why didn't you ever—'

'Come for you before now? I was curious,' he said, leaning back in his chair. He drummed his fingers rhythmically on the table top. 'I wanted to see what you'd do with your newfound magic, which,' he added, sighing, 'was bitterly disappointing, I can assure you.'

'Then teach me,' Jenyfer said, setting down her fork.

Melodias ran a hand through his black locks. 'Didn't your human parents teach you the magic word?'

She grit her teeth, contemplating stabbing him with the fork she had discarded. 'Please.'

He chuckled. 'That's better. First, ask your questions.'

'What questions?'

'Don't play games with me – you aren't very good at them,' he said smoothly. He picked up a piece of the fish and popped it in his mouth.

'I know you are simply burning with curiosity.' A pause, his eyes locked on hers. 'Ask me about her.'

Jenyfer swallowed. She had already decided she would play the game, but she wasn't sure she wanted to know about her mother. The Master of Songs and Death – her *father* – was examining his black-scaled fingers, his face the perfect picture of boredom, but Jenyfer sensed he wanted to tell her, and that it was strangely important to him. And, if she was being honest, it was important to her as well. She could barely remember the woman who had given life to her. Her last moments with her mother had been filled with blood and screams, before she had been dragged away.

'Tell me about my mother.'

'Elowen was the most beautiful woman I'd ever seen. I saw her one night, through the portal—'

'What portal?'

Melodias' eyes flashed with irritation. 'Don't interrupt. I saw her and I knew I had to have her—'

'People aren't toys to *have*—'

'Again, don't interrupt.' He waved his hand and when Jenyfer went to speak, her voice was gone. She looked at him in panic. 'Relax. It's temporary. Anyway, where were we? Yes, that's right. Your mother liked to walk along the shoreline at night, so I disguised myself as a human man and put myself in her path. I didn't trick her other than that, so you can stop glaring at me like that. I never used my magic on her.'

Liar, Jenyfer said with her eyes.

He sighed. 'Believe it or not, it doesn't matter. I loved her and she loved me in return. But I couldn't stay in the human world – I had a realm to run, a job to do. The black lake you've seen, that holds the souls of all those who have not passed into the Otherworld. All those souls who, for some reason, Ankou denied entry but did not send elsewhere. They are given to me, to keep and to guard and ... anyway, back to your mother. I told her what I was, who I was,' he said softly. 'Being a faery is one thing, but being the Master of Songs and Death is another. She wasn't keen on me after that.'

He stopped to take a sip of his drink, then continued, his voice tight. 'She didn't tell me she was pregnant – I didn't even know it was possible. Male humans can impregnate a syhren, but the other way around?' He shook his head, glancing at Jenyfer, sitting mute and angry across from him. 'Most human-syhren half-breeds are without power, but you? You're a miracle. I knew the moment you were born – I felt it. I felt your magic enter the world. I could not leave to claim you, so I sent some of my guard but, by the time they got there, you were hidden from me. But it was human magic and I knew eventually it would fade. So, I waited.'

Jenyfer opened her mouth to speak and then remembered she couldn't, so she glowered instead. Melodias chuckled, waved his hand, and removed the magic that bound her voice.

'It didn't fade – she released the spell – to save me,' Jenyfer told him snappily.

'Does it matter?' Melodias asked. 'You're here now, where you belong.'

She looked him in the eyes. 'I don't belong here.'

'We'll see.' He stood and tucked his chair in, every movement as fluid and graceful as water, as the most beautiful music. 'Come,' he said, stepping back into the dining room. Jenyfer pushed back her chair and hurried after him, heart pounding. She followed him into the dark, blue-tinged hall. Melodias talked as they walked.

'We can transform if we want – when we swim, our legs can become tails—'

'Like mermaids?' Jenyfer asked. The dead mermaid in the town square in Kernou flashed into her mind, followed by Bryn's face, the pride, the arrogance.

'Ugh, no. We are nothing like those fish-people,' Melodias spat, then he threw her a smile over his shoulder. 'We're better – stronger, faster, much more powerful. We can manipulate water, move through water at incredible speeds, breathe underwater. But all of this is secondary to your song, Jenyfer.'

They continued in silence, encountering no one but a few grey-clad servants – half-breeds, Jenyfer realised. They kept their eyes on the floor and moved past quickly. She realised all the syhrens she had seen were female.

'Are there male syhrens?' she asked.

'No. Why?' Melodias asked, turning to look at her curiously. 'Looking for a mate, darling?'

'I just wondered,' Jenyfer muttered. Her thoughts shifted to Ordes, but she kept her expression calm. 'So all syhrens are female? Why?'

Melodias resumed walking. 'It is the way it is,' he said. 'There are male mermen, and a male of almost every species in the sea, but not syhrens.' He paused at a set of ornate double doors, indicating them with a flourish of his hand.

'What's in there?' Jenyfer asked warily.

'Your answers. Some of them, anyway, until you start asking the right questions.'

Beyond the doors was a library. She was under the sea, in a library. She stood, dumb and mute, and let her eyes soak up every detail of the room. The room was lined floor to ceiling with books, lit by orbs of softly glowing light with delicate trailing tentacles, like luminous jellyfish, floating above their heads.

Like the library in Avalon, it was a room of exquisite, existential delights; a room that dripped with the secrets of the world, with knowledge, something Jenyfer had always desired but didn't understand how much until she first stepped inside Niniane's library. Being denied books, denied knowledge other than that presented in the Decalogue, Jenyfer had spent most of her childhood imagining the things she could discover, if only she was allowed. She thought briefly of the book she had taken from Ordes. She'd never read it, and had left it in her cabin on *The Excalibur*. She wondered absently if he'd found it.

In the library of Lyonesse, there were glass cabinets tucked between the shelves.

'What else is in here?' Jenyfer breathed.

'Stuff,' Melodias answered.

'Stuff?' she repeated flatly.

He sighed. 'Relics, antiquities ... My library is rivalled only by the library on Avalon, as I'm sure you know. You can explore later. Come on.' Melodias led the way deeper into the room, passing between shelves that towered above Jenyfer's head, stopping at an expansive open space, filled with a long table and chairs. Hovering above them were more jellyfish-like orbs of blue and silver light. Melodias waved his hand and a book came floating towards them, falling to the table in front of them. He didn't speak as he held his hand above it and the book flew open, the pages ruffling until they stopped suddenly.

He stepped back, pulled out a chair, and indicated Jenyfer was to sit. She swallowed, but obeyed, sliding into the chair.

'It's all there,' Melodias commented. He was standing behind her, and she wanted to turn and look at him, but she didn't. She focused on the book instead. 'You can read, can't you?'

'Of course I can read.'

'Very well, just checking. Our true magic is in our voices, which I'm sure you've already worked out,' Melodias explained. 'What have you done with your voice so far?'

'I thought you were keeping tabs on me?'

'I can't see you on land,' Melodias said, so Jenyfer told him about the man in the market in The Vale, then about what happened in Port Leore, keeping her eyes on the pages in front of her. She did not mention Ordes and what her magic had done to him.

'It upsets you. Why?' Melodias asked neutrally.

Jenyfer gaped. 'I made a man stab himself!'

'So?'

She shook her head and turned back to the book.

He sighed. 'This is going to be a problem,' he stated, slinking around the table to sit opposite her.

'What is?'

He ignored her question, gesturing at the book. 'You can read it for yourself, but to give you a summary. There are different songs for different purposes, and each one contains a different sort of magic,' he said. 'There are songs to make someone fall in love with you, songs to make someone forget, to put someone to sleep,' he paused. She kept her face calm, but was thinking about that moment on *The Excalibur*, about the magic she had unknowingly used on Ordes. 'Songs for drowning and for compulsion, songs for sorrow, and songs for death.'

'Death?' Jenyfer said sharply. 'Do you mean how syhrens can make a man drown himself?'

'No. I mean a song to kill, crafted for that very purpose. Drowning a man is one thing, but a song of death, designed to stop a man's heart in his chest, to stop the flow of blood through his pitiful human body ... I fear that it is a song you will never master.'

'Why not?'

'Because before you do, you have to let it all go, Jenyfer,' Melodias said softly.

She swallowed. 'Let what go?'

'Your humanity.'

'I'm half-human,' she reminded him bluntly.

He waved her away. 'Yes, yes. It's very unfortunate, but I can only work with what I have.'

Jenyfer sat back and folded her arms. 'And what is that?'

He studied her across the table, those sea-storm eyes, so like hers, sweeping her features, trying to see inside her. 'I'm not sure yet. Every syhren has their own song. A song that lives inside them and is theirs alone – no syhren song is the same. It is that melody that you sing when you work your magic,' he explained. 'The combination of your song and the words you sing is what gives you your power.'

'Teach me the other songs then, the ones for forgetting and compelling and—'

'It's not that simple,' Melodias cut in, shaking his head. 'It's not like reading some words and singing them, Jenyfer. You can learn the words, but to learn the magic, to weave those words into your melody ... you have to practise. You have to control your emotions.'

'What do my emotions have to do with anything?' she asked.

'You've spent your life with the weight of your emotions threatening to drown you. You've warred with anger and pain and love and frustration and all the while your magic was growing. Am I right?' Melodias asked.

Jenyfer blinked. He was right. She was terrible at managing her emotions, letting them sweep her away, letting fear and anger rule her, the starting point for every stupid decision she'd ever made, every rash moment in her life.

'You're a creature of water, my darling,' her father said. 'And you never truly knew it. It isn't surprising that you let your base human emotions get the better of you.'

Jenyfer ignored the insult. 'If I learn to control my magic, will it help?'

'Yes,' Melodias whispered, his eyes shining. 'Once you learn what you can do, you'll never have to feel scared again. You'll never have to fear your magic because you will own it. And therefore, you will own yourself.' He stood quickly. 'Come with me.'

Jenyfer scrambled to her feet, following her father from the library and down the corridor in the opposite direction they had come. Melodias led her into an empty, cavernous room. The ceilings reached high above their heads, much like the sea caves of Carinya.

'What is this place?'

'This is where you will practise your songs,' he said simply. 'This room has been designed for this purpose – the acoustics in here are fabulous, don't you think?' he added, then opened his mouth and sang.

While the magic in his voice had no effect on Jenyfer, the music that poured from his lips did. The sounds swept into every corner of the room and curled around her body at the same time, sinking inside her, *changing* her. Each note, each beat, each shift in timbre, from joy to sorrow, major to minor, the layers she could hear in her father's song made her want to weep. Each sweeping crescendo, each subtle shift in tempo, had her inner song pulling at the core of her, wanting her to sing, to open her mouth and let the music come.

When he stopped singing, the music remained, echoing from the stone walls, the final notes resonating and pulsing through the air, until they slowly faded.

'Impressive, isn't it?' Melodias said simply, and Jenyfer wasn't sure if he was referring to his voice or the acoustics of the room. She could only nod. 'You will need to develop your songs; your compositions will be unique to you – the words may be the same but the way it is sung, the melody, the arrangement of the notes – that will be yours alone,' Melodias said quietly. 'You are the conductor of your opus.' He paused, his eyes sweeping over Jenyfer's face.

She knew he could see it. The storm that had been shaken loose inside her.

'Now,' he said, coming to stand behind her. He placed his hands on her shoulders. 'Sing.'

'Here? Now?'

'Yes. You won't harm me with your song, however much you might wish to. You've spent so long thinking you can't do this, but you need to trust in the magic inside you. Let it come. Let it make its way free of you,' Melodias whispered. 'Let go of fear, Jenyfer.'

'But what do I sing?'

'Whatever comes to you.'

Jenyfer closed her eyes, trying to still her mind, slow the furious thundering of her heart. She had to find that space within herself, that place she knew was waiting. She took a deep breath, pulling the warm, watery air into her lungs. She could feel the magic beneath her skin, the tingle, the anticipation. Now, instead of pushing it away like she had been, she let it sing, let this place of shadow and lightning, of wonder and darkness, of music, pull that magic from her body. It swirled around her, coiling gently, caressing her body, droplets of water wrapping themselves around her like a cloak.

Behind her, she sensed Melodias smile.

'Now,' he said. 'Sing for me.'

Buried beneath the layers of her mind, the layers that had been wrapped around her for her whole life, Jenyfer found the eye of her storm. She had been so tied up in her secrets and lies, so tangled in pain and anger and so haunted by a lifetime of hiding what she was.

Melodias squeezed her shoulders in encouragement.

She opened her mouth.

A tempest of sound rose from the marrow of her bones to take its place in the world.

CHAPTER 34

A jumbled mass of shining black rocks jutted out of the ocean and waves threw themselves with violent abandon onto a shoreline littered with the corpses of ships and debris. Ordes squeezed the small boat in between the wreck of *The Lady's Breath*, the lettering on the side of the craft still visible but almost worn away with age, and what he realised too late was a pile of bones, bleached white from the weather.

'Fucking syhrens,' Kat mumbled, scowling at the bones.

'I didn't think you'd be worried,' Ordes mused as she jumped out and stood with her hands on her hips. She glared at him as he hauled the boat as high as he could, trying to avoid stepping on any bones.

'I'll have you know,' Katarin began, 'I only hunt those who deserve to die a miserable death, and,' she said fiercely, before Ordes could interrupt, 'I send them to sleep before letting them sink to a watery grave.'

'Who decides who gets to die?' he asked her, narrowing his eyes against the sharp bite of the wind.

Katarin checked her weapons were in place. 'My crew. Those we target are men who've committed crimes against women. Why do you think we spend so much time in the towns, Ordes? We're collecting information. Taverns are the best place for such talk, you'd know that. It's one of the ways we learn about where and when a Magic Wielder will die.'

'I wasn't judging, Kat,' he said quietly.

She gave him a curt nod, and turned away. 'Are you sure about this?'

There was nothing on the island except rocks and bones. No buildings, not a syhren or anything fey to be seen. Ordes swallowed uneasily. 'I'm sure,' he said. 'Jen is here somewhere.'

'Yes, your destiny, or whatever you want to call it,' Katarin said.

'I didn't ask for it, and neither did she,' Ordes said simply.

The Captain of *The Night Queen* gave him an interested look. 'Did you know, though? When you first met her? Love at first sight and all that?'

'Not exactly,' Ordes answered, sighing. 'I'm not—'

'If you're about to say you're not in love with her I might punch you in the face, Ordes,' Katarin said, rolling her eyes. 'Because if you're truly not, what are we doing here?'

He said nothing.

Katarin grinned. 'Come on then, lover boy. Let's go and find her. Do you think Melodias has a door somewhere we can knock on?'

'There's meant to be a portal,' Ordes said. 'At least, as far as I understand it there is. The island isn't big – we should be able to find it.'

'Hopefully before anything finds us,' Katarin mumbled.

For hours, they clamoured over rocks and more heaps of bones, over pieces of ships and scattered driftwood. Jenyfer was alive, Ordes knew – he could feel it. He reached up to touch the space where his collarbones met. His fingers tingled as his mother's magic beat against them, a steady thrumming under his skin. He shot a quick glance at Katarin, who had stopped to wipe her forehead with the back of her hand. If anything happened to her because of him, he'd never forgive himself.

Between two columns of towering rock, they found the portal – a shimmering wall of blue light suspended in mid-air. Music rose and fell like a wave around them, but Katarin's expression did not shift.

'Can't you hear that?' Ordes asked.

'I hear nothing. Come on,' she said, stepping towards the portal. Ordes grabbed her arm.

'Wait. We have no idea what's on the other side of that thing, or even if we can get out. Maybe I should go while you wait here and if I'm not back—'

'Less talk, more action.' Katarin shook off his arm, and stepped through the portal.

Ordes sighed, and followed her.

He was falling towards something, the world turned to blue and silver and black around him. Magic ran like a river over his skin and his insides screamed, his blood burning and freezing at the same time. There was no sign of Katarin. No sign of anything. He could have been anywhere.

He closed his eyes and continued to fall.

Ordes was lying on his back, staring up at a dark sky blanketed with clouds. Forks of silver lightning danced around inside them, an endless rolling storm. He sat up slowly, rubbing at his head. A groan from nearby made him swing around in panic.

Katarin was lying not far from him, blinking up at the sky. 'Fuck,' she said.

'That's one way to put it,' Ordes mumbled. 'Are you alright?'

'In one piece,' she said, pushing herself onto her elbows so she could look around. Everything was dark and flat. Nothing grew out of the ground and the air was strangely thick and humid. 'Any idea where we should go?'

Ordes closed his eyes, focusing on Jenyfer's heartbeat, noting how its volume changed depending on which direction he turned his head. 'This way,' he said eventually, climbing to his feet, helping Kat to stand. She brushed her hands on her backside and pushed the hair from her face, but said nothing.

Jenyfer's heartbeat led them to the gaping mouth of a tunnel.

'Not too late to turn back,' Ordes whispered.

Katarin scoffed and unsheathed the dagger at her hip. He did the same.

The tunnel was dark, the walls flecked with glowing shards of ocean blue. Ordes' senses were screaming, hands sweaty where they gripped the blade. Behind, and Kat was muttering under her breath.

He had no idea how long they had been on this island. He had lost his sense of direction as soon as they'd fallen through the portal and stepped inside the never-ending darkness of the tunnel – east, west, north, south – all were scrambled together. He wondered whether Kat was feeling as claustrophobic as he was; they were both children of the ocean, of the open sea and open sky. Ordes' stomach was rolling violently.

'Kat,' he whispered.

'What?'

'Thanks for coming.'

'If I die, I swear I will haunt your arse until the end of time, Ordes,' she promised.

'I believe it.'

The tunnel did not have any branches but Ordes was still certain they were lost. His eyes were strained from peering into the darkness, his hands numb from trailing along the cold walls. Every placement of his feet brought a moment of fear.

They walked on through the darkness. Ordes couldn't hear his footfall, or Kat's, and the ground was slightly squishy. Several times, though, they had crunched over something hard; the first time, he'd crouched and felt around on the ground. More bones. Eventually, the tunnel finally began to widen and a soft blue light shone at the end. Ordes paused. His heartbeat thundered in his ears, and he could feel the hectic pulse of the blood through his veins. He took a deep breath, trying to be calm.

'Don't you flake on me,' Kat hissed, coming up behind him.

The light at the end of the tunnel shimmered and danced, another curtain of magic. Ordes watched it, stomach still rolling. Kat sighed and pushed past him, approaching the curtain and holding out her fingers. She yelped and jumped back.

'What?'

Scowling, she rubbed her hand on her thigh. 'Just a tickle. Won't kill us.'

Before he could say anything, she squared her shoulders, tightened her grip on her blade and stepped through. He followed, fists clenched, his thoughts locked onto Jen. Not realising Kat had stopped, he barrelled into her. She pushed him away, but when he lifted his head, any words he had for her fell away.

The landscape beyond the veil was populated by trees of coral, their spindly branches like fingers. Ordes licked his lips, tasting salt and seaweed. A damp wind ripped across the open space between the tunnel and the coral forest.

'Are you sure she's worth it, Ordes? I mean, this place ...'

Above them, the sky was dark blue and grey, like the ocean under a storm. Ordes took a deep breath and marched towards the graveyard of skeletal coral trees, Kat following. As they walked, Ordes knew they were being watched.

The coral forest thinned, and they found themselves standing on the edge of a marshland, a great stretch of water covered in swirling fog. Swallowing, Ordes approached the edge, pulling his cutlass free and poking it into the dark water. A skeletal hand shot free of the soupy water. Kat choked back a scream as Ordes stumbled away from that hand, his stomach in his throat, nerves quickly withering as more hands broke the surface. A stone path pulled free of the water, stretching out into the marshes.

'Oh look, he's rolling out the stone carpet for us,' Kat tried to joke, but her voice shook. Ordes touched her arm.

'I'll go first.' He placed one foot on the crumbling path, not looking at the sea of dead hands, not thinking about the fact they seemed to be reaching towards him as he took another step. He heard Kat step onto the stone, sucking in a breath. 'You good?'

'Can we hurry up?'

Music was woven beneath the thunder and forks of lighting that lit Melodias' realm.

They were taking too long to cross the marsh. A feeling of desperation overtook Ordes and he started running, expecting something with claws and teeth to leap out of that horrible dark water and rip into him at any moment. Kat was close behind him, her breathing sharp.

They cleared the marshes, feet finding solid ground again. In the distance was a castle. A high stone wall surrounded it, the entrance a set of heavy-looking metal gates. There were four towers, one higher than the others, stretching into the sky, each tower covered in tall, wide windows that gaped at them like black mouths. A bridge lay between them and the castle. It didn't appear to be guarded, and the gate at the end was open like an invitation.

Ordes' head screamed in warning.

'The castle,' Kat mumbled. 'Look at it, Ordes.'

Glistening amongst the dark stones were pieces of white. Bones. Jen was in there, somewhere. Ordes approached the bridge, Katarin close behind him; the bridge was wooden, suspended above a river as black as the sky. The water was smooth and still, a mirror reflecting nothing.

Ordes put one foot on the bridge.

Loud music burst into life around them, filling the air. Katarin put her hands over her ears.

'What the fuck?' she shouted, but Ordes shook his head. He could feel the music pulling at him, but his mother's magic kept it from making him throw himself into the river. He glanced down – the surface of the river rippled. A head of silver hair broke through, then another, and another.

'Kat,' he said.

'Shit,' she hissed.

Syhrens. Too many to count. They began to climb the steep gorge, moving swiftly, their silver skin and hair glowing in the darkness. The music continued, louder and more forceful.

Hand shaking, Ordes reached behind him for Katarin. Finding her shirt, he pulled her towards him. 'In the Captain's cabin on *The Excalibur* is a copy of the map. The one on mine and Jenyfer's skin. Take it to my parents.'

'What are you—'

'You need to get out of here.' The first of the syhrens appeared over the edge of the gorge. Ordes shuffled backwards, forcing Katarin to move. One syhren became three, then ten, then he lost count. All were singing, their unearthly beautiful faces expressionless.

Katarin gripped his arm. 'Ordes ...'

'Get the map, Kat,' he said firmly. 'Arthur needs it. Now get out of here.'

'But—'

Whatever she was about to say, Ordes didn't hear. He shoved her towards the marshes and the tunnel. She looked at him, her face stricken, then she spun around and ran.

Ordes adjusted his grip on his cutlass. He would fight for a moment, knowing already it was pointless; his magic coiled around his fingers but he knew that, too, would be useless. There were too many of them. But, as the first syhren reached him, something shifted in the air around them. The syhren froze, her inhuman face strangely peaceful in its arrested state. Curious, Ordes waved his hand in front of her eyes. She didn't blink, and he realised they were all frozen like that.

He put his cutlass away and moved forward, stepping around one sea faery, then another, carefully edging towards the bridge, his heartbeat threatening to drown him. He had no idea what was going on, but he'd take the win. As he put one foot on the wooden bridge, the air in front of him shimmered. He stumbled back, fumbling for his weapon as a figure in a hooded cloak materialised in front of him.

A chuckle echoed in his ears as he pulled the cutlass free again.

'Pointless,' a voice said. 'And I thought you might actually be clever.'

'What are you?' Ordes demanded.

The figure reached up and slowly removed their hood. A skeletal face, no hair, eyes as black as the depths of night, skin that shimmered and shifted out of focus, as if Ordes was not supposed to see them properly; he could not tell if the mysterious figure before him was male or female, or something in between. 'You tell me, faery.'

'You're a wraith?'

'That's one word for it, I guess. I'm many things, Ordes,' the wraith said, coming closer to him; he jolted at the casual use of his name. 'You know me, and you have always known me.'

'I don't—'

'You are the only one outside of the Old Ones to have witnessed my journey across the water, towards this place. You are the only one to have seen the Bag Noz,' the wraith said.

'You ... you're the helmsman of the Night Boat?'

'I am.'

He sucked in a breath. 'Why can I see you?'

'Because of what you are. Because you were born in the space between the worlds, where magic comes from. The one who stands between the worlds shall bear the weight of them both,' the wraith said softly.

'The prophecy,' Ordes breathed. 'What do you know about it?'

'Many things,' the wraith said. 'My master has watched these things unfold.'

'Ankou?'

The wraith nodded, and leant their skeletal face close to his. 'He has things to share, secret things, important things.' They pulled back. 'But they are not for your ears. They are for *hers*.'

'Whose?'

'She who shall reshape this world with her voice.'

'Jenyfer?'

'That is her name, yes,' the wraith said.

'Where is she?'

'She is here,' the wraith replied, waving a hand at the inky sky above them.

'You said she will reshape the world. Do you mean Teyath?'

'No, I mean *this* world – Melodias' realm,' the wraith said.

Ordes frowned. 'But how?'

'I cannot say,' the wraith answered. 'And you cannot say. Understand?'

He nodded. 'Can you help me?'

'No. You need to play this game, Ordes. Play his game, for a while,' they added, pale bloodless lips curling into a smile. 'Melodias likes games. And he likes her – he will not let her go easily. You need to understand that. You need to decide if this is worth what he will ask you to give.'

Ordes swallowed. 'She's worth it, if that's what you mean.'

The wraith tapped a translucent finger against a bony chin. 'Let me ask you something. If you had to choose, between her and the rest of the world as you know it, what would you choose?'

'There is no choice,' Ordes said. 'I'd rather be with her in a world reduced to nothing, than be without her in a world that is whole.'

The air around the wraith shimmered and flickered. 'She will have to make a choice as well. Would she drown the world for you, I wonder?'

'So do I,' Ordes mumbled, not realising he'd spoken out loud until the wraith chuckled. They clicked their fingers and sound rushed back into the world, the syhren song deafening. Ordes let his cutlass fall to the ground and did not fight when a hand closed over his arm.

CHAPTER 35

The cooking area was deserted. Arthur frowned. The fires were lit, and stew was bubbling in a large pot dangling over the coals. Earthen bowls were stacked up waiting. Silence hung over the village; in the distance, Arthur heard a horse whinny, heard small feet racing through the trees.

He closed his eyes, concentrating. His magic moved through his veins as he listened to the world around him.

Come, the trees called. *This way.*

Following the voice of the trees, Arthur walked away from the cooking area, into the forest. The sun was setting; ribbons of gold and red stretched through the forest like flames. Something moved beneath the trees up ahead. He quickened his pace. He could hear voices, human voices now.

Leaning against a tree further along the path, was Mordred. He pushed himself upright.

'You took your time. My mother had me wait in case you didn't work it out for yourself,' he said. 'Hurry up.'

'Where is everyone?' Arthur asked his cousin.

Mordred's smile was dark as Arthur fell into step beside him. 'Up ahead. But, before we get there, is there anything you want me to tell him?'

'Who?' Arthur asked as they reached the end of a line of people winding through the trees. Flaming torches were being carried by those at the front of the crowd, and Arthur wondered whether the whole village was out here beneath the trees. He had no idea where Jalen was, or the High Priestess.

'The sacrifice,' Mordred said simply.

'The … what?' Arthur stammered. Mordred shook his head, pushing through the crowd, moving towards the front. Arthur followed him, struggling to keep up with his cousin's longer strides, until everyone began to move again, spreading out until they had formed a large circle around the edge of a clearing.

The High Priestess was standing in the middle of the clearing. Morgause was wearing a headdress of feathers and leaves, her hair braided around it. Her arms were bare, swirling blue painted on her skin, and the skin around her eyes was blackened. The glyphs on her forehead appeared to have been freshly done, the white markings bright against the caramel tone of her skin. She scanned the watching crowd, pausing as her eyes found Arthur's, before they moved to Mordred, who stepped from the circle and approached her.

Arthur had no idea what was going on. Orange sparks from the torches leapt into the night sky, shooting into the trees before they vanished.

At that moment, the crowd at the edge of the clearing stepped aside, and two of the Inborn came forward, dragging a man between them. His hands were bound, and a gag was stuffed between his lips, pulled so tight the skin around his mouth was curled back and Arthur could see his teeth. The man looked around wildly.

The Witchfinder. He was wearing his red cloak.

Arthur sucked in a breath. 'What is this?' he asked the person nearest him.

'Inanna's justice,' the man answered. Before Arthur could say anymore, the Witchfinder was dragged into the middle of the clearing and dumped at the High Priestess' feet as someone pushed through the crowd to stand at Arthur's side.

'Lamorna!' he breathed. 'You shouldn't be here.'

'Why not?' she said. She looked away from him, watching as Mordred crouched before the Witchfinder, tipping the man's face towards him. 'They call them the Sheletari here,' Lamorna said quietly. 'They who devour. Did you know that?'

'No,' Arthur said. 'I mean, I didn't know what the word meant.'

Morgause lifted her hands towards the sky; the crowd did the same, except for Arthur and Lamorna. 'The Sheletari are many,' the High Priestess declared, her voice ringing through the forest. 'But we are not afraid of the darkness. The Sheletari hide behind their god. We walk side by side with ours. Yet, the Sheletari and those in the Sacellum believe their way is the right way. But, I ask you this – who gets to decide what is the right way?'

'Inanna,' someone shouted. 'Ask Inanna! Ask the Old Ones!'

The High Priestess nodded, moving in a slow circle around the Witchfinder on the ground. 'Tonight, we will feed the enemy to the Gods.' The crowd murmured their assent. 'Tonight, we will show the Old Ones we are their servants and that we continue to honour them for the gifts they give us – magic, and strength. We will prove to the Old Ones we continue to fight for them, as they wish us to, and they will reward us as they have already rewarded us. The prophecies of the Myrddin have promised us a new world, a world shaped by the hands of a king who is on our side.' She paused, her gaze falling to the Witchfinder. 'This man is our enemy, as he is the enemy of all those with magic in their veins. This man's life will be given to the earth so that new life will rise!'

Arthur jolted, every muscle tensing.

'It's you, isn't it?' Lamorna asked. Arthur had almost forgotten she was there. 'This king they talk about. It's you.'

'Yes, it's me,' he said, realising that was the first time he had admitted it so freely. Lamorna stared at him for a moment. She opened her mouth to say something else, but in the circle, Mordred raised his hand.

'As the leader of the Inborn, it is my job to protect you,' he said, his voice lifting into the night, flowing over everyone. 'It therefore falls to me to wield the knife and make this sacrifice on your behalf. With the blood that I spill on the earth this night, know that this is my promise to you all – when the new world rises from the dust of the old, when the Old Ones walk the earth once more, you shall always have me as your shield. You shall have me as your weapon against that which hides in the darkness!'

Arthur trembled as those words rushed through him.

'That's the pledge of the Inborn,' a voice murmured. Arthur felt Jalen's fingers wrap around his. 'The Inborn are the shield and the spear of the world.'

'Did you bring the Witchfinder here?' Arthur whispered.

'Yes.'

'Why?'

'For this moment, Arthur,' Jalen said quietly. 'It has to happen. If we are to stand a chance against those that want to see magic gone from the world, we need Cruithea behind us. You need them. You need to watch this, and you need to accept it.'

Arthur shook his head. 'There must be another way.'

'There isn't. Don't think all of the stories you've heard about this place are untrue. There will be more blood spilled in Cruithea yet,' Jalen said, his fingers tightening on Arthur's. Arthur kept his eyes on the Witchfinder, noting the state of the man's robes, his hair, which was messy and wild, the pallor of his skin. When they had left Avalon, the Witchfinder was in the care of the Priestesses. He was healthy, unharmed, but this man …

Lamorna was watching everything intently, eyes shining. Arthur wanted to tell her to turn away, to not watch what was about to happen to a servant of the One God, but at that moment, she looked at him, as if she knew what words were dancing on his tongue. She held his gaze, then turned back to watch as Mordred unsheathed a blade from a scabbard at his hip.

The Cruitheans cheered.

'How long has he been here?' Arthur asked.

'A while,' Jalen answered.

You didn't think we sat them down and had a polite chat, did you?

Mordred ran the blade across his palm, closing his fist. He moved to stand behind the Witchfinder, who was on his knees now, his eyes closed, bound hands clasped at his chest and Arthur knew that if the man's mouth was able, it would be shaping the Word. Mordred opened his fist, dipped his fingers in the blood there, and wiped them across his forehead, repeating the gesture on the Witchfinder. The man jerked away from the leader of the Inborn in horror, but did not open his eyes.

'With the blood, Mordred is promising the Old Ones that this man will be returned to them,' Jalen explained.

'But ...'

'He may be a follower of the One God, but the Sheletari is still of the earth, Arthur,' Jalen said softly. 'He will still take the journey across the water in the Bag Noz and he is still Ankou's to judge before he passes to the next world.'

There were no more words spoken, not by Jalen, or the High Priestess, or her son, who held his blade aloft, his fingers weaving through the bound man's hair. At a nod from Mordred, one of the Inborn approached and cut the ropes from the Witchfinder's hands and removed the gag from his mouth. The man gasped, and Arthur expected him to immediately begin reciting the Word, but as Mordred pulled the Witchfinder's head back, pressing his blade to the Witchfinder's throat, Arthur saw it – the mark on the man's forehead, between his eyes, like someone had tried to remove what had once been there.

He was Cruithean, one of those taken, one of the ones Mordred had spoken of.

The Witchfinder's eyes opened, his chest rising and falling rapidly as he looked up at Mordred – and nodded.

He spread his hands wide, palms to the sky. Slowly, light began to pool in his hands. Arthur tensed, but instead of trying to fight his way free, the Witchfinder released his magic into the sky as Mordred pushed his head over the blade and cut his throat.

Arthur expected a cheer from those watching, but it was a murmur, soft and reverent.

A prayer.

'By the earth and wind and fire and rain, blood of our blood and bone of our bone, blessings to the next life, until we meet with you again.'

Lamorna sucked in a ragged breath, and when Arthur looked, she was gone.

CHAPTER 36

Everything the Master of Songs and Death did was musical.
Every word held its own melody, every step he took held its own
rhythm, and every frustrated noise and sarcastic sigh sounded like
a song. He had taken Jenyfer back to the cavernous room with the great
acoustics, waiting while she turned in circles and noticed all the things
she had failed to see before – the way the walls sparkled, the way the
water that dripped down the walls to kiss the floor, and the way her bare
feet resonated against the slick stone floor.

'To understand your magic you need to understand music,' Melodias
said, stopping her mid-turn. 'You need to understand its depth, its
candour, its grace. You need to be able to grasp the power of it, be able to
visualise it and then create the layers that music contains – a note can be
polyphonic, for instance. You need to learn about dynamics, tempo, and
timbre. About pitch, and the difference between major and minor scales,
chromatic and diatonic scales, harmony and—'

'I get it,' Jenyfer muttered, her good mood vanishing. 'I have lots to
learn.'

Melodias smiled. 'It will come naturally to you.'

'How can you be so sure?'

'You're my daughter,' he said simply, as if that explained everything. 'Once you have mastered the theory, you will put it into practice, and then, you will find the true magic in your voice will roll off your tongue.'

'Why is it so important to you that I can do this?' Jenyfer asked.

Melodias' lips curled. 'What father doesn't want to help his daughter reach her potential? And as to the why – this is about power.'

'Power?' Jenyfer echoed.

Melodias nodded. 'The one thing that everybody wants and the one thing hardly anybody gets. Power makes or breaks us. It will be the making of you.'

Jenyfer shook her head.

'Think about the power you already had in your pitiful human life up there,' Melodias paused and waved his hand vaguely through the air.

'What power?' Jenyfer answered.

'Exactly,' Melodias murmured, his eyes burning with excitement. 'Think of what it will be like to go back there and show all those who ever doubted you, who thought you were nothing, that you are something. That you are power, perfected and brutal. They will cower before you,' Melodias promised. 'They will bow to *us*, daughter.'

Jenyfer said nothing, let him read her thoughts on the issue in her face, wondering what it was he truly wanted from her, why he had brought her here. She was convinced it had nothing to do with years of missed parenting.

He clicked his fingers and a desk, chair, and a mountain of books appeared. 'Your studies.'

Jenyfer stared in dismay at the towering stack of books. 'I have to read all those?'

'I have someone assigned to help you, don't worry. Andromache will join you shortly,' Melodias announced, and then he was gone, vanished into nothing, and Jenyfer was left in the cavernous room with the beautiful acoustics, and the stack of leather-bound books. Alone, she hummed to herself, the sound creeping into the air, bouncing from the walls. A smile spread across her face, so she sang, just nonsense, words that weren't even words, but her voice! In this space it was glorious. Jenyfer wrapped her arms around herself and continued to sing, then flung her arms out and spun in slow circles, head tipped back.

'That's the quickest way to ruin your voice.'

The speaker's voice was low and husky. Jenyfer stopped so suddenly she almost fell over. A syhren sauntered into the room. The faery snapped her fingers and another chair appeared on the opposite side of the desk. She gestured to it. 'Sit.'

'You're Andromache?'

'I am,' the syhren said. 'And your father has given me strict instructions. You are to learn to use your voice properly. You are to learn about music.' Andromache took a seat, arranging the skirt of her deep blue gown around her legs, turning aquamarine eyes on Jenyfer. Her eyebrows furrowed in displeasure, and Jenyfer hurried over to the other chair, plonking herself down without a shred of the grace the other syhren had demonstrated.

Andromache was the most beautiful creature Jenyfer had ever seen, more beautiful than Katarin and even Niniane. Like all syhrens, Andromache was long limbed and moved like she was made of water. Long silver hair tumbled over her shoulders, shifting like it was caught in a current. Her skin had a silver sheen. Jenyfer had noticed some syhrens wore their scales all the time while some, like Andromache, let them decorate their long fingers and temples. And when Andromache spoke, it was like music, so melodic and pure. Powerful.

Andromache taught her the words to the songs, but Jenyfer could not craft her own melodies. Something was holding her back, no matter how much she tried.

'No,' Andromache snapped when Jenyfer's song failed her again. 'Again.'

'I can't.'

'Again,' the syhren demanded. 'And mean it.'

'I'm trying!'

Andromache shook her silver head. 'You're not. You're scared of your song, of what it can do, of what it has done already. But, think about what you could do with some control, Jenyfer. Think about the power you will have.'

Jenyfer closed her eyes. Her song was right there, hovering on her tongue, and she finally understood what it was. It was daggers plunged into guts. It was dazed looks and glassy eyes. It was whispered commands and obedience. It was death. It was the power her father spoke of and it hummed in her veins, cool and dark and filled with opportunity.

Her syhren song.

Unique to her.

Her blood warmed; her song purred.

But she did not let it out.

When Jenyfer wasn't at her music lessons with Andromache and her hard words, she would explore, until the dark halls of her father's castle and the dripping spaces outside of it were as home to her as the streets of Kernou had been, however much she had felt like an outsider. That had been a choice, Jenyfer realised as she turned from the window in her room and pulled on the dress that had been laid out for her by one of the servants. She could easily have done as Lamorna did and given herself over to the One God and all he, no, *she*, represented, but she now understood why she never did – the part of her that belonged in the watery, music-saturated world would not allow it.

But she didn't belong here either, not really.

She left her room and headed down the corridor. Her presence had been requested, and when she entered the room with the black lake, Melodias was not perched on his throne like he usually was.

He was waiting by the edge of the lake, staring into its blackness.

Jenyfer joined him.

'It's time to show me what you have learnt,' her father said. 'You will sing for me again.'

Jenyfer frowned. 'If syhrens are immune to one another's songs, how do we practise?' she asked, her breath catching at the realisation that was the first time she had referred to herself as a syhren.

Melodias indicated the lake. 'With them.'

'Them?'

He waved his hand; the surface of the water stirred and slowly, the ghostly form of a woman appeared. As Jenyfer watched, the woman's body became solid, yet her expression was blank. Jenyfer gasped as the truth hit her.

'You use *people* as practise?'

'They're already dead, Jenyfer,' Melodias said. 'Their souls belong to me – a deal I made with Ankou – so you can't really hurt them. But, there is enough of the human left in them that our magic has an effect.'

Jenyfer stared at the dead woman, at her vacant eyes. In life, she imagined her to have rosy cheeks and plump, berry-coloured lips. She imagined the wet slick of blonde hair blowing in the breeze.

She shook her head.

The woman reminded her of her sister.

'No.'

'No?' An eyebrow lifted at her tone. 'Whatever do you mean, no?'

'I mean just that – no.' Jenyfer turned and raced from the room, out into the corridor, running towards the main door to the castle, and from there, she hurried into the garden, grateful to be outside and away from her father and that ghastly lake, even if outside was still beneath the ocean. She liked the garden and its strange plants; she couldn't name a single one, but they were beautiful in their floral horror.

Jenyfer stopped. A gate. There had never been a gate in the garden wall before, she was certain of it, but she'd noticed things often appeared on a whim in this place, like in Avalon. Doors, an extra hallway, and now, wrought iron gates. There was no lock, so she eased the gate open and stepped outside the garden walls, into a landscape that was barren and dead. A wasteland, nothing but skeletal coral trees rising from the rocky ground.

'So, you're the heir to the bone throne.'

The voice made Jenyfer jump; she felt her water magic swirl into her palms and droplets of it curled around her arms. The voice chuckled.

'Who's there?'

'You're his daughter, there is no doubt about that.' The voice came from the air around her, touching one ear and then the other, an echo that rebounded off nothing.

'Show yourself,' Jenyfer demanded.

A breath touched Jenyfer's ear. 'As you wish.'

The air before her rippled and then, a figure draped in a black cloak, a hood covering their head, stood before her. Jenyfer took a hasty step backwards. 'Who are you?'

The figure reached up and removed the hood with pale, slender hands. 'I'm Ophine, the helmsman of the Bag Noz.'

Ophine shimmered in the strange blue light of the world beneath the sea, and Jenyfer was unsure whether the creature standing before her was male or female. Ophine's skin was translucent, so Jenyfer could see the bones that rested beneath, with eyes as black as the darkest night. Bloodless lips and a pointed chin. Jenyfer was startled to see Ophine was bald.

'What are you?'

'A wraith, sort of.'

'You're from the Otherworld?'

'Technically, yes,' Ophine's voice was like paper, dry and whispery, but somehow soft. 'Ankou is my master.'

'What are you doing here?'

'Looking for you,' the wraith said.

'Why?'

Ophine sighed and ran their fingers over the leaves of the nearest plant; they withered and died. The wraith shrugged. 'He was so sure about you.'

'Who was? Melodias?'

'No. Ordes.'

Jenyfer's heart surged. 'Ordes? You know Ordes?'

'We've met.' The wraith's tone was casual. 'But tell me this – how is it you don't know where he is, when he was certain he could find you?'

'What … where is he?'

Ophine smiled. 'Let's see if you can work that one out, Jenyfer. After you're done with this place and with prophecies, my master will speak with you. He has many things to share.'

Then the helmsman of the Night Boat was gone, vanished as if they'd never been there. Jenyfer stared at the world outside her father's walls, blinking in confusion. She gasped, then closed her eyes and concentrated, pushing aside the music that swam through her, digging deep into the heartbeat that rested alongside hers. It was strong, stronger than it should have been. Jenyfer frowned. Ordes' heart was never that strong, not unless …

Her eyes flew open and she turned and ran, stumbling over herself, through the garden and up the stairs into the castle. She raced through the halls, barrelling through two servants carrying silver trays, ignoring their cries of displeasure. She tore through the dark halls until she found her father, sitting on his throne near the black lake.

Panting, Jenyfer rested her hand on the wall, pushing the length of her hair from her eyes.

Melodias raised his eyebrows. 'Yes?'

'Where is he?'

Her father sighed.

Chapter 37

Lamorna had not been able to stop thinking about the Witchfinder. She had heard things while being in Cruithea. She had heard Witchfinders were actually Magic Wielders, but she had not believed that. Not until she had watched the way golden light had poured from the Witchfinder's palms into the night sky moments before he had his throat slit and his blood washed over the ground.

It had made her stay awake most of the night, her eyes on the kibitkas flap, clutching her blankets and waiting, waiting for the ghost of the Witchfinder to come to her, because surely the One God had not taken him to the next world, not if he was a Magic Wielder. But the sun had risen just as it did every other morning, with no ghosts or signs from the One God.

Lamorna had stayed in the kibitka all the following day, unable to gather the courage to leave. She hated this place, this country, these people. She hated the suffocating density of the forest, with its wild animal and damp earth smell. The only thing Lamorna truly liked about

Cruithea were the horses. She'd discovered them corralled in a circular pen at one end of the village when she had forced herself to explore her temporary world. Lamorna had only ever seen a horse once, and that animal had been a proud and haughty beast with a nasty eye.

The horses in Cruithea were different. There was a wildness to them that drew her in as much as it repelled her. She'd learnt Cruitheans rode with no saddles and only used a simple bridle. Her aunt had explained the horses were bonded to their riders.

'Through magic?' Lamorna had asked.

Tamora had shaken her head. 'Through trust.'

Lamorna had spent hours watching the animals, the way they interacted with each other, working out which one was in charge of the small herd. And they watched her back, those liquid eyes boring into hers. Part of her was uneasy knowing about the bond between horse and rider. She wished Tamora had not told her about it, because if these animals, who were so strong and powerful and intelligent, trusted their riders ...

Then there were the faeries she had seen lingering around the horse pen. Piskies. She had wanted to scare them away, thinking they must surely frighten the horses, but the animals did not mind, and the piskies were smiling, petting the horses and braiding their manes and tails with swift little fingers.

But even though the death of the Witchfinder had unsettled her, Lamorna could not stay locked up forever, so she had gotten up and dressed, had eaten her breakfast and now, with nothing else to do, she had gone in search of the horses. She wondered if it were possible to learn to ride one while she was here. There were no horses in Kernou. Only boats and fish, and she had no desire for either of those things. Not that she would have been allowed to learn to sail, or learn how to catch fish, she realised.

There were five horses in the holding yard today. Lamorna rested her hands on the fence and watched them. She liked their manes and the way they flicked their long tails to brush away insects. She did not see any piskies, but she could see where the faeries had braided the horses' hair. She smiled. Piskies were not very good at braiding. One of the horses, a big black one, lifted his head to look at her.

Lamorna felt a spark in her chest. She held out her hand. 'Come here,' she called, but the horse stared at her, then tossed its head and went back to eating, and she was surprised by how disappointed she felt, how rejected, by an animal.

'They don't want to go to anyone except for their riders,' said a small voice at her elbow.

Lamorna glanced down. A young boy was standing there. He was shirtless, his hair wild around his face, and he had no shoes on, but his face was bright and friendly.

'How does someone get to be their rider?' she asked him.

The boy shrugged. 'All I know is you have to bond with them when they are babies. Then, when they trust you, they will let you ride them.' He smiled up at her. 'Come with me. I have something better to show you than horses.'

'What could be better than horses?' Lamorna said.

The boy rolled his eyes, reaching for her hand. She stiffened as his fingers closed around hers, but he didn't notice. He tugged on her hand, and she let him drag her away from the horse pen and into the forest.

'Where are we going?' she asked him. 'Is it dangerous?'

'Not where we're going,' the boy said.

'Why?'

'Because the Inborn will be there.'

Lamorna sucked in a breath, and let herself be led between the trees, the boy's hand warm in hers. Soon, she could hear a melodic clanging. She could hear a voice, giving instructions. A voice she recognised from the night the Witchfinder died.

Her heart stuttered. 'I don't think we should go,' she said quickly.

The boy ignored her, pulling on her hand. He was strong for a small child. She glanced over her shoulder. She thought she knew where the village was, but she had not come this way before. Swallowing, Lamorna followed the boy through the trees – at least if they were going to see the Inborn, no faeries would get her and someone would be able to tell her how to get back to the village.

In a clearing up ahead were the Inborn. The men were bare-chested, their muscled arms and torsos gleaming with sweat, even though, to Lamorna, it was chilled beneath the trees. The Inborn were mostly men, but there were a few women present, and they were swinging swords and axes and other weapons Lamorna did not know the names of with deft efficiency.

She swallowed. There were no weapons in Kernou, not like this. The Red Hand carried daggers, but she didn't think any of them actually knew how to use them.

Not like the Cruitheans did anyway.

The boy bounced up and down on the balls of his feet, almost bursting with excitement. His agitated movements made Lamorna's arm shake, and made her laugh. She clapped a hand over her mouth – she never laughed; the sound was so foreign to her ears it scared her. But the boy's excitement was strangely catching, and she found herself smiling.

She was watching the boy and not what was going on, and it wasn't until someone was kneeling on the ground before them that she realised they were no longer alone.

Mordred was there. He was watching the boy.

'Who's your friend, Lyr?' he asked gently.

The boy leant forward so he could whisper in Mordred's ear, and Lamorna desperately wanted to know what he said about her. A smile crawled across Mordred's face. 'I see. Well how about you go and see your father and I will look after your friend.'

The boy let go of Lamorna's hand and rushed over to the other Inborn, who had stopped their training and were now drinking from waterskins and talking.

'Lyr says you want to ride a horse,' Mordred said, his face amused. Slowly, he stood, all supine muscle and flowing grace. He was taller than Lamorna by a head. She had to peer up at his face, before she remembered she shouldn't, and dropped her eyes, making him chuckle. 'This isn't Kernou,' he told her quietly. 'Those rules don't apply here.'

'I know,' she mumbled, still not looking at him.

'Are you afraid of me?' he asked.

'No,' she said quickly.

'You were there the other night, weren't you? I saw you.'

'Yes,' she whispered. 'I was.'

'And you don't approve?' Mordred asked her.

'I don't know what to think,' she whispered. Then, because the thought rushed into her head and startled her, 'Is Arthur Tregarthen really going to be a king?'

'Perhaps,' Mordred said, but Lamorna thought she detected something in his tone – jealousy maybe. Mistrust. She looked at him then, wondering. The leader of Cruithea's Inborn held her eyes, not looking away, and it made her realise she had not looked a man in the eye for a long time, perhaps ever, not like this. She lifted her chin a little, studying Mordred boldly. She decided she liked his eyes; they were the colour of soil, deep and rich, and his skin was like the darkest honey from their hive in their garden in Kernou.

Another of the men came and offered Mordred a waterskin. He took a drink, wiping his mouth with the back of his hand, and then held it out for her. Cautiously, Lamorna took it, aware he was watching every movement she made. She did not look away from him as she took a small sip and passed the waterskin back.

'Can you find your way back?' he asked her.

'I think so,' she said.

'I'll get you an escort,' he said, turning and calling for the boy, Lyr, over his shoulder. The child raced back to them, grabbing hold of Lamorna's hand again. 'Make sure she gets back safely, Lyr,' Mordred told the boy seriously. 'I'm giving you the job of protecting her,' he added. Lamorna went to remind him that Lyr was a child and she was probably better at protecting him, but Lyr puffed his chest out proudly, so she fell silent.

Without another word, Mordred returned to his training and Lamorna and Lyr began the walk back to the village. She thought she could feel eyes on her and when she glanced over her shoulder, Mordred was watching. She swallowed, and turned her face away.

Arthur held the training sword Halymere had given him between his hands. The weapon was not heavy, not like the dragon sword Arthur had held in his dreams. Halymere had walked him back to his kibitka, but Arthur had not gone inside. Instead, he had headed into the forest with the sword, determined to get the hang of it. He needed to master this.

The day was late, shadows long and stretching through the trees like dark fingers. Arthur found space between the trees and planted his feet, finding what Halymere called his 'centre'. Arthur shifted around until his feet were shoulder-width apart. Halymere had told him he needed space and leverage, so that he could use the sword to better attack as well as defend himself. The sword had to feel like an extension of his arm; if it didn't, Arthur wasn't holding it correctly.

He rolled his shoulders around, letting his muscles stretch and become fluid. The sword made a hissing sound as Arthur swung it through the air in front of him. He could see his shadow, see the graceful arc the sword made as he moved it.

'You look good with a weapon,' a voice commented.

Arthur did not turn to face Jalen. 'I have a long way to go.'

'Yes, but that doesn't mean you don't look good.'

With a smile, Arthur let the sword drop.

'Do you need a sparring partner?' Jalen asked. He clicked his fingers, and was suddenly holding a sword, identical to the one Arthur had.

Arthur smiled. 'Are you offering to let me chop you up?'

'Of course,' Jalen replied, swinging the sword in front of him. He shifted his weight, found his feet, then nodded. 'Come on, Arthur. You can't hurt me, remember? What better training partner is there?'

'Alright,' Arthur concurred. He repositioned his feet and checked his grip on the sword.

'Draw my attention to where you want me to attack,' Jalen said. 'Use the sword to draw my eye. Let me watch your arms and hands, and let me anticipate your moves, then do something completely different.'

Arthur took a deep breath, keeping his eyes on Jalen's face which, he soon discovered, was a mistake, because all he wanted to do was kiss him and not worry about the sword. Jalen's lips quirked.

'Arthur,' he reprimanded.

'Sorry.' Quickly, Arthur feinted left, making Jalen lunge, before coming in to attack from the right. He thought he had it, but Jalen was swift, the storm demon sliding easily out of the way and going on the attack, forcing Arthur to bring his sword up and around to block the blow.

'Good,' Jalen murmured. 'Again.'

They returned to their beginning stances, their movements slow, deliberate, until Jalen struck faster, harder, and Arthur had to think on his feet, darting out of the way and countering the attack.

'How do you know how to sword fight?' he asked when they were catching their breath.

'I learnt a long time ago, starting just where you are now,' Jalen explained. 'Again, Arthur.'

For the next thirty minutes, until the sun had slipped away and the forest was almost dark, Arthur feinted and dodged. He thrust, cut and sliced until sweat ran down his face and into his eyes.

'I'm dripping,' he exclaimed with a laugh, setting the sword aside and peeling off his shirt, using it to wipe his face. 'Halymere doesn't make me sweat this much.'

'I should hope not,' Jalen murmured.

Arthur laughed and tossed his sweat-soaked shirt at Jalen, who snatched it from the air and slung it over his shoulder. His eyes walked Arthur's skin, travelling over the line of his torso, his shoulders, his arms, down to the fingers curled around the hilt of the sword.

'If this is a distraction technique, it's working,' the storm demon said. He let his sword drop to the ground. 'Come here,' he said softly. Smiling, Arthur went, leaving his own sword behind on the leaves. Jalen kissed him gently, then ran his fingers down Arthur's chest, his touch light. 'When you're King—'

'A king should know how to use a sword,' Arthur cut in.

Jalen shook his head. 'Not necessarily. A king will have people who will fight for him.'

'I don't want to be that sort of king,' Arthur said. 'I don't want others to have to risk themselves for me, if I wouldn't do the same for them.'

Jalen nodded. His fingers slipped beneath the waistband of Arthur's trousers. 'Right answer,' he said softly, leaning over to press a kiss to Arthur's mouth. 'A leader should lead by example.'

'So I should keep practising,' Arthur said, gesturing at the sword behind him, but he didn't move.

'A leader should also know when to stop,' Jalen said.

'Is that your way of telling me I'm terrible at this?' Arthur joked.

'It's my way of telling you to take a break,' Jalen replied. Arthur's breath caught as Jalen dropped to his knees on the forest floor. 'And a king, especially, should allow his subjects to show their devotion.'

Jalen pressed his lips to the tender skin on Arthur's belly.

'I would like to devote myself to this part right here,' he declared.

'Just that part?' Arthur managed. He ran his fingers through Jalen's hair, aware of how fast his heart was beating, how quickly his chest was rising and falling and of the fire that was burning in his blood. His fingers trembled.

'This part as well, I suppose,' Jalen replied, kissing Arthur's belly again, a little bit lower.

Arthur bit his lip. 'I guess I can get used to devotion.'

'What about worship?' It was a whisper, a breath brushing Arthur's flesh. 'I don't get on my knees for just anyone,' Jalen added, fingers curling around Arthur's hip bones.

Arthur swallowed his thundering heart. 'Well, in that case, worship away.'

CHAPTER 38

Time had lost all meaning in the darkness. At first, Ordes had tried to count the hours, but he had quickly given up. He could hear the faint strains of music. He'd seen no one since he'd been locked in here, except for a woman who brought him scraps of food. She was tall and slender, with dark hair bundled on top of her head. Silver dripped from her ears and her face was soft and beautiful. A syhren, or maybe not. There was something about her that reminded him of Jenyfer and his eyes widened as he realised what it was – she was partly human. She hadn't spoken to him.

Ordes had examined the bars of his cell with fingers and magic, but there was no way out. Katarin hadn't been dumped in the cell next to him, so he could only assume she got away. He could only hope she got away.

Footsteps, slow and steady, made their way through the darkness. A sphere of blue light floated down the hall and a man stepped into view. Hair the colour of the darkest night sky tumbled over his shoulders, shifting like waves, and his features were cut sharp, his cheekbones high, the line of his jaw like a razor. He was dressed in all black, silvery skin flecked with scales. But it was his eyes that hit the hardest, because they were exactly like—

'Where is she?' Ordes asked.

Melodias smiled. 'Shouldn't we make introductions first?'

There was something predatory about the Master of Songs and Death. Ordes could feel Melodias' power, like he could feel his mother's, but while Niniane's magic was sunshine and warmth, Melodias' magic felt like the deepest, darkest heart of the ocean. Wild and strong, unpredictable. Dangerous.

Melodias leant against the opposite wall with casual grace. 'Why did you come here? Did your mother send you?' At Ordes' startled look, he smiled. 'I know exactly who you belong to, boy.'

'I belong to myself,' Ordes managed.

'Do you now?' Melodias murmured. 'What did your dear mother have to say about me?'

More footsteps echoed down the hall – fast, furious, bare feet shifting across the stones. Jenyfer rushed into view, dropping to her knees in front of the cell. 'Ordes,' she breathed, then turned to Melodias. 'Let him out.' Jenyfer's voice was coloured with anger. 'Now.'

Melodias rolled his eyes. 'If I must.'

Jenyfer's expression was wild, eyes burning, her skin burnished silver-blue in the light suspended above them. The delicate scales on her temples and arms glimmered. She thrust her hand between the bars; Ordes closed his fingers around hers. At her touch, his blood exploded, his magic swirling beneath his skin. She was wearing a black dress that pooled on the ground behind her. The neckline was plunged low enough that the curve of her breasts was visible, and the dress hugged every part of her, leaving her arms bare. Shells and glittering pearls decorated the neckline of the dress.

'You're okay,' he murmured.

'What are you doing here?'

'Did you really expect me not to come?'

Melodias sighed. 'Ugh. If I let him out, can you stop with the heartfelt platitudes?'

Jenyfer scowled.

Melodias clicked his fingers. The bars of the cell vanished. Still holding Jenyfer's hand, Ordes got to his feet. Jenyfer stood up beside him.

'She's done nothing but mope and complain and make threats since she learnt you had come to visit. It's the most unfortunate timing – she was doing so well with her lessons,' Melodias said.

'What lessons?' Ordes asked.

Jenyfer shook her head at him – a warning.

'Come,' Melodias said simply. He pushed himself off the wall and walked off down the hall. Jenyfer gave Ordes' hand a squeeze, and nodded.

'You're really okay?' he asked her as they walked.

'He hasn't hurt me,' she said, her voice sad. 'Kat?'

'Alive.'

Jenyfer swallowed tightly and nodded again, the corners of her mouth turned down. Melodias led them up a flight of stairs and through a door that opened into a wide and lavishly decorated hallway. Melodias glanced at them over his shoulder, a small smile tugging at his mouth as he ran his eyes over Ordes.

'You look like your father.'

'What do you know about my father?' Ordes asked quietly.

'A lot more than you, I'm assuming,' Melodias replied. He stopped and turned, arms folded, disappointment stamped all over his inhumanly beautiful face. 'For the children of prophecy, you're both rather … lacking,' he drawled, then sighed. 'Jenyfer, show our, ugh, *guest* to his room.'

Jenyfer shook her head. 'No. He stays with me.'

'Whatever for?' the Master of Songs and Death asked, dark eyebrows raised.

'I want to play with him a bit,' Jenyfer answered. 'You said I needed to practise, so, I'll practise. He'll let me, won't you, Ordes?' she added, throwing him a look.

'Sure,' he replied. Her face relaxed a fraction.

Melodias waved them away. Jenyfer tugged on Ordes' hand; he followed her down a hallway that glistened with shadows, the walls dripping water, around several corners, taking him deeper and deeper into the castle. He had wanted to memorise his surroundings, get his bearings, but she was moving too quickly. They stopped abruptly, and she pushed open a door, nudging him inside. He saw a bed, draped in a black coverlet, a window with a charming view of a silver and blue-tinged sky, and a dresser. The walls were hard stone and the floor was covered in a luxurious rug the colour of night.

Once she closed the door, Jenyfer turned on him, smacking him in the chest. 'Are you insane? What were you thinking, coming here?'

'He can't hurt me,' Ordes said softly.

'Ordes—'

He undid the buttons on his shirt, placing one hand below the apex of his collar bones. He flexed his fingers – slowly, painlessly, the stone Niniane had given him slid free of his skin, until he could hold it in his palm.

Jenyfer was gazing at the stone in wonder. 'What's that?'

'Protection. Against syhrens.'

She narrowed her eyes. 'Who gave you that?'

'Niniane,' Ordes replied.

Jenyfer folded her arms. 'Your mother gave you a magical stone to protect you against me, didn't she?'

'Yes,' Ordes said simply as the stone sank back beneath his flesh. 'She did.'

'Well that's lovely,' Jenyfer muttered. 'You shouldn't have come, protective stone or not,' she whispered. Then, 'I'm glad to see you,

Ordes. I really am. But you can't do anything to piss him off. Melodias is dangerous. He's powerful and he has this way of getting inside your head. And he's—'

'Your father,' Ordes cut in gently; Jenyfer's face paled. 'Kat told me.'

'Right.'

'We don't get to choose our parents, Jen,' Ordes said. He could hear the pounding of her heart, could see the worry on her face. 'It doesn't change anything. It doesn't make you anything but yourself.'

She nodded, but her expression was still tight. 'You need a bath. And you should sleep.' There was a door tucked into the far wall opposite the bed. Jenyfer disappeared in there, and moments later, Ordes could hear water. He wandered over, leaning in the doorway as Jenyfer held her hand above a shining metal tub. Her brow was gently furrowed as she used her magic to fill the tub. When steam was rising from the water, she stopped, glancing over her shoulder. Catching him watching her, her cheeks coloured slightly.

'I'll find you a towel,' was all she said, and left. He had just removed his shirt when she was back, a fluffy towel clutched in her hands. Her eyes moved over him, tracing the lines of the map on his flesh. 'He can't see that you've got that,' she said. 'He hasn't said anything about mine, but ...'

Ordes nodded. 'I promise to wear a shirt in your father's presence.'

Her lips twisted into a wry grin. 'I'll get you some clothes and something to eat,' she said, and was gone again. Ordes heard the door to her room open and close. With a sigh, he stripped the rest of his clothes off and slid into the tub, groaning in relief. The water was so warm he fell asleep, waking when someone touched his arm.

Jenyfer was crouched by the tub. Her face was sad.

Without thinking, Ordes reached out a dripping hand and touched her cheek. Her eyes closed and she leant her face into his palm. His thumb stroked her skin gently.

'I need to get you out of here,' she whispered.

'Not without you,' he said. He could hear the pounding of his heart, of her heart, of the world around them. The heat of her slipped beneath his skin. Sparks danced in his belly. 'I'm not leaving here without you, Jen,' he added firmly.

She sighed, opening her eyes. 'Dinner?'

'I think I want to go to bed,' Ordes murmured.

'Well,' she said lightly, 'don't snore.'

'When have I ever snored?'

'In The Vale,' she shot back, the smile freezing on her face.

Ordes let his fingers drop from her cheek, moving closer to her, the memory of that night slamming into his brain in such painful clarity he could taste her, could feel his tongue curled against the heart of her body. 'I don't remember snoring,' he said, holding her eyes.

Jenyfer's breathing deepened; she swallowed, and the look on her face told him she was thinking exactly what he was. She shifted a little closer, placing her hand on his cheek, tracing the curve of his jaw, his ear. He closed his eyes, wondering how long it would be until she pulled away. Her hand came to rest over his heart, where a flame was smouldering.

He wanted to be broken over and over, made anew with the press of her lips, of her breath, the touch of her hand, silk upon his skin.

The heartfire has a mind of its own, Ordes. You won't be able to keep the truth from her. Remember that. Niniane's voice, although he could not recall her speaking those words.

But love was a feathered hope, a nest lined with the words he couldn't bring himself to say.

'Jen—'

'Your clothes are on the chair,' she said, standing and sweeping from the bathing room. He heard her fussing about in the bedroom, and closed his eyes again, lying back, his head and heart on fire.

CHAPTER 39

T he *Excalibur* crawled towards the timber jetty leading like a finger
to the mist-cloaked island. It was a sheltered cove, closed in on
each side by the gentle curve of hills. The navigator, Kayrus, bit his
lip in concern when Katarin insisted he bring the ship through the gap.

'It's too shallow at the moment,' the man argued. 'We should wait for
the tide.'

She raised her eyebrows. 'It's fine. Trust me.'

He looked like he was about to dispute her words, and she was ready
for it, ready to pull rank, to remind them that with Ordes gone, she was
in charge of this ship. The quartermaster hadn't even opened his mouth
to protest when she'd returned to the ship alone and let them know the
new arrangement, and she sensed Iouen was happy to give up control of
The Excalibur to her.

Kayrus did as she asked, the large vessel sliding effortlessly to a stop
alongside the jetty. Katarin didn't say *I told you so*. Instead, she cleared
her throat, her fingers closing tightly around the copy of Ordes and

Jenyfer's magical map. She would deliver it to Niniane, explain what had happened, and then leave.

'Thank you,' she told Kayrus.

'Do you think he'll be alright?' he asked. She could still hear the questions, the accusations, the crew had thrown at her when she returned, soaking wet and shivering, without Ordes.

'I hope so,' was all she said, leaving the helm, calling for the gangplank to be lowered. Those of her crew still alive were resting below deck. She would organise for the Priestesses to have them brought from the ship to the island, where they could receive proper care. Her thoughts drifted to Aelle. The loss of her friend brought a rush of tears to Katarin's eyes, but she blinked them away. There would be time to deal with it later.

Katarin hurried down the gangplank, not bothering to leave instructions that they wait for her. She knew they would. Tahnet would make sure of it, at least. As the mist closed around her, she breathed a sigh of relief. Home. She was home and, somehow, she needed that now.

She was still chewing over what she would tell Niniane about her son, when a figure emerged from the mists.

Tymis.

His eyes moved past her.

'Where is he?'

She shook her head, her stomach clenching uncomfortably at the look on the Captain's face.

Tymis shot forward, fisting his hands in Katarin's shirt and pulling her against his body. 'Where is he, Katarin?' he asked in a deadly tone.

She shoved him away roughly, continuing down the jetty, Tymis following, throwing questions at her, so many that by the time she reached the castle and hurried inside, her head was spinning with them and she was doubting herself. She should have stayed. She should have fought them. She should not have left Ordes behind. She *never* left people behind, especially not family, and, she supposed, that was what he was to her now.

It wasn't until the moment he threw her behind him and demanded she leave that she realised it. Guilt had dug its claws deep and, although she'd tried, Katarin could not shake the beast off. She'd been in dangerous situations before, had fought her way out of them, but in Lyonesse, she had experienced something she was not accustomed to.

Fear.

She'd been scared; no, more than scared, terrified, as that army of syhrens advanced on them. It was fear that made her run, and she made a vow to herself that if Ordes didn't return, she'd find her way back there and blast every sea faery into dust, and then Melodias could do what he wanted with her.

Niniane was sitting on her throne in the courtyard. Her face showed no surprise as Katarin strode in, Tymis on her heels. She could feel his glower, the heat of his eyes between her shoulder blades. She ignored him and directed her attention at the Goddess whom she served. 'I thought you'd like to know, your son elected to stay in Lyonesse.'

'I know.'

'You what?' Tymis snarled, turning his anger on Niniane, before swinging back to Katarin. 'What were you thinking? Do you have any idea what you've done? What you've put in jeopardy?'

'Fuck the prophecy.' Katarin drew herself up. She would not be intimidated by the Captain of *The Excalibur* and she would not show fear, not in front of any man, regardless of who he was. 'If you truly know your son, you'd know he's a stubborn bastard who does whatever the hell he wants.' She tried to step around Tymis, but he blocked her path again. She'd never been this close to him, she realised, and she could feel the magic trapped inside him. A burst of sympathy shot through her, anger following quickly on its heels.

Tymis spoke between clenched teeth. 'And you *left* him there?'

'He didn't give me much choice.' Katarin's voice rose. Her fists curled and she readied her magic. She'd flay Tymis alive if he so much as thought to challenge her. 'He saved my life, if you must know. Melodias' syhrens were coming for us and Ordes—' she paused, shaking the images from her head. 'He made sure I got away, and he *let* them catch him. Here,' she said, shoving the map at Tymis. 'He said to give you this.'

'The map?' Niniane asked.

Tymis laughed bitterly, the map clutched tight to his chest. 'You're finally interested are you? Your son is deep in the belly of Lyonesse, having the gods know what done to him, and all you care about is ...' He shook his head and marched up the steps of the dais, glaring at Niniane.

She did not cower under his anger. She reached up a pale hand and touched his cheek. 'Melodias will not harm him.'

'You know this for certain, do you?' Tymis shot back.

Niniane held his gaze, her face stern, and eventually he turned away from her, muttering to himself. Katarin looked from one to the other, a prickle of unease shooting along her spine.

'You need to go to Cruithea,' Niniane told her.

'Do I?' Katarin challenged.

'Katarin, darling. There is nothing you can do for Ordes at the moment,' the goddess said softly; Tymis ground his teeth. 'But you can help your brother. Arthur must begin his search for the Treasures as soon as he is ready, and he will need a ship. There is no faster way to travel.'

'I'm pretty sure he has his own mode of transport,' Katarin said.

'Jalen's attachment to Arthur may mean that he is not the best one to offer advice. Arthur needs his sister. He needs friends. Family. He cannot do this alone. If he is to find his strength and complete this quest, he needs people around him who he can lean on. He needs guidance,' Niniane added.

The unease skittering along Katarin's spine increased as Tymis gave Niniane a sideways glance and she was suddenly exhausted by the whole thing – prophecies, Treasures, mysterious maps, the loss of *The Queen* and her crew. Lyonesse beat at her brain with tiny, damp fists. She pushed them all away and drew herself up.

'Fine, but if I'm going to be of any use to anyone, I need a ship,' Katarin said swiftly.

Niniane nodded. 'Keep the one you arrived on.'

'That's my ship,' Tymis said, hands on his hips.

'Actually, it's *my* ship,' Niniane returned. 'And it's mine to give.'

'What about my crew?'

'They're Katarin's crew now, Tymis,' Niniane said simply. 'I'm sure she will take good care of them for you.'

Tymis slowly turned to Katarin. 'I'll speak with them first. If you so much as—'

'You think I'm stupid?' she snapped. 'I've been onboard your ship for over a week, Tymis.' She took a deep breath and recounted the attack on *The Night Queen*, Jenyfer's capture and the rescue of what remained of her crew by Ordes and *The Excalibur*, her throat tightening when she mentioned the loss of Aelle. 'But I guess you already know all of that. I want those who need healing brought from the ship.'

'Of course,' Niniane answered. She clicked her fingers, and a robin was resting in her palm. The Goddess stroked its head with a slender finger. The bird ruffled its feathers, and vanished. 'The Priestesses will make them comfortable.'

Katarin nodded.

'I'm sorry for what happened to your people, Katarin.' Tymis held her eyes, his expression shifting into one of acceptance. 'It's a loan, you understand? That ship belongs to my son.'

'I understand,' Kat said softly. 'You think I'm happy with leaving him behind? Regardless of what you might think about me, *Merlin*, I'm not heartless. I don't leave my crew – my family – behind. But Ordes—'

'I know,' Tymis mumbled. 'Did you see Jenyfer at all?'

Kat shook her head. 'But I'm pretty certain Melodias didn't send his syhrens for her because he wanted to play happy families. Is it the map?'

'Possibly,' Niniane answered.

'And now he has both halves of it,' Tymis reminded her.

Katarin was looking at Niniane. Her skin prickled again, her magic tingling.

Niniane rearranged the skirts of her gown, then stood and stepped down from the dais, coming to stand in front of Katarin. 'Jenyfer is more important than any of us guessed, although I knew that this day would come, eventually.'

'Are you talking about the Grail?' Katarin asked.

'Yes, and no. Many years ago, Merlin spoke of three who would reshape the land – one with a foot in the sea, one with a foot on the land, and one with a foot in both worlds,' Niniane said.

'I know this already,' Katarin responded impatiently. 'Jenyfer, Arthur and Ordes.'

'But they are not the only ones interested in the Grail, or its power,' Tymis said. 'Melodias would want it because it's shiny, and he likes shiny things. In other words, we don't know what his game is. He cannot wield the Grail, and he knows this, but now that he has Jenyfer *and* Ordes ...' Tymis let his voice trail off.

'Let's hope Ankou does not realise they are in Lyonesse. Melodias wouldn't want him to know that.' Niniane's voice was soft, for Tymis' ears only, but it filled the room.

'Why?' Kat demanded.

Silence was her answer. She scowled. There was nothing else she could do, not for Ordes, or Jenyfer, at that moment, but she could do something for Arthur. 'If there is anything else I need to know, you need to tell me now, because you have two minutes before I walk out of here.' She hesitated, not wanting to voice the words, but knowing she had to, if only so she had. 'Can we trust her?'

'I hope so,' Tymis said softly.

Before she left, Katarin glanced over her shoulder. Tymis and Niniane were having a low, furious conversation. 'One more thing,' Katarin called;

they looked at her, no surprise on either face. 'Melodias has an army. I thought you might want to know.' She turned and left before either of them could say anything more.

Her head, and her heart, were bruised enough.

After her injured crew had been moved to the House of Priestesses for care, Katarin called for them to raise anchor and move off. Tahnet stood with her, watching the Priestesses ferry their friends, their family, away. The blonde woman's arm was in a sling, and bruises coloured her features, but she had refused to leave. Katarin was secretly glad – even though Tymis had stood on deck not long ago and told the men Katarin was their Captain now, she needed an ally. She needed someone who understood her, understood how she thought.

Understood what she felt, and understood why she couldn't talk about it.

'What's our bearing?' Tahnet asked softly.

Katarin frowned. 'We should go to Cruithea and find my brother, but ...'

'You want to return to Lyonesse?'

Katarin nodded. 'Just for a few days, and if they don't show up, then we sail north.'

Tahnet nodded. 'Alright. I'll let Iouen know.'

Katarin raised her eyebrows.

An uncharacteristic blush stained Tahnet's cheeks. 'He's been kind to me. He even brought me sweets yesterday. Some chocolate,' she added almost defensively, jamming her uninjured hand on her hip, making Katarin laugh. If there was one thing she knew about Tahnet, it was that chocolate was a fast way to her heart. Iouen had gotten lucky.

As Tahnet hurried away to find the quartermaster, Katarin folded her arms. Mist clung to the water around them, and the scent of apples floated on the crisp breeze. She went over what Niniane and Tymis had said about Melodias and the Treasures. Then, there was the vague reference to Ankou, something Katarin knew she wasn't meant to hear.

Something was being kept from her.

CHAPTER 40

The path was slippery, the leaves underfoot soaking into a carpet of thick moss, damp with dew. The world beneath the trees was an orange and gold one, leaves glimmering with moisture, the dark brown of the bark blending into the wall of autumn. Mist cloaked the early morning, swirling around Lamorna's boots. She knew it would lift once the light and warmth of the sun made its way between the trees, but that didn't stop her muscles from tightening or her nerves bunching with apprehension.

Birds erupted in a flurry of wings from a nearby shrub, disturbed by her passage. Lamorna jumped, her hand over her mouth, the bucket she carried tumbling from numb fingers. Annoyed, she scooped the bucket from the ground and continued on. Tamora had given her a chore – fetching water. She had gone with her aunt on several occasions to the stream and Tamora had decided Lamorna knew the way well enough by now, so the water was to become her job.

The stream appeared, meandering through the trees up ahead. Lamorna followed it until she found the dip in the granite rocks that formed the border between the water and the forest. She moved carefully, not wanting to fall in. It was chilly beneath the trees still, and she did not fancy getting wet. Besides, she could not swim.

She dropped into a crouch, heat staining her cheeks at the way she was positioned, her legs splayed, her weight on her haunches. It was most undignified, but she dutifully dipped the bucket into the stream and filled it, heaving it up and over the rocks to rest on the ground while she straightened, ignoring the twinge in her back. She was not used to tasks like this. In Kernou, there was no squatting beside streams that threatened to pull you in.

'You shouldn't be out here alone,' a voice said from behind her. Lamorna bit her lip to stop from crying out and turned to face the speaker.

Mordred. He smiled, teeth bright against the rich tone of his skin. His expression was amused and Lamorna quickly recovered herself, hefting the bucket. The sun was higher now, pushing through the trees to touch the forest floor, and the mist had almost vanished, only remaining in patches that clung desperately to the base of the trees. Lamorna headed back towards the village and Mordred fell into step beside her, so casual, so calm, while her heart was racing at his closeness, at his very presence.

She watched him from the corner of her eye. She was not supposed to be alone with a man, especially a man like him. It had been different before – the rest of the Inborn were there. She ignored the fact his arms were bare, and did not look at the swirling ink that decorated his flesh, keeping her eyes on his face, even as her brain screamed at her to look away, to behave properly.

Confidence radiated from every part of him. At his belt, he carried a dagger and a small axe, a reminder that he was dangerous. She knew that already, thinking again about the Witchfinder, and then about what she witnessed that day in the forest with Lyr. Mordred stepped in front of her suddenly, blocking her path, his eyes raking her face, seeming to soak up every detail of her.

'You shouldn't be wandering, Lamorna,' he said.

'I'm not wandering,' Lamorna replied, trying her best to sound important. 'I'm collecting water.' She held out the bucket as evidence, then edged past him. Mordred caught up to her easily, reaching down to take the bucket.

'I can manage,' Lamorna said sharply.

'Let me help.'

'Collecting water is women's work.'

'Collecting water is everybody's work here,' he responded neutrally. 'It doesn't matter who you are – woman, man, child, warrior, or priestess – if you need water, you get it.'

'I bet your mother doesn't collect her own water,' Lamorna said, her tone clipped.

Mordred's fingers brushed against hers; she jumped and let him take the bucket as her cheeks heated.

'No, she doesn't.' He headed off down the path, turning to look at her. 'Come on. You shouldn't be wandering,' he added again.

'Why not?' Lamorna asked, quickening her pace to catch up to him. 'It's just trees,' she said lightly, trying to ignore the prickling of her skin. The expression he gave her was one of disbelief.

'Has your aunt taught you nothing about the ways of the fey folk?'

Lamorna tossed her head. 'I don't believe in faeries.'

Mordred chuckled darkly. 'You should.' When she rolled her eyes, his expression became serious. 'They can be dangerous, Lamorna. Deadly. If you insist on going into the forest alone, you need to know how to protect yourself.'

She bristled, unable to help it. He was nothing but a heathen, a savage – as were all the people here – and she did not like the way her belly warmed when he looked at her. 'The One God will protect me,' she snapped, then shut her mouth, shooting him a worried glance. He was watching her curiously.

They had stopped walking. She could hear the gentle sounds of the village in the distance, could hear the horses, their snorts and soft wickers. She had planned to go and watch them after she delivered the water to her aunt, entertaining more thoughts about what it would be like to climb on the back of one, to earn its trust. But animals didn't usually like Lamorna. It was her sister all wild things, natural or not, were drawn to.

Mordred was watching her. 'Tell me,' he said quietly, 'about the One God.'

She almost fell over. 'What?'

He shrugged. 'I'm intrigued. I'm curious about what it is that holds half of this continent in thrall. I know that worship of this god has spread, so, tell me.'

Lamorna's heart skipped a beat. 'What do you want to know?'

'Whatever you want to tell me,' he said simply. She nodded, and a broad smile crept across her face – before she remembered her place and let it fall, let her tone become soft and reverent, as was expected. By the time they had reached the village, she had filled his ears with as much as she could, everything else forgotten.

That night, as the sky darkened and people gathered around the cooking fires, Mordred sought her out again, finding her lingering at the edge of the crude village square, a bowl between her fingers. Steam rose from the stew, curling gently into the air, the food cooling quickly.

'Not hungry?' he asked her.

Lamorna shook her head. 'Not really.'

'There are things you need to know, if you are to survive here.' His voice was like spider silk, weaving its way around her head, the strands tightening as he looked at her. She made herself hold his gaze. She made herself be brave.

'Like what?'

Mordred glanced around, his eyes sweeping over the people gathered around the cooking fires. No one had noticed them yet, too busy with their meals and conversations. She had no idea where her aunt was. Tamora was different in this place, Lamorna realised. She smiled more, laughed more, and both her and Keraine had slipped into life in Cruithea with an ease that caused jealousy to burn like a fire in Lamorna's heart.

'Everyone here has a place,' Mordred said, his voice low, his words echoing the thoughts in her head. She glanced at him suspiciously; he flashed her a quick smile, making her belly flop. People did not usually smile at her like that. She liked his smile, and there was a soft roughness to his voice. Lamorna decided she liked that as well, then bit her lip, pushing the thoughts out of her head.

'If you wish to fit in here,' he continued, bending his head so his voice and the warmth of his breath touched her neck, 'even under pretence, you will have to find your place, find what it is that makes you useful, makes you important.'

'But I don't know what that could be,' she answered with a frown.

His eyes, as dark as the soil of her garden in Kernou, crinkled at the edges when he smiled. 'You are skilled at fetching water,' he quipped, and her frown deepened, making him chuckle. The sound of his laugh sent a trickle of heat through her. 'We shall think of something,' he declared.

'Why would you help me?'

'Why wouldn't I?'

'No one else has offered to help me,' she said, unable to stop the bitterness from bleeding into her tone. 'So why would you?'

'Because I know what it is to feel out of place,' Mordred answered gently.

'You?'

That smile again. 'Yes, me. I'm a warrior, an Inborn, but I am also the son of the High Priestess, and that carries its own dilemma.'

'Such as?'

He shook his head. 'I don't expect you to understand.'

Lamorna frowned again. Nobody expected her to understand anything. They never had. Except the One God. She understood Him. She smoothed her frown away with her fingers and stood up straighter. 'I will accept whatever help you can give me,' she told Mordred, not looking at him.

'And you, in turn, will help me,' he replied.

A flutter of something inched along her spine. 'Help you do what?'

'Perhaps you will be the one to show me a different path.'

Hope bloomed in her chest again as she thought of her task. 'Yes,' she said simply. 'Maybe I will.'

He smiled at her, then left, and she was alone again. Lamorna found a place and sat, balancing her bowl on her knees. So warm had been Mordred's smile that she didn't even mind she was sitting on the ground like an animal. Across from her, a group of children had given up on their meals also and were playing, chasing each other about. One of them waved his hands, causing the leaves at his feet to dance around, the others laughing and grabbing at them.

Lamorna chewed the inside of her cheek. They *seemed* happy.

She spied Arthur Tregarthen on the other side of the communal area and hoped he wouldn't see her. She'd been avoiding him after their conversation, as much as was possible; but now he handed his bowl to the blonde-haired man who was always with him and skirted the edge of the cooking area until he could sit, uninvited, in the dirt at her side.

Lamorna did not know what to say to him. She snuck a glance, running her eyes over him quickly. His hair was wild, brown curls falling across his forehead and into his eyes, and he was dressed like the Cruitheans were in bark-brown trousers, sturdy boots and a goat-leather vest over a tightly fitted brown shirt.

He didn't speak and Lamorna's eyes returned to the children. 'Is everyone here a Magic Wielder?' she asked eventually.

'No,' he said.

Still with her eyes on the children, Lamorna said in a low voice, 'But you are. Bryn said.'

'Did he?' Arthur murmured. 'I wonder what else he said.'

'Can you show me?' she asked.

He looked at her in surprise, and then he waved his hand and a warm breeze caressed Lamorna's cheeks. She watched him, noted the fierce concentration on his face as he lifted a leaf from the ground with his magic, catching it gently between long fingers.

Lamorna set her stew aside, deciding to ignore the magic for now. She would think about it later, about what it meant. 'How did you get here?' she asked, and then listened as Arthur recounted his story – running for his life from Kernou, his father and the Witchfinder unconscious, the Konsel tracking him, until he stowed away aboard Katarin Le Fey's ship. He didn't look at her when he spoke about the Captain of *The Night Queen*, and Lamorna wondered what he wasn't saying.

'And you?' Arthur said. 'Have you put aside your belief in the One God, Lamorna?'

'Have you?' she shot back, her cheeks heating. She did not want to answer the question.

Arthur held her eyes, something he had never done before. 'I never believed.'

'But—'

'I played my part well, I guess,' he mumbled, turning away from her. 'And now, I have a different part to play.'

'That silly prophecy?' she demanded.

'I saw you talking with Mordred,' he said instead, changing the subject to one that made her even more uncomfortable than the magic and the trees that were all around her.

'What of it?' Lamorna said, tossing her head, trying for her sister's nonchalance in the face of such a probing statement.

Arthur's expression was stern. 'Be careful around him. He is a powerful Magic Wielder, and I'm not certain his motivations are, well, the right ones.'

Lamorna wanted to ask what he meant, but instead she stood, collecting her bowl from the ground. 'I don't know what you mean,' she said lightly, turning and hurrying across the communal space before he could stop her. She left her uneaten stew near the cooking fires and returned to her kibitka, where she lay down on her bedroll and pulled the blankets up over her head, her heart thundering.

CHAPTER 41

Andromache was waiting, tapping her bare foot against the dark grey stones, arms folded. Jenyfer swallowed and muttered out an apology. The syhren made an exasperated noise. The room was bare today – no table and chairs, no towers of books. Jenyfer had left Ordes sleeping, sprawled on his stomach, the sheets bunched around his hips. She suspected he'd been awake as she climbed out of bed, but he hadn't said anything and she was glad.

'Today,' Andromache announced. 'You're going to prove to me that you aren't totally worthless.'

'Fantastic,' Jenyfer mumbled. She rubbed at her chest. It was hot. Her back was hot as well. Without having to think about it, she knew Ordes had been pressed against her at some point during the night, his arm draped over her middle, his face buried in her hair. She had fallen asleep to the sound of his breathing.

'Pay attention,' Andromache snapped. Jenyfer jumped. The syhren rolled her eyes. 'Today, I want you to sing again.'

'Sing?'

'Yes, Jenyfer. You're a syhren. That's what we do. We sing and we enjoy it,' Andromache replied. She did not come any closer to Jenyfer, just watched her with those piercing eyes. Her silver hair was swept off her neck in an elaborate style. Pearls were woven through the thick strands, catching pieces of the muted light that eased into the cavernous room from high above their heads. Andromache's gown was deep blue, fit tight to her torso before flaring over her hips to pool on the ground. Silver scales flecked her skin.

'You enjoy sending men to their deaths?' Jenyfer said, folding her arms around herself. Her gown was also a deep blue, and her feet were bare. She wasn't sure there were any shoes in Lyonesse. The floor beneath her feet was slightly damp, as it always was, and water slid slowly down the stone walls.

'Of course,' the syhren said simply. 'Now, your father thought you might need some motivation to draw out the magic he is convinced you possess.'

'I'm not practising on human souls – I don't care if they're already dead,' Jenyfer snapped.

Andromache's lips thinned into an unimpressed line. 'Your voice is a gift and you don't want to use it.'

'A gift?' Jenyfer scoffed. 'It's a weapon!'

'Yes, it is,' Andromache snarled, her silvery skin colouring. 'It's the most powerful weapon in the world, Jenyfer. It can compel, coerce, destroy, or kill!'

'You do realise those aren't good things?' Jenyfer argued.

'Your voice can make a man fall in love with you, even if that man is a faery,' Andromache said, her voice lowering, her smile cat-like and sly. 'I know all about him.'

Jenyfer swallowed. 'I didn't know what I was doing. I didn't want that to happen.'

'Didn't you?' the syhren asked. 'Your magic knew what you wanted, even when you didn't. It will always know, because it is tied to your instincts and your desires. You cannot change that, so there is no point in trying to pretend it doesn't exist. You might as well learn to control it. Not that I care what happens to you,' Andromache added nastily.

'I never thought any differently,' Jenyfer retorted.

'Your father has given me a task, and I will succeed in that task,' Andromache said simply. 'If you won't use a human soul, then perhaps this will be enough to tempt that song of yours into its true existence.'

Before Jenyfer could ask what she meant, Andromache waved her hands. Water rose from the stones at their feet and slid across the floor. It was pulled from the walls and the very air around them, droplets colliding in the middle of the room. They swirled around one another, a wild vortex of liquid tinged with blue and silver and, slowly, a shape took form.

A very human shape.

With a very familiar face.

Bryn.

Jenyfer sucked in a breath. 'How ...'

'He hurt you,' Andromache declared.

'Yes,' Jenyfer whispered, closing her eyes. She could feel his weight, even now, could smell the salty scent of him, could feel the calluses on his hands as they spread across her flesh. She could hear him, the almost animal sounds he made. Her fists clenched.

'He tried to catch you and drag you back to that pitiful town,' Andromache continued.

Jenyfer nodded.

'What would you do to him, if you could see him right now, Jenyfer?' Andromache whispered. Her voice came from all around, echoing softly, a whisper that promised pain and vengeance.

'I'd ...'

'Yes?' Andromache said softly.

Jenyfer shook her head.

Fingers touched her throat and she jumped as Andromache's slender hand closed around her neck, but the syhren did not squeeze like Jenyfer expected. She stroked, her fingers gently moving over Jenyfer's skin. 'Would you make him stab himself, like the other man?'

Jenyfer didn't ask how she knew, like she didn't ask how Andromache knew about Bryn, or Ordes, or anything Jenyfer had done with her voice.

Andromache put her mouth close to Jenyfer's ear. 'Would you make him slit his own throat? Throw himself to the sea? Steal the breath from his lungs? Stop his heart?'

Jenyfer opened her eyes.

'Look at him,' Andromache urged, 'and do what your instinct tells you to do.'

The watery-Bryn was perfectly rendered. Transparent and slightly shifting, it did not stop Jenyfer from being able to see him as he was in the flesh – the tanned skin, the freckles across his nose, the lines around his eyes. The sandy-coloured hair tumbling over his forehead, teased by an invisible wind. The breadth of his shoulders, the bulk of muscle there. His arms. His hands, the ones that had held her down while he did what he had been instructed.

That mouth, which had spoken words she never thought she'd hear him say.

Jenyfer's song rushed up her throat with a roar of fury, sweeping her away completely as she opened her mouth and sang, the music ripped from her throat, from her bones. Her heart. She sang until her eyes were burning and her lungs felt like they would burst, until her body felt light and heavy at the same time, until she felt like she was made of water and stone, of salt and sand, of silver light and the power of the fiercest oceanic winds. Jenyfer sang, never taking her eyes from the water-Bryn, and into her song she poured her grief and all the things she had been unable to say, all the words she had swallowed down into the depths of her, not wanting to acknowledge them, not wanting to give them space in the world.

Anger was liquid fire in her veins as her song soared into its crescendo. On the final note, Bryn exploded.

Gasping, Jenyfer stumbled backwards, unable to stop looking at the place where he had been. Water slicked the stones. Her voice still bounced off the walls, slowly fading until there was nothing but the sound of her ragged breathing and Andromache's sharp intake of breath.

'Well,' the syhren said softly.

Jenyfer could not move. Long after Andromache had gone, she stayed in the cavernous room, staring at the place where Bryn had been, wondering and wondering. Beneath her skin, in her blood, her magic was purring; her song swirled inside her, stronger and more powerful than she had ever felt it.

Jenyfer barely ate at dinner, pushing food around her plate, rearranging it over and over, her father watching her closely but saying nothing. There was something about his expression that made Ordes' stomach clench and caused his magic to swim to the surface to rest in his fingertips. The look Melodias gave him told him the Master of Songs and Death could sense the magic, so Ordes pushed it away. Jenyfer had told him not to taunt her father, so he wouldn't.

Jenyfer drank two glasses of dark red wine, then poured herself a third. Her cheeks were rosy, eyes shimmering in the candle light.

'Andromache tells me you made a break-through today,' Melodias said casually. For Ordes' benefit, he added, 'With her music. Yes, she was very impressed, Jenyfer.'

Jenyfer mumbled something.

Her father sighed. 'You wanted this. You wanted to understand what you are.'

Jenyfer's head shot up. Her fingers tightened on the stem of her glass. 'Not like this. She manipulated me!'

'Of course she did,' her father said, smiling. 'She's rather good, isn't she?'

'She's a sadist,' Jenyfer snapped.

'Did she hurt you?' Ordes demanded without thinking. He didn't know who this Andromache was, but the heartfire surged in his chest.

Melodias burst out laughing. 'And what, exactly, would you do about it, faery? Do try – I'd love to see it.'

Ordes opened his mouth to argue, but Jenyfer shook her head at him. 'Don't bother,' she said, her voice flat. She took a large gulp of her wine, then looked at her father. 'If you're done with us for this evening, we're leaving.' She stood up, collecting the half-empty bottle of wine and her glass, and marched towards the door. Ordes followed her; he could feel Melodias' eyes on them as they entered the hall. Jenyfer handed him the wine and didn't speak again, not until they were in their room and she'd drained her glass.

'Jen,' Ordes murmured as she poured another glass. She shot him a furious look, then drained the wine in one go. When she went to pour another glass, the bottle was empty. She frowned at it, then headed for the door.

'I'm getting more wine.'

Ordes closed his hand over her bare arm. 'Stop. I don't know what's going on, but I don't think drowning yourself in wine is going to help.'

She shook herself free.

'What happened today?' he asked.

Jenyfer pulled at her hair and stalked across the room, her legs getting tangled in the length of her skirt. Cursing, she grabbed the material and ripped into it, tearing it so the dress was now split to her thigh on one side. Satisfied, she slumped onto the bed and put her head in her hands.

'Has your magic ever made you want to hurt someone, and enjoy it?' she asked him.

'Maybe,' Ordes replied.

Jenyfer sighed and flopped onto her back, fingers picking at the scales on her wrists. 'I don't want to be this,' she mumbled. 'Andromache thinks it's wonderful, being a syhren, having the power to kill with your voice. She thinks it's a gift.'

Ordes went to sit by her. She shifted so she could rest her head in his lap and his fingers automatically moved into her hair, stroking against her scalp.

'Did you know a syhren can stop a man's heart?' Jenyfer asked quietly, closing her eyes. 'Did you know a syhren can drown a man in his own blood? Fill his lungs with it until he can no longer breathe? I could do that, if I wanted.'

Ordes said nothing, continuing to stroke her hair.

'You know what frightens me the most about my power? Not that I can do these things, but that I might like it if I did.' She yawned. 'Does that frighten you?'

'No,' he said.

'Such pretty lies, Ordes,' she murmured, before sighing and falling asleep.

CHAPTER 42

Arthur put his energy into the sword. Thanks to the training he'd been doing with Jalen, he could hold his own against Halymere now, his wrists more flexible than before, the muscles in his arms and shoulders stronger than they were when he'd arrived. He no longer curled his shoulders when he walked; now, his spine was straight, his stride more confident. But when Melhala asked him why he was walking around puffed up like a rooster, he realised that perhaps swagger wasn't his style.

'Be yourself,' the water wielder told him. 'Your cousin has enough swagger for the whole continent,' she'd added in a biting tone.

After the evening meal, Arthur decided to visit his aunt. The High Priestess was surprised to see him, but welcomed him to sit by her fire. 'Is something wrong?' she asked him.

He shook his head. 'No, but I have questions that I hope you can answer.'

'If I can, I will,' she told him.

'Tell me about Ereshki,' Arthur said, watching his aunt's face carefully.

Morgause held his eyes and, for a long moment, Arthur thought she was not going to speak, but she sighed softly. 'Ereshki is the sister-goddess to Inanna. Once, she was worshipped here freely, but things changed.'

'Is this about the Treasures?' Arthur asked.

'The Treasures? No. The Treasures were lost a long time ago, Arthur. Many hundreds of years. What I am talking about happened much more recently,' Morgause said. 'Ereshki is sometimes called the Dark Mother. If you imagine people as a set of scales, like these.' The High Priestess waved her hand at the flames and a set of scales, like the ones Arthur had seen the Konsel apothecarist using while measuring out the bitter medicines given to the sick in Kernou, appeared and hovered above the flames. 'Everything is about balance, Arthur. We all carry light and darkness inside of us. Ereshki is that darkness.'

'And Inanna is the light?' he asked.

'Not necessarily. Inanna is the goddess of war and fertility – life and death, Arthur. And in both of those things there is darkness and light. Ereshki represented all the things people desire – love, companionship, peace, but she is also the darkness. She is grief and pain, longing and loss, the unconscious shadow we all carry. It was Ereshki's role to help man maintain the balance, the counterpoint to her sister, but Ereshki was jealous of Inanna. She didn't want to share the worship and devotion of the people and, eventually, her darkness became man's darkness,' Morgause explained. 'We do not speak of her here anymore.'

'Why?'

'Because we decided the things that she was offering were no longer what we wanted in our world,' Morgause said, frowning. 'Greed, envy, lust for power, corruption … the sort of things that people kill for, that they have started wars for. The sort of things that would cause a brother to try to murder his beloved sister.'

'Enyon and Eseld,' Arthur murmured.

'Yes.'

'The prophecy mentions the Red Ones,' Arthur said slowly. 'And Goerika told me Ereshki was called the Red Serpent. Do you think there is a connection?'

Morgause stared into the flames. 'In the Dead Woods, two days travel away, is the Ossuary, the House of Bone.'

Arthur jolted. 'Forever entombed in the House of Bone …'

Morgause stared into the flames. 'The House of Bone was the centre for Ereshki's worship. You have to understand, Arthur, the Red Sisters, the most devout of her followers, practised magic that is dangerous – for body, mind, and soul.'

'What sort of magic?' he asked.

'Blood magic,' his aunt said in a low voice. 'Ritual slaughter and sacrifice—'

'Like the death of the Witchfinder?'

'No, not like that,' Morgause snapped, then rubbed her eyes. 'I'm sorry. The first thing I did as High Priestess was outlaw the worship of Ereshki and forbid the practising of blood magic. It was not a decision made lightly, but blood magic changes a person, and with the Sheletari on the rise … I was thinking of my child, of all our children. Some argued that it was blood magic we needed to defeat the evil rising from Malist and the Sacellum, but I did not agree.'

'The House of Bone?' Arthur asked.

'The Red Sisters are still there, and they still practise their magic as they have always done. We have a … truce, I suppose. But no one is to go there,' Morgause added, looking at him as if she expected him to rush off into the Dead Woods searching for blood witches and dangerous magic. 'I do what I have to do to keep my people safe.'

Arthur watched the flames. 'If the Red Ones are part of the prophecy …'

'Then they will have a part to play,' Morgause said. 'But I don't know what that part is.'

That night, with Jalen tucked against his back, an arm draped over his middle, Arthur's thoughts were a jumbled mess. Goerika had warned him that the line between truth and lie was easily blurred; the story she told him about Ereshki was different to the one the High Priestess had told him, and Niniane had barely mentioned the banished goddess.

Arthur wondered where she was, and then stopped.

Kernou perhaps? Or was it Malist she had chosen? The seaside or a city of stone? Perhaps she wasn't in either, but had turned her back on man and was deep in the Dead Woods with those still devoted to her and her magic.

Arthur drifted into sleep and was immediately swept into a cave damp with water-spray. The Fisher Queen was waiting for him, the Grail balancing on her knees.

'Hello, Eseld,' Arthur said, bowing.

Her face did not change. 'So, you know.'

'I do. I'm sorry for what happened to you,' he replied gently.

Eseld ran her finger lightly along the edge of the Grail. Arthur heard music, sweet and gentle, before it changed into screams. He put his hands over his ears.

'Who is that?'

'Are you ready to learn a truth?' Eseld asked him, still stroking the Grail. The screaming continued until it was a high-pitched moan that echoed on and on, rebounding off the walls of the cave and smashing into Arthur's skull.

'What truth?' he managed.

Eseld's finger paused and when she spoke her voice was sad. 'We all have a beginning,' she said, and then Arthur was tumbling through blackness, the stars whirling around him, until he landed on his knees outside a simple cottage made of white-washed stone walls and a thatched roof. He could smell the ocean; looking down, he saw he was kneeling on sand, pale gold grass poking through. He ran his fingers over the grass, feeling the sharp texture of the blades.

Inside the cottage, someone screamed. A girl.

Arthur leapt to his feet and pushed at the door, not bothering to knock, the sound of the child's wails lifting the hair on the back of his neck. He tumbled through the door, and stopped.

A girl on the verge of being a woman sat on a simple chair near a rough wooden table. Kneeling at her feet was a man with sandy blonde hair, tanned forearms resting either side of her legs.

'Nessa, you need to tell me who,' the man said, and Arthur felt his knees give out.

He knew that voice.

Jalen.

'I cannot,' Nessa whispered. Tears stained her cheeks. 'Please, don't make me.'

'Nessie, you have done nothing wrong,' Jalen said firmly, peering up into her face. There was a bruise colouring her cheek, Arthur noticed, and she had the same sand-coloured hair as Jalen.

A sister?

Jalen ran his hand through his hair in a gesture that was painfully familiar to Arthur. He took a step forward, Jalen's name on his lips, but the floor fell away and he was falling again, landing heavily in a forest. It was night. Trees stretched into the air above him and the moon was hidden by a layer of clouds.

A man's voice floated through the darkness. 'Nessa, Nessa. Come out little rabbit. Don't make me wait for you.'

Arthur held his breath as a man stepped into the clearing. The man looked around, but did not see him.

'Nessa!' the man's voice was impatient now.

Footsteps crunched over leaf and twig, and it was not Nessa that entered the clearing, but Jalen. The other man's face hardened, and then he laughed as Jalen withdrew a dagger from his belt. 'Am I supposed to be afraid of you, Jalen Rowe? Where's your sister? I have missed her, sweetling that she is.'

As Jalen moved towards the unnamed man, Arthur took a step forward. He wasn't sure what he could do, but he wanted to help—

He was falling again, landing this time on wet sand. A crowd was gathered on a beach. Storm clouds painted the sky blue and grey and purple. A boat bobbed past the breakers.

A girl screamed. 'Jalen!'

Nessa. Arthur turned, finding her in the arms of a woman with the same blonde hair, tears running down her face. Nessa broke free of her mother, running along the beach, plunging into the water, her brother's name on her lips.

Arthur swallowed.

In the boat were three men.

Thunder rumbled as one of them stood, then was pushed into the water by the others.

Arthur sat up, gasping. 'Jalen,' he whispered.

A hand touched his back. 'I'm here. What's wrong?'

'I ...' Arthur began, but could not find the words. Images were tumbling through his brain, loss and pain and *grief* pulling at him. He didn't know what was real and what wasn't. He took a deep, shaking breath, Jalen's hand moving along his spine in long, comforting strokes. Arthur turned, reaching for Jalen with a sort of desperate urgency that was at once familiar, and not, because it wasn't fear, or longing, or blind desire that drove him this time.

It was something more, something deeper he could not name. He didn't say anything, closing his hands over Jalen's cheeks, and when their lips met Arthur pressed himself as close to Jalen as he could, until he thought their flesh might meld together.

Jalen didn't speak either, kissing Arthur back, ferocious and gentle at the same time, his fingers threaded through Arthur's hair and his teeth scraping the tender skin of Arthur's throat. Each time Jalen touched him, no matter how many times he'd done so before, it was like a jolt, an exploration of senses that Arthur had forgotten had already been awoken. Each time was a claiming and a reclaiming of him and everything he was able to give and take, it was falling over the tallest cliff to smash onto the rocks below as the ocean crept over him. All the broken pieces of him came together with the touch of lips and tongue, the press of fingers into flesh, and the melody of burning gasps and moans that shrank the world to nothing but a whirlwind of pleasure.

With each intoxicating second, Arthur was swept away and remade.

'I dreamt of you,' Arthur said. Jalen was lying across his chest. Sweat slicked his forehead, beads of it catching on Arthur's fingers as he stroked damp hair from Jalen's face.

'Did you now?' the storm demon mumbled. His teeth closed over Arthur's nipple gently.

'Not like that,' Arthur said breathlessly, wondering how it was possible that he wanted Jalen again so soon, that he craved the feeling of Jalen's arms around him. He swallowed, his fingers moving along Jalen's scalp. 'They drowned you,' he whispered, the dream pulling at him urgently.

Jalen became very still. 'Yes,' he said, his voice nothing but a breath against Arthur's skin.

'But I thought …'

Jalen sighed and sat up, running his fingers through his messy hair. 'I was human once, Arthur. Just a man. I barely remember my life as it was. But I did something in that life that needed to be punished.' Jalen did not look at Arthur as he continued speaking. 'I killed a man. He hurt someone I loved. My sister. She was only a child, and he hurt her.'

Arthur recalled the blonde-haired girl he had seen in his dream.

'When she told me what had happened, I can still remember, even now, hundreds of years later, the rage that coursed through me, so hot and potent it burnt. She did not want me to do anything, but she deserved revenge, and as she would not seek it herself, I claimed it on her behalf,' he said, pulling his knees up to his chest and closing his eyes. 'I convinced her it would be alright. She told the man she wanted to meet with him, on the pretence she wanted to lie with him again, but instead of her, he found me. I broke his hands, the hands that had touched her, then slit him from belly to breast bone,' Jalen explained. He opened his eyes, pinning Arthur to the pillow with the pain there. 'In my village, to take a life meant you had to give one. That was the rules, to maintain the balance. I would not let them take my sister, so I let them take me instead.'

'I know,' Arthur whispered. 'I saw.'

'I had a choice, you see – burn, or drown. I had seen a man drown once. He panicked for a moment but, then ... he looked strangely peaceful. And I thought it would be better, for my sister and my mother, to not have to watch me burn.'

'Jalen ...' Arthur reached out his hand and Jalen took it, squeezed it tightly.

'But, when I reached the Otherworld Ankou did not send me on. He sent me back – as this.'

'Why?'

'I don't know.'

CHAPTER 43

Ordes found himself sharing a drink with the Master of Songs and Death. He'd not long woken, and he'd woken alone. Heart hammering, he'd dressed and gone in search of Jenyfer. The beating of her heart had led him down a darkened hall dripping with water and straight into a cavernous room with a long wooden table covered in candles.

'You've just missed her.'

The God of the Seas was seated on a wrought iron chair on a small balcony, the doorway bare of curtains. 'She's busy, in case you're wondering. She is studying and is not to be disturbed.'

'How long have I been here?' Ordes asked.

This time, Melodias looked at him, glancing over his shoulder, dark hair shifting like they were under water. 'Does it matter?' He gestured to a second chair. 'Join me.'

Cautiously, Ordes approached, stepping out onto the balcony. Lyonesse was stretched out beneath them like a jewel, a black river slithering like a serpent across the landscape. Far in the distance, where the river disappeared into a wall of mist, was a small boat.

'You can see it, can't you?' Melodias murmured.

'Yes.'

'Interesting.'

'Why?'

'Sit,' the Master of Songs and Death commanded; Ordes did. Jenyfer's father terrified him.

Melodias waved his hand and a cup appeared, filled with black liquid. He nodded, indicating Ordes was to take it. 'Poison isn't my style. If I wanted you dead, you'd be dead already.'

'Good to know,' Ordes mumbled, picking up the cup and taking a small sip. It was slightly salty and bitter. Tea, Melodias told him. Ordes looked out over the landscape again – everything shimmered, like he was watching the world through a watery sheen. It should have been comforting, but it wasn't. He lived on the water, not in it – or beneath it.

Melodias set his cup down. 'If I were a human man and you'—he raked his eyes over Ordes disdainfully— 'had shown up on my doorstep with an interest in my daughter, what would I say to you?'

'But you're not human, so it doesn't matter, does it?'

Melodias considered him with interest. 'No, I'm not, and neither are you.'

'I'm half—'

'My boy, there is nothing human about you. Not one little bit. Mother not tell you that?'

Ordes felt like he'd been punched in the gut. 'I don't believe you.'

Melodias sighed. 'If you want to keep lying to yourself, fine, but back to our other matter. If you can keep her, what then? And I don't mean keep her in your bed. When the comfort of you and her is no longer enough, what then, faery?'

'No longer enough for whom?' Ordes managed. His head was spinning. Not human?

'For her. Heartfire or not, she is not like you,' Melodias replied softly. Ordes jolted and Melodias smiled.

'She may not know yet, but I can see it. I can practically taste it. It's sickening, if you ask me.'

Ordes' fingers tightened on his cup. 'I didn't.'

'She is not made from the same things you are made from. She is darkness and light and the very essence of her is fluid, ever-changing. You cannot hold back the tide, so why would you try and hold back her? Will you build a dam to contain what she is? Because, I can tell you now, no dam wall will be enough to hold what is living inside her. So,' Melodias added, 'when she casts you aside, when you are longer enough for her anymore, I want you to remember this conversation and this moment as one of warning, not threat.'

'And what about promises?'

Melodias raised a dark eyebrow. 'What about them?'

'What about the promises I have made to her? To myself? Do you expect me to push those things aside?' Ordes set his cup on the table and turned to the Master of Songs and Death, wondering if it would be the last thing he did. 'Because that is not the sort of man I am.'

'Sometimes we have to change what we are,' Melodias replied. 'I know you hear the heart of the ocean. I know you feel it, as she does. But what you are and what she is are two vastly different things.'

'You don't know her,' Ordes argued.

'Don't I? I fear she is more like me than she wants to accept,' Melodias mused.

'She isn't like you,' Ordes said. 'She feels. She cares about others.'

'But you worry she doesn't care enough,' Melodias said simply. 'For you, that is.'

'She cares for me,' Ordes said, sitting back. 'What do you really want? Is this about the prophecy? Do you want the Treasures of the Gods?'

Melodias drummed his fingers on the tabletop. 'I want my Stone back, the rest I don't much care for. Not yet, anyway,' he added, then sighed, his gaze sliding to Ordes again. 'You're an idiot.'

'Thanks.'

The power Jenyfer had unleashed on the water-Byrn had left her shaken, and it had taken everything she had, every ounce of control, to push it away and not let it come screaming into the world like it wanted. She didn't know what Andromache had told her father, but she had not seen the syhren woman since that day.

When she wasn't with Ordes, the library was her haunt; no matter how many books she read, there was always something she was not finding. No other syhrens would speak to her – the part-humans avoided looking at her, and when she did manage to catch their eyes, they ducked their heads, but never quickly enough. They knew who she was and who she belonged to. She supposed they all did. Apart from Andromache, Jenyfer had not had a conversation with a single syhren. She wasn't sure they could speak – their expressions were always strangely serene, verging on vacant.

Jenyfer did not go to the library today. She went searching for her father. Maybe she could make some sort of deal with him? He let Ordes go, and she'd …

She took a deep breath. If it meant Ordes was free of this place, then she'd stay – for now, at least. That he'd come here, for her, both warmed and chilled her blood. That he would take such a risk for her was thrilling … and terrifying.

Would she do the same for him? Jenyfer stopped walking, resting her palm against the wall, going over every minute she had spent with him, each moment washing through her like a wave.

Yes, she realised. She would.

Her heart felt strangely warm. She rubbed at her chest.

She would exchange herself for his freedom, pretending to become what her father wanted her to be – and making sure she never left this place in the process, never had the opportunity to unleash her song on the world. There was nothing else she could think of that ended with Ordes both free and alive; the powerlessness of her situation made her grit her teeth. She pushed herself off the wall, pulled her shoulders back, and made her way to the throne room, finding her father there. Jenyfer skirted the edge of the black pool.

And stopped.

There was another throne of bones sitting beside her father's.

Melodias gestured to it. 'Yours.'

Jenyfer made herself smile. Made herself play the game. 'Thank you,' she said, lifting the hem of her ridiculous gown and ascending the stairs. She could feel him watching her as she settled herself on the throne, arranging her skirts while she collected her thoughts.

'I know what you're going to ask—' Melodias began.

'Are you in my head?' Jenyfer accused.

He chuckled. 'It's all over your face. You want me to let him go.'

'Yes.'

Her father sighed, drumming dark-scaled fingers against the arm of his throne. 'You place a lot of faith in someone who is keeping things from you.'

Jenyfer's heart paused. 'What are you talking about?'

The tapping continued, rhythmic, musical. 'He hasn't told you, has he?'

'Told me what?' Her skin prickled uncomfortably.

'It'd be for his own reasons, and I'm sure they're adequate enough, but I would want to know if it was me. I'm sure it's nothing about you, Jenyfer,' Melodias added. 'I mean, I'm sure you haven't done anything *wrong*. You can't help what you are.'

Jenyfer froze.

'We're not made for loving,' Melodias said, lifting his shoulders in a shrug. 'We can love, sure, but it's not easy to love us back.'

'Stop,' Jenyfer whispered. 'I know what you're doing and it isn't going to work.'

'I'm only trying to help you see how important it is to put your trust in someone who trusts you back,' her father said.

'He trusts me,' she snapped.

Melodias turned to her, and his voice was low when he spoke. 'Ask him about the heartfire, then ask him how long he's known and why he hasn't told you.'

Ordes was in their room, sitting by the window. He glanced over his shoulder as Jenyfer entered, and gave her a smile. She couldn't smile back and didn't give him a chance to get to his feet or ask her what was wrong before she fired the question at him.

'What's the heartfire?'

His face froze and her heart sank.

'What is it?' she asked again.

Ordes dropped his eyes. He looked at the floor for such a long moment she didn't think he was going to answer; when he lifted his head, his expression was deeply conflicted. 'I didn't keep it from you on purpose,' he said softly. 'Well, I did, but not because I wanted to deceive you, Jenyfer.'

'But what is it?' she said. Her chest was hot. She rubbed at it, irritated. Ordes followed her actions with his eyes.

'Ever since I met you, there has been something pulling me towards you – something I couldn't name and didn't understand. Even now, all I want to do is touch you. It's as if my hands are outside of my control.' He smiled, but it faded when she didn't smile in return. Ordes ran his hand through his hair and she noticed his fingers were trembling. 'The feelings I have – the yearning, the longing I can't shake, that I don't *want* to shake, that connection we share,' he said, shaking his head, frustrated with his explanation. 'It's not this map, Jenyfer. The thing that keeps us together, it's not the map, the Grail, or the Treasures. We're connected because something bigger than us has decided it should be. That's the heartfire.'

Jenyfer couldn't breathe.

'You're my soulmate,' Ordes said softly. 'The other half of me.'

She swallowed. 'You kept this from me? For how long?'

'Since Avalon. My mother ... she's the one who told me and ...' his voice trailed away. 'And I asked her not to tell you about it.'

'Why?' Jenyfer managed.

'Because I know how important it is that you make your own decisions, Jen.'

'But I can't, can I?' she shouted, making him jump. 'I can't because this heartfire has already decided for me. You knew this, and you didn't tell me?'

'I'm sorry,' Ordes said. 'I should have told you.'

'How can I believe you?' Jenyfer whispered.

Ordes slowly climbed off the bed but did not move towards her. 'If you asked me to tear out my own tongue, or rip out my eyes, I'd do it, Jenyfer, because that is what it means,' Ordes said. Then, 'You do have a choice. You're not under any spell or compulsion. You can make your own decisions, but ...'

'But what?' she demanded, almost afraid to hear the answer, but needing to know.

'You will never be able to love anyone else. The magic of the heartfire won't allow it.'

'Then how is it a choice?' Jenyfer said flatly. 'Be with you, or be alone? That's what you're telling me, right? I have to choose you because I can't choose anyone else!' She let her head fall into her hands. 'This is ridiculous. First Bryn, and now you? What have I ever done to deserve this?'

'Nothing,' Ordes mumbled. 'Except being born what you are, the same as me.'

She knew her words had hurt him and regret stabbed at her, but she shoved it away ruthlessly. 'You're okay with this? With this lack of choice?'

'Of course I'm not,' Ordes said fiercely. 'But it doesn't make any difference, for me, anyway, because I'd already decided, Jenyfer. Before I knew about the heartfire, before I knew what it meant, I'd already decided that it was you. You who I wanted to see the rest of this life with. Don't you understand?' he said, finally moving closer to her. 'I'd already decided I—'

'Don't,' Jenyfer whispered. Her song slithered beneath her skin as he took another step closer, then another, until she could touch him if she wanted. She bit her lip and looked at the floor.

Ordes' fingers curled beneath her chin, forcing her to look at him. 'Why not?'

She shook her head.

'I could be dead next week and I'm not going to die without letting you know how I feel.'

A lump lodged in her throat, so tight and so thick she couldn't speak, couldn't breathe.

Her chest burnt.

Ordes cupped her face in both hands. 'You don't have to say it back. I don't expect you to, but you need to know you are worth it. You the person, not you the syhren, or you that the prophecy speaks of. You, Jenyfer, just as you are.' A pause. He took a deep breath. 'I love you.'

Those words sank inside her, burrowed deep into her blood, into her bones. She heard them, felt them brand themselves on her insides. Felt them burn and latch onto her and those same words, those three little words, began the climb up her throat. Her song was purring alongside them, urging them on; but, as they slid onto her tongue, Jenyfer swallowed them away, smothering a gasp at the pain of it, the pain of denying it.

'You should have told me about the heartfire,' she said instead.

Slowly, Ordes let her go. 'I was afraid to say anything, because I knew we'd end up here, having this moment, and I thought … I guess I thought that, with time, you might …'

'I might what?' she breathed.

He looked at her quickly, then away again. 'It doesn't matter,' he said finally. He went to step past her, to leave, but she blocked his path, shaking her head.

'It does matter. If you expected something from me, it does matter, Ordes,' she said.

He put his head in his hands. 'You're killing me, Jen,' he whispered. 'I came here for you. Did you ask me to? No. Did you expect me to? Probably not, but I came *for you* because I couldn't leave you here alone. But if this is where you would rather be, you need to tell me.'

'I don't know,' she whispered.

Ordes dropped his hands. 'Let me know when you do, then.'

'Why am I suddenly the bad guy?' Jenyfer asked, folding her arms. 'You're the one who kept something as important as a soulmates bond from me. I'm not the one who lied.'

'No, you're the one who can't tell the truth,' he bit out.

'Do you want to hear me say I love you? Is that what you want? Because if I said it, I wouldn't be telling you the truth at all,' Jenyfer shot back, her voice rising. 'I won't lie to you. If you can't … if you push me, Ordes, you might never hear those words from me.'

If a heart could break, she would have heard his snap down the centre. Her chest burnt, but she ignored it, not taking her eyes from his face.

He opened his mouth, closed it again. This time, she let him leave.

CHAPTER 44

The Fisher Queen's cave was lit by the flames flickering gently from the fire-pit before her. Golden light played over her features. She inclined her head in greeting when Arthur stepped inside. He sat beside her without a word, holding out his hands to the flames, frowning.

'I can't feel their heat,' he said.

'You won't,' she told him. 'Like many things, the fire is not real.'

'Is this place real?' he asked.

'It is,' she confirmed. This time, the Grail was not resting in her lap. Arthur looked around the cave, his eyes searching the gold-touched shadows, but he could not see it. He could feel it, though, could hear its song. 'You can see it anytime you want,' Eseld told him. 'If you dream of it.'

'I can't dream when I'm already dreaming,' Arthur said.

'Is this a dream, though?' the Fisher Queen asked.

He jolted. Of course it was a dream. Wasn't it?

Eseld was watching him. 'When you dream, when you come to me, it is not a dream at all, Arthur. Can't you sense that?'

'If I'm not dreaming, then where am I?' he asked.

'You are in the space between the realms.'

He swallowed. 'How do I get here?'

'The world of magic knows what you are – it knows what you shall be, what you shall do. At least, it knows what it wants you to do, but you have a choice, Arthur,' the Fisher Queen told him. 'The Grail is yours to wield, as you wish, but be aware of the consequences of your choice.'

Arthur frowned. 'What do you mean?'

'Darkness and blood will come for you before the end, when the battle is waged in the skies, in the seas, and on the land, darkness and blood will come for you,' Eseld whispered. Her mouth was turned down at the corners.

Goerika's words. The demi-god's warning.

'Seek the Grail,' Eseld said. 'Let it show you what you need to see.'

Arthur took a deep breath and closed his eyes, picturing the Grail as he had last seen it, and, slowly, an image formed in his mind. Hands he knew – his – rested on one side of the vessel. As he watched, another set of hands joined his. Slender, female, and flecked in scales.

Jenyfer.

Arthur opened his mouth to speak to her, even though he could not see her face, but another set of hands reached out to touch the Grail.

Three sets of hands upon the stone …

Arthur sucked in a breath, unable to take his eyes off the third set of hands. A man's hands. Sun-browned skin, long fingers, the knuckles marked with strange symbols he had never seen before.

'The language of the Old Ones,' Eseld's voice whispered. Arthur did not take his eyes from the Grail, afraid that, if he did, Jenyfer's hands and the man's hands would vanish.

'Who is he?' Arthur asked Eseld.

The Fisher Queen's hand came to rest on Arthur's forearm; her skin was cool, slightly damp. 'You know him already, although you have never seen him. You know him because you are tied to him by prophecy, as you are tied to Jenyfer. The three of you are bound in this together.'

'Can I see his face?' Arthur breathed.

'If you wish. This is your dream, Arthur. You control it. *This* is your gift,' Eseld added, making him frown. He wanted to ask what she meant, but he needed to see this man's face. Slowly, his vision expanded, until hands became forearms, Jenyfer's decorated with glorious silver scales. Arthur let his gaze travel along her arms until he reached her face. She was as he remembered – fierce, strong. Determined.

Swallowing, he let his eyes move to the man who stood at her side.

Arthur knew this face, like an instinct.

Eyes like molten silver. Skin burnished by the sun. Hair like a raven's wing, brushing the broad expanse of his shoulders.

'Who are you?' Arthur mumbled.

Silver eyes met his. 'So,' the man said, his voice oddly disjointed, but still powerful. Arthur could feel the magic in that voice. 'You're the saviour of the world. But which world?'

Then, Arthur was barrelling backwards, past the Fisher Queen in her cave, until he slammed back into his own head, gasping. The kibitka swam into focus around him as he struggled to control his breathing.

This is your gift.

What did that mean?

Jalen stirred, rolling over to sling his arm across Arthur's chest, but Arthur could not sleep. When dawn came, he was still staring at the canvas ceiling, Eseld's words and the image of the silver-eyed man tumbling through his head.

Chapter 45

Jenyfer's fists curled, fingernails biting into her skin. With an irritated growl, she shook her head, taking her place next to her father. His smile was a knowing one.

'To be a fly on the wall …'

She narrowed her eyes at him, making him chuckle, then launch into a lengthy explanation about how his realm worked, what his role was, what her role was to be, but she wasn't listening. Ordes hadn't come back to their room and she hadn't gone looking for him. She should have. She should have apologised for her words, for her cruelty, but pride and fear had kept her curled up in a ball on the bed, her eyes on the door, waiting for him to come back.

He had told her he loved her. If she closed her eyes, all she could see was his face, his lips moving as he spoke. All she could feel was the burning in her chest that she was trying to ignore and all she could hear was her heart beating alongside his. Her fingers twitched; she wanted to touch him. She shoved her hands in her lap, wedged them between her knees and grit her teeth.

Melodias snapped his fingers in front of her face. 'Pay attention.'

'I am!'

He sighed. 'This is why I hate the heartfire. It turns people into idiots.' He sat back, one long leg crossed over the other. Jenyfer watched him out of the corner of her eye. 'I've been thinking,' he said, tapping his fingers against the arm of his throne of bones, 'about your request, and about this very interesting map on your skin. I'm sure you've worked out, or someone has told you, where it leads?'

Jenyfer swallowed tightly, forcing her heart to be steady. 'Maybe.'

'They all think they can fool me,' Melodias mumbled, then sighed, waving his hand at the door. It flew open, and Ordes was dragged into the room by two syhrens. His expression was dazed and for a moment Jenyfer's heart stopped, but then she remembered the charm in his chest. But she did not dare relax, not with the way her father was watching him. 'I'll have that map, thank you, and then we can discuss your other request.'

With effort, Jenyfer dragged her eyes from Ordes to her father. 'And how do you propose to get it?'

'Hopefully without drama, although, if I've learnt one thing about you people,' Melodias said, indicating her and then Ordes, 'it's that you love some drama.' His fingers still drummed against the chair – musical, like everything he did. 'It's simple, really. You need to give it up.'

'Give it up?' Jenyfer repeated. Her fingers gripped the arms of her throne; Melodias' eyes lingered on them, then rose to her face. His lips curled into a cruel smile and he clicked his fingers. Ordes was forced to the ground. He fought, but the syhrens who held him were stronger.

'Stop,' Jenyfer cried as his cheek was pressed against the cold stone floor. She cast a desperate look at her father. 'Stop this.'

'Just how much do you care about him?' Melodias was still smiling, enjoying the spectacle before him. 'Give up the map.'

'How?' Jenyfer asked.

Ordes swore as the syhren holding the back of his neck squeezed hard. If he were human, Jenyfer was certain his spine would have snapped under the pressure.

Don't fight, she silently begged him. *Please. Please, don't fight. I'm sorry.*

'As I said, it's simple,' Melodias drawled. 'You give me the map, and I won't kill him.'

'How do I know you won't kill him, and me, anyway?' Something was clawing its way through Jenyfer's insides, some deep instinct she couldn't name. 'You won't find the Treasures without us,' she reminded him.

He ran his hand through his hair, his eyes irritated. 'I don't want to kill either of you. You're Magic Wielders and, therefore, you're important.' He shifted his gaze from Ordes, still pinned on the floor, to Jenyfer. 'All you have to do is wish that map free of your skin, and it will be. But he has to do the same,' Melodias added. 'Half a map is no use to me, is it?'

'If you want the map, you will need to let me talk to him. Let me convince him,' Jenyfer begged. 'Then, once you have it …'

'Yes?'

'He can go? He can leave this place?'

Melodias nodded.

Jenyfer swallowed, forcing herself to rise and walk down the small flight of stairs to where Ordes was still struggling like an animal caught in a trap.

Ordes' cheek was crushed against the floor, the rocks slippery and cool. He couldn't see anything except the bare feet of the syhren who held him, her webbed toes inches from his face. He struggled, but was not strong enough to fight the fey strength of the sea faeries. The syhrens didn't speak, much like that day near the bridge – before the wraith had appeared.

He'd love for them to come and work their strange magic now.

Another set of feet, human feet, came into view. Jenyfer knelt beside him, lowering her head so she could whisper in his ear and her hair tumbled down to brush against Ordes' cheek. 'He wants the map.'

Ordes grit his teeth. 'We can't.'

'Please,' Jenyfer whispered. Then, to the syhren whose fingers were threaded through Ordes' hair, 'Let him up.'

Ordes' head was wrenched upright, so sharply his neck pinched. Jenyfer remained crouched beside him, looking at Melodias over her shoulder. The Master of Songs and Death was watching them, a small smile tugging at his mouth. If Ordes could move, he'd wipe that smirk right off Melodias' face. His magic swelled beneath his skin, and the heartfire was aflame in his chest.

Jenyfer stood and put her hands on her hips. 'I can't talk to him like this. Let him up.'

Melodias rolled his eyes, then clicked his fingers and Ordes was free. He jumped to his feet, his magic dancing across his knuckles, his eyes locked on Melodias; but, before he could take a step, Jenyfer put herself in front of him.

Facing him.

A barrier between him and her father.

He stared at her, unable to believe this was happening, that she would do this.

'Ordes, please listen to me,' she said urgently.

'Punish me as much as you like, be as angry with me as you want, but don't do this, Jenyfer,' he hissed.

Jenyfer stepped closer, her face tight with worry. 'He'll kill you,' she said, glancing at the two syhrens, 'and I can't watch you die.' She placed her hand on his chest and the heartfire surged at her touch, burning a trail through the guts of him.

'I *won't* watch you die. I won't let it happen. I can live with your anger, Ordes, but I can't live with your death.' Her voice broke around the edges but she kept her eyes on his and slowly moved closer, her hands sliding down his arms so she could wind her fingers between his. His magic curled around their joined hands. 'Trust me, please.'

Ordes let his head drop into the curve of her neck, crushed by a wave of defeat so potent he could taste it, and let his magic fade.

Finally, he nodded.

He gripped her hands tightly. He would not let her go, would hold on with everything he had no matter what happened next, no matter that she didn't love him back. He could live with that, but he couldn't live without her. The heartfire wouldn't allow it – *he* wouldn't allow it.

Jenyfer took a deep breath, not looking at her father, not letting go of Ordes' hands, keeping her eyes on him. 'We agree.'

Melodias wasted no time. He waved his hand; a burning, tingling feeling crawled over Ordes' body as the inky lines of the map freed themselves from his skin, then from Jenyfer's. He watched in amazement as the black lines joined, the map forming itself in the air above their heads. He tried to hold that image in his mind, stamp it there, but everything was happening so quickly. The map floated towards Melodias. He held up his hand and the moment it touched his skin, it vanished; and with it, their path to the Grail.

Jenyfer sighed in relief, turning to her father, her movements stiff, her shoulders curled in on themselves. 'Can he go now?' she said.

With a sinking in his gut, Ordes realised it wasn't only the map she had just given up. He pulled her back against his chest and folded his arms around her.

'What have you done, Jen?' he whispered, squeezing her to him.

Melodias started laughing. 'Go?' he said, cocking an eyebrow. 'Why would I let him go?'

'You promised!' Jenyfer shouted, and Ordes knew what Melodias would say before he said it. Jenyfer didn't know the rules, the way of the gods and the fey, but Ordes did. How could he have been so blind?

The God of the Seas was not bound to anything because he had not *agreed* to anything.

'I said no such thing.' Melodias chuckled.

'You tricked me,' Jenyfer said, her voice low, a growl – a warning. Ordes could feel her magic shifting beneath her skin and music barrelled through his mind.

Melodias rose from his seat, expression lethal. He snapped his fingers, and all the light was sucked from the chamber. Ordes clutched Jenyfer tightly as they tumbled into blackness.

CHAPTER 46

The sun poked through the canopy, pieces of gold against the dark green of the leaves. At least, Lamorna thought, it wouldn't rain on her today. She knew the way now and didn't need someone with her; she'd brushed off concerns about faeries, even though Mordred's warning was still ringing in her ears and had her jumping at every sound for days afterwards.

Collecting water was one of the only times she was alone and one of the only times it was *quiet*. Everyone here was so loud. They talked in loud, boisterous voices, verging on rude in the way they spoke. So Lamorna didn't complain about her trips into the forest; she could recite the Word and not have to worry about being discovered, but she always made sure to keep her voice low, nothing above a whisper. It didn't matter to the One God that she was almost soundless in her reverence, only that she continued her worship.

She hated that she had to keep it secret. Her task weighed on her, but she had seen no possible way she could succeed with these people.

Perhaps, she thought, kneeling by the stream, the One God had made a mistake in choosing her for this mission.

Two days ago she had sent a letter back to Kernou, to the Chif, disguised as a letter to her friend. Lamorna knew she didn't really have any friends, not in the way her sister had Bryn. The young women in Lamorna's prayer circle didn't consider her a friend, she knew that. It didn't bother her. Mostly. All mail entering the village was given to the Chif and the Konsel, who read each and every letter before passing it on to the recipient. Lamorna smiled wryly – Jenyfer would hate that.

It had taken many sly questions to find out how she would get a letter sent; in the end, she'd resorted to begging one of the young boys in the village to help her. She'd thought about asking Lyr, but knowing his father was a member of the Inborn made her forget that idea. She found another youngster and he'd been keen to assist her – she'd worked out the younger children didn't have much of a role in Cruithea, aside from helping their mothers. Too young to train to be warriors, they were filled with a wild and restless energy that Lamorna realised she could use, and three of the young lads had bounded off into the trees. She had no idea where they were headed and didn't ask, just glad her message would be delivered.

Lamorna dipped the bucket into the stream, letting it fill gently, then heaved it out. She wasn't strong by any means, but the task was getting easier, so she assumed her strength was improving. She no longer sweated on the walk to and from the stream.

She was part of the way back to the village when someone stepped from behind a tree.

'Mordred! You scared the life out of me!' she said, setting the bucket down. He wasn't smiling today – just looking at her strangely. 'What is it?'

Slowly, he reached into the pocket of his trousers and withdrew a piece of parchment. It was creased and smudged with dirt, but Lamorna's heart sank as she recognised it.

'Where did you get that?' she asked breathlessly.

'You do know what I do here, don't you, Lamorna? What my role is?' he asked her.

'Yes,' she whispered.

'So, you'd know that no message leaves this village without my permission,' he said, tucking the letter away. He regarded her a moment, then circled her once, like an animal – a predator – might. 'Imagine my surprise when a couple of boys were caught on the border carrying a very interesting—'

'You read it?' she asked, wringing her hands as fear gripped her in its claws.

'I did.'

Lamorna closed her eyes. She could feel him looking at her still and she swallowed her rising stomach. She would not disgrace herself by vomiting in front of him, no matter what.

'They don't know, do they?' Mordred asked softly. 'Your aunt and her lover. They don't know you're still serving the One God and the Chif.'

Lamorna's heart was thunder, so hard and fast it was painful. 'Will you tell?'

He considered her, then, after what felt like an age, shook his head. 'No. I won't.'

She had to ask. 'Why?'

'Because,' he said simply. 'If you need to get letters to Kernou, I can arrange that.'

'You can?'

He shrugged. 'There are people I trust here – people who will do what I need without asking questions. Do you understand?'

She nodded.

'But,' he said. 'I want something in return.'

Her breath hitched. 'What?'

He stared into her eyes. 'I want you to teach me. What you told me before, about the One God, has made me think that perhaps … perhaps things here are not … right.' He paused and rubbed at his cheek; Lamorna could see the conflict in his eyes. 'Where you come from, power is different, is it not? I mean, the power of your god is given freely. No one has to work for it, continue to push themselves and receive nothing in return.'

Lamorna frowned. 'You don't like it here?'

'It's not that I don't like it, it's that I wish things were different. For me,' he added in a low voice. 'My mother is powerful because she is the High Priestess, and that is something I will never be. I have spent my life bowing to the Goddess and it isn't that she's given me nothing – she gave me my magic, she gave me this body that has allowed me to prove myself as a warrior, but ...'

'You want more than that,' Lamorna said softly. He nodded, but would not look at her. 'There is no shame in that, Mordred.'

'Isn't there? I thought your god did not encourage people to want beyond what life had dealt them,' he responded, still in that conflicted tone.

'That is true,' Lamorna admitted. 'But, there is a difference between wanting more than you should get, being selfish, and wanting to be something else, especially if you feel the One God has set a path for you. There is nothing wrong with wanting to walk that path.'

Mordred looked at her then, his expression curious. 'Have you ever wanted to be something else?'

'No,' she said simply. 'I am happy with what I have been given by the One God.'

'The Chif holds you in esteem?'

'He knows I am valuable to him,' she said, then stopped, wondering if she had committed a sin in voicing her own importance. 'I mean, I am trusted. He knows I hear the Word, and he knows I obey the wishes of the One God before anything else.'

Mordred stepped closer to her, so close she would be able to touch him if she wished. 'And what does the One God wish for you, Lamorna?'

She swallowed and found herself having to hunt for the words. Mordred was so close to her, intimately close. It made her body feel light and her cheeks heat. She dropped her gaze so she would not be distracted by the colour of his eyes, or the shape of his jaw, finding herself looking at the expanse of his chest instead, which was no better.

She shut her eyes. 'I am His soldier. One of many, but still His. I might not wield a weapon, like you, but I am still devoted to fighting His fight.'

'And would he like me, this god of yours?' Mordred's voice was low, soft. She wanted to look at him, but she didn't. Words were difficult, so she settled on a nod instead. 'Would He let me fight for Him?'

Her eyes flew open then. 'You would do that?'

'I do not know,' he answered. 'I would have to know that I would be rewarded.'

'Oh, you would be,' she said, unable to help smiling.

Mordred returned her smile. *His whole face transforms when he smiles,* she thought, then shoved it away guiltily.

'It's settled then,' he said smoothly, picking up her bucket. She did not object this time. 'We will meet here, after dark each night, and you will teach me.'

'I will have to sneak away from my aunt,' Lamorna said as they walked.

'Is that a problem?'

'No,' she affirmed. 'No, it isn't. This is what the One God wants, so I will make it happen.'

The following night, after Tamora and Keraine had fallen asleep, Lamorna eased the blankets back and hunted around on the ground for her boots. Her heart was thundering and her mouth was dry. She wondered if Jenyfer had felt the same, all the times she'd crept out of the cottage to do whatever she did on those nights.

With one eye on her aunt's sleeping form, Lamorna pulled her boots on, collecting her coat from the end of the bed. She walked backwards carefully, barely daring to breathe until she was outside the kibitka, the chill of the night curling around her. Slowly, she looked around. Everyone appeared to be in bed – she had no idea what time it was and hoped she hadn't left it too late, that Mordred hadn't given up on her.

He was waiting for her, exactly where he said he would be. Her heart skipped a beat at the sight of him, but she forced the feeling away. She needed to concentrate. He was dressed warmly, like she was, and looked up as she approached, a smile sliding across his face.

'I was beginning to think I was not worthy,' he said lightly.

She shook her head. 'You are worthy, and I will help you to absorb the Word.'

Mordred nodded. 'Yes, I'm sure you will. Shall we begin?'

They sat on the ground, opposite one another. Lamorna could feel him watching her as she arranged her skirt, making sure she was maintaining her modesty. 'I do not have a copy of the Decalogue with me,' she began, suddenly strangely nervous.

'I suspect you know the book off by heart,' Mordred said, again with that smile, the one that caused a fluttery feeling in her belly. Lamorna cleared her throat. She wasn't sure how to respond to the praise in his voice, so she ignored it.

'The rules of the One God are not complicated,' she said, and he nodded. She had told him the rules already, but would go over them again. She had learnt, through prayer circle, that sometimes people needed to hear the rules more than once, especially in the beginning. She began to recite them, but he shook his head.

'I remember, Lamorna,' he said gently, not unkindly. 'No other gods, no killing or stealing, no adultery,' he threw her a wink that made her stomach tighten. 'Jealousy, pride, greed, lust, and hatred are sins and the One God favours temperance, humility, and diligence in all things.'

She beamed at him. 'Well done.'

He dropped his eyes for a moment, toying with the leaves on the forest floor, his fingers rustling through them, tiny flecks of gold left in their wake – his magic. Lamorna sucked in a breath, and his eyes shot to hers again. 'But tell me the last ones again, about women. Those rules are very interesting to me.'

Lamorna cleared her throat. 'Women are the bearers of sin—'

'No, not that one. The one about authority,' Mordred cut in.

'A woman shall not hold authority over any man,' Lamorna quoted softly.

'And in Kernou, in your world, this is true?' he asked.

She nodded. Mordred didn't say anything else, and a thoughtful silence fell between them. Lamorna wasn't sure what to say next. She was surprised that he'd remembered everything she'd said to him that day – she'd been speaking so fast, so excitedly, even though she tried not to.

'You haven't asked,' he said suddenly.

'About what?'

'Letters,' he answered, his voice low, warm. He pulled his lip between his teeth, chewing on it as he thought about her situation. 'You cannot very well hand them over to me in the middle of the village. We need a better plan.'

Lamorna frowned. 'Could I leave one somewhere, a place only you know?'

'Done this sort of thing before, have you?' Mordred asked.

'No!' she objected, and then realised he was smiling. Teasing her. She managed a small smile back.

'You could always give them to me here,' he said. 'If you think I am a worthy pupil and will continue to teach me?'

She nodded, her heart leaping in triumph.

'So,' he said. 'What do we do now?'

'Well,' Lamorna began, shifting until she was kneeling. 'Now, we pray.' She motioned for him to copy her movements. Even kneeling, he was so much bigger than she was, a hulking presence within the reach of her hands. Lamorna clasped her hands to her chest – he did the same. 'We close our eyes,' she told him. 'I will recite the Word for us.'

Lamorna closed her eyes, trusting he would do the same, and began her recitation of the Word. She had gotten to the part about saying the Word daily when she sensed something wasn't right. She opened her eyes and looked up, her voice faltering when she realised Mordred did not have his eyes closed.

He was looking at her.

'Sorry,' he said sheepishly, reaching up to rub at the back of his neck. 'I got distracted.'

'By?' Lamorna asked, irritated, then she remembered this was new to him and she needed to guide him, not berate him.

That smile again. 'You.'

The butterflies in her stomach burst back to life, beating against the inside of her so hard she thought she might be sick. 'Me?'

'Is that so hard to believe?'

She cleared her throat and looked at the ground.

'Lamorna, look at me.'

She did.

'I am afraid I have sinned, just now,' Mordred said, his voice as soft as clouds, as silken as a gentle breeze. 'Should I confess?'

'If you like,' she whispered. 'What is your sin?'

'I have had … lustful thoughts. That's a sin, isn't it?' he asked, a little frown between his brows that she suddenly wanted to smooth away with her fingers. Lamorna made herself nod, swallowing tightly. Her breathing felt strange.

She cleared her throat, remembering why they were there. 'What are these thoughts?'

Mordred's lips curled wickedly. 'I'm not sure I should voice them, considering the object of those thoughts is right in front of me.'

Lamorna stopped breathing as her insides flooded with warmth, so much of it she waited to burn, waited for her body to turn to ashes as Mordred climbed to his feet, flashed her another of his smiles and stretched luxuriously, as sinuous and graceful as a cat.

'Tomorrow? Another lesson?'

She nodded, not trusting herself to speak, and then he was gone, leaving her with the dark forest and the moonlight surrounding her.

CHAPTER 47

Stone walls and floor, cold to touch, and slightly damp. A low ceiling. No windows. Bars. Jenyfer sighed, letting her head fall into her hands.

'Your father is an arse,' Ordes said from somewhere behind her.

'Yes,' she agreed. 'How long have we been here?'

'No idea.' His tone was clipped.

'I'm sorry,' she whispered. 'I just wanted him to let you go.'

Ordes sighed, reaching for her in the dark, a calloused thumb finding her cheek.

Footsteps, slow and steady, casual, echoed in the distance, gradually moving closer until the Master of Songs and Death was standing on the other side of their cell door. His eyes moved over them and he shook his head, something like regret dancing over his face.

'I really do hate the heartfire, you know.'

Jenyfer scowled. 'You've got the map now, but why? What do you want? The Treasures? The Grail? You can't wield it – no one but Teyath's King can do that.'

'Yes, I know,' Melodias said curtly. 'I was there when this stupid prophecy was spoken. Perhaps it's time I went and found this King myself. Do you think if I invited him for tea he'd accept?'

'No,' Jenyfer snapped.

'Pity. I'd like to know what he plans to do with this world,' Melodias said simply, examining his black-scaled fingers. 'You think you can figure out where the Treasures are and just go get them?' He chuckled. 'You're a pair of fucking idiots.'

'The prophecy—' Jenyfer began.

Melodias slammed his hand against the bars of their cell; the force of it rattled the stones around and beneath them. Jenyfer swallowed, her magic pooling in her hands as her song crept up her throat.

'The prophecy conveniently leaves important information aside,' Melodias declared, rubbing scaled fingers against his cheekbone. He turned his liquid gaze on Ordes. 'You, in particular, are an idiot. She at least has an excuse, spending her life with *humans*, ugh. You, however, have no excuses for being so ignorant about the ways of your own kind.'

'Fuck you,' Ordes mumbled.

'If only your father had taken the time to actually educate you, instead of spending the last thirty years running around pretending to be a pirate, one of you,' Melodias said, waving a hand at Ordes and Jenyfer collectively, 'might have some idea of what you're about to do. Even if you could find these Treasures – which you won't, now – you would still have to collect them. Each Treasure is guarded.'

'Guarded?' Ordes asked. 'But no one else ...' his voice trailed off.

'Finally working it out, are you?' Melodias murmured. 'You can't trust any of us, faery, not when it comes to this. Your father, your mother, me ... we're all capable of being untruthful, regardless of what rules bind us. But,' he said, his tone becoming serious, 'those who guard the Treasures are not going to hand them over just because you ask nicely or bat your eyelashes.'

'What guards them?' Jenyfer asked. A shiver skimmed its way down her spine.

'Ancient beings,' her father responded. 'When the Red One took the Treasures, she gave them into the keeping of some of the oldest and most powerful fey creatures in the world. And she left instructions that have nothing to do with any prophecy. Ereshki was smart, if not reckless.'

'And the Grail?' Jenyfer shifted closer to the bars and ran her finger down one – magic hummed beneath her touch.

'Guarded by the shade of a long-dead Queen. Ereshki ran off with the Treasures and hid them around the land, and the rest of us decided to hide the Grail from her,' Melodias said, then sighed. 'But, once again, things were not as clear cut as they should have been. Merlin gave the Grail to the Fisher Queen and she promptly vanished.'

'My father helped hide the Grail? Why?' Ordes asked.

'That is something I have asked myself many times over the last couple of hundred years,' Melodias said. 'The Treasures are imbued with our magic, the same magic that was used to create the world. They were made by us, but they don't belong to us. They have taken on a life of their own.'

'And the Grail can't be found until the Treasures are retrieved,' Jenyfer said.

'Darling, I worry about your comprehension skills. The prophecy – or prophecies, if you like – say no such thing,' Melodias replied. Jenyfer opened her mouth to argue, and then stopped. Her father chuckled.

'Does this mean we can find the Grail without the Treasures?' Ordes asked.

'The Grail will not allow itself to be found, or its guardian will not allow it to be found, at least, until the others are collected and in your hands. Like calls to like,' Melodias explained. He looked between them again, rolling his eyes at their expressions. 'You've been ordered to find the Treasures by Niniane, I gather?'

'Yes,' Ordes answered, to Jenyfer's surprise.

'And you trust everything that comes out of your mother's mouth?'

'Should I trust what comes out of yours?' Ordes shot back.

Melodias laughed. 'Not at all but, as your instincts up to this point have been completely useless, I'll say this – only a blind man goes through life letting others lead him.' He leant forward, his gaze pinned to Ordes' face. 'Are you a blind man, faery, or something else?'

'I can see just fine,' Ordes said through his teeth.

A thought barrelled through Jenyfer's mind, a memory of a dream. An army of syhrens on a beach. Every muscle in her body tensed. 'War? Is that what you want?'

'You think *I* want war?' Melodias asked incredulously. 'My dear, war is messy. I don't like mess. For a long time, I've been trying to work out whose side I'm on. I was hoping that this Once and Future King of the Myrddin's might be able to help me decide. This map'—he patted his chest— 'that I now wear on my skin will give me leverage. Both sides want it, so I will use it as a bargaining chip and see what they have to offer me.'

'You said both sides. Who is on which?' Ordes asked.

Melodias gave him a look of pity. 'Your parents must be thrilled with how you turned out,' he said. 'But, if you must know ... on one hand, supposedly wanting peace and goodwill and magic to be returned to the world, we have your mother, the Green Knight, and the Goddess of Fate, annoying bitch she is. And on the other, Ankou, Inanna, and Ereshki, wherever she is, and whatever face she is wearing now.' He paused, ran his eyes over both of them. 'You think you know the truth of things because you've been told a few stories, but you know *nothing*, either of you,' he said. 'You think the Red One was the one to betray this world? Think again, and start asking the right questions.'

Then he was gone, nothing but the sound of his laughter echoing through the water-tinged darkness.

When Jenyfer next woke, a skeletal face was peering at them.

The wraith placed both hands on the bars. 'I haven't got all day.' Their whispery voice slid across the stones.

Jenyfer scrambled upright, cursing as her legs became tangled in her dress.

Ophine chuckled. The air shimmered and the bars vanished. 'You'd better be quick,' the wraith said. 'I can't hold this for long.'

Heart pounding, Jenyfer picked up the hem of her dress and hurried out of the cell, Ordes on her heels. Ophine stepped back and the bars snapped into place.

'Follow me.'

'Where are you taking us?' Jenyfer asked in a whisper.

The wraith sighed. 'You want to get out of this realm and off this miserable island?'

'I could kiss you right now,' Ordes said. Ophine glanced at him over a cloaked shoulder, looking him up and down.

'Sorry, faery. You're not my type,' was all they said. Then, 'Move. If we're lucky, we won't encounter any of Melodias' brain-dead syhrens. Puppets, all of them,' they added scathingly.

Jenyfer couldn't agree more. They followed Ophine through an archway at the end of the hall, passing more cells, all of them empty. The wraith led them to a small door hidden at the end of the outer hall. Jenyfer stared in dismay at the lock, but Ophine simply clicked thin fingers and it tumbled free. Ordes' hand shot out, catching it before it could clatter on the stones.

'Not just a pretty face, are you?' Ophine said, then pushed open the door. The darkness in the narrow tunnel was so thick Jenyfer couldn't see anything at all.

'Where are we?'

'Between your father's realm and my master's,' Ophine answered. 'You will hear things the deeper we move into this space. Ignore them all. If you follow those voices, you will be lost here and not even Ankou will be able to find you.'

Jenyfer swallowed, reaching behind her. Ordes closed his fingers around hers.

'We will cross a bridge of stone, over a pit of fire,' Ophine told them.

'Why are you helping us?' Ordes asked.

Ophine's chuckle drifted back to them. 'By all means, faery, you're free to go back.'

They walked in silence for some time, their surroundings never changing, until Jenyfer felt heat. Ophine led them around a corner and they emerged from the darkness to find themselves standing at the edge of a deep ravine. Flames danced below them, and the heat was so intense Jenyfer felt the moisture flee her skin. Wordlessly, Ophine moved towards the bridge of stone that would let them cross the pit, cloak shifting in the wafts of mind-numbing heat that floated up at them.

Jenyfer swallowed. The One God's Pit. It was *real.*

'Don't look down,' the wraith instructed.

They moved onto the bridge in single-file, Jenyfer sandwiched between Ophine and Ordes. The bridge was narrow, with chunks of stone missing in places. Heart in her throat, Jenyfer kept her eyes straight ahead, following Ophine, shifting as the wraith did to avoid the places where the bridge was dangerously slim.

As they neared the centre of the bridge, the voices began.

Voices urging them to throw themselves into the pit, to throw each other into the pit, to run, to flee, to join them, join them, *join them.* Voices that promised power, glory, and everything anyone could ever desire. Voices that issued warnings – don't trust the wraith, trust us. We know what you want, Jenyfer. We know what you are. We know what you fear. You can trust no one but us.

On and on the whispers went, and even when they had left the bridge behind and had stepped once more into a dark tunnel, Jenyfer was convinced they were lost until, eventually, watery light appeared above them. Jenyfer held her breath, fingers feeling along the wall.

A ladder, cut into the stone.

'Climb,' the wraith ordered.

'You go first,' Ordes said, his voice oddly shaky. Jenyfer nodded, knotting her skirts around her thighs awkwardly. The ladder sloped gently, each step taking her closer to the light. She could hear the ocean smashing against rocks, could smell the briny scent of the sea, and her magic surged, giving her a burst of strength. Heart hammering, she emerged into a world bathed in sea-spray and a cloud-streaked sky. But it was the sky, the real sky. She tipped her face to it and sighed in relief, then took in her surroundings. She was standing amongst a scattered assortment of rocks, some as big as cottages, others nothing more than tiny pebbles, but it wasn't the rocks or the fresh air that made her heart soar.

The ocean.

Water stretched to all corners of her vision, dazzling and dark beneath the cloudy sky.

Ordes emerged next, blinking, and then Ophine appeared, the wraith somehow paler in the real world. Ophine scowled at the light, pulling the hood of the cloak higher so it dropped over their face. Only thin, colourless lips could be seen.

The light revealed something else, something Jenyfer had not noticed about Ophine in the dark, watery world of Lyonesse. 'You have scales,' she whispered. They were small and delicate, scattered around the wraith's jaw and neck.

Ophine's lips curled into a small smile. 'You have much to learn.' The wraith glanced up at the sky again. 'I have to go. I have done all I can. You will have a head-start, at least. That was what my master wanted.' The smile fell. 'They will come for you. Perhaps not yet, but they will, I can promise you that.'

'What do we do?' Jenyfer asked. Ordes had wandered away and was peering over the edge of the cliff. Ophine nodded in his direction.

'The faery has worked it out,' they said.

'Thank you,' Jenyfer whispered. 'I don't know how to repay you.'

The wraith was silent. Slowly, they reached out a skeletal hand and touched Jenyfer's cheek. 'Stay alive. Change is coming, and it might not be what you are expecting. Swim, sister,' they said, and then they were gone.

Jenyfer hurried over to where Ordes was standing, her head spinning with more questions, but they would have to wait. Below them, the ocean beckoned, waves rolling against the base of the cliff and sliding over rocks. Jenyfer's song purred away beneath her skin as she suddenly understood. She stepped back and stripped off her dress, tossing the hated thing away, sighing as the salty wind brushed her flesh.

She felt Ordes look at her.

'I'm still mad at you,' she said.

'I'm not thrilled with you, either.'

Jenyfer nodded and peered over the cliff again; her skin prickled as her scales jumped to life. 'Do you trust me?' she asked. Then, 'No, don't answer that.'

'I trust you, Jen,' Ordes said without hesitation. 'With my life.'

'I don't know where we'll end up – that will be up to my magic,' she said. Her song purred in anticipation. 'Don't hit any rocks. I'll go first.

Ordes caught her hand. 'We go together.'

Jenyfer nodded.

As one, they dove from the cliff top to plunge into the welcoming arms of the sea.

CHAPTER 48

Arthur's dreams were damp, full of water and music. He had expected to find himself in the Fisher Queen's cave, but instead he was standing on top of an island of rocks. The waves slammed against the shore, spray coating his face and catching in his hair. There were bones on this island, he realised with a shudder.

He had no idea where he was, where his dreams had brought him this time. The sky above him was dark with storm clouds, and the wind was so fierce he had to shield his face with his hand.

The music continued, growing louder.

The fingers of Arthur's other hand were wrapped tight around something hard and firm. He glanced down. He held the Sword of the White Dragon again, but it was so heavy he could not lift it.

The music paused, and then rushed forward, melodies tumbling over one another, the low notes vibrating through the stones at his feet, pushing through the soles of his shoes and into his body. Those notes rattled his bones and curled around his organs and the Sword of the

White Dragon grew heavier. It was not happy. It did not want to be here, wherever here was.

The ocean was all around him and, as he watched, the waves stilled and the water began to creep over the rocky shore, a tide rising inexplicably fast. Swallowing, Arthur glanced around, spying a pile of rocks in the middle of the island. They were high. Surely the sea wouldn't rise that high?

The sword was leaden. He had to drag it along the ground, the scraping of metal against rock blending with the music and hurting his ears anew.

'I'm sorry,' he told it, sensing its displeasure at the treatment. Wind pulled at his hair and clothes, grabbing at him, trying to force him back towards the water. Panic rose in Arthur's throat. The sword was so heavy, too heavy, but he could not leave it behind. The water was rising faster; the place where he had just stood was now covered in a dark ocean, still as glass. He knew he'd be able to see his reflection in it if he looked.

The sword did not want to move anymore.

Arthur tried to free his hand, but his flesh was stuck to the hilt.

The water continued to rise. It crept over his ankles; when it soaked through his trousers to touch his skin, the music rose to a terrible crescendo, piercing and drilling into his head, but he could not cover his ears.

Water reached his knees.

Can I drown in a dream? Arthur wondered.

Suddenly, the water stopped. It lay around him like a sheet of glass, reflecting the sky and the purple underbelly of the storm clouds.

Something moved in the watery mirror. Arthur frowned.

A woman's hands. Scales licking her skin. Slowly, her face was revealed. Dark hair, pale skin, more scales, and eyes like the ocean.

Jenyfer.

'Jen!' he called, but she could not hear him. 'Jenyfer!'

Another face appeared. The man with the silver eyes. Arthur's magic twitched beneath his skin and he frowned. He did not recall having magic in any of his other dreams.

'Hey!' Arthur called. 'I see you!'

'They can't hear you,' said a voice.

Arthur jolted, stumbling back, using the sword for balance, not wanting to fall into the strange, dark water.

A figure wearing a hood was standing in the water with him. He could not tell if they were male or female, or neither. The voice spoke again. 'You should not be here.'

'Where is here?'

'Between the worlds, King Who Shall Be.' The voice was raspy, light.

'How do you know me?' he asked.

'You should not be here,' they repeated, then looked towards the sky. Arthur caught a glimpse of a skeletal face as the wind increased. 'He is coming for you. He should not be here, either,' the creature added with a slight shake of the head. 'Fool. Always has been a fool.'

A gentle splash. The water shifted around Arthur's legs.

'We need to go,' Jalen commanded.

'How are you in my dream?' Arthur asked, his heart swelling at the sight of the storm demon.

Jalen was not looking at him. His eyes were on the mysterious figure in the cloak. 'This isn't a dream – not really, anyway. Come.'

'But—' Arthur objected.

Jalen shook his head, reaching up to touch Arthur between the eyes, and Arthur was hurtling backwards, tumbling over and over, until he slammed back into his bed, head spinning and stomach churning. He groaned.

Jalen was sitting up, watching him, a frown on his face. It was light outside – morning.

Arthur blinked, then sat up, gasping as his dream images swirled and shattered and then reformed into two faces. 'We need to get them out of there!' he said breathlessly. Then, 'You brought me back? Where was I?'

'Lyonesse,' Jalen said softly. 'And I should not have done that, but I had to.'

'But how—never mind. Who was that creature?' Arthur asked. 'The one in the cloak. Were they real?'

'Very real. That is Ankou's servant, but also the least of our problems at the moment,' Jalen said with a sigh, climbing off the bed and pulling on his clothes. 'Jenyfer and Ordes should not be there, either.' Jalen's face was worried.

'Ordes? That's his name?' Arthur asked urgently. Jalen's mouth twisted, as if he'd said something he wasn't supposed to, but Arthur pushed it aside. 'We have to go and get them.'

Jalen ran his hand over his face, his frustration evident. 'You don't understand … They are in Melodias' realm, and Melodias *cannot* get his hands on you. He cannot find the Treasures.'

'Then we do nothing?'

Jalen shook his head. 'I didn't say that. The Master of Songs and Death isn't a threat to me. He has no power over me,' he added in a low, scathing voice that Arthur had never heard before.

Arthur scrambled off the bed, hunting for his clothing, chewing his lip as he dressed. 'I thought the Old Ones had, well, control over you.'

Jalen shook his head. 'Regardless of which one of them created us, we can choose our allegiance. I gave mine to the Witch of the Mists many, many years ago. Ankou was rather unhappy with me for that, but that doesn't matter. Niniane is the only one who can command me to do anything.' He paused. 'Except you.'

'Me?'

'Yes.'

Arthur took a deep breath. 'Will you go to Lyonesse?'

Jalen kissed him, although his eyes were worried. 'Anything you ask.'

Katarin rested her elbows on the railing, peering over the edge into the water. The ocean was smooth, the water so clear she could see the sand below. Small, silvery fish darted in and out of *The Excalibur's* shadow. She glanced over her shoulder to where the sails were limp. The sun was directly above them, and the sky was free of clouds.

'This ship hates me,' she said with a sigh. They'd been dead in the water for two days, and not even Katarin's magic would make *The Excalibur* move. She couldn't communicate with the ship the way she could *The Night Queen*. Kat rubbed her eyes. She missed her ship. She missed her crew. Tymis' men were alright, she supposed, for a bunch of human sailors. They worked hard, and they had followed her instructions without complaint. She hadn't learnt all their names yet, and wasn't sure she would, not knowing how long this ship would be hers.

Tahnet sighed and rested her hands on the railing. The blonde woman gave Katarin a faint smile, looking out to sea. Tahnet's arm was finally free of the sling she'd been wearing and Kat watched her flex her fingers gingerly.

'Better?' she asked.

'Getting there.'

'I guess the chocolate is helping,' Kat said with a smile.

Tahnet scoffed, then gasped. 'Kat, out there,' she said, pointing. 'Is that …'

Katarin frowned. On the horizon, where the ocean met the sky, something moved. She squinted. 'I can't tell what it is,' she said.

'Iouen!' Tahnet called.

The quartermaster hurried over, then shimmied up the rigging once Tahnet gestured to the horizon. 'Is it them?' she called, shielding her eyes from the sun as Iouen secured himself and removed a spyglass from his pocket, quickly lifting it to his eyes.

Katarin held her breath.

'It's them!' Iouen called, lowering the spyglass.

Katarin sighed in relief. Tahnet grabbed her hand and squeezed it, the act bringing a hot rush of emotion to Katarin's eyes. She blinked furiously.

'Sorry,' Tahnet whispered, eyes dancing with cheek. 'I don't think anyone saw.'

Katarin laughed, shaking her head.

'Should we go and get them?' Iouen asked. Before anyone could answer, wind ripped across the deck and teased the sails. 'What the ...'

Iouen's words were stolen by a whirlwind. The crew drew back with a collective gasp, making Kat smile. For the crew of a magical ship, Tymis' men were shit at actually dealing with magic. Kat kept her eyes on Jen and Ordes, watching as they dropped below the surface of the water. She did not turn to watch the storm demon materialise fully on the deck, did not acknowledge the whispered awe of the crew as they realised who, and what, now stood amongst them.

Jalen came to stand at her side as two dark heads emerged from the water, close enough now that Kat could see their faces clearly. Ordes grinned and waved. Laughing, she waved back.

'Took your time,' she shouted. Then, quietly to Jalen, 'Why are you here?'

'Arthur sent me,' he replied.

'*You* were going to go to Lyonesse because my brother asked you?' Katarin said quickly.

'I was going to go to Lyonesse because my *King* asked me,' Jalen answered snappily.

'Sailing a bit close to your maker, aren't you, demon?' Kat shot back. 'I hear Ankou still has the shits with you.'

Jalen scoffed, but said nothing, folding his arms, his jaw tight.

Katarin watched her brother's lover from the corner of her eye. Niniane's words swam through Katarin's mind. 'Tell me,' she said, her voice low, 'can demi-gods die?'

He didn't look at her. 'Are you threatening me, Katarin?'

'Not at all,' she rejoined, shifting her gaze to the water. 'But if you hurt Arthur, I will find a way to end you. That's a promise, demon.'

Ordes and Jen emerged below where Katarin stood. Jenyfer's face was milk pale. Ordes pulled her against him and, with the flick of his hand, conjured a wave to lift them both from the water. They landed on the deck, Jenyfer's knees giving out. She was naked, hair slicked to her body, scales shining in the sun, a brilliant mixture of blues and greens and silver. Without Katarin having to ask, someone brought a blanket and draped it over Jenyfer's shoulders.

The syhren's teeth were chattering, the skin around her lips blue.

'Is she okay?' Kat asked Ordes. The crew had gathered around them but stepped back as Ordes scooped Jenyfer into his arms. Her eyes slid closed, water dripping from her skin and hair.

'She ... I don't even know where we are ...' Ordes whispered.

'Off the coast of Carinya,' Tahnet told him quietly.

He shook his head.

'How long have you been in the water?' Katarin asked, looking at Jenyfer in concern.

'That's the thing.' Ordes looked up, meeting Katarin's gaze. 'A few hours.'

'How...' Katarin's eyes fell to Jenyfer again, and she suddenly understood. She stepped aside, indicating the deck. 'Welcome back, Captain.'

'Kat ...' Ordes began.

She shook her head. 'We'll talk later. There are clothes and whatever you need in the Captain's cabin. Don't argue, Ordes,' she added, then turned to the storm demon. 'Niniane needs to know they're alive and safe. And, demon,' she added, 'return when you're done. You can sail back to your King with us.'

Jalen nodded; the tightness in his jaw had not relaxed. Wind closed around his body like a hand and he was gone.

CHAPTER 49

Lamorna tied her hair back in a knot at the base of her skull. She knew it wasn't how people wore their hair here, but she didn't care. That morning she had woken with a longing to return to Kernou. She hadn't felt it so strongly for weeks, but now her belly churned with it. She found a coat to pull on over her dress. Her legs were often cold beneath her skirts, but she couldn't bring herself to wear pants like a man.

'Where are you off to?' Tamora asked as Lamorna seated herself on the end of her bedroll.

'We need water,' Lamorna answered.

Tamora nodded. 'I'm sorry I don't have a lot of time to spend with you, Lamorna,' she said, stirring an overly generous dollop of honey into her tea. 'I'm kept busy here, much more than I was in Kernou. At least here, I can work.'

Tamora was a healer and a midwife, or she had been before Kernou changed; but Lamorna could not remember the town being any different than what she had grown up in. She pushed away the unease that spread through her. It was different there now, she could not deny it, and wondered what else had changed in the time she had been away.

The Chif's – the One God's – mission sat heavy on her shoulders.

'Have you made friends?' Tamora was saying.

'Not really,' Lamorna answered as Keraine pushed the flap of the kibitka aside and strolled in, arms laden with wood for their fire. 'I mean, I have one, I suppose.'

Keraine, overhearing the end of the conversation, exchanged a look with Tamora.

'What?' Lamorna demanded.

Tamora's expression was filled with concern. 'Do you mean Mordred?'

'Is that a problem?' Lamorna asked, not looking up as she pulled her boots on. 'He's the High Priestess' son, the leader of the Inborn. A Magic Wielder. I thought you'd be pleased?'

Her aunt cleared her throat. 'He's very … experienced, Lamorna,' she said diplomatically.

'Experienced in what?' Lamorna asked lightly, lacing her boots. Her heart had begun to thunder and her body tingled. She swallowed, checking her laces with grave intensity.

'Don't pretend to be naive,' Keraine cut in. 'You know exactly what she means.'

Lamorna gave the other woman a dirty look. 'We don't all think of sex and … and … whatever else, like you, Keraine. Don't think I don't know what goes on when I'm not around.'

'Lamorna!' Tamora scolded, but Lamorna tossed her head and strode from the tent, collecting the water bucket on the way. Her cheeks were hot, and she wasn't sure what had angered her more – the suggestion that she thought about Mordred in *that way*, or the relationship between Tamora and Keraine; one that, now they were here, in a land buried deep in blasphemy, they threw in Lamorna's face.

At least that was how it seemed.

I have had lustful thoughts.

Lamorna paused, those words smashing into her, before she swallowed them away and stomped into the forest, heading for the stream, not caring how much noise she was making as she walked. She'd been told to be as silent as possible in the forest – Mordred himself had warned her about the things that lurked there – but she was too angry to care. Let them come, she thought fiercely. She was not going to be frightened of any faeries, even if they were creatures of the Beast. She would trust in the One God to protect her, to send any abominations back to the Pit from where they came.

She knew the way to the stream well by now. Lamorna scowled to herself, dropping to her knees beside the water. She had to admit, it was lovely here, with the clear water and the way the light caught on the surface of the stream and made it sparkle. Except, there was no light today. She glanced up at the canopy; a slice of dreary, grey sky peeked through, making her scowl deepen, before she let her face relax with a sigh.

The sooner she did what she had come here to do, the sooner she could return to Kernou and her life, whatever that was now. Perhaps the Chif would reward her? Lamorna dipped the bucket into the water. The moment she did, the stream stopped flowing. She paused, hovering over the edge, one hand gripping the bucket tight, the other balancing her weight on the smooth rocks that bordered the water.

The forest had stilled around her. Silence rang out, loud and ominous, and her heart sped up. She swallowed, still hovering, unsure of what to do, what was going on.

'You need to move back – slowly,' said a deep voice. Mordred. She hadn't heard him approach, and if she wasn't so frightened she'd demand to know why he was following her.

'Do as I say, Lamorna,' he continued, his voice tight, urgent. Swallowing, she moved backwards, dragging the bucket with her. When she was almost clear of the stream, something emerged from the water.

It was a horse's head, black and glistening. A pair of brilliant amber eyes stared at her. She blinked. The head moved closer. She was vaguely aware of Mordred behind her, his footsteps over the forest floor, and she knew she should get up, get away from this ghastly thing, whatever it was, but she couldn't move, caught in the power of its stare.

For a moment, nobody moved – she was frozen, the horse still staring at her and, without turning, she sensed Mordred had paused as well. The creature moved closer and from the water appeared a long neck. Lamorna had the urge to pet it, reaching out her hand. The horse inched its head nearer and she stretched out her fingers. She could nearly touch it!

There was a voice in her head, telling her to jump into the stream, telling her to climb on the horse's back, to ride. Lamorna had never ridden a horse, but she desperately wanted to ride this one.

Just before her fingers touched that silken black nose, Mordred was there. He pushed her away roughly and she fell with a cry, slicing her hand on something sharp on the ground. The pain of it broke whatever spell she had been under. She gasped, scurrying backwards, eyes wide, terror flooding her throat as she watched Mordred. He was standing in the water; he spoke words in a language she didn't recognise and the horse … the horse glared at him before sinking back beneath the water. Lamorna swore its eyes flashed bright green just as they vanished below the surface.

She made a little sound in her throat. Mordred climbed out of the stream and hurried over to her, kneeling at her side.

'What was that?' she whispered, unable to take her eyes off the water – which was now flowing like it usually did. She should find the bucket.

Mordred gave her a little shake, his fingers like claws, digging into the soft fleshiness of her upper arms. 'Lamorna, focus on me.'

She did. His face was worried. She wanted to touch it, not realising she actually had until he grasped the hand she placed on his cheek.

'You're hurt,' he said, examining her palm. The cut was shallow, but she sat still while Mordred tore a strip off the bottom of her skirt and bandaged her hand. 'You're lucky I came along when I did,' he said, sitting back and running his eyes over her, as if checking for other injuries. 'You just met the colpach – a water horse,' he explained. 'If you'd have climbed on its back, you wouldn't have been able to get off and it would have drowned you.'

Lamorna shuddered. 'I want to go back to the village.'

He nodded, standing and offering her his hand. She let him pull her upright; she staggered a little, and he slipped his arm around her, holding her steady. Lamorna was too shaken to be embarrassed, to think about how improper it was that he was touching her. She sagged against him, pressing her face into the firm muscle of his chest, his skin so warm—she pulled back, realising what she hadn't even noticed before.

He wasn't wearing a shirt.

She swallowed and went to step away, but he trailed his finger down the side of her face, gently tracing the curve of her cheekbone. Her skin burnt where he touched her.

'No one has ever told you that you're beautiful, have they?'

Pleasure seeped into her before she quickly tried, unsuccessfully, to squash it. Her belly twisted and she was twitchy. She knew she should push his hand away, or move out of his reach, but she didn't. 'Vanity is a sin,' she said, her voice low.

He chuckled. 'Is it really?' His finger moved along the line of her jaw then up, hovering over her lips. 'Would you like to know what my lustful thoughts were?'

She needed to step away from him, but she stayed where she was.

'Has anyone ever kissed you before, Lamorna?'

'No. Desires of the flesh are—'

'I know,' Mordred mumbled. 'Sins. Let me tell you what I was thinking the other night.' His finger touched her bottom lip and she jumped as sparks shot through her veins. 'These lips should be kissed. They *deserve* to be kissed. The One God would not have made your lips so pleasing if He didn't want them to be shared with another, would He?'

Lamorna's heart was thundering so loudly she knew he could hear it. She swallowed, throat tight; slowly, she shook her head, then frowned. 'I don't know.' It was a whisper escaping in a rush of air. She didn't know. What he said made sense, but then ...

She could feel Mordred's eyes on her face but would not meet his gaze. His finger remained on her lip and it carried the weight of the whole world. Slowly, he traced the outline of her lips, first the bottom, then the top.

Her mouth opened a fraction. She wanted to speak, but there were no words. The world narrowed to the gloom of the forest around them, the sound of the water trickling over rocks, the horror of the water horse niggling at the back of her mind; then, everything faded away and there was nothing but the suddenly warm air and the sweat that had gathered on the back of her neck.

Nothing but Mordred's eyes.

'I'd like to kiss you,' he whispered. His breath touched her face – he was so close to her, closer than any man had ever been. Closer than anyone had been for a long time.

'Can I kiss you?'

Lamorna closed her eyes. Her belly was tight now, burning, that heat slowly spreading through the rest of her body until she felt like every part of her was on fire. This was what it must feel like to be in the Pit with the Beast, she thought. For a moment, she could feel the flames on her flesh as they began to devour her, to consume her for her lust and perversion, for wanting this forbidden moment.

'Can I kiss you, Lamorna?' Mordred asked again.

Some deep part that she had never acknowledged thundered through her, so strong and savage in its desire. It wanted to know what it was like, just once. That part that she had been taught was wicked and sinful – it wanted to *know*.

It can't hurt, she thought guiltily. *It's just a kiss. Just one.*

Before she could change her mind, Lamorna nodded.

Fear flooded her as Mordred gently curled his palm around her cheek, sliding his finger beneath her chin so he could tip her face towards his. She kept her eyes closed and held her breath while butterflies assaulted her stomach and her blood burnt; she was slowly melting when he hadn't even kissed her yet and then—

He did.

His lips were soft, softer than she'd imagined they'd be. He touched them to hers lightly, so lightly it was like a whisper, a cloud passing over her mouth for the briefest moment.

She didn't know what to do, so she remained still, but her hands itched to touch him, to know how warm his skin was, to run her fingers over the swell of muscle carved from his upper arm.

Mordred stopped kissing her. Lamorna frowned.

'Again.' The word escaped her lips without consent as that wicked part of her rose up and took control. He chuckled low in his throat, then pressed his lips to hers again, harder this time, one of his arms snaking around her back.

He didn't pull her into his body – she went willingly, falling against him like a leaf shaken from a branch. His fingers dug into her lower back; the strength in them made her gasp against his lips. His tongue swept inside her mouth, filling her with fire that shot right to the core of her body, making her tremble in his arms.

She wound her arms around his neck, pushing herself onto her tiptoes; he was so much taller than she was, but she needed to be closer as her body shuddered and burnt and melted.

Gently, he broke away from her. She sighed – in relief, in wanting – making him laugh softly and rest his forehead against hers.

'Now,' he whispered, his breath fanning her face. 'You've been kissed.'

'Yes,' was all she could say. 'Yes, I have.'

They continued the nightly prayer sessions and Lamorna continued to pass over her letters. Mordred did not try to kiss her again, and part of her was relieved. The other part was burning and writhing and waiting, waiting, waiting for him to do it again. On the third night after the kiss, when they'd spent close to an hour sitting facing one another, Lamorna reciting the Word, Mordred's deep voice chiming in every so often, her thoughts strayed, shaken and tumbling over one another. This time, it was her who did not close her eyes to pray. This time, it was her who watched him.

This time, the lustful thoughts were hers.

'I have a confession to make,' she whispered when Mordred finally opened his eyes, the silent prayer he'd been engaged in over.

His eyebrows rose. 'What is your sin?'

'Lust,' she breathed. Some bold, foreign part of her held his gaze.

He stared back at her and, slowly, his lips curled into a smile. 'How would the One God punish this sin of yours?'

'I don't know,' she said. 'How do you think he should punish me?'

That smile deepened, and something wild and wicked entered his eyes. 'If the One God was truly wanting to punish you, he'd remove the object of your lust so as not to tempt you anymore.'

'He would,' she agreed. The butterflies in her stomach were flapping, flapping, flapping with burning wings. She took a shaky breath and went to move back, to remove herself from the temptation, but his arms closed around her before she could back away.

Slowly, gently, he urged her forward, closer until, still kneeling, she was pressed against him. Her breathing was ragged, throat dry. She licked her lips, looking up at him, and then he was kissing her again, those strong fingers threaded through her hair, tugging and drawing a moan from her lips, the twinge of pain combined with pleasure sending a heady rush through her body, straight between her legs. Mordred continued to kiss her and she kissed him back, not caring that she barely knew what she was doing, not caring that he was more experienced in this than she was. All Lamorna wanted in that moment was him.

Each night from then on, they spent less time at prayer and more time kissing – just kissing – but every time a new part of her body would tingle. She was soft and feverish and wild and relaxed. She ached and ached to touch him, to have him touch her in places she had never even touched herself; but each time he would kiss her, and nothing more.

It wasn't enough.

Chapter 50

Jenyfer's fingers trembled around the mug of warm tea she held. She had not been allowed out of bed, so she was smothered in blankets while everyone else was gathered around the desk in the Captain's cabin. Part of her was cross at the mothering, but the other was happy to be warm and dry.

Katarin was sitting in Tymis' chair, her booted feet up on the desk. Her eyes slid to Jenyfer and away again, and Jenyfer didn't know what to think about that. She hadn't asked Ordes about the crew of *The Night Queen* when he'd arrived in Lyonesse, not wanting to know the details, not wanting to know who was dead and who had managed to survive, to acknowledge the role she had played in the destruction of the ship and, therefore, the loss of Kat's crew. But she couldn't ignore it anymore. She resolved to speak to Katarin about what had happened the night they were attacked. She needed to apologise, even if she didn't know what was going on.

Aelle was absent, Jenyfer realised suddenly, and it hit her. Aelle had stuck to Katarin like a burr; for the fey woman not to be here ... she took a gulp of her tea, the hot liquid scalding her throat. She managed to cough twice before Ordes was there. Scowling, Jenyfer batted his hands away.

'I'm fine,' she hissed.

His face creased up, but he said nothing, returning to the table where a map was spread out. Jenyfer swallowed another mouthful of tea, trying to wash away the taste of guilt. While those syhrens had hold of Ordes, she couldn't think for the fear that gripped her and, behind that fear, riding in on a wave, was anger and a savage desire to protect him. She hadn't realised what it was she was feeling at the time but now, she knew instinctively what it was.

The heartfire.

She sighed, turning her attention to the tall man leaning against the wall near the window with his arms folded and a frown on his face. He was familiar to her, but she couldn't place him. Katarin told him bluntly to stop sulking.

'You can leave if you wish,' she said. 'I'm sure Arthur is missing you as well.'

The man ground his teeth, making Katarin smile smugly. She removed her feet from the desk and unrolled a map, laying it out over the other one with a dramatic flourish.

'I told you to give that to my parents,' Ordes said, frowning.

Kat shot him a look. 'I did. This is a copy. I thought it might be useful to have more than one, which was a good idea, considering ...' Her voice trailed off, eyes sliding to Jenyfer once again.

Jenyfer cleared her throat. 'Is Arthur in Cruithea still?' she asked. When Kat and the man nodded, Jenyfer set her tea to the side. 'Then that's where we're going?'

'Yes,' Kat said. 'Unless there is somewhere else you'd rather be?'

'Kat,' Ordes warned. She waved him away with a sigh.

'It's alright.' Jenyfer climbed off the bed, keeping the blanket wrapped around herself, and padded across the timber floor to stand by Ordes' side. The ship rolled beneath them. She let her eyes move over the map. 'Has anyone worked any of this out?'

'No,' Katarin answered.

'Melodias called it a bargaining chip,' Jenyfer said softly.

The blonde man's voice was low and coloured with anxiety when he spoke. 'What did he say to you? Melodias? Did he tell you anything?'

'He said there were sides to whatever is going on here. He said he hadn't chosen a side yet.' Jenyfer paused, watching his face closely. Her song niggled at the back of her brain. The tightness to his face, the tension she could see in his jaw, puzzled her. Ordes was frowning as well but, when no one spoke, Jenyfer went on, shifting her attention to Katarin. 'You're practically Niniane's daughter. Are there sides, Kat? Is there something else going on that we don't know?'

'Yes.' It was the man who answered. 'The Old Ones don't exactly have a shared vision of what the new world will look like.'

'Isn't that Arthur's choice?' Ordes asked. 'That's what the prophecy says – the Once and Future King shall see the land healed. Isn't that what that means? The bit about healing?'

The man nodded.

He was handsome, his jawline strong and sharp, and there was something in the way he stood ... He met Jenyfer's gaze and she realised where she had seen him before. 'You were a fisherman in Kernou,' she said. 'I know you. I mean, I saw you sometimes.'

'I was,' he said. 'Well, I was pretending to be, anyway.'

Kat scoffed. 'This is Jalen, the storm demon your town used to leave offerings on the beach for.'

'You don't look like a demon,' Jenyfer said, hiding her surprise.

Jalen's smile was tight. 'What does a demon look like, anyway?'

'What sort of world do you think Arthur should build?' she asked him. 'I mean, if you're the demon of storms, you're hundreds of years old. You would have seen the world as it once was. Is that what Arthur should want? A world where magic rules?'

'Is that what your father wants?' Katarin cut in, her voice cool. She sighed, sitting forward, elbows on the desk, her eyes on Jenyfer's. 'Can we trust you, syhren?'

'Of course you can,' Jenyfer said, surprised. 'I know I made a mistake but—'

'Can we?' Katarin cut in sharply. 'I mean, you've spent some quality time with daddy dearest and—'

'Kat,' Ordes said sharply. 'Enough.'

Kat sat back, holding up her hands in surrender. 'Alright. I was just asking.' She turned her gaze on Jalen. 'So, are you going to tell her? What the world was really like when ruled by magic.'

'I thought you'd know the stories,' Jalen said.

'I want to hear them from you,' Katarin said firmly. She rolled up the copy of Jen and Ordes' map, revealing a map of Teyath beneath it. Her eyes found Jenyfer's again, then slowly moved around the table. Katarin trailed her finger along Teyath's coastline, passing Kernou, around the southern tip, skirting the Pearl Coast, before moving north again, towards Malist. She paused for a moment, and then kept going, her finger tracing the many islands of The Teeth; here she stopped again, her eyes flicking to Jalen's, before she moved her finger to Cruithea.

'Tell them,' she said, 'of the things that once existed in this world.'

Jalen sighed; the look he gave Katarin was an angry one. 'Magic has two sides,' he said. 'Light and darkness, and from those two sides the fey creatures of the world were born. I'm a demi-god, only new to this world, really, compared to some of the things that no longer exist.'

'They exist,' Katarin mumbled.

'The point is,' Jalen said. 'As magic left the world, as belief in magic changed, the world changed as well. Not the world you see – the rivers and the mountains, the forests – but the world beneath that world. Before I was what I am now, the forests and the seas were full of creatures we did not have names for. They were beautiful and terrifying and powerful, but now they are gone.'

Ordes tapped his chin. 'And if magic rules the world again?'

Jalen shrugged.

Katarin was watching him carefully. 'Which side are you on, Jalen?'

'I'm not on any side,' the demon shot back. 'I will support whatever Arthur decides.'

Jenyfer slept, and woke, and slept again, finally waking feeling more alert than she had in days. The ocean outside the window was painted with the golds and reds of dawn. Ordes was up and dressed, standing near the desk with his arms folded. His attention was on the map, and Jenyfer wasn't sure which one he was looking at.

She was about to clear her throat to let him know she was awake but his gaze found hers.

'Morning.'

'Morning,' she whispered back. They stared at one another. Jenyfer could feel his heart, strong and steady; she could also feel his hurt. 'Where did you—'

'In the chair.'

'You didn't have to do that.'

'Didn't I?' he mumbled.

Jenyfer sat up, pushing the mass of her hair over her shoulder. Her stomach was tight, muscles curled in on themselves, but she could feel everything starting to fray around the edges, like an old rope about to give in. About to let go.

Ordes had walked into her father's realm for her, even when he didn't know if she truly cared for him or not. He let himself be captured so he could find her. But he did all that without knowing if they would ever get out of there. It was the biggest risk anyone had ever taken for her. Destroying Andromache's watery rendering of Bryn had shaken something loose in Jenyfer – more than her magic. Where she had been tied up in knots, angry and hurt and broken, she felt calmer, more resolved. She would never forgive Bryn for what he did and what he let himself become, but she could forgive Ordes. She could stop punishing him for caring about her. For loving her.

'I'm sorry,' she said. Ordes' eyes snapped to hers. 'I'm sorry for pushing you away. None of it is your fault. I understand that now. You weren't the one to hurt me. You've been patient with me – I just hope you'll continue being patient with me while I work it all out.'

Jenyfer rubbed at her eyes. They burnt, almost as much as her heart. 'Besides my aunt and my sister, no one has ever …' Her voice trailed off. Bryn's face dropped into her mind. She swallowed and shoved it away, but could still see it, like some terrible emotional after-image. Ordes was watching her. He hadn't moved. He was so still, like he was carved from stone. But inside, he was like glass. Fragile and breakable, and Jenyfer knew that glass part of him was cracked.

Jenyfer took a deep breath. 'Thank you for coming to get me. I know I said it before, but I mean it. I want you to know I mean it.'

'I do,' he said quietly.

She managed a smile. He smiled back, a small smile, but it was enough. 'Let's go to Cruithea, find Arthur and … I don't know. Work out what to do next, I suppose', she said. 'I wish I knew what my father was going to do with our map. I can't imagine him out and about in the world searching for Treasures – I get the feeling he doesn't like to get his hands dirty.'

'He has an army for that,' Ordes muttered.

'Have there been any sightings of syhrens? Ophine told me they would come for us – for me, anyway,' Jenyfer said, breathing a sigh of relief when Ordes shook his head. She wrapped a blanket around herself and went to stand by the window, running her hand along his arm as she went, unable to help it, even though her head – and her heart – were a mess. They stood close together, not touching. The ocean sparkled in the morning light, golden tongues licking the hull of the ship.

Ordes shifted his weight. She glanced at him, then back to the ocean.

'What did you hear? When we crossed that pit of flames?' His voice was low, worried.

'Just whispers. Nothing important. What about you?'

'Whispers,' he replied. 'But … and this is going to sound crazy, they knew who I was. They said my name, and they told me … they told me I belonged with them.'

Jenyfer nodded. 'Ophine said they would try and confuse us.'

Ordes was silent; his arms were folded, his face tense.

'Have you ever been to Cruithea?' she asked. Before he could answer, someone pounded on the door and Iouen's voice rang out.

'We're here, lovebirds. Ready yourselves. Katarin said to tell you it's a two day walk from the harbour to the village, so get your boots on.'

Jenyfer groaned, moving away from the window and beginning the search for the clothes Kat had left her. As she pulled a coat from the floor, she stopped. 'Ordes, is this yours?'

It was a book. Old, battered, the title barely readable, the gold leaf long worn away. Jenyfer scooped it from the floor, frowning. It wasn't very thick and, as she held it, it vibrated in her hands and a faint melody floated through her brain. Ordes peered over her shoulder as she ran her fingers over the title text. 'I can't read it,' she said. 'I don't know this language. Is it from Avalon?'

'Commonly we call it the language of Avalon but, really, it's the language of the Old Ones,' Ordes answered. 'Tymis taught me to read it when I was a kid. The title says, *The Otherworld*. It's not my book, or my father's. I have never seen it before.'

Jenyfer stared at it, heart pounding, then flipped open the cover, dismayed to see all the text was in the language of Avalon. 'I can't read this!'

'I'll teach you,' Ordes offered.

Jenyfer set the book on the bed with a sigh and continued the hunt for her clothes.

CHAPTER 51

It was nearing dusk, but they weren't meeting in the forest today.

The One God's Word echoed through her mind but, for the first time in her life, Lamorna ignored it. She didn't even care if anyone saw her. With her fingers threaded through Mordred's, she let him lead her into the warmth of his kibitka, let him sweep her into his arms and carry her across the floor towards the bed. She didn't look at it, didn't want to think, so she kissed him instead, making him laugh and his footsteps stumble a little.

She liked his laugh. It made her feel warm inside, warmer still that *she* was the cause of it.

But those feelings slipped away when he set her gently on his bed; she found she couldn't look at him, studying her hands clasped tightly in her lap.

She shouldn't want this, but she did.

Mordred knelt on the floor at her feet, his hands resting on her knees. 'Lamorna.' His voice was soft and warm. 'Look at me, please.'

She did, unable to resist the pull in his voice.

The flecks of gold in his eyes shone in the lantern light. She wanted to touch him, so she reached out a trembling hand and ran her fingers down the side of his face. 'I'm alright,' she heard herself say, but she didn't know if it was the truth or not. 'I'm alright,' she repeated, stronger this time. He nodded, then sat back on his heels to remove his shirt.

Part of her wanted to look away, but it didn't stop her staring at him, at the lines of ink that decorated his flesh, the hard muscle of his chest and arms, the broad shoulders and strong neck. She let her eyes drift lower, over the sculpted stomach. The sharp outline of his hips was visible through his trousers and—

Lamorna closed her eyes.

She knew nothing about being intimate with a man. It was something she never imagined she would experience. She had no idea what she was supposed to do, how she was supposed to feel, whether the warmth spreading through her – that had been spreading through her for weeks – and her short, sharp breaths were normal or not.

'You can look at me,' Mordred said softly. She sensed him stand, heard his fingers move over material, a shuffling, muffled, and then, 'I want you to look, Lamorna.'

She swallowed before she slowly opened her eyes again.

He was completely naked before her.

'I want you to see what *you* have done to me,' he said simply.

She couldn't look at his face when he spoke. She couldn't take her eyes off his body, off one particular part of his body that she realised she didn't even have a name for, because she had never spoken about it. She knew the mechanics of what was about to happen, because even though they weren't supposed to talk about it, women did; usually in hushed voices after prayer circle – and Lamorna had listened while pretending not to. Looking at Mordred, though, she couldn't begin to understand *how* it worked.

'Do you want to touch me?' he asked.

Lamorna shook her head. She did, but she was afraid, so terribly, terribly afraid, even though her body was burning and the place between her thighs was aching, pulsing with an urge she also could not name, an urge that frightened her.

'Come here,' Mordred said, the words a gentle order. She swallowed and stood, but did not move closer. He came towards her, taking her face between his hands and kissing her, and kissing her, until she was gasping and had put her arms around him, clinging to him. He kissed her as he undid the laces on the front of her dress, sliding the material from her shoulders until she was bare-chested.

He dropped to his knees again, easing her dress over her hips and down her legs, until it pooled on the floor at her feet. Then, he stood and stepped back, his eyes moving over her naked flesh, his gaze making her burn and tremble and want to cover herself. No one was supposed to see her body like this, not even the man she married.

When she went to hide her breasts, Mordred caught her hands and shook his head. 'You're beautiful. The One God knew what He was doing when he made you,' he murmured, then scooped her off the ground.

Lamorna didn't have the chance to reply, because he was kissing her again and lowering her to the bed, his body covering hers; she felt so small, so fragile, beneath the bulk of him. He kissed her jaw, then his lips were on her throat. She could feel his teeth nip at her skin and it made her gasp and arch her back, her body moving without thought, the flesh between her legs throbbing, her belly heavy and hot with anticipation.

Mordred kissed his way down her body, making her blush as he caught first one nipple, then the other, between his teeth. Just as she was about to tell him to stop, because it was too much, he kissed her belly, her hips, and then, she bit her lip to stop from crying out in shock. Any shame she'd been feeling about being naked in front of him vanished as he continued to do whatever it was he was doing between her legs. She didn't even know this was something people did! And how it felt! She moaned, then clapped her hand over her mouth.

'You're allowed to feel,' Mordred said from between her thighs. 'Pleasure is not a sin, Lamorna. It's one of the greatest gifts we've been given. The ability to feel,' he paused, pressing an open-mouthed kiss to the spot that had been burning and aching, making her cry out, 'is something to be revered, not shamed. The body, *your* body, is to be worshipped. Do you understand?'

'Yes,' she breathed.

'Then I'm going to continue to worship it,' he said simply.

She nodded and let her head fall back onto the pillow, biting her lip until her hips were moving on their own and sparks were dancing behind her eyes. But it wasn't enough. She wanted more.

When she said so, her voice low, unrecognisable, laced with desire, he positioned himself over her, reaching between their bodies to slide his fingers inside her. When she began to writhe and gasp he removed his fingers, keeping his eyes on her face. She waited, panting, her chest rising and falling, her body burning and tingling. Then, Mordred covered her body with his again; slowly, gently, he pushed himself inside her, a little bit at a time, and she closed her eyes against it, the stretching and burning, the stab of pain.

Soon, though, it floated away and she was swept up in a great wave that sent her barrelling over the edge of something completely outside of her control as he moved, pulling out of her then sliding back in, so strong and steady, his hips never faltering, his breath in her ear, her name on his lips. Lamorna was neither here nor there, nothing but a heartbeat inside a cage of flesh and bone, nothing but pleasure and more pleasure washing over her, flooding her until she completely lost who she was.

Lamorna slept and when she woke, curled in the blankets, it was to find Mordred watching her. She stared at him, not knowing what to do or say. The reality of what she had done threatened to sweep her away – the shame of it! – but then she remembered what he had said, about her body, how it should be revered, worshipped.

No one had ever said that about her before. She had never been told she was beautiful, had never considered for one moment that anyone would find her desirable or pleasing. She wasn't supposed to think those thoughts about herself. Even so, she felt warm inside, like something was buzzing in her belly.

As she lay there, Lamorna glanced around the kibitka so she didn't have to look at Mordred. His kibitka was much larger than the one she shared with her aunt and Keraine. There were animal skins on the floor, spotted deer by the look of the hide, and a small table and several chairs set to one side, no doubt where Mordred took his meals or conducted whatever business a Cruithean warrior general did. In the lantern light she could see he had an area for washing, with a large metal tub and a washstand, not unlike the one in her cottage in Kernou, and the floor in Mordred's kibitka was not bare earth. Instead, beneath the hide was timber – another thing that told her how important he was.

But he didn't believe that. She knew that, even if he hadn't said it.

'I should probably go,' Lamorna whispered finally. She didn't want to leave – she wanted to stay curled against him all night and wondered whether that would be possible, but her aunt would no doubt come looking for her. And, she realised with a little jolt, Tamora would know exactly where to find her. Lamorna stared up at the ceiling, at the intricate crisscrossed wooden poles and domed centre, the crown partially open, acting as the chimney for the wood-burning stove extending through it. The kibitka was still warm, but the fire in the stove had burnt down to nothing.

Magic, she realised with a shiver.

Mordred tucked a length of hair behind her ear. 'Although I'd much rather you stay here with me, it's probably best if you go back to your kibitka.'

Lamorna cleared her throat. His head was propped on one elbow, tattooed skin shining golden in the light from the lanterns set on the desk. He was beautiful, and fierce, and wild; and she wanted to tell him, but she didn't know where to start. 'I ...'

He kissed her gently on the mouth. 'Go,' he whispered. 'I'll see you tomorrow.'

She nodded and slipped from the bed, feeling his eyes on her naked body as she found her clothes and dressed quickly. She gathered her cloak under one arm, her boots in her hand. Heart thundering, she glanced at him before leaving – he was still watching her, smiling. She gave him a little smile in return and ducked out into the night.

He'd been gentle with her but still, the place between her thighs burnt and throbbed. Despite the pain that pinched at her as she walked, Lamorna smiled widely, her face hurting with it. She couldn't remember the last time she'd smiled like that.

It was chilly, the air wrapping around her to burrow beneath the thin layer of clothing she wore. She snuck through the camp as quietly as possible. As she came around the edge of a kibitka, she found herself face to face with a man not from the village. She gasped, her hand flying to cover her mouth. He tipped his head to one side, studying her with interest, and she knew how she must look – wild hair, no shoes, clothing bundled in her arms.

'Well,' he said, at the same time she recognised him as the pirate from the market in Kernou. A grin crawled across his face. 'Looks like someone bent you over their knee.'

Lamorna blushed, then reminded herself she had done nothing wrong. She lifted her chin, trying to think of what to say as, behind him, a voice rose from the darkness, sharp and full of shock.

'Lamorna? What are you doing here?'

The pirate stepped aside and Lamorna was looking at her sister.

They had moved from the shadows between the kibitkas into the wavering light of the cooking fire. Lamorna could feel the pirate watching her, his strange, silvery eyes on her face. His hair was long, messy curls brushing broad shoulders. She stared back, wondering at him, and when he reached up to tuck his hair behind his ear, she gasped, catching sight of the pointed tip.

'He's a faery,' she whispered, more to herself than anyone else, but Jenyfer smiled.

'He won't hurt you, I promise,' she said. The pirate's eyebrows lifted sardonically.

Lamorna could not remember his name. Her head was spinning. Jenyfer was different, so very different to the last time Lamorna had seen her – right before she was tied to the stake and given to the ocean. Jenyfer was as fierce as ever, but there was something else, something that Lamorna could not put her finger on.

She watched Jenyfer and the pirate, the way their eyes moved between one another, as if they couldn't help it. The way his body was angled toward Jenyfer's ... Lamorna stifled another gasp, now having some understanding of how things between men and women worked.

They were lovers. Bryn had told the truth.

'Where have you been?' Lamorna asked, her throat tight.

'Where have you been?' Jenyfer retorted, then threw her arms around Lamorna's neck, almost knocking her to the ground. 'I thought you were dead.'

'I ... thank you,' Lamorna whispered. Jenyfer pulled back to look at her in surprise. Lamorna held her sister's gaze. 'I know what you did, and I know that's why I'm alive. So, thank you.'

Jenyfer looked like she'd say something, but she just swallowed, gripping Lamorna's hand tightly. There were *scales* on Jen's temples, shining delicately in the firelight. Lamorna wanted to touch them, but Jenyfer frowned, her eyes sweeping over Lamorna's body. 'Why are you half-dressed?' she asked as she pulled Lamorna to sit with her by the fire.

The pirate chuckled and Lamorna was glad of the half-darkness so they couldn't see her heated cheeks. She said nothing, avoiding Jenyfer's eye. Eventually, her sister asked after their aunt. 'I'm assuming she's here. I can't imagine you travelling all the way here alone. What happened in Kernou?'

Lamorna pulled her hand free. 'Too much to explain right now. I'll go and get Tamora. She'll be happy to see you.'

'Don't wake her – it's late,' Jenyfer said gently.

The pirate stretched long legs out towards the fire. 'Who's in charge here anyway?'

'That would be me.'

All heads turned as the High Priestess stepped into the light. Behind her was a red-haired woman with an irritated expression. Despite the masculine clothing she was wearing, she was one of the most beautiful women Lamorna had ever seen; but no one bothered to introduce her. The High Priestess' eyes swept over Lamorna quickly, as if she was unimportant, nothing to be bothered with. Normally it didn't bother her, but tonight it did. Lamorna clenched her hands into fists that she kept hidden beneath the cloak bundled in her lap. Morgause's gaze moved over the pirate's face as the red-haired woman muttered something.

Lamorna waited for Morgause to say something sharp and scathing, and then nearly fell over when the High Priestess of Cruithea *bowed* her head towards the pirate.

'Born of the Myrddin and the Goddess of Magic,' Morgause said, never taking her eyes from his face. 'A child of prophecy. We are ready.'

Lamorna's head spun. The Witch of the Mists was his mother? Did that make him a god? She shook her head slightly. No, there was only the One God. The pirate was nothing but her sister's lover, a fey thing. Dangerous and to be watched. Lamorna swallowed. She had not lost sight of her mission, regardless of what she had done.

'For what?' the pirate asked, those unnaturally-coloured eyes narrowed in suspicion.

'To teach you, of course,' the High Priestess replied. 'To guide you in becoming what you need to become.'

He shook his head.

'Ordes,' Jenyfer said softly. That was his name, Lamorna remembered.

He tossed Jenyfer an irritated look.

Morgause nodded at Jenyfer. 'We have prepared for your arrival as well. Now all three of you are here, things can begin. But,' Morgause added firmly, indicating Jenyfer and Ordes were to stand, 'we will discuss this in the morning. We have a kibitka ready for you. If you would follow me.'

'Wait …' Lamorna began.

'Tomorrow,' Morgause affirmed.

'If you don't mind,' Jenyfer said softly. 'I'd like to stay with my family.'

Lamorna saw something cross the pirate's face and wondered if she had made a mistake in her assumption. Morgause simply nodded, and then she, Ordes, and the beautiful red-haired woman dressed like a man disappeared into the night.

Jenyfer turned to Lamorna. 'Now, we can talk.'

CHAPTER 52

Lamorna led the way through the maze of tents. Jenyfer followed her silently, noting all the things that were different about her sister. Lamorna walked differently; in Kernou, she had taken short, sharp steps, like she was always in a hurry. But here her stride was loose, more casual, longer, and her hair – Jenyfer could not recall the last time she saw her sister's hair free. Even when she slept, Lamorna had kept her hair bound in a plait so tight no strands escaped.

And she was barefoot … and half-dressed.

Jenyfer bit her lip.

What else has changed? She wondered as Lamorna stopped briefly in front of a simple tent at the edge of the village. She glanced at Jenyfer over her shoulder, but Jenyfer caught her arm before she could go inside.

'Lamorna—'

'I've been walking,' her sister said, keeping her voice low. 'I couldn't sleep.'

Jenyfer nodded; she knew that tone, the urgency in it, the worry. 'Alright,' she said softly.

Lamorna was looking at her. 'Are you really a faery?'

'Yes,' Jenyfer said. 'I'm a—'

The tent flap was thrown open and Tamora appeared, long red hair tumbling over her shoulders. Her eyes found Lamorna first, her expression one of deep worry. 'There you are! Where have you been? We've been worried sick. I was about to go searching—' she broke off abruptly, noticing Jenyfer. 'Jenyfer?' she whispered.

Jenyfer didn't know where the rush of emotion came from, but suddenly she was crying, and Tamora folded her in her arms and held her against her chest, making little shushing noises, her hand on the back of Jenyfer's head. Wordlessly, she led Jenyfer inside, making her sit by the fire and pressing a mug into her hands. Tea.

'I'm fine,' Jenyfer managed, as another voice cut through the darkness.

'Did you find her?'

Jenyfer glanced in the direction of the voice as Tamora hurried to light the lanterns. A head of dark hair popped up from the bedclothes. 'Hello, Keraine,' she said softly.

The other woman's face registered her shock, before she smiled and sat up.

'They're lovers,' Lamorna whispered in her ear.

'I know,' Jenyfer whispered back. 'I've always known – suspected, anyway.'

'And you didn't tell me?' Lamorna's voice dripped with annoyance, making Jenyfer smile. She had missed her sister. She had missed Lamorna's snark, her disapproval of everything in the world. Despite their differences, they were family. Tamora was watching them both, her expression conflicted, and Jenyfer knew she wasn't sure where to start: quiz Lamorna on where she had been, and with whom, or choose Jenyfer.

'I'm alright,' Jenyfer said, drawing her aunt's attention to her. Lamorna looked like she needed a moment to get her story, whatever it was, straight.

'I can see that,' Tamora said fondly, settling herself near the fire. 'I knew you would be.'

Keraine had made her way out of bed. She carried a blanket with her, which she draped over Tamora's shoulders gently. Tamora reached up and squeezed her hand; Jenyfer sensed Lamorna look away.

'Jen—'

'Me first.' Jenyfer set her tea aside. 'What happened in Kernou?'

Tamora sighed, rubbing at her face, and then told Jenyfer about the increased hold the Chif had on the town. She spoke about accusations and burnings, of people fleeing town, as they had done. When she got to the part about the Red Hand of God, she faltered.

'Bryn is a member,' Lamorna said.

Jenyfer swallowed away the memory of him. 'I see.'

'He says you made Alric stab himself with your magic. Alric died,' Lamorna said, while Tamora scolded her, but Jenyfer nodded.

'He tried to capture me in Port Leore. He'd hurt Ordes ... he was going to hurt me, so I did what I did,' she said calmly, although her heart lurched. She had not thought about the Konsel man's fate, only what she had done. 'I didn't know he'd died. I didn't want that to happen.'

'You did what you needed to do,' Keraine said. 'Don't apologise for it.'

'You would say that,' Lamorna muttered.

'Have you been with Tymis Merlyni since leaving Kernou?' Tamora asked, frowning when Jenyfer shook her head. 'Then where?'

'Avalon,' Jenyfer said – Tamora and Keraine sucked in a breath. Then, her voice low, a whisper, 'I met him, Aunty. I know you told me to stay away and I did, but ...'

'Who?' Lamorna demanded. 'Who are you talking about?'

Jenyfer took a deep breath. 'The Master of Songs and Death, the God of the Seas.'

'You went to Lyonesse?' Tamora asked sharply.

'Not by choice.' Jenyfer explained the attack on *The Night Queen*, and everything that happened while she and Ordes were under the sea, leaving out some details she hadn't reconciled with herself. 'But we escaped him, and now, here I am.'

'Jenyfer,' Tamora breathed. 'Oh, Jen. I'm sorry I didn't tell you. I couldn't, because if you knew—it was your mother's wish that you didn't know, not until you were ready, and she was my sister. I had to honour that, for her, but also for you, because Melodias …'

'I know,' Jenyfer said. 'And I understand. I'm not angry, Tamora.'

Lamorna was practically bouncing where she sat. 'Will someone tell me what is going on?'

'You're my sister, Lamorna. My family and I love you,' Jenyfer said. 'But your father, the man who died at sea, was not my father.'

'What?' Lamorna gasped.

'My father is Melodias. The Master of Songs and Death,' Jenyfer said. Lamorna stared at her, the hectic colour that had been painted on her cheeks when Jenyfer first saw her bleeding away. Lamorna opened and closed her mouth, before scrambling to her feet and racing out into the night. Jenyfer stared after her in dismay.

'She will need a moment to process that,' Tamora said. 'She won't go far.'

Jenyfer nodded. Keraine cleared her throat, reaching over to touch Jenyfer's knee. 'Let me make you a bed. There isn't much room here, but we shall find somewhere.'

'Thank you,' Jenyfer whispered. Her eyes drifted to the tent flap, ears straining, listening for Lamorna, waiting for her to come flouncing back inside.

But she didn't.

Lamorna didn't care that she was sitting in the dirt, or that her feet were bare and her hair a wild tangle down her back. She had spent the rest of the night in the forest with nothing but the trees and the night animals for company. It had been freezing and she hadn't slept, too busy shivering and worrying at every creaking branch and padded footstep she heard. She had felt things watching her and the tang of fear had been sharp in her mouth. She could still taste it, even though the sun was up and light glinted through the treetops.

Scowling, she picked up a stick and dug at the ground, poking and driving the stick deeper and deeper until a worm appeared. Lamorna paused, staring at it for a moment, wondering at the strange, segmented body, before she drove the point of her stick through its fleshy softness. The worm did not make a sound, though it twitched and writhed; she couldn't remember if worms had voices or feelings. Did it even know what she had done to it? She had heard once that if you cut a worm in half it would not die, but regenerate and where there was one worm, there would be two.

She didn't know if that was true and couldn't recall who had told her.

It was Jenyfer, she remembered suddenly.

Lamorna stabbed the worm again, and again, until it had stopped moving.

Footsteps crunched over the leaves behind her, but she did not turn around, nudging the remnants of the worm aside and resuming digging at the ground.

'Your aunt has been looking for you,' Mordred told her softly.

Lamorna said nothing.

'I've been looking for you.' He eased himself down beside her, sitting cross-legged. She stole a glance at him, barely able to believe it had only been last night that they had … she turned away, looking out over the forest instead. 'You've made quite a considerable hole, Lamorna.'

She shrugged, then tapped her stick against her shin, enjoying the sharp sound it made against her bone, the tingle of discomfort she got from it.

'Your sister—'

'She isn't my sister!' Lamorna snapped, whipping around so she could glower at Mordred through narrowed eyes. 'She's a faery! And she lied

417

to me! They all lied to me – my whole life. I bet even that nasty Keraine knew the truth.'

Mordred did not look away from her anger. 'A faery isn't such a bad thing, Lamorna.'

'She's a syhren,' Lamorna shouted, the volume of her voice startling her. The One God did not permit women to raise their voices, and she had raised hers a lot since being in this wicked place. A bird took flight from the trees above them, lifting into the morning air in a flurry of wings and protesting squawks. 'The God of the Seas or whatever he is is her father. I heard them talking about her being part fey – why didn't I realise what that meant?' she added to herself.

Because you're an idiot, the little voice whispered.

'Are you sure that's what she said?' Mordred asked slowly.

Lamorna nodded furiously. 'She's been in Lyonesse, with … him.'

'Melodias,' Mordred murmured, and Lamorna scowled. She had not told Mordred about what had happened in Kernou, and what had happened afterwards, things she could barely remember, so she told him now, letting the words spew out of her, not looking at him as she spoke, worried he would not believe her. She told him about being in the darkness, where it was damp and filled with music, and she told him what the Chif and the Konsel had done to her.

Slowly, Mordred lifted her skirt; his fingers stroked the scars on her knees gently. 'I had wondered about these. I'm sorry. They should not have done that to you.'

Lamorna nodded, shoving her stick viciously at the ground. 'She isn't my sister at all.'

'You survived Melodias, and Lyonesse, Lamorna. Not many people can make that claim. That makes you, and your sister – sorry, not-sister – very interesting indeed,' Mordred said simply. He moved a little closer to her, until he could press his arm against hers, and her skin flamed at the touch. Lamorna heaved an exasperated sigh, letting her cheek rest against his arm. 'Did your not-sister come here alone?'

Lamorna lifted her head to look at him in surprise. 'You don't know?'

'Know what?'

'Jenyfer came with a pirate, from *The Excalibur*. His name is Ordes, and your mother was happy to see him,' Lamorna said. Mordred's expression hardened. 'She said the Witch of the Mists was his mother.'

Mordred's lips twitched but he neither smiled nor frowned. His face was impassive, but Lamorna knew he was thinking. She had learnt that about him; when he was thinking, he became very still.

'Who is the Myrddin?' she asked.

Mordred looked at her then. 'Where did you hear that name?'

'Your mother spoke it. She said Ordes was the Myrddin's son as well. Is that important?' Lamorna asked, running the tip of her finger down Mordred's arm. The longer he sat near her, the more she wanted to touch him and feel his body against hers again.

Mordred caught her hand, lifting it to his mouth so he could kiss it. 'Do you believe in prophecies, Lamorna?'

'No,' she answered. 'I don't believe in anything that is not part of the One God's Word.'

He gave her a wry smile. 'The Myrddin is a prophet. Many hundreds of years ago, he spoke four prophecies and—'

'Wait,' Lamorna interrupted. 'Hundreds of years? That isn't possible.'

'There is much about the world you do not know,' Mordred said sharply. 'You're so willing to believe in a god who is not what you think he is, but you are not willing to accept magic and faeries and prophets when they appear before your eyes?' He chuckled and shook his head, leaning over to plant a kiss on her forehead. Lamorna pulled away from him, stung; he reached out and smoothed her tangled hair from her face. 'I like you like this – feral and wild. Like you're part of the forest.'

She batted his hand away. 'What are these prophecies then?' she demanded. 'Everyone talks about them but no one has ever told me what they are.'

'Your aunt never told you?'

'Maybe, when I was small, but I don't remember,' Lamorna said, turning from him and picking up her stick again. She did not poke it into the ground, but clutched it between her fingers tightly. She wanted to ask what he meant, that the One God was not what she thought, but she didn't, biting her lip instead. She would ask later. Mordred rested his hand between her shoulder blades, and she let him. When he spoke again his voice was low.

'For the serpent to become the dragon, it must consume itself and be reborn. Three sets of hands upon the stone, one set of hands to pass alone. A song shall sing the Red Ones home, forever entombed in the House of Bone; and, the last, Only on Camlann Field, will the red dragon yield, and the Once and Future King shall see the land healed.'

Lamorna was very still, the words worming their way inside her. Had she heard them before? She closed her eyes, digging through the pieces of her mind, searching for anything about dragons and stones and Kings. Deep inside, in a memory she had made herself forget, there they were, but in her mind, those words were full of music and the never-ending drip of water.

'Lamorna?'

She shook her head. 'You believe these prophecies?'

'Yes,' Mordred said.

'But what do they mean?' she pressed.

'Change,' Mordred responded.

CHAPTER 53

Ordes had half-hoped Jenyfer would find her way to his bed after seeing her family. He hated that he knew she wouldn't, hated that he had even thought she might, and hated that he didn't see in her eyes all the things he was feeling, the things he knew she would be able to see in him when he looked at her. He had ignored his mother's warning, Kat's warning, and he kept the truth from her – and it had reared up and bitten him on the arse, not caring that he'd done it to protect her from the truth of it, to let her choose to love him or not.

She'd chosen now.

Ordes rubbed the fuzziness of sleep from his eyes as he glanced around the kibitka he had been given. It was much larger than was necessary, but he'd been too stunned to object when the High Priestess had escorted him inside. She had called him a child of prophecy, as Melodias had.

Whispered words from the pit of flames raced into his head.

The one who is born between the worlds shall bear the weight of them both.

Even demons knew the prophecy.

Ordes sat up swiftly.

His father had said he was born on the edge of the lake in Avalon. Niniane had confirmed it.

'A foot in both worlds,' Ordes mumbled. 'What the fuck does it mean?'

This was more than finding some Treasure.

The flap of his kibitka trembled, and then Jenyfer stepped in; seeing him still in bed, naked, she bit her lip, then frowned, taking in his expression. 'What?'

'Nothing.'

'There is someone you have to meet,' Jenyfer told him softly. 'He found me just now, on my way here.' She didn't wait, slipping back outside and leaving him to dress.

When Ordes stepped into the muted green light of the forest, his head a scrambled mess and his heart slowly burning his insides to ash, there was a young man with messy, bark-brown hair and soft green eyes standing with Jenyfer. He was tall and lanky, not much muscle on his frame, and his smile was nervous, hesitant in a way Ordes could understand.

Jenyfer made the introductions but Ordes knew exactly who was standing before him without having to be told. His magic hummed and purred and filled him with warmth. 'So, you're the saviour of the world.'

Arthur Tregarthen's face paled, as if he'd heard those words before. 'Please don't call me that,' he said quietly, then suggested they find somewhere to sit, somewhere more private to speak. Ordes hadn't noticed until then, but a small crowd had followed Arthur and were watching him, their faces eager.

'Your admirers, I take it?' Ordes said.

'Unfortunately, yes,' Arthur mumbled, glancing over his shoulder. 'Come on.'

They followed Arthur through the forest, ducking beneath low hanging branches and untangling themselves from the claws of bushes with little white flowers, until they found a small clearing large enough for the three of them to sit.

Ordes stretched his legs out, bumping into Arthur and almost tripping Jenyfer, who was pacing awkwardly in the small space, her head narrowly missing a branch. 'Sit down,' he murmured. 'You're making me dizzy.'

She shot him a look but did as he asked, plonking down next to him. Close, but not close enough; she tucked her knees up to her chest, then sighed in irritation, stretching her legs out across Ordes' thighs. His hands automatically came to rest above her knees. Her eyes brushed his face, but when he went to move his hands, she stayed the movement and shook her head; a tiny gesture, but it made him smile.

Arthur was looking back the way they had come, as if checking that they hadn't been followed, before he sat as well, tucking his knees up to his chest, his long legs awkward in the small clearing. He held Ordes' eyes for a moment, before his gaze shifted to Jenyfer, and his face collapsed. 'I wanted to help you, when they locked you up, but I couldn't risk it. I'm sorry.'

'There's no need to apologise, Arthur,' Jenyfer answered softly. 'It's okay.'

'It isn't,' he argued, shaking his head. 'What my father did, is doing, is wrong. He's got everyone under his thumb, even Bryn. I thought I could get through to him. I thought he'd help you.'

'You asked him to help me?' Jenyfer's voice was nothing more than a breath.

Ordes' hand tightened on Jenyfer's leg, a silent promise that there would be retribution for all that had happened to her.

Arthur nodded. Then, softly, painfully, 'I could tell how scared you were when ... I could feel it. I'm—'

'You don't need to apologise for that either, Arthur,' Jenyfer interrupted. 'It wasn't your fault. I'm not going to judge you because of the way your father behaved – you were as trapped in that place as I was. Your cage was different, but a cage all the same.'

They spoke no more about Kernou and the things that had gone on there. Ordes studied Arthur Tregarthen as subtly as he could, wondering about this young man, who couldn't be any older than his early twenties, and the role he was to play. Had Tymis known what sort of weight he would be throwing onto a then-unnamed man's shoulders? Had he known what sort of pressure he would be placing on the three of them when he made his prophecies? Arthur rubbed at the back of his neck, a nervous gesture that Ordes recognised, and he felt the overwhelming desire to apologise for his father's words and the tremendous burden they carried.

Arthur cleared his throat, sensing the scrutiny, and his eyes came to rest on Ordes' face even as his hands fidgeted against his knees. 'How long have you known about this prophecy?'

'All my life,' Ordes replied. 'But my part in it was kept from me until very recently.'

'I assume you're like me? Completely unaware and baffled by the whole thing?' Arthur asked Jenyfer, who nodded.

'I still don't believe it,' she muttered. 'What are we supposed to do with the Treasures when we find them?' She glanced at Ordes. 'If we can find them.'

Arthur frowned, reading something in their expressions. 'What do you know that I don't?'

Jenyfer shifted uncomfortably. 'I'm assuming Kat has told you everything by now, so you know where we've been, and with whom,' she said, and Arthur nodded. 'My father told us the Treasures were guarded by ancient and powerful fey beings who might not want to hand them over.'

'And that was as forthcoming the Master of Songs and Death would be,' Ordes added. 'We don't know who or what they are, or even where they are – they could be anywhere on the whole continent.'

Arthur, the Once and Future King, put his head in his hands and groaned.

'You're not alone in that feeling,' Jenyfer said softly. 'When I left Kernou, I could never have predicted any of this would have happened and I can't help but feel it's because of me that it is happening now. If I hadn't ...'

'Your sister would have died, Jen,' Ordes said gently.

'I know,' she mumbled; her fingers closed over his, and he ran his thumb over the back of her hand, feeling the delicate scales there. 'But, it's done and I can't change it. I guess we have to see this, whatever it is, through. Do you know which Treasure is yours?' she asked Arthur.

'The sword,' he mumbled. 'I keep dreaming about it.'

Before anyone could say anything else, footsteps crashed through the forest. Ordes' hand dropped to his hip, but he'd left his dagger behind. His magic danced over his knuckles instead. He could feel Arthur watching him.

Katarin came bursting into their hiding spot. 'Well, this is cozy. Do you know how hard you were to find?'

'That was kind of the point, Kat,' Arthur said.

She laughed, then sketched a bow. 'Apologies, your Majesty.'

Arthur scowled.

'I have a message for you, Ordes,' Katarin announced. 'Aunt Morgause says you're to visit the Temple. Tomorrow. You're going to learn how to use your magic. You might finally be useful for something,' she added cheekily, before stalking away, cursing when the tails of her long coat got snagged on some branches.

They reluctantly climbed to their feet and followed Katarin, who was waiting for them near Ordes' kibitka. She and Arthur left, walking close. Familiar with one another. Ordes watched them curiously.

'She's his sister,' Jenyfer said softly.

'Poor Arthur.'

Jenyfer's lips twitched; before she could leave, Ordes reached for her hand, drawing her close to him then, when she didn't resist, into the kibitka.

425

'I know you're angry – I'm angry – but I want you here, with me.'

Jenyfer sighed and rubbed at the scales on her temple. 'Lamorna ran off and didn't come back last night, after she found out about Melodias being my father. I need to talk to her,' she added softly, but didn't pull away from him.

'I'm going to the Temple tomorrow,' he reminded her. 'Whatever and wherever that is.'

'Are you scared?' Jenyfer asked.

'No,' Ordes said, shrugging. He ran his thumb over the back of her hand. 'I'm intrigued. And, okay, maybe a little worried. What if the Priestess is mean to me?'

Jenyfer raised her eyebrows. 'That's what you're worried about?'

Ordes laughed, then his smile faded and a frown pulled at his face. 'I'm worried something will change. That I won't be me when I come out.' The whispered words from the pit of flames still tugged at his mind.

'You'll still be you,' Jenyfer said quietly. She went to sit on his bed, glancing around the kibitka. 'Annoying and—'

'Charming and—'

'Gods-damned messy. You've been here one night, Ordes, and there's already clothes on the floor.'

'If I knew I would be entertaining, I'd have cleaned up,' he joked, watching her face carefully, seeing if she remembered those words, and the moment he'd said them to her in his cabin on *The Excalibur*.

Something flashed across her face, something he couldn't read fast enough.

'I'll see you when you get back,' she said, and then she was gone.

The morning air was crisp and smelled of the forest. Ordes wrinkled his nose. Wet earth, decaying leaves, animals – so very different to the smells of the ocean. He was surprised to see Arthur waiting for him outside his kibitka. With Arthur was a young woman with dark hair.

'This is Ethinne,' Arthur said. 'A Priestess of the Temple.'

'I'm still training,' she reminded Arthur. Then to Ordes, 'I'm here to escort you.'

The deeper they went into the forest, the more frenzied the butterflies in his stomach became. Or were they birds, swooping and pecking at his insides? Ordes thought he'd be sick. He had no idea what to expect, and he hated going into something blind. Even stepping through that portal with Kat on Lyonesse he'd had at least some idea of what he was going to encounter, but this ... the Temple was something he had read about, had heard about, but he still didn't know a thing about it or about the Priestess who he was going to meet.

Arthur walked quietly beside him. There was a calmness that radiated from him, a sense of quiet authority, untapped, like the man who would become a king had not realised it yet.

'Wait!' a voice called.

Jenyfer was hurrying through the forest towards them. Her hair was a mess, as if she'd just tumbled out of bed, and she was dressed in the Cruithean style in brown trousers and a close-fitting shirt. She carried a dagger at her hip and her face was tight with worry. Ordes didn't say anything as she caught up to them, just slipped his hand in hers. Her face relaxed and they continued walking until Ethinne stopped in a clearing.

The forest had grown deadly silent. There was no medley of insects or birds. Ordes saw no fey creatures, no animals either, and the absence of life sent a chill down his spine.

'We are here,' Ethinne announced, turning to face them.

Ordes looked around. 'We are?' There was also no sign of any temple. There was nothing but trees. She smiled at his expression, then bent to collect a stone from the forest floor. She cupped it in her palms and blew on it gently.

The ground beneath their feet shifted and the air in front of them shimmered.

'You might want to step back,' Arthur told Ordes and Jenyfer as Ethinne placed the stone on the ground, her hands moving through the air before her. Slowly, the fabric of the forest shifted, a ripple passing through it. The stone shuddered and then grew and unfolded, spilling to cover the ground as a building took shape, pulling itself together from the ground up, until it reached above their heads.

Ordes gaped. 'What the …'

Jenyfer's breathing was thick. 'This is—that's incredible!'

Ethinne turned to Ordes. 'If you are who and what the High Priestess says, magic like you have never seen is yours to wield – and much, much more.' She stepped past them, reaching for the door to the temple, nothing more than a large slab of granite. At the touch of her hand, it swung open, revealing a dark hall.

Ordes turned to Jenyfer; her face was creased. 'Worried I won't come out?'

'No,' she murmured. Then, quietly, so only he could hear, 'I regret it.'

'Regret what?'

'What I said to you,' she whispered. 'In Lyonesse.'

'Well,' Ordes said softly. 'You'd better make me miss you. I could be gone for days.'

'You're an arse,' she said. But before he could kiss her like he wanted to, she gasped, staring into the trees, batting away his hands.

'What's down there?' she demanded, nodding at the forest.

'Trees,' Ordes suggested. Her grip on his hand tightened.

'The Ossuary,' Ethinne said softly. 'The House of Bone.'

'The House … of Bone?' Jenyfer whispered. 'What is that?'

A song shall sing the Red Ones home …

Ordes sucked in a breath.

'When the Red One was banished and the people of Cruithea turned from her, those who would not give up their devotion chose to leave Nimus Arbores. They have lived in the Ossuary, in the Dead Woods, ever since,' Ethinne explained.

Jenyfer took a step towards the treeline.

'Jen?' Ordes squeezed her hand; she jumped. 'What is it?'

'I can hear music,' she whispered.

Ethinne eyed the Temple. 'You have to go, Ordes. It will not wait for you – *she* will not wait.'

'Right,' he said. Jenyfer was pale; she trembled in his arms. He kissed her gently, folding her against his chest. He met Arthur's eyes and the other man nodded at the silent request.

'Come on, Jen,' Arthur said. 'I'll walk back with you.'

She nodded, letting herself be drawn away from Ordes. He gave her a smile, and then turned and followed Ethinne into the darkness, his blood tingling. As soon as he stepped inside the Temple, his magic started dancing and twirling and tugging at him. The Priestess did not speak again, nor did she light their way with any torch or magic, the soft fall of her feet the only guide Ordes had. Even his fey senses did not cut through the darkness. The air was chilled inside the temple, and the smell of damp earth was stronger the deeper they went.

The hallway stopped suddenly, opening up into a wide, square space. Torches sprang to life from sconces positioned along the walls. Waiting for them was another Priestess, her face draped in shadow. 'I am Goerika,' she said in greeting. Her voice was like the sea – gentle and rough at the same time, dripping with power. 'The Priestess of the World's Door.'

'Hi,' Ordes managed.

Goerika made a little noise of disapproval, but she turned to the other woman and bid her leave. 'Follow me,' she told Ordes. He did as he was told.

She led him into another dark corridor. 'You will stay here until you have mastered your gifts,' she said simply.

'How long will that take?' he asked.

'I do not know. That will depend on you.'

'I'd like to knock this over in a day, if I can,' Ordes responded.

She stopped, turning to face him. He couldn't see her face, but could feel her eyes crawling all over him. 'I do not think so.'

'How long then?'

'A week. Maybe more. You will stay here until then.'

'A week? In this place?' Ordes stopped walking and shook his head. 'You know what. I've changed my mind. I'm completely at ease without having mastered any gifts you think I might have.'

'You will stay here,' was all the woman said. 'Follow.'

CHAPTER 54

Arthur's head was full of words. The Green Knight's. Goerika's. The things Jenyfer and Ordes had told him about Lyonesse. Katarin's story about the loss of *The Queen* and people Arthur had known. He felt their deaths, absorbed his sister's silent grief and wished he could undo it.

More than anything, though, he wanted to get moving. He wanted to do something. There was a sense that everything was about to change and he was filled with restless energy. As the sun rose, Arthur crawled from his bed, leaving Jalen sleeping, and went in search of Halymere. Perhaps throwing a sword around for a few hours might help him still the turmoil in his head, help him be able to answer some of the questions that were digging at him.

When Arthur arrived at the communal cooking area, he was told Halymere was waiting for him in the space the Inborn used for training. He was given directions and headed off past the horse pens. He had never met Halymere in this part of the forest, and was still mulling over what it might mean when he entered a clearing.

Halymere was not there.

'I gave him the morning off,' Mordred said. Arthur's cousin was leaning lazily against a tree. His hair was bundled on top of his head, and his arms were bare, the warriors tattoos visible. Today, Mordred carried no weapons in his belt, but it was not a wooden practice sword dangling from one large hand.

It was a real sword, the steel glinting welcome in the morning light.

'It's about time you handled a real weapon.' Mordred nodded at the sword. Arthur could see another tucked in a scabbard his cousin wore across his broad shoulders. 'Take it.'

It was a challenge. Arthur swallowed, thinking back to the last time he and Mordred had stood across a clearing from one another.

Mordred must have been thinking about that moment as well. 'No magic,' he promised. 'Just this.'

'And what is this, exactly?' Arthur's heart was pounding painfully and he pushed a steadying breath from his lungs. There was no avoiding this moment. Arthur could see that in Mordred's face. To walk away from this would be to concede defeat in a battle he did not understand. Mordred did not move, he did not even blink as Arthur approached him and closed his fingers around the hilt. Mordred released his hold on the weapon; it was heavier than it appeared and Arthur tried not to let his surprise show.

'Let's see what you can do,' Mordred said. His expression was calm as he drew his blade; the sword hissed as it slid into the morning air. Mordred swung the weapon in a graceful arc. Arthur did not take his eyes off it as his cousin shifted his feet, finding his centre, letting his weight rest in his thighs.

Arthur copied his movements, keeping his breathing steady, trying to still the thunderstorm in his chest. All the moisture fled his mouth. He licked his lips, pushed another breath from his lungs, and hoped Mordred could not see his trembling hands.

'No two sword fights will ever be the same,' Mordred told him. 'Your inexperience may, in fact, save your life.'

'How could it possibly save me?' Arthur asked in disbelief.

'If you don't know what you're doing, you're less likely to overthink it – you're more likely to act on instinct,' Mordred explained. 'You're more likely to fight to survive.'

'Alright,' Arthur said. He lifted the weapon again, adjusted his grip.

'No,' his cousin barked. 'Forget what you think you know. If you need to fight to live, you can't spend time thinking. Until you master the sword, until it becomes an extension of your arm, of your will, let your instinct guide you.'

Arthur nodded. 'Instinct. Right.'

'Never had to fight to survive, have you?' Mordred said casually. He took a step closer, his sword raised slightly. Arthur did not take his eyes off it. 'Eyes on me, Arthur.' Mordred's voice was low, firm. 'Don't watch the weapon. Read my intent in my face.'

Before Arthur could read anything, Mordred struck, the sword swinging towards him with such speed he only just managed to step out of the way. Mordred said nothing, swinging the sword again, the weapon lower this time, aiming for Arthur's middle. Arthur stepped back again.

'You can't always get out of the way,' Mordred said. 'Defend yourself, or you die.'

'I am.'

'Sometimes, to defend, we need to attack.'

Mordred's next blow was high, the sword swinging in a downward cut; Arthur lifted his weapon. The blades clashed against one another, the sound echoing through the forest. Arthur kept his eyes on Mordred's face, and as Mordred prepared for his next attack Arthur thrust his sword forward, taking a step backwards at the same time, putting distance between them and forcing his cousin to parry the blow.

'Better,' Mordred commented, 'but weak. Your weakness will see you dead.'

'You don't know a thing about me,' Arthur said furiously. He lunged.

Mordred blocked the blow easily, coming in with a counterattack that rattled Arthur's bones. 'Let me guess – you've always done what you've been told. You've never broken the rules, never spoken out of turn—'

Arthur laughed. 'You think I didn't want to? You have no idea what would have happened to me if I did,' he replied, gritting his teeth as Mordred swung the sword at him again. A muscle twinged in Arthur's jaw as he dodged the blow.

'You're a puppet, Arthur,' Mordred snarled, and his anger made Arthur frown.

'I don't understand you at all,' he managed, blocking his cousin's next strike. He swept Mordred's sword out of the way, adjusted his grip and ignored the sweat sliding down the side of his face.

'Nothing but a puppet,' Mordred continued. 'Whose puppet will you be now? Who will be your master?'

'I'm my own master!' The words left Arthur's throat in a shout, and the sound of his voice, the volume of it, made him jolt. He could not remember the last time he shouted, or raised his voice even.

Mordred adjusted his grip on his sword. 'Prove it. Make your first decision.'

With gritted teeth, Arthur went on the offensive. He thrust and cut, over and over, his movements becoming more fluid as he went and, soon, he moved without thinking, deflecting Mordred's next strike, sweeping his cousin's sword out of the way again.

'If you wish to be obeyed, if you wish me or any man to obey you, you need to know how to command,' Mordred said. 'Could you do it, Arthur? Could you command someone to kill for you, to die for you, to turn themselves to dust for the world you want?'

'You and I have a different opinion on what a leader should be,' Arthur said. He waited, but Mordred did not attempt to strike him again. Arthur did not relax his grip on the blade. 'Why should I have to command anyone to do anything? Why can't it be simpler than that? If I have to command people to believe in me—'

'If you won't command people, how do you expect to lead them?' Mordred cut in.

'I don't know,' Arthur admitted. 'What would you do?'

'What needs to be done.'

'Which is?' Arthur asked. He drove the point of his sword into the ground, and ran his hand over his face, pushing the hair from his eyes. 'You're right. Everything you said before is right, Mordred. I *was* a puppet. I wasn't free to make my own decisions – I didn't have the courage to stand up for myself. But I do now,' he added. 'I don't know if I am the right person for this task but, for some reason, something greater than you and me and anyone here has decided I am. Am I supposed to ignore that?'

'How do you know for sure it's you?' Mordred asked. 'Because my mother told you so?'

'You think she's lying to me? That a goddess is lying to me?' Arthur said softly.

Mordred's gaze was shrewd. 'What did she in the temple have to tell you? I know you went there – everyone knows. They have taken it as one more sign that you are the King of prophecy, but I want to know what she said to you.'

'If you must know, she told me to trust my instincts, much like you just have,' Arthur answered. 'She told me ...' He sighed. 'She told me the Red One was not the one to betray the world.'

'Do you believe that?'

'I don't know what to believe when it comes to the Old Ones and prophecies. I'm only starting to learn who I am, Mordred.' Arthur hesitated, wondering if he should say any more. The world of magic and gods and prophecies was still so new to him, but to Mordred ... this was his world. 'She told me darkness and blood would come for me before the end.'

Mordred's face did not shift.

Arthur took a deep breath, and went on. 'When the battle is waged in the skies, in the seas and on the land, darkness and blood will come for you,' he said. 'They were her words. Ereshki is caught up in this somehow. The Red Ones, the House of Bone. I don't know what these things truly mean, but *you* do, Mordred. This is your world,' Arthur added. 'I'm a stranger to it.'

'The prophecy also mentions a serpent,' Mordred said slowly.

'For the serpent to become the dragon, it must consume itself and be reborn,' Arthur murmured. 'What does it mean?'

'Have you ever seen a snake shed its skin?' Mordred asked him. 'Do you know why they do that?' He didn't wait for Arthur to respond. 'As a snake's body grows, its skin does not, so it needs to rid itself of what no longer fits.' Mordred sank to the ground, sitting cross-legged. After a moment's hesitation, he gestured to the leaves, an invitation for Arthur to join him.

Heart hammering, Arthur sat.

'The serpent consuming itself – rebirth. Just like the shedding of a skin that no longer fits, if we want to be something different, something *more*, sometimes we have to consume part of ourselves in order to emerge renewed,' Mordred explained. 'Some believe this is about light and darkness, or the shadows within ourselves. Some believe the serpent consuming itself is a symbol of death.'

'Death?' Arthur echoed sharply. Goerika's words came rushing back to him.

Mordred's lips curled. 'Not literal death, but the death of part of ourselves. The shedding of a skin that no longer fits.'

'And the dragon?'

'Power,' Mordred said.

'It all comes back to power, doesn't it?' Arthur mused.

'Why should it not?'

Arthur was silent, his thoughts shifting to his father. Ulrian's quest for power had led him to do horrible things. It had changed him, stripped away any compassion he may have had in his earlier life. Arthur shook his head. He was not his father, and would never be, but he was still deciding *how* he was supposed to become a man that others looked to – a man who was capable of ruling over others. 'What is it you want, Mordred? From your life?'

Mordred was silent and, for a moment, Arthur thought he would not answer him, but his cousin sighed. 'I want more than what I've been given. Is that selfish? Perhaps. Your father's god would say it was, but I feel like I was put on this earth for *more*.'

Arthur smiled. 'I can understand that.'

'Can you?' Mordred said furiously; his anger made Arthur lean away from him. Mordred shook his head, frustration in every line of his body. 'We don't need soft rains and gentle skies, Arthur. We need thunder and power. We need a whirlwind to rip the world to pieces and shape it into what it should be.'

Arthur kept his eyes on Mordred's.

'We need a man who knows who he is, not a confused boy who is playing at being a man.' Mordred paused. 'When you can show me what sort of man you are, show me what sort of king you will be, and show me you can be the whirlwind, I'll bend my knee to you, cousin, but not before then.'

CHAPTER 55

Lamorna made her way through the forest, keeping her footfall light. She was not collecting water today. She was simply walking. She needed to clear her head. There were too many words in it, too many things she didn't understand, and she didn't like it. She didn't like being made to feel she knew nothing.

Mordred believed in the prophecies he told her about, and she knew he was smart, so if a smart man believed in them so passionately, did that mean they were real? Or was it like her and the One God? Was the strength of his beliefs nothing more than faith, like hers was?

Or had been.

Lamorna knew her faith had slipped recently. She had not forgotten her task, but it seemed less important than other things going on around her.

Like her sister being a syhren.

Lamorna stopped walking, chewing on her lip. Did it matter? Did it truly matter? She was still Jenyfer. She just … had scales.

Yes of course it matters, a voice whispered in her ear. *Syhrens are deadly. They are dangerous. They sing men to their death. That's probably how your father died. Yours, not Jenyfer's, because she isn't really your sister.*

'Shut up,' Lamorna muttered. 'Jenyfer saved me.'

Did she? the voice asked. *I thought she abandoned you to the darkness and music and water. I thought she abandoned you to the Master of Songs and Death.*

'Lamorna!'

Jenyfer's voice. Lamorna turned, watching her sister as she approached, her dark hair wild around her face. Jenyfer was light on her feet – she had always been that way, but there was something different about the way she moved now – like water, fluid and graceful. Powerful.

'Where are you going?' she asked.

Lamorna gestured vaguely at the forest. 'Just for a walk.'

'Can I come?'

'I suppose,' Lamorna said, and continued walking, not waiting to see if Jenyfer followed her. Her sister didn't try to speak to her, and Lamorna was both grateful and angry. Why hadn't Jenyfer apologised yet? Why had she taken days to approach her? Lamorna bit her lip, gnawing on it as they stepped their way over fallen branches and ploughed through the leaves. Well, she did. Jenyfer barely made a sound as she walked. No faeries would get her.

Because she is a faery, the voice reminded Lamorna.

'Shut up,' Lamorna hissed.

'I didn't say anything,' Jenyfer said.

'Not you,' Lamorna mumbled.

Jenyfer stopped, closing her hand over Lamorna's arm, halting her in her tracks. Jenyfer's hand was cool. Lamorna looked at it, her eyes tracing the pattern of scales that decorated the back of her sister's hand. Slowly, she reached out and touched them, unaware of what she was doing. They were soft.

'You didn't come back the other night,' Jenyfer said. 'Where were you?'

'I slept in the forest.'

Jenyfer made a little noise of surprise. 'You slept in a forest? All night? By yourself?'

'Yes,' Lamorna said, shaking her arm free.

'I never lied about my father, Lamorna – I didn't know. I mean, I knew I was a Magic Wielder, but everything else – it was as much a shock to me as it was to you.'

Lamorna nodded, although she didn't agree. They kept walking, coming to the stream where Lamorna collected water. She sat on the soft grass at the edge, but did not lean over to touch the water. Jenyfer eased herself to the ground beside her, and they sat in silence, like they used to in their cliff-top garden in Kernou. Eventually, Lamorna could no longer stand the quiet.

'What happened with Bryn?' she blurted. It wasn't what she wanted to ask, but it was the first thing that came out.

Jenyfer's face stiffened. 'I don't want to talk about that,' she whispered, and Lamorna sucked in a breath, the truth hitting her in the face and she didn't know why she didn't realise it before.

'He forced you, didn't he?' she said slowly. Mordred had asked to kiss her. He had asked her what she wanted. He had not forced her to do anything.

Jenyfer's cheeks coloured with anger. 'I didn't think it mattered,' she snapped. 'Isn't that what you said? That I had no choice but to obey my husband? That if he wanted to lie with me it didn't matter what I wanted?'

'I ...'

Jenyfer shook her head, tucking her knees up to her chest and resting her chin on them. Her face was hard. 'I hate him for what he did to me. When I saw him in Port Leore, I wanted to hurt him so badly. If Ordes hadn't been injured, I'd have let him kill Bryn. He said he would, if I asked him to, but until I saw Bryn standing there I hadn't truly thought about it.'

'And Ordes?' Lamorna asked. 'Is he …'

Jenyfer sighed, her face softening a little. 'It's complicated.'

'But you like him?' Lamorna pressed.

Jenyfer smiled. 'Yes, Lamorna, I like him.'

Lamorna picked up a fallen stick and poked the ground with it. She didn't like Jenyfer's tone – it was patronising, the sort of tone a mother might use with a child who didn't truly understand what was being talked about.

But Lamorna did know.

'I like someone too,' she said, sneaking a glance at her sister, looking long enough to register the surprise on Jenyfer's face, before she turned her eyes to the water.

'Who?' Jenyfer demanded. 'Someone from Kernou?'

Lamorna shook her head.

'Someone *here*?'

'Yes.'

Jenyfer was silent for a long time, and when she spoke, her voice was light, but Lamorna could hear the worry beneath it. 'Are you going to tell me who?'

Lamorna shook her head. She tossed away her stick, and climbed to her feet. 'I'm going to go back now,' she announced, brushing the leaves from her backside. 'I've never been further than this stream. The forest isn't really safe,' she added sternly, walking away. She heard Jenyfer scramble to her feet and follow, and her sister said nothing all the way back to the village; at the edge of the square, as people were beginning to gather for the evening meal, she grabbed Lamorna's arm again.

'I didn't think you …'

Lamorna tossed her head and freed her arm. 'Were worth anyone liking?'

Jenyfer's mouth dropped. 'No, Lamorna, that isn't what I meant.'

'Isn't it?' Lamorna snapped as that dark and vicious part of her that she'd been struggling to keep hidden rushed to the surface, riding in on a wave of anger. 'I think it's easier for you to think of me that way. Poor, stupid Lamorna, indoctrinated and brainwashed. Blind and ridiculous Lamorna. Who would ever care for her besides her god?'

Jenyfer's face collapsed, but before she could answer the whinny of a horse floated across the square. Lamorna turned, her heart jumping, then surging and tumbling off the tallest cliff as Mordred arrived on the opposite side of the cooking area. She wasn't sure what pleased her most – the horse, with its shining black coat and wild mane, or the sight of Mordred on its back.

His eyes found hers and he smiled.

Jenyfer looked between them, her expression tight, Lamorna's nasty words still branded there. 'Lamorna—'

Lamorna strode away from her, straight up to Mordred and the horse, not caring who saw her. She rested her hand on the animal's neck, surprised at the warmth of its skin, and the feeling of the muscle shifting beneath her fingers. 'Where are you going?' she asked.

Mordred had been watching Jenyfer, but he dropped his eyes when Lamorna spoke.

'I was going to patrol the borders,' he said, and it was then Lamorna noticed the daggers at his hips. She had the sudden urge to touch one.

'Can I come?' she asked.

'I'll be gone all night.'

'I don't care,' she said, stroking the horse, liking the velvet-softness of its coat.

'What if we meet someone there?'

'Like who?' she demanded. She could sense Jenyfer watching. *Let her work it out for herself*, the voice whispered.

'The enemies,' Mordred answered with a chuckle.

'Then you'll protect me, won't you?' Lamorna replied.

The leader of Cruithea's Inborn held out his hand for her. 'Of course.'

Lamorna put her hand in his and he pulled her up behind him, the horse standing patient and steady as she arranged herself and her skirt. If there was ever a day for her to wear pants, it was today, she thought, struggling with the thick fabric of her dress. When she was settled, Mordred nudged the horse forward, telling her to hold on to him. She did, resting her cheek between his shoulder blades, breathing deep the smell of him.

As they moved away, Lamorna glanced over her shoulder, searching the crowd.

Jenyfer was gone.

Lamorna rubbed at her backside. Mordred chuckled from where he was crouched near the fire he had made. They had ridden for ages and she had no idea where they were, or which direction the village lay. A shiver of fear shot through her – if Mordred were to leave, she would be lost. She'd die out here without him.

'Where are we?' she asked.

'The Hunter's Forest. The Nemhain mountains lie to the west and south of us, the Moon's Bite and the Greenstone Sea to the north, and Nimus Arbores to the east. Carinya is three days from here on horseback.' He smirked at her over the flames. 'Why? You want to run away together, Lamorna?'

Lamorna blushed and shook her head, wondering if she should say yes instead. When she didn't come home, Jenyfer would tell Tamora what had happened, and Tamora would know without having to ask.

Mordred held out his hand. 'Come here. I'll make you feel better.'

Smiling, she went, letting him pull her into his lap, his hands sliding beneath her skirt to squeeze her thighs. Lamorna sighed in relief. He kept going, massaging her flesh, his hands moving higher until they closed over her hips.

'Better?' he whispered.

Lamorna studied his face in the fire-licked darkness. He did like her, didn't he? She wasn't sure how to tell, and knew she could never ask such a direct question, not one like that, so she kissed him hungrily, hoping he could tell how much she liked him through her mouth.

'A little better,' she whispered against his lips, feeling bold and wicked. 'But I think you missed the aching part.'

'Oh? Is it a bad ache?'

'Terrible,' she breathed, as the heat from the fire made its way inside her.

'We can't have that,' Mordred murmured, making her moan and shift her thighs further apart as his fingers dropped to stroke the core of her body before they plunged inside her. Soon, she was lying on her back, the stars in her eyes, Mordred's weight covering her and a wave of pleasure washing over her as he drove himself into her, again and again, harder than he had before. She decided she liked feeling how strong he was, how powerful.

Yes, Lamorna thought smugly, he likes *me*.

Chapter 56

Ordes was not a good student, and the look the Priestess of the Temple was giving him reminded him strongly of the face his father was wearing the day Ordes got himself tangled in the rigging. For failing to pay attention, Tymis left him dangling like bait on a hook for an hour before helping his eight-year-old son down.

'You have no idea what you can do,' Goerika said, her frustration with him evident. 'Do you truly know who you are?'

'Is that a trick question? Because I'm really not in the mood for mystical shit right now,' Ordes replied. He was tired and cranky, hungry, and the Temple gave him the creeps. If he was being honest, this whole country gave him the creeps. There were too many trees, caging the sky and the blocking the horizon, and ever since they'd arrived, he'd felt trapped, had longed for the water, the wide-open space of the ocean, and a salty sea-breeze on his cheeks. And now, all he had was the very solid stone walls of the Temple closing him in.

The Priestess blinked at him, shaking her head. 'Born of a Goddess and, well … who is to say *what* Tymis Merlyni actually is.'

Ordes' heart seized and suddenly, he was all ears. 'What do you mean?'

'Do you know what your father is?'

He wasn't sure how much to tell this strange woman peering at him in the darkness. He wasn't sure how to put the truth of what his father was into words. 'I know who he is, but I'm not sure what he is.'

The Priestess clicked her fingers and all the candles in the Temple surged into life. 'Merlin is not human, not really. It is difficult to explain, because part of him is human – or it was, once.'

'Born of a mortal woman and a being not of this earth anymore,' Ordes mumbled, repeating his father's words to him in the Captain's cabin of *The Excalibur*, words that ripped Ordes' world to pieces in a few short moments.

'Yes,' Goerika confirmed.

'This … being? Do you know what it was?'

Goerika gave Ordes a serious look. 'Perhaps this is not knowledge you need right now.'

'I think I'm the best person to judge that,' Ordes countered. 'If you know, tell me, because whatever he is, whatever he came from, that's part of me as well, isn't it? And if I am to master whatever gifts you think I have, wouldn't it help to know their origin?'

'Very well,' the Priestess agreed. 'But you may not like what you learn.'

Ordes' insides squirmed but he nodded in acknowledgment.

'Have you ever heard of demons?' Goerika asked. 'True demons. Beings that were once human, but who were so dark and twisted in the time they spent living that, on their deaths, Ankou deemed them not fit to enter the realms of the Otherworld. He sends them to a place of never-ending darkness and fire—' she paused when Ordes jolted. 'You know of this place?'

'I had a short visit,' he mumbled. Whispers filled his head again.

We know you, Ordes.

Goerika watched him, waiting, and then continued when he did not speak. 'They are left in the flames as punishment for their wicked natures.

But, sometimes, not even a realm created by a god is strong enough to hold them, and some manage to find a way out, so strong is their will. Most do not make it back to the world of the living,' she paused, holding Ordes' eyes, 'but one did. One who had managed to amass tremendous power while in Ankou's pit.'

'What sort of power?' Ordes asked.

We can give you power. You can be a god.

'The sort of power that was used to create this world and everything in it. Magic like the Old Ones possess. You see, when the Old Ones created the realms they unintentionally left behind pieces of their magic, and that magic can be tapped into, if one is clever enough to learn how to do it,' the Priestess explained.

Ordes swallowed. 'Are you telling me Tymis was fathered by a demon?'

Welcome home.

'That is exactly what I am telling you.'

'So his magic ...'

'Dark and light exist in perpetual balance, Ordes,' Goerika said softly. 'Within every one of us there is dark and light and many, many shades of grey. Sometimes, one outweighs the other. Sometimes, we exist within the grey spaces only. There is a darkness in your father, as there is darkness in you, in the syhren you love, in the boy who will be a king. Even in me. Your father's magic is the magic of the Old Ones, *all at once*. Do you understand what that means?'

Ordes bit his lip, his mind flying. Niniane controlled magic; the Green Knight the earth; Melodias the seas; Ankou the realm of the dead; Morrigna – fate; Inanna and Ereshki ... he sucked in a breath. 'Everything,' he said quietly. 'My father's magic is the magic of *everything*. This realm, the Otherworld, the space between the realms ... the beginning and the end ...' What did this make his father? What did it make him? 'How can someone have that inside themselves and not go mad?'

The Priestess said nothing. Ordes' heart felt like it would burst from his chest.

'Am I human at all?' he asked, needing to know. He had always thought himself more human than fey, clinging to that part of himself, letting it be the face he showed the world, taking comfort in it.

Goerika was silent for so long, by the time she spoke Ordes was squirming where he sat, his magic twitching beneath his skin. Absently, he was aware of Jenyfer's heartbeat – even here, deep in the Temple – and he let the steady, rhythmic drumming soothe him.

The Priestess shook her head. 'You are not. The form you wear is the form you choose to wear. You could be whatever you wished, look however you wished, if that was truly what you wanted.'

All the air rushed from Ordes' body, his lungs seizing – were they even lungs? Did he even need to breathe? If he held his breath, would he die? Questions, assumptions, denials rushed through him too quickly for him to grasp any of them.

What he was able to rip from the swirling storm of emotions was anger, so hot and potent it was blinding. 'You know what? I want to leave. I don't want to talk to you anymore,' he snapped, glaring at the Priestess. 'This is all bullshit, and I don't know how much more of it I can take! My whole life has been turned upside down and, in case you hadn't realised, I'm well and truly pissed off about it! I don't want to be anything special. I don't want whatever it is you, or the Old Ones, or some gods-damned prophecy is offering me!'

You're an idiot, boy. Melodias' voice. Ordes shut his ears to it.

'Very well,' Goerika said, and vanished, and he was left sitting in a darkness that swelled with magic and whispered things to him he could not understand.

'Fuck!'

He was left in the darkness for days. Maybe. Maybe it was a week. Ordes had chewed his lip so much it was swollen. Had tugged at his hair until his scalp burnt with it. Had slept. Had woken with something clawing at his belly, at his skin.

He wasn't human. Not even half-human.

His mother was a Goddess.

His father … was there even a word for it?

He wasn't human.

Not human. Not one part of him.

Did it truly matter? He had no idea, but something deep inside him sighed in profound relief, as if it had been waiting for this moment, for this acknowledgement. For so long Ordes had wondered about his magic, about his mother, about the deep place at the core of him, where he knew the heart of his magic lay. A place that he had only dipped his toes into.

What would happen now if he dove straight in?

Fear flooded him.

Demon, Goerika had said. The whispers from the Pit echoed through his ears. Was some of that destructive power alive in him?

Darkness and light and all the grey areas in between?

Ordes put his head in his hands. He had told Jenyfer not to be afraid of what she was, not to let the things she had read in a book shape her. To trust in who she was, in what she could feel inside. He needed to take his own advice.

He pulled a steady breath into lungs that he wasn't sure he needed, and straightened his spine. 'Alright. I want to know what I can do,' he told the empty darkness.

The air rippled across his skin and Goerika was back, sitting exactly where she had been before his outburst. She leant forward and took hold of his chin, her eyes scanning his face. She nodded, having come to some conclusion, and sat back.

'Your father can control the elements, summon darkness and light, change his shape at will, see through time, *move* through time, call things into being. It stands to reason that his gifts are also your gifts, Ordes. What can you do?'

Ordes closed his fist and when he opened it, a sphere of water sat there. 'I can control water best,' he said.

'Because you entered this world in it,' the Priestess said. 'But you can do much more than that.' She closed her eyes and the air around her shifted, four points of light erupting into the space between them, like stars in the night sky. The candles went out and, slowly, each star unfolded until a flame, a ball of water, a feather, and a leaf hung in the air between them.

The four elements.

'What are you?' Ordes asked.

'I am a demi-god,' Goerika said. 'There are two of us who remain. I have existed here, in this space, for aeons. I am almost as old as the Old Ones, and I was put on this earth to help those like you become what you were supposed to be.'

'Those like me?' Ordes mumbled.

'The children of prophecy. Although no one knew it then, not even the gods.' Goerika's 'stars' vanished, and the candles flickered back to life. 'Prophecies are neither truth nor lies,' she said softly. 'Their power resides in how they are interpreted, and by whom. One man's truth is another man's lie.'

'What does that mean?'

'Trust your instincts.'

Start asking the right questions. Melodias' voice.

'Why did Ereshki steal the Treasures of the gods?'

Goerika's face did not shift. 'To protect what she loved.'

'Which was?'

'Humanity.'

Ordes frowned. 'I thought people turned their backs on the Old Ones.'

'They did, but that was long after the Treasures were taken.'

Ordes kept his eyes on the demi-god's face. 'Are they worth finding?'

'Yes.'

He had one more question, one that pulled at him from that deep place within, where his magic lay. A question that rushed up his throat. 'Will Arthur reshape the world for the better?'

'One man's truth is another man's lie, Ordes,' Goerika repeated softly.

Ordes lost track of how long he'd been in the temple, sitting across from the Priestess who was actually a demi-god. He knew he had used a lot of magic, but where he would usually feel drained, he wasn't – he felt refreshed, renewed, and *ready*, whatever that meant.

Goerika had him juggling the elements, over and over, until he could manage them all and shift between them with barely a thought. He still liked water best – water was calm and powerful at the same time. Earth was steadfast and patient, while fire caused his belly to warm and flicker with light. Air was a breeze that ruffled his hair and teased the candle flames.

'Each element does not exist without the other,' Goerika told him. 'Earth cannot survive without water to quench its thirst, and without fire to cleanse it. Air feeds fire, and when the water runs from the mountains into the creeks, the rivers and eventually, the ocean, it takes with it nutrients that replenish the seas.'

'Can I summon anything I want?' he asked her.

'You have already been doing this your whole life,' the Priestess replied. 'When you want a mug that is out of your reach. When you want the lanterns lit but don't want to get up. But, as for anything you want? If it is connected to the elements, if it exists in some form of a natural state, you can call it to you.'

Ordes fingered his chin. 'Could I, say, drop a rock on someone's head?'

Goerika raised her eyebrows. 'Balance, Ordes,' she reminded him. 'Light and dark.'

He nodded, grinning. Slowly, the Priestess smiled back, and it made her seem so much younger. Ordes flexed his fingers. His magic felt different – he felt different. He had not reached the bottom of that deep well of power, still holding back, still afraid of what might be waiting for him at the very limits of his magic. Within the safety of the Temple's walls, Ordes had shifted himself through time and space, disappearing and reappearing somewhere else minutes later. The sensation left his skin prickling, and his insides feeling scrambled as every part of him broke apart and reformed itself somewhere else, and he had no memory of where he had been or what had happened to him in the minutes he was not physically present.

He did it again, snapping from one side of the cavernous room to the other and back again. This time, the nausea was a little less.

'How do you feel?' the Priestess asked. Goerika was sitting cross-legged on the stones. She had not shifted her position in all the time they had spent together, except for when she disappeared after his tantrum.

'Alive,' Ordes said without thought. 'I feel … I feel *whole*. Almost,' he added.

She nodded. 'One last thing. I want you to change your form.'

He had done everything she had asked, but this was something well outside of his comfort zone. 'What if I get stuck as a mouse or a bug for the rest of my life? No thanks.'

Her lips twitched. 'As you wish. Know that the power to shift your form is yours, if you ever need it.'

'I can go?'

'Yes.' Goerika waved her hand and the Temple of the World's Door dissolved into thin air, leaving him blinking at the brightness of the day, the forest silent around him. Ordes turned to thank the Priestess, the demi-god, but she was gone.

CHAPTER 57

While Ordes was in the Temple, Jenyfer had been introduced to Melhala, a water wielder, who proceeded to drill Jenyfer on the basics of her water magic, but she had barely been able to concentrate. She was worried about her sister. The Lamorna she knew was prim and proper. This new Lamorna was … Jenyfer didn't know yet, but the afternoon her sister had ridden out of the village with the leader of the Inborn, Jenyfer knew for certain that something had changed in Lamorna.

The Lamorna she knew would never climb willingly on the back of an animal, not even to get away from Jenyfer. The Lamorna she knew wouldn't have gone within a metre of a Cruithean Magic Wielder, yet the way she had looked at that man, and he at her …

Jenyfer wondered if their aunt knew.

But she couldn't blame the entirety of her distraction on her sister.

She missed Ordes. Despite being angry, her insides hurt with the absence of him.

'Are you coming, Little Morsel?' Katarin called.

Jenyfer nodded, picking up her pace, until she was following in Katarin's shadow as they trekked through the forest. It was weapons work today. Up ahead, Arthur and Melhala were discussing magic, and Halymere was stalking through the trees to the side of them, eyes alert. He met Jenyfer's gaze, nodded, and turned his attention back to the forest. Katarin was silent and Jenyfer's thoughts wandered again, back to the book on the Otherworld she had left in her kibitka.

The book that had mysteriously appeared on *The Excalibur*.

She'd considered leaving it on the ship but, at the last minute, driven by something she didn't understand, she'd stashed it in her pack and it had become her companion, her comfort, while Ordes was gone.

Even now, with the book tucked beneath her bed, she could hear it singing to her and she knew without having to think about it that when she returned she'd pull that book into her lap again. She couldn't read it, so mostly she rested her hands on it, or flicked through the pages gently, careful not to tear them. There were pictures, drawings in great detail, so she studied those; but, without being able to read the captions, she wasn't sure what she was looking at.

Jenyfer stopped, sucking in a breath. Ordes was in the Temple no longer. She knew it. She could sense him. He was somewhere close, and moving closer. Jenyfer glanced over her shoulder, but there was nothing except for trees, leaves raining down gently. She frowned, turning back to the path, when the air in front of her shifted, and Ordes appeared.

Out of nothing.

Jenyfer stumbled back, tripping over herself and falling hard on her arse, too stunned to worry about the pain of it. 'What the ...'

He smiled, and it was the most beautiful thing she had ever seen.

'New trick,' he said, offering her his hand. She took it, and could immediately feel the *power* that flowed beneath his skin. She let him lift her to her feet. The air around him was shimmering with waves of silver.

'How?' she whispered.

He did not let go of her hand. 'All my life I've felt this deep, dark space inside me, where I knew my magic lay. I had dipped into it a few times, mainly in defence of the ship, but I hadn't jumped in there, you know? I was scared,' he admitted softly. The silver of his eyes glowed under the trees.

'And now?' Jenyfer asked.

He winked, and vanished. She spun around, unable to stop herself from gaping.

'Ordes? Where are you?'

'Here.' His voice touched her ear and she jumped. 'Sorry.'

'No, don't apologise. It's amazing,' she told him, turning in his arms so she could look at his face. 'You're amazing,' she said softly, pushing herself onto her tip toes so she could kiss him. She didn't think, she just did it, her body sighing in relief. 'I missed you,' she whispered against his lips. She felt his surprise; his hands tightened where they were pressed into her lower back. He kissed her, slow and deep, setting a fire burning under her flesh, and she wondered if it was possible to kiss him forever.

'Absence makes the heart grow fonder?' he asked, resting his forehead against hers.

'Something like that,' Jenyfer agreed.

Up ahead of them, somewhere beneath the trees, someone laughed.

Jenyfer slowly pulled away. 'When you disappear, where do you go?'

'I don't know, exactly. The Priestess of the Temple told me it was the space between the worlds.' Ordes ran his hand through his hair, his expression suddenly tight, worried. 'Jen, my father is not what I thought he was.'

They walked side by side, hand in hand, as he told her what he had learnt about Tymis Merlyni. 'What does that mean for you?' Jenyfer asked.

'I haven't worked that out yet,' Ordes said. He lifted his free hand, flexed his fingers. Silver light, stronger than Jenyfer had seen it before, rushed over his knuckles. 'Everything is much easier. I thought it was easy before, natural, but now ...' He stopped, turning to her. 'What's your favourite flower?'

'What?' she laughed.

'Your favourite flower. Tell me,' he insisted.

She laughed again. 'Alright. It's a bee orchid. Not a flower really, I suppose. They grow on the moors near Kernou. There isn't any here, though. They're a pinky colour—'

'I know it,' he said, then closed his fist. Jenyfer watched the air around his hand shimmer, like it had that night he'd broken her out of the cage in Kernou and, when he opened his fist, nestled in his palm was a perfectly formed bee orchid.

Jenyfer looked at him in shock.

'It's real,' he said. She didn't say anything, standing still, her heart thundering as he tucked the orchid into the length of her braid.

'Ordes,' she whispered. 'That's ...'

He shrugged, his cheeks colouring. 'Come on,' he said, taking her hand again, and they walked in silence until they caught up with the others, where Ordes took a moment to show off until Katarin burst out laughing.

'At least you're useful now,' was all she said.

Jenyfer folded her arms, resting her shoulder against the trunk of the nearest tree. She watched Ordes, the easy smile that graced his face, the way people looked at him when he spoke. The way he made people laugh, made them smile.

She sighed, tucking her dagger away and untying her hair, shaking it loose from its braid, making sure to catch the tiny bee orchid before it hit the ground. Carefully, she tucked it in the pocket of her coat.

Everything had become much easier for her magic-wise, but being in the company of other Magic Wielder's was not. No one had done anything wrong exactly; it was the way they looked at her. Whenever Jenyfer opened her mouth, she could almost sense them cringe, sense them waiting for her to do something with her voice.

Footsteps crunched through the leaves and Jenyfer glanced over her shoulder to see Katarin approach. The Captain was wearing her long coat and cutlass, but instead of looking out of place off the water and beneath the trees of Cruithea, Katarin was as fierce as usual. 'You look lost,' she commented.

'I can't do what he does. He makes it look easy, talking to people, even when he's … whatever he is now,' Jenyfer mumbled, nodding at Ordes, who now held Arthur and Halymere in thrall with whatever tale he was spinning them. Halymere was relaxed, sword slung casually over his shoulder.

Kat followed her gaze, and then sighed. 'Come with me.' She didn't wait for Jenyfer to agree, turning and walking deeper into the forest. Jenyfer tore her eyes from Ordes and followed Katarin. They didn't speak as Katarin led them between the trees towards a stream. She plonked herself down at the water's edge, stretching her legs out.

'Sit,' she commanded. Jenyfer did. She waited, but Kat didn't say anything, staring moodily at the water. The pirate Captain flashed Jenyfer a quick look, but before she could speak, Jenyfer jumped in.

'I'm sorry,' she said quietly. 'For what happened with *The Queen*. I know you think it's my fault.'

Katarin sighed and rubbed at her cheek. 'I did think it was your fault, at the time, but I know it wasn't. Melodias is now at the top of my list of power-hungry arseholes I'd like to have a chat with,' she said fiercely. 'And I know what happened with the map wasn't your fault, either. I know what it's like to be in the presence of an Old One – although, Niniane isn't a cunt.'

Jenyfer smiled. 'No, she isn't,' she said. Then, 'I'm sorry about Aelle, and the others.'

'Thank you,' Kat acknowledged quietly. 'I miss them. I miss *her*.'

'You loved her?'

Katarin rubbed at her cheek. 'We shared a bed for a time, and I know she loved me, but I ended things before … I wasn't good for her,' she said softly. 'I couldn't give her my heart. I haven't ever given it to anyone, but Aelle … she understood why. She didn't hate me for it. I should have loved her for that alone.'

'I'm sure she knew you cared,' Jenyfer said.

In the distance, they could hear the sound of steel on steel. Training had begun again. Jenyfer went to get up, but Katarin's hand closed over her forearm.

'You don't have to wear it like a badge, Little Morsel.'

'What?'

Katarin scooped up a rock and tossed it into the stream. 'Ordes is a good person, for all his faults. And he loves you.'

Jenyfer said nothing, concentrating on the pattern of scales at her wrist.

Another stone hit the water; ripples spread out, pushing tiny waves against the shore line on both sides of the stream. 'He went to Lyonesse for you. Even when your father's army of rabid syhrens were coming for us, he still went. He didn't turn back.' Katarin sighed and rubbed at her cheek. 'Ordes is a fool in most things, but he's honest, Jenyfer. Yes, he didn't tell you about the heartfire, but he was trying to protect you.' Katarin added softly, 'If I was a different sort of person, I'd have taken what he was offering me, but I couldn't let him love me either.'

'What do you mean?' Jenyfer managed.

'Ah.' Katarin rubbed at the back of her neck; a blush crept across her cheeks.

Jenyfer felt like someone had punched her in the gut.

'For two years we met once a month, in Newlyn. We bickered about useless shit, we sometimes spent the night together, I was a bitch, and that was it,' Katarin answered plainly. 'I knew the moment he'd met you because he was different. He was all broody and puppy-eyed.' She sighed. 'Love is different for the fey, for people like us, like Ordes. We have one person that is our other half, one person out of all the people in the world. Some never find them, their other half, but for those that do, they will love that person, be bound to that person, forever.'

Jenyfer kept her gaze on the water. 'The heartfire.'

'Yes.'

'Do you wish it was you, and not me?'

Katarin's reply was swift. 'No. I've done terrible things—'

'So have I,' Jenyfer argued.

'Like what?'

Taking a deep breath, Jenyfer told Katarin about Alric, and what happened in Port Leore. 'He's dead because of me. My magic killed him.'

'It sounds like he deserved it,' Katarin said simply.

'But—'

Katarin whirled to face Jenyfer, her expression as fierce as a storm. 'No, don't you dare. It was self-defence. You were defending yourself, and you were defending others. Don't ever let anyone make you feel bad for that, Jenyfer, you understand me?'

Jenyfer swallowed, and nodded.

'You're not like me,' Katarin said, her voice softer. 'Which is a good thing, for you, and for Ordes.'

Jenyfer picked up a stone and threw it into the stream. 'I—'

'Don't make me slap you again,' Katarin warned. 'Do you not see the way he looks at you? It's sickening, if I'm being honest.'

Jenyfer swallowed. 'I don't know why I keep pushing him away. I don't want to, but I do, and I can't stop myself.'

'You know though, deep down,' Katarin said. 'I know about the man in Kernou.' She smiled sadly, seeing Jenyfer's expression. 'No one told

461

me. When you've been around enough women scorned, enough women who have been ill-treated, you get a sense for it. Ordes is not like him, whoever he was.'

Jenyfer looked at her hands. 'I know.'

'Then work out what you want,' Kat said.

'I wish it was that simple.'

'It is,' Katarin argued. 'You're making it complicated. We all come with a past, with things that have hurt us, but that doesn't mean things have to be that way.' She stood, dusting her backside free of leaves and dirt. When she turned to leave, Jenyfer called her back.

'Are you going to take your own advice?'

'What are you talking about?' Kat put her hands on her hips challengingly.

'You've not noticed the tall, dark, and handsome Cruithean warrior who's been looking at you all day?' Jenyfer said casually.

Katarin sighed.

Jenyfer laughed. 'His name is—'

'Yes, I know his name, thank you,' Katarin grumbled. 'I also know his shoe size and how he likes his eggs.' She snatched a stone from the ground and threw it violently into the water. 'This is why I prefer my ship. There are no ex-lovers there. Not anymore,' she added, then stomped away.

Jenyfer turned back to the water but, instead of tossing a stone in, she waved her hands and pulled one from the creek bed. It was water-worn, smooth and shiny, white with lines of charcoal grey running through it. She stared at it a moment, then tucked it in her pocket with the orchid.

A sweaty and tired Jenyfer, Ordes, and Arthur wandered into the cooking area. It was too early for dinner, but Jenyfer's stomach grumbled at the thought of food. Halymere had put her through her paces, a snarky Katarin watching and calling out unsolicited advice. Jenyfer had suspected she'd wanted to annoy her Cruithean ex-lover, but Halymere was like a mountain buffered by the wind – steady and strong, not worn down one bit. He hadn't even glanced at Katarin, focused on his task: making Jenyfer's muscles ache.

'I stink,' Jenyfer declared. 'I need a wash.'

'You smell like water,' Ordes told her. 'You always do.'

The conversation with Katarin swirled around Jenyfer's mind. There were things she wanted to ask, but also, things she knew she didn't truly want to know. Katarin had made it seem like it was nothing, and maybe for her it was. Jenyfer pushed the words away, and pulled a smile on instead. 'How long until someone cooks me something?'

Arthur grinned, wiping the sweat from his face. 'I'll cook something,' he said, wandering over to the fire pit, setting his sword aside and reaching for a pile of fresh timber, which he dumped into the pit, frowning as he arranged it, then hunted around for the flintstones.

'Need some help?' a voice rumbled.

The fire burst into life. Arthur stumbled back.

The leader of the Cruithean Inborn, the man Lamorna had ridden off with, was standing not far from them. He was a lot larger on the ground than he'd appeared on horseback. Tall, muscled arms covered in swirling tattoos, a glyph between his deep brown eyes. 'Are you going to introduce us?' he asked Arthur, nodding at Jenyfer and Ordes, and Jenyfer did not like the way Arthur shrank under the man's gaze.

'I'm sure you know who they are already, Mordred,' Arthur mumbled.

Mordred laughed, his braided hair slithering like snakes over his broad shoulders. He took his time running his eyes over Jenyfer. Ordes tensed; before he could do or say anything, Mordred's gaze crawled over his face. The Cruithean stroked his chin thoughtfully.

'Well, I know what you are,' he said, nodding at Jenyfer. He looked at Ordes again. 'But what the fuck are you?'

'And you?' Jenyfer demanded. Her skin was itching, her magic tense, putting her on edge. Adrenalin pooled in her mouth, coating her tongue. 'What are you, apart from an arsehole?' she challenged. Arthur looked at her like she was mad, and maybe she was. Mordred could probably crush her skull with his fingers.

His smile was sly, cruel. 'Your sister told me all about you.'

'Did she?' Jenyfer bit out, her fists curling.

'I don't think she has appreciated being lied to for all these years,' Mordred went on. 'That's something that always fascinates me about people who have been wronged – what they are willing to do to make things right again.'

White-hot anger ploughed through Jenyfer's veins. She lunged for the leader of the Inborn; Ordes closed his arms around her middle, pulling her back against his chest. She barely heard his warnings over the music in her head. 'Stay away from my sister,' she hissed.

Mordred laughed. 'She's very sweet,' he said, giving Jenyfer a knowing wink.

Jenyfer's song rushed up her throat. She opened her mouth, felt the air around her shift as her magic prepared to unleash.

Ordes swore and tightened his grip on her.

'Sing to me, syhren,' Mordred whispered. 'I dare you.'

'Enough!' Arthur's voice, louder than Jenyfer had ever heard it. 'Mordred, leave them alone.'

'Whatever you say, cousin,' the Cruithean said. He turned and walked away, leaving Jenyfer a seething, trembling mess in Ordes' arms.

CHAPTER 58

Arthur watched as golden light danced across the backs of his knuckles. He still wasn't sure what it meant, though. Mordred had asked him which element he was strongest in, but so far none of them felt stronger than the other. If his magic had a true purpose, Arthur didn't know what that was yet.

As the light played across the backs of his hands, his thoughts moved to Jenyfer and Ordes. He'd watched Jenyfer manipulate water, make shapes of it and command it. He hadn't heard her sing, but he knew what her voice could do. And he'd watched Ordes *disappear* into thin air, only to reappear moments later. He was the son of the Myrddin, the prophet Arthur was yet to meet. The need to know about the one who had long ago spoken words that would shape Arthur's destiny burnt like a flame in his chest. He'd tried not to think too much about the prophet of the gods, focusing his energy on learning how to fight and how to use his magic, but he could feel something tugging at him, an urgency he didn't understand. He was not usually so full of restless energy.

Perhaps that was what made Arthur head for Ordes' kibitka, what made him not hesitate, stepping inside. Ordes was sprawled across the bed. Arthur thought for a moment he was sleeping, but he sat up, pushing his hair out of his eyes.

The two men stared at one another, and Arthur could feel his nerve sliding away.

'Sorry, I can—'

'Do you want to be a king?' Ordes asked him quietly.

Arthur blinked. The question had taken him off guard. 'I don't know,' he admitted. 'Every time I think I've decided, something happens to make me change my mind.'

'What happened this time?'

'You.' The word came from deep inside, and Arthur hadn't realised he'd been thinking about it until he spoke it. Now that he'd said it, he couldn't take it back and it hung there between them; such a small word but one that, at the moment, carried such tremendous weight.

Ordes' silver eyes were wide. 'Me?'

Arthur nodded. He came further into the kibitka, stepping over a pile of clothing to get to a chair. 'I've seen what you can do. You're powerful, and confident, and—'

'And I have no fucking idea what I'm doing,' Ordes said with a laugh. 'I sometimes wish I'd never gone into that temple,' he added. 'At least before, I could be a fuck-up and have an excuse. Now, I feel like I should know what to do. It's clear that this magic of mine is meant for something – only, I don't know what.'

Arthur nodded. 'I can understand that.' He flexed his fingers and the golden warmth of his magic slid free. 'I can't do a thing with mine.'

'Maybe it's like mine,' Ordes told him gently. 'There, but out of reach. Maybe you should go and see Goerika again.'

'No thanks,' Arthur said quickly, making the other man smile. 'Did she say anything strange to you?'

'Everything she said was strange,' Ordes muttered. 'I've gone over it and over it until I've given myself a headache but I can't make sense of some of the things she told me.' He uncurled his legs, shuffling to the edge of the bed and swinging his feet onto the floor. 'I don't think we can trust in everything we've been told, Arthur.'

'Why?'

Ordes shrugged. 'Call it an instinct, I don't know. But somewhere in the middle of everything we've been told by Old Ones, and demi-gods, and my father is the truth.'

'But whose truth?' Arthur mused. 'And why would they lie at all?'

'Because they can. This world is new to you. I don't mean anything disrespectful by that – I just mean the world of magic is not always simple. And gods are definitely not simple.' Ordes rubbed at the back of his neck. 'I never knew who I was – who my mother was – but my father told me all the stories. I've heard about the Grail, and Old Ones, and prophecies my whole life. I've heard about *you* my whole life – only I never knew you were actually real.'

'Let me guess – you're as disappointed as my cousin is?' Arthur said, unable to help sounding bitter. Mordred's dislike of him was something he could still not understand. He didn't for one moment believe his cousin was jealous of him. Of the idea of power, maybe, but not of Arthur himself. Even though they had come to some sort of understanding, he couldn't shake the foreboding from his bones. Goerika's warning rang through him – *darkness and blood will come for you before the end.*

Ordes tucked his hair behind his pointed ears. 'I think if there was to be a king, I'd not want him to be an arsehole. I've known arseholes, Arthur. You don't strike me as one.'

Arthur's cheeks warmed. 'Thank you.'

Silence lapsed between them; Ordes' face was creased into a frown, and Arthur remembered the true reason he had come here. 'Tell me about your father.'

Ordes' eyebrows lifted. 'Are you sure you want to ask that?'

'He's the Myrddin. His prophecies are about to change our lives – have already changed our lives. Yes, I want to know,' Arthur said. 'If you'll tell me.'

'Up until recently, he was just my father – Tymis Merlyni, pirate, Captain of *The Excalibur*, nothing special. A Magic Wielder who had his magic stolen by a goddess. I had no idea who he truly was,' Ordes said quietly. 'And I've barely had a chance to think about it myself. He's my father,' he said, hands spread in a gesture of confusion. 'He's always been there. He's cranky, and moody, and has a terrible sense of humour, but I've watched men drop to their knees for him, open the skin on their palms, and give him their lives. I thought that was normal, but I'm beginning to understand it's not, that not everyone's fathers are like that – men that, despite their flaws, command respect, because that is what he does. It isn't forced, he doesn't ask for it, yet he gets it.' He paused, shooting Arthur a proud look. 'I respect him, and I was one of those men on my knees for him. For all his faults, and for all our disagreements, I love him.'

'I envy you,' Arthur said softly. 'For being able to have that relationship with your father.'

'I'm sorry your father is … what he is,' Ordes said.

'Thank you,' Arthur whispered.

Silence lapsed between them.

'So … a storm demon?' Ordes' smile was crooked, playful.

Arthur blushed. 'He was just a fisherman. I didn't know until after …'

Ordes laughed a little humourlessly. 'I understand better than you think.'

'Jenyfer?' Arthur asked softly.

Ordes nodded. 'We haven't spent a lot of time together lately,' he admitted, and Arthur could hear the hurt in his tone. He sighed and fell back on the bed, linking his hands behind his head. 'I thought that once she found her sister she'd be happier, but …'

'Lamorna is not an easy person,' Arthur supplied.

'That's one way of putting it. I happen to think she's absolutely wretched,' Ordes said simply.

'It's not her fault,' Arthur said.

Ordes sat up again. 'No, I guess it isn't. But she still had choices, like you, like Jenyfer.'

'She chose to believe,' Arthur replied.

At that moment, Jenyfer barged into the kibitka. She froze, her gaze shifting between the two of them. 'What?'

'Nothing,' Ordes said, giving her a radiant smile.

Jenyfer's eyes narrowed. She let her gaze move around the kibitka, as if something there would give away what Arthur and Ordes had been talking about; not that they had anything to hide. Arthur watched Jenyfer, noting how, no matter how hard she tried to look somewhere else, her eyes kept returning to Ordes. Eventually, she sighed, shedding her jacket and setting it neatly on the table, before crossing the room to fall face-first onto the bed.

Her voice was muffled by the mattress as she said, 'Can anyone remind me why I didn't just let my sister drown?'

And Arthur couldn't help himself – he laughed.

CHAPTER 59

Tamora was wringing her hands, her expression worried, but beneath it was excitement. The whole village had been engulfed in a shroud of excitement and anticipation. People had been bustling about all day, and what looked like a massive bonfire had been built in the place usually reserved for cooking. All the pots and utensils had been moved.

'What is it?' Lamorna asked.

'Tonight is Fire Night,' her aunt said, her tone agitated. 'It's a celebration of the turning season. You must have noticed the days had been getting warmer, and longer? Winter will be over soon.'

Lamorna nodded. She hadn't realised it had been winter here, only that it was colder.

'Well,' Tamora continued, 'in Cruithea, celebrations are held to honour this time, because summer means good hunting and full-bellies. So, tonight they will light the bonfire and there will be singing, and dancing, and music.' She shot Lamorna a look and Lamorna knew what her aunt was thinking – these were all things considered unnecessary for a full life in the eyes of the One God.

Lamorna made herself smile. 'It sounds like fun,' she said.

Tamora frowned. 'It is fun,' she said, 'But it is also—'

Keraine swept into the kibitka, her face alight with laughter. 'The festivities will start as soon as it is dark.' She paused, taking in Tamora's face and hurrying over to her, touching her cheek gently. Lamorna made herself watch. 'Has something happened?'

'I was telling Lamorna about Fire Night.'

Keraine laughed again, turning to Lamorna. 'You could do with a night of drinking and debauchery.'

'What?' Lamorna said as Tamora sighed and mumbled she hadn't gotten to that part yet. Lamorna listened as her aunt explained the symbolism of this night – it was about fertility, about encouraging new life in all things. 'Tonight is about unity.'

Keraine, with her hand in the small of Tamora's back, turned serious eyes on Lamorna. 'You need to be careful out there.'

'Why?'

'Because you're young, and inexperienced, and—'

'I'm not stupid,' Lamorna retorted with a toss of her head. She pushed her hair back from her face. If they knew, if any of them knew, they wouldn't call her inexperienced. They wouldn't think she knew nothing about the world. *No*, the voice whispered. *They'd see you for the sinner you are.*

The sound of drums floated into the kibitka from outside. 'It sounds like it's starting,' Lamorna said, heading towards the entrance. She paused, looking back at her aunt and Keraine. 'Are you coming?'

She didn't wait for their reply, taking a deep breath and stepping out into a world turned orange. The bonfire had been lit; from her kibitka, Lamorna could see the flames reaching for the sky. She followed the stream of people headed towards it, finding herself swept up in their excitement. She had no idea whether Tamora and Keraine were behind her. She caught sight of Jenyfer, whose eyes widened when she saw her sister. They had not spoken more than a few words to one another since their argument, and part of Lamorna was sad, but another part revelled in it, in the burning anger in her belly.

Leaving Ordes, Jenyfer pushed through the crowd until she could grip Lamorna's hands. Lamorna let her. 'You probably should—'

'Why does everyone keep saying that?' Lamorna muttered crossly.

'Alright,' Jenyfer said softly. The sound of drums echoed over the village, spiralling up into the trees to be swept away by the fading light. She tugged on Lamorna's hand. 'Come and join us.'

Lamorna was about to agree, but then she saw Mordred. He was moving through the crowd, heading straight for her, his eyes on her face, a smile on his lips. Lamorna shook her head and he stopped, noticing Jenyfer, and then he was gone, melted into the throng of people.

She allowed Jenyfer to lead her to where Ordes and Arthur Tregarthen were standing. With them was the beautiful red-haired woman she had seen that first night, and a few times since then. Mordred had told her the woman's name was Morgaine, and she was his cousin. She was still dressed like a man.

'She doesn't look old enough to be out here,' Morgaine said, looking at Lamorna.

Jenyfer laughed and the sound of it made Lamorna want to punch her sister. 'She'll be fine. We'll look after her, won't we?'

Lamorna was looking at the red-haired woman, who smiled, a slow sensual smile.

'She has no idea who I am, does she?'

'You're obviously not as famous as you think you are, Katarin,' Ordes drawled.

Lamorna smothered a gasp as it sank in.

'There we go,' Katarin Le Fey mumbled.

'I thought your name was—' Lamorna faltered under the look the pirate Captain gave her.

A young woman with a blissful expression wandered over to them, a tray of mugs in her hands. 'This is more like it,' Katarin announced, her smile becoming wicked as she took a mug. Everyone took one, even Lamorna.

She sniffed it and was about to take a drink when Arthur gently took the mug from her hands. Lamorna put her hands on her hips, but he shook his head, his expression kind, worried, like it always was. The man she knew as Arthur's lover appeared and slipped an arm around Arthur's shoulders, pressing a kiss to his temple. Lamorna turned away, not wanting to see, only to find Morgaine-Katarin had vanished and Jenyfer was finishing her drink.

Ordes burst out laughing, then covered his mouth with his hand. 'That's definitely not faery wine,' he observed. Jenyfer laughed and kissed him. He pulled away, surprise scrawled across his face, before he kissed her back and they seemed to forget where they were, glued to each other in an obscene way, considering there were people all around them.

Lamorna turned away from them, the drums echoing in her ears, the sky bled to black around the edges of the world, the glow of the bonfire exploding around them. She suddenly realised her sister and the pirate were not the only people stuck to each other.

This is about unity.

Lamorna sucked in a breath as the reality of Fire Night hit her.

This was the sin and blasphemy of the Old Ways being shoved down her throat.

She wanted to go back to the kibitka. 'Jenyfer,' she said loudly, but her sister was too busy to listen, her fingers undoing the buttons on Ordes' shirt and her lips on his throat. The pirate gave Lamorna a lazy smile, his eyes unfocused and half-closed. Arthur and Jalen had disappeared into the darkness somewhere. Lamorna did not want to think about what they might be doing, so she pushed her way through the crowd that had begun to dance to the pounding drums, heading for her kibitka.

She had almost made it when someone pressed a mug into her hands.

Lamorna hesitated.

'Drink,' Mordred whispered.

At least Mordred didn't think she was too young, or too naive, to be enjoying Fire Night. Lamorna pushed her thoughts about the Old Ways aside and drank. The liquid was warm and slightly bitter, with an earthy taste she couldn't place. She could taste honey and herbs beneath the sharpness on her tongue. Lamorna finished the drink and when she looked around, Mordred had gone.

The mug fell from suddenly numb fingers, landing on the ground at Lamorna's feet. A giggle escaped her lips and she clapped a hand over her mouth. Her head felt strange and her body was weightless, like she was floating above the village, tangled up in the canopy, as light and fragile as a leaf. She drifted through the crowd, moving closer to the fire, her hands held out. Her skin was golden and orange. She turned her hands over and over, watching the light dance across her flesh.

The drums were still beating out their rhythm, and Lamorna gasped as that rhythm slipped inside her, settling beside her heartbeat, thundering and drowning and burrowing inside her. She laughed and spun around, then stopped. She couldn't see properly – everything was blurry. She blinked, but the world started to spin as people whirled around her, their faces sharp and pointed, devilish, in the light from the bonfire. Heat wafted her face and lifted her hair. Lamorna paused, watching the golden-orange sparks drift into the night sky and, inside her chest, in her blood, was the pounding of the drums, on and on.

She stumbled through the crowd. She saw Arthur Tregarthen and the storm-demon. She saw her aunt and Keraine. She saw debauchery wherever she looked and those images clamoured over each other, burrowing into her brain and urging her to … Lamorna did not know. All she knew was the drums kept pounding and pounding and pounding and her head spun and tingled like it was full of exploding stars.

She needed to find Jenyfer. She wanted to go to bed, to sleep, but her head was soft like cotton wool now and the press of bodies around her was too much. She walked backwards, stumbling over something and landing on her backside in the dirt. A hand touched hers.

Lamorna looked, then scurried away.

A man and woman, or was it woman and woman? She wasn't sure but, whoever they were, they were a tangled mass of partially naked limbs, glistening with sweat in the firelight. Swallowing, she dragged herself to her feet and moved further away from the fire, from the drums, from the sounds of pleasure that suddenly came from all around her.

The forest sang to her, dark and welcoming at the edge of the blazing circle of light. The trees moved in time to the drums, branches swaying, bark slowly peeling and leaves raining down on her head as Lamorna stepped between their trunks. She placed her hand on one – the bark was smooth, soft, but she knew somewhere in her mind that it should be rough to touch.

The sounds of the night raced out to meet her, drawing her deeper into the trees.

Where was Jenyfer?

She called out. Or she might have called out. She didn't know.

There were voices in the trees, whispering and calling to her, telling her to come, come. Come deeper. Lamorna followed the voices, her vision wavering, her feet moving on their own as she kept walking. The trees were thicker now, their branches dark. The full moon winked down at her in snatches of white light and the trees stopped, opening up to a clearing that dipped into the earth.

She could see a person. Or was it two people? A man and a woman.

Lamorna paused, reaching out to wrap her arm around the nearest tree for support. She could still hear the drums in the distance, could still feel that music pulse through her. Her mouth tasted strange; bitterness sat heavy on her tongue and she tried to swallow but couldn't.

Where was Jenyfer?

As she watched, gripping the tree for support, the man and woman embraced, and then they were moving, like they were dancing. They were so graceful, so beautiful that she wanted to join them; but she had never danced and didn't know how. It was only when the woman flung back her head and laughed that she realised it was Jenyfer, and the man was Ordes.

Jenyfer pulled away from Ordes and Lamorna watched through hazy eyes as her sister slowly removed her clothes until she was naked under the night sky and the watchful gaze of the forest. With her dark hair covering her breasts and tumbling down her back like a cloak, Jenyfer wound her arms around Ordes' neck and pulled his head down so she could kiss him.

Lamorna watched, as the drums continued to beat out their steady, pulsing rhythm. She watched the pirate, who could possibly be a god or possibly not, she wasn't sure because there was only One God.

'I want to swim,' Jenyfer announced, spinning in circles, her head tipped to the stars peering down on them. Lamorna expected them to leave the clearing, to go to the stream, her stream, where she and Mordred had first kissed.

But they didn't. Ordes held both hands towards the earth, and suddenly, water bubbled up from the ground around them, splashing and surging, until it covered their ankles and kept climbing, higher, until it was around their waists and there was a lake where before there was none.

Jenyfer laughed in delight and threw her arms around him.

'Sing for me,' he said, and Lamorna frowned. Jenyfer did not sing, surely he knew that. She watched Jenyfer rest her hand on his chest – and then she sang. Lamorna stared and stared, her ears almost breaking with the sound. It was beautiful. She did not understand the words, but she could feel the song, feel its sorrow and its joy and could almost see the way her sister's voice rose into the air, the way it wove through the trees and floated on the surface of the water.

The song ended and Lamorna wanted to tell her sister to sing again, but Ordes had his arms around her and they were kissing and kissing and his hands gripped Jenyfer's flesh. He lifted her into his arms and then walked them to the edge of the lake he had somehow created. Lamorna watched as he lay Jenyfer down and covered her body with his, like they had done this a thousand times before. Lamorna's belly tightened and twisted and desire flared inside her and the drums, the drums, the drums …

An arm slid around her middle and something warm and wet touched the shell of her ear.

'I've been looking for you.' Mordred's voice was soft. He saw where Lamorna's gaze lay and chuckled. 'I didn't know you liked to watch.'

'I don't,' she protested quietly. 'At least, I don't think so.'

Mordred stood there with her, his chest pressed into her back, and watched along with her. 'Your sister is very beautiful.'

Something sharp speared through Lamorna's chest. 'You said I was beautiful,' she mumbled before she could stop herself.

His fingers trailed down the side of her face. 'You are. So very beautiful.'

'This lake is beautiful, too. Ordes made it. And did you hear Jenyfer singing?' Lamorna asked excitedly. She needed to tell their aunt that Jenyfer could sing!

'No. But I can see her scales,' Mordred pointed out.

Lamorna looked and looked and there, on Jenyfer's legs, on her arms, were scales, glinting in the moonlight. 'She's a syhren,' Lamorna whispered. 'I forgot.'

'Yes, she is. And he just became much more interesting,' Mordred murmured. Lamorna thought she could hear worry in his tone. 'Come with me.'

She obeyed, and let him lead her away from her sister beneath the trees towards the raging heat of the bonfire and the press of bodies. But they didn't stop. With her hand firmly in his, Mordred led her away from the revellers and the chaos that was Fire Night until they reached his kibitka. Lamorna clenched her thighs together as he pushed aside the flap, that spark in her belly growing larger and larger until she wondered if it would burn her to pieces from the inside.

Mordred held the flap open for her and she ducked beneath his arm and went in, only to stop and stare.

Sitting on his bed was a man. Lamorna wasn't sure if she had ever seen him before. Or maybe she had.

While she was trying to work it, trying to hunt through the scattered parts of her brain, Mordred placed his hands on her shoulders. 'I like to watch as well,' he whispered.

'Like to watch what?' she replied. Her mouth didn't feel right. She licked her lips. 'I'm thirsty.' He let her go, moving away from her while the man on the bed, who she realised was naked, watched her. When Mordred returned he pressed a mug into her palm.

'Drink, Lamorna,' he said, his voice washing over her.

She did. Soon, her vision had wavered further and her body did not feel like it belonged to her anymore. Mordred took the mug, setting it aside, before he cupped her face and claimed her mouth. His kiss was hungry, and she thought he might swallow her. She giggled against his lips, but kissed him back, wound her arms around his neck and pressed herself as close to him as she could without crawling beneath his skin.

He walked them backwards until they reached the bed – she'd forgotten the other man was there. He was still watching her through eyes that appeared black in the semi-darkness. Mordred released her and she swayed a little, unsteady on her feet. The man patted the bed beside him and she sat. His mouth moved but she didn't hear what sounds he made because the only sounds she could hear were her heartbeat and the drums, the drums, the drums.

Then, Mordred touched her cheek gently before he turned to the man, holding his face like he'd held Lamorna's, and kissed him.

She blinked – she could not look away, could not tear her eyes from the way their mouths fit perfectly together, or how the man ran his hands over Mordred's shoulders the same way she liked to. She did not look away as Mordred reached for her hand; she placed her fingers in his and let him draw her closer, closer, until he could run his fingers through her hair.

'Such beauty is a thing to be shared,' he whispered. 'Don't you agree?'

She could only nod.

'Lie back,' Mordred ordered. She did. She'd do anything he asked, she thought with a smile. A giggle escaped her as his hands moved over her body, removing her clothes one piece at a time until she was naked and stretched out on the bed.

She frowned, suddenly remembering it was not just her and Mordred. The other man was still there. She went to say something, to ask who he was, but he was standing now and Mordred put his arms around him and kissed him again. All she could do was watch the way their bodies moved against one another, the way their hands, both so strong, gripped at each other's flesh and muscles in a way that made her glad they weren't grabbing her like that but, at the same time, she wanted them to put their hands on her.

Perhaps she said so, because soon they were lying on the bed with her, one on either side, but when the strange man went to kiss her, she pulled her face away.

'No,' she murmured. Her tongue was thick and heavy in her mouth.

Mordred touched her face. 'Don't you like him?' he whispered.

Lamorna frowned. 'I do … I think. I don't know,' she managed. 'I like you more.'

Mordred said nothing; the other man did not move. Lamorna glanced at him – he was watching Mordred, not her. Lamorna held her breath. Eventually, Mordred nodded, and the man was gone.

'Is it better now that it's just us?' Mordred asked, tracing the outline of her lips with the tip of his finger.

Lamorna nodded. 'But you like him, don't you?'

'I do,' Mordred admitted. 'But I like you more.'

He kissed her, swept her away, and soon his mouth was between her legs and she didn't know who or where she was, only that she was pleasure, and sin, and flesh, and lips, and burning, and the drums that beat, beat, beat into the night.

When Lamorna woke, she was naked and exposed to the morning air, Mordred's arms like a cage around her. Her memory was a scattered, tormented thing and her head hurt. Her body ached all over. There were bruises forming on her arms. She didn't remember what had happened for her to have them.

She pulled away from Mordred and sat up, tucking her knees beneath her chin as flashes of what had happened last night came back to her.

'Lamorna?' His voice was low, rough with sleep.

She could not look at him. 'What was in that drink?'

'It was Fire Night,' he answered, as if that explained everything. 'Everyone drank it. It's custom.'

'But what was it?' she pressed. She needed to know.

He sighed lightly. 'Fermented juice and a mushroom that only grows in a particular place at this time of year. We dry it, grind it into powder and add it to the juice. It makes you ... well, you know, don't you.'

Lamorna scrambled from the bed, taking the blanket with her and wrapping it tightly around herself. Her eyes were still not working properly. Mordred's face was blurry. 'You should have told me!'

Mordred stretched, so casual and calm, then came towards her. She wanted to step away but she didn't. 'What we did was not sinful, Lamorna. It was not wrong. It is never wrong to enjoy pleasure.'

Lamorna closed her eyes against the burning spark of memory of being on all fours like a beast. 'I need to go home,' she whispered.

'Back to Kernou?'

She nodded.

Mordred sighed. 'I think maybe that is best.'

Lamorna said nothing, but her heart – it hurt! So much she thought she might die.

'What would you say if I wanted to come with you?'

She did look at him then. 'Why?'

He shrugged. 'I'd like to meet your Chif.'

'But you're not a believer. You don't believe in the One God,' she said firmly, successfully keeping the hurt out of her voice and lacing it with anger instead. 'You've been pretending. You lied to me.'

'I did,' he agreed, running the tip of his finger down her bare arm. 'I don't believe in the One God, but I believe in power, Lamorna. And if your One God, your Chif, truly has the power you say he does, then I want to meet him. I want to know him.'

'What will your mother say?' she whispered. 'What will you tell her?'

Mordred smiled and the edges of her anger melted. 'Leave the High Priestess to me, my love.' He took her arm and led her back to the bed. 'Now, you should sleep. It's a long journey back to Kernou. I'm sure you're looking forward to being home.'

'Yes,' she said softly. 'I am.'

CHAPTER 60

Birds. There were birds in her head.

Jenyfer groaned, rubbing at her face with shaking fingers as she forced her eyes open. The world spun and the birds continued to chirp. If she could get up, she'd wring their feathery necks. She had no idea what time it was, but a slice of light eased into the world. She blinked, but the blurriness around the edges of her vision remained, so she closed her eyes again, listening.

The village was silent.

Her memory was a fractured, spiralling thing, thoughts and images forming and shattering only to reform again, then fade into nothing. Opening her eyes, she took a deep breath, held it, and let it out slowly.

The world shifted into focus. A kibitka. But not the one she'd been sharing with her family.

A warm body was pressed against her back, an arm draped over her middle. Slowly, Jenyfer peeled back the blankets.

Skin the colour of rich honey. Tattooed knuckles.

'Fuck,' she said, her voice clawing its way clear of a throat that felt like sand.

'If you want, though, my head hurts,' Ordes said, voice raspy.

Stomach churning, Jenyfer rolled over to face him. His eyes were open, glowing silver in the morning light. Deep shadows rested beneath them. 'What happened last night?' she demanded.

Ordes shifted onto his back. 'I don't remember a bloody thing after drinking whatever that was,' he said. 'You?'

'Nothing.' Jenyfer climbed from the bed, taking the blankets with her and ignoring his protests. She stared in dismay at the clothing and blankets scattered over the floor. 'Ordes, where are my clothes?'

'How should I know? Maybe you tossed them away in a fit of passion.'

Jenyfer blinked again and the world sharpened further. She sucked in a breath and closed her eyes against the flash of memory – trees, water, his hands. The press of his lips, his weight covering her. Music. The chirping birds had fled. There were drums in her head now, a steady, pounding rhythm, ceaseless and insistent.

'I can't remember *anything*.'

Ordes sighed and climbed out of bed, rummaging through the piles of material on the floor, until he found a shirt and trousers. He dressed, keeping his back to her, while she stood there with the blanket wrapped tightly around her, unable to think of what to say. Steps stumbling slightly, he splashed his face with water from the basin on the washstand, then proceeded to hunt for his boots.

'Where are you going?'

'I can't do this anymore. This. Us. Whatever the fuck this is.'

'You said you'd wait—'

'And I will, but I can't keep doing *this*!' His voice rose. 'Having you pull me close only to push me away because every time you do a part of me breaks, Jen, and I've got this burning in my chest that I wish I could stop! If you don't want me, then I'll find a way to live with that, I will, but I can't do this. I can't spend the night with you and then have to wait for you to tell me it was a mistake, that you just want to be friends.'

Something pinched sharply in Jenyfer's chest. If she let him walk out now, she knew, instinctively, that it would all be over between them, heartfire or not. That she'd have lost him.

'Ordes—'

'I can't do it so I won't anymore because this isn't just about your feelings – it's about mine as well,' Ordes continued. His voice was broken. His face was broken.

She had broken him. The realisation of it crashed over her, leaving her breathless.

'Ordes,' she said again.

'You're protecting yourself, I get that, but I need to protect myself as well. I think for now it's best if we—'

'I love you.' The words came from deep inside, pulled to life, and once they were free all the tension fled Jenyfer's body. His eyes shot to hers in shock. 'I love you, Ordes. And I'm sorry. I'm so sorry. I've been so scared of giving myself to what I felt, but that isn't your fault. I know you're not Bryn and I know you'd never hurt me. You've been there for me every time I needed you and—'

The air snapped as he vanished, reappearing in front of her. His eyes walked her face, searching for a hint of a lie. There was a wariness to his expression that she understood, that she knew she deserved.

Jenyfer took a deep breath. She placed her fingers against his lips, tracing first the top, then the bottom lightly. The warmth of his breath curled around her skin and made her shiver. 'I can't promise I'll be any good at this – I've been terrible at it so far,' she said. 'How is it supposed to work?'

Ordes slid his finger beneath her chin, lifting her face to his. 'I don't know. I've never been in love, but if this feeling in my body isn't love, then I don't know what it is.' His fingers trailed over her jaw, curled over her ears and into her hair until he was holding her face between his hands. 'I love you. You have woven yourself around my bones, my heart.

You're in my blood. If I wanted to get rid of you, I'd have to rip myself open and pull you out piece by piece. But I choose not to.'

Choice. There it was again. Jenyfer's whole life had been shaped by choices, by the consequences they had left her with. Should she have made different choices? Maybe, but then she knew she wouldn't be where she was right now.

Ordes had always let her choose. He always would, and she knew that, possibly always had. Jenyfer wanted her choices to reflect the future she wished for, not the future she had feared. Katarin had been right – the memory of Bryn and what he had done had been stopping her from truly moving forward.

In her mind, Andromache's watery rendering of the man who had once been Jenyfer's confidante, her friend, exploded again, and with it her fear washed away.

'I've been so scared of losing the power to choose. I was so focused on what the heartfire had taken from me, I didn't stop to think about what it had *given* me,' Jenyfer whispered.

Ordes smiled. 'Because I can't remember last night either, I'm going to kiss you now.'

This moment was different. Somehow, her declaration, her commitment to him and to them had changed things. As his lips pressed against hers, Ordes scooped her into his arms and tossed her onto the bed. Jenyfer laughed as he crawled over her and peppered her face with kisses. Still laughing, she untangled herself from the blanket and rolled them over, straddling his hips. His hands immediately gripped her thighs and her breath caught at the feeling of him pressed between her legs, the sudden warmth of his body, like the sun had been absorbed into his skin.

Every one of his breaths, every inhale, was ragged, ripping into her as she bent to place her mouth on his chest, her tongue moving against his skin, slow and languid, the taste of him sending sparks shooting along her spine.

She sucked in a breath at the power of the aching in her chest, the force of it, the heat that coursed through her. The feeling of him beneath her palms, beneath her body, burned so deeply that she couldn't remember where she ended and he began. She kissed him until her insides had melted.

Ordes broke away, sitting up so he could close his arms around her and pull her closer. She sought his mouth again, kissing him deeply, like she could crawl her way beneath his skin, or drink in every part of him. The kiss slowed, became deeper still, rhythmic, musical almost, as tender and gentle as a soft ocean breeze, as a lullaby. Jenyfer's song was suddenly silent, the absence of sound deafening, until she understood.

This was all her.

All him.

This was not magic.

This was the heartfire.

Her blood was burning, her heart was a flame teetering on the edge of crumbling to ash.

'Are you alright?' Ordes whispered.

She nodded, unable to speak, not knowing how. She rested her forehead against his, her breathing deep, broken and ragged, as something inside finally fell away. The very core of her split open and was devoured by the flames that raced through every part of her. A moan clawed its way free of her throat, the sound fading to a whimper; his hands tightened against the small of her back.

'Jen?'

'I feel it,' she whispered, placing a trembling hand on his chest. 'The heartfire. I can *feel* it. Is it meant to feel like this?'

'Like you're burning? Like you've been ripped apart and put back together? Yes,' Ordes answered gently.

'This is …'

'I know.'

With his arms around her, Ordes flipped them around, pressing her back into the mattress. Then, so slow, so tender, he kissed her again, until she was almost crying from wanting, from needing him. From the weeks of tension, the storm slowly building inside her, so powerful and strong she thought it would wash her away as he kissed his way down her body.

'I'd burn this world down if you asked it,' Ordes breathed, his voice brushing her belly. Magic curled around his body, rising from his skin like a silver mist. 'I'd boil the seas, rip the earth to pieces until there was nothing left but bones and ash, and then I'd build you a new world, Jenyfer. Whatever you wanted.'

She couldn't speak.

As his magic surrounded them, she swore she could see a pair of wings rising from his back.

Jenyfer lay with her head resting on Ordes' chest, his heartbeat thundering in her ears, and in her chest was a fire. In her veins was fire. In her blood, her bones. Fire curled around her organs.

Around her heart.

It was fated from the beginning that they should meet when they did. Her disobedience became the catalyst for something she would never have predicted.

Jenyfer smiled, shifting onto her side so she could see his face. His grin was goofy, his eyes half-closed, shadows still coating the skin beneath them. He did look like shit, and she guessed she was no better. She chuckled.

What? he asked.

The smile slipped and a frown pulled at her forehead.

You're looking at me very seriously. Should I be concerned?

His voice was in her head. Jenyfer swallowed.

Ordes smiled, reading her face. 'You're not imagining it.'

'Is this some new trick of yours?' she asked.

'It's the heartfire,' he said softly. 'I first heard your voice in my head in Avalon. I thought I was losing my mind.'

Jenyfer kissed him. 'How does it work, then? Does it mean we can read each other's thoughts? Or just hear them?'

'I don't know, but I know where you are at all times,' Ordes said. 'I can feel it.'

'Me too,' she admitted. 'I mean, I can sense where you are when you're not near me. I didn't know what it was, until now.'

'Does that bother you?' he asked quietly. She ran her fingers down the side of his face, tracing his cheek bone, then his jaw, the shape of his lips, unable to stop herself from touching him. Ordes caught her fingers and kissed them, his eyes flicking to hers, his face expectant, and she realised she hadn't answered his question.

'No, it doesn't, not anymore. When you're near me, I feel ... warm. Content, but also, alert, if that makes sense.'

'Niniane told me that the heartfire might make us a little overly protective of each other,' Ordes said, a smile tugging at the corner of his mouth.

'In a crazy sort of way?' Jenyfer asked.

'Maybe,' he said, rolling onto his side, mirroring her pose.

Oh, she said. Then, *This isn't so bad.*

No, it isn't.

CHAPTER 61

Jenyfer guarded the book about the Otherworld obsessively, holding it in her lap whenever she could; but without being able to read the words, it was all lost to her. Her face was constantly creased in annoyance but she hadn't yet asked, and Ordes hadn't offered again.

He was afraid of what he might read there, and he wasn't sure why. There were secrets in those pages, things Ordes could sense they all needed to know but he hadn't opened the book. His insides twisted as the Pit of flame roared to life in his mind. He shoved it and the voices away ruthlessly.

Jenyfer was sitting on the bed with the book in her lap when Ordes swept into the kibitka. He'd been with Arthur and Halymere, and was sweaty. He ignored her protests, running his sticky nose along her neck and pressing a kiss to her forehead.

'I need to know what is in here,' she muttered, stroking the spine of the book. 'You said you could read this. So, read it to me.'

'Now?' Ordes asked, his muscles going rigid. 'Can I wash first?'

'Please. You smell,' she rejoined, grabbing his chin and kissing him.

He made himself grin, pull on the mask. 'Want to wash my back for me?'

Jenyfer waved him away. 'You can manage,' she said, turning her attention back to the book, so he washed, taking his time, not caring that the water was freezing. He could have heated it, he supposed – a tiny flame leapt to life on the tip of his index finger, but he let it die, wrapping the towel around his middle and returning to Jenyfer.

She snatched the book away from his dripping hair. 'Careful!'

He raised his eyebrows. 'It looks like it's been wet before, Jen, the pages are all crinkled – but okay, fine.' He ran his fingers through his hair; steam rose into the air, and moments later, his hair was dry, curls bouncing around his shoulders. 'Better?'

'Show off,' Jenyfer mumbled. 'You need a haircut.'

'Do I now?'

'Yes. I woke up with your hair in my mouth. Find me something sharp and I'll cut it for you. But later,' she said, indicating the book. When he settled beside her, she passed him the book, unable to take her eyes off it. 'Does it … does it *sing* to you?'

'Sing? No,' he said, looking at her curiously.

'I can't explain it,' Jenyfer began. 'I can almost hear it, calling me.'

'Alright,' Ordes said softly, opening the book carefully. 'It's old,' he said, running his fingers lightly over the first page – nothing jumped out at him. No thoughts, no feelings. Nothing but a fuzzy blackness in his mind. 'I can't sense anything from it. My touch magic is picking up nothing.'

'Is that unusual?'

'Before I went into that Temple I would have said no, but now …' he chewed his lip. Jenyfer's gaze flitted between Ordes and the book, waiting, waiting, until Ordes could sense she was almost ready to burst. Eventually, he sighed, turning back to the book, running his eyes over the pages. 'I can't read all of this, Jen. There are words here I don't know, but we can try and fill in the gaps, I guess.'

She nodded, picking at the scales on her wrist, then didn't take a breath the whole time he was reading.

'"The Otherworld is also known as the Realm of the Dead, or Anaon. It exists in a parallel world alongside the mortal realm. It's a mirror world, reflecting reality. Souls enter Anaon by travelling along the Black River from the realm of Lyonesse, in the Bag Noz. They will pass through a mist, and find, in the middle of a swamp, an island covered in apple trees",' Ordes read. 'Apples grow in the Otherworld? Who'd have thought?'

'Keep going,' Jenyfer pressed. She shifted her position so she could peer at the book over Ordes' shoulder. He turned the page gently; the paper rustled like whispers and secrets. Something inside him told him to stop, to put the book aside, but something else urged him to keep reading, a smooth voice whispering in his ear. It sounded like Melodias. Ordes scowled.

On the next page was an illustration. A skeleton man in black robes, with flowing white hair and a white hat, the brim tipped to cover his face. In one hand he held a set of scales, and in the other, a scythe, the sharpened blade pointing upwards. At his feet were two hounds, one black and one white. The dogs had hollow eyes and stared out of the picture.

'Ankou,' Ordes said.

Jenyfer tapped the caption beneath the picture, written in tiny text.

'The hounds represent light and darkness,' Ordes explained. He'd known about Ankou's hounds his whole life.

'So Ankou is the God of Death?' Jenyfer asked.

Ordes shook his head. 'No. It says here he is not death, but a servant of Death. He does not choose who dies.'

'Then who does?'

'Perhaps no one. Death just is, I suppose,' Ordes said.

'Melodias calls himself the Master of Songs and Death,' Jenyfer began. 'But if Death is its own master, then that isn't correct, is it?'

'No,' Ordes replied.

Jenyfer shifted impatiently. 'What else does it say about Ankou?'

Ordes was silent as he read. 'To give you a summary – the Otherworld was given to Ankou by the Creator. She saw that he was morally just, and once it was obvious that humans were to die, the Old Ones created the Otherworld to house their souls. The Creator chose Ankou to guard them, because he was not swayed by emotions – because he was able to judge and remain objective.'

Ordes turned the next page, and frowned. 'I can't read a lot of this, but this seems to be the rules,' he said, giving Jenyfer a quick look. 'For the Otherworld and how it works.'

'Can you read any of it?' she asked, sounding disappointed.

'When a soul is judged, they will move on to one of three places – Anaon, where they will live in luxury in a world like their own, to Melodias' black lake, the one we saw,' he added, 'or they are sent to the Pit.'

'The Pit?' Jenyfer echoed sharply. 'The One God's Pit?'

'I don't know. All it says is it's called the Pit,' Ordes replied. His ears were full of whispered voices. He closed the book, fingers curled around it tightly.

'We were always told that if a soul ended up in the Pit they would be there for eternity,' Jenyfer said. 'We were lectured about it obsessively. All to scare us, but now, after actually seeing it …'

'Apparently demons can get out.' Ordes set the book to the side; his mouth tasted like ashes. 'Why do you need to know all this stuff anyway, Jen?'

'I don't know, exactly,' she answered. 'But why else would this book have shown up on *The Excalibur* when it did? Plus, Ophine told me Ankou wanted to speak with me. Why though?' She sighed, running a hand through her hair, then indicated the book again. 'Does it say anything about the Treasures of the Gods, or the Red One? Anything about the One God? Ereshki?'

Ordes flipped open the book again, scanning each page quickly. There were more pictures, but he ignored them all, until he sucked in a breath.

They were looking at a full-page drawing of the Bow. Ordes ran the tip of his finger along the curved limb. There was a caption beneath it.

'The Bow of Mists,' he murmured. 'It belonged to my mother.'

'Then it's yours, right?'

He nodded. 'It says here the bow is not always corporeal, that it is made of mist and magic. It can only be wielded by one in service of the Once and Future King. No one else can touch it or it will turn to mist and vanish. The quiver of arrows never runs out, and whoever uses it will never miss their mark.' He stopped and chuckled. 'We'll have to see about that.'

'You should ask someone to teach you how to use one, while we're here,' Jenyfer suggested.

'The Bow of Mists always seeks the truth,' Ordes said. 'What does that mean?' He turned the page, and they were looking at the Singing Stone. It was round and smooth, with a small hole in the centre. 'The Singing Stone is the Stone of the Once and Future King, but it can only be heard by someone with the power of music in their blood. It's Melodias' Treasure.' On the next page was the Sword, Arthur's Treasure.

'The Sword of the White Dragon,' Jenyfer said softly.

'No one can escape from the Sword once it is drawn,' Ordes said. 'It is the Sword of the King and it can kill a god. There's something else here but I can't read it – something about hands.'

'When were they made?' Jenyfer mused. 'I mean, were they created before or after your father's prophecies? Because the Once and Future King links them all. And your mother said we needed to find the Treasures before Arthur could find the Grail.'

Ordes turned the next page, but it was blank. There was no drawing of the Grail.

'That's helpful.'

'Maybe we aren't meant to know what it looks like?' Jenyfer said. 'It's Arthur's to wield.'

'But it's ours as well,' Ordes argued. 'Three sets of hands upon the stone ...'

Jenyfer sighed and lay back, linking her arms behind her head. 'We should show Arthur this book.' Ordes was still flipping through the pages. 'What are you looking for?'

'The Pit,' he said. 'Demons.'

She was looking at him, her expression concerned.

'Goerika told me my father was born of a mortal woman, and a being who escaped the Pit. A demon,' Ordes added quietly.

Jenyfer sat up, slipping an arm around him. 'You're not a demon.'

'How do you know that? I don't know what I am.'

She rested her head between his shoulder blades. 'We were taught that demons were darkness personified. That they lived in the Pit with the sole aim of tormenting souls for eternity. Even though it's probably a lie, part of it makes sense, doesn't it? And you,' she said, kissing the back of his neck. 'Are not like that.'

He sighed. 'Goerika told me Ereshki stole the Treasures not for power, but to protect the thing she loved most – humans.'

Jenyfer frowned. 'But how would stealing the Treasures protect anyone?'

'I'm not sure,' Ordes said quietly, then, 'is it possible your father was right? Have we got this all wrong?'

Jenyfer snorted.

'I'm serious. He said we weren't asking the right questions. And he warned us not to believe everything we were told,' Ordes continued.

'My father is a liar,' Jenyfer said firmly.

'According to him, all the Old Ones are liars,' Ordes replied.

'Come on,' Jenyfer said, climbing off the bed. She scooped the book from Ordes' lap. 'We're going to see Arthur.'

CHAPTER 62

Arthur's kibitka was crowded. Jenyfer was gnawing on her fingernails, perched on the edge of his bed, while Ordes was pacing in the small space left to him. In his lap, Arthur cradled the book Jenyfer had thrust at him. Jalen stood behind him, looking over his shoulder.

'The Otherworld?' Jalen said, his tone puzzled. 'Where did you get this?'

'It appeared on *The Excalibur* on the journey here,' Jenyfer told him.

'Can you read it?' Arthur glanced at Jalen. The demi-god's face closed up tightly and he shook his head. Something squirmed in Arthur's belly but he said nothing. *Trust your instincts*, a voice said. Goerika's. Arthur ignored her. Jalen wouldn't keep anything from him. If it wasn't for Jalen, he wouldn't even be here. It was Jalen who had given him the courage to run, even when Arthur had no idea what was about to unfold on the path for him.

Katarin was sprawled in the other chair, feet up on the table. 'This isn't about a book, is it?' she demanded of Jenyfer and Ordes. The latter rubbed at his face and shook his head.

'Then what?' Arthur asked softly. He turned the book over in his hands gently.

'We know the Treasures are guarded,' Jenyfer began. She was chewing on her lip now. 'My father hinted in his annoying way that these guardians weren't going to hand them over easily.'

Something walked the length of Arthur's spine. 'What else?'

'Are you serious?' Kat interrupted loudly. 'Melodias is a liar.'

'Melodias is an Old One,' Ordes put in. 'He can't lie, remember, only bend the truth, like they all can,' he added, his voice dropping. 'Goerika said the same thing, but not in those exact words.'

'Are you implying your mother is a liar?' Jalen demanded of Ordes and everyone jumped at the storm-demon's tone. Arthur had never heard Jalen sound like that – cold, challenging. Threatening. Arthur cleared his throat.

'No one is saying that,' he said softly.

'I am,' Ordes said simply; Arthur sensed Jalen bristle. 'Melodias implied the map was useless.'

'But we need it to find the Treasures,' Kat argued. She unhooked her feet from the table and sat up straight, a frown creasing her features. 'Don't we?'

'Honestly, I don't know anymore,' Ordes said. 'Melodias took it from us to use as leverage, remember? But if it's useless, why did he take it?'

'Because maybe no one else knows that,' Jenyfer answered. 'It makes sense, doesn't it?' she added when no one agreed with her. 'If everybody thinks the map is important, they'll all want it, and Melodias knows that. But … if it really is useless, I don't understand why it would appear at all.'

Arthur groaned. 'Alright – forgetting for a moment why the map exists if it leads nowhere – let's say Melodias is telling the actual truth.' He opened the book, flipping through the pages carefully. 'What does all this say and why is it important?'

'The title is misleading,' Ordes replied. 'Yes, there is information about the Otherworld in there, but also about the Treasures. More information than anyone has bothered to share,' he added, shooting Jalen a look. Arthur heard Jalen's teeth snap together.

Katarin sighed and tapped her fingers on the table-top. 'So the Treasures are guarded? By something nasty, no doubt.'

'Ancient beings, Melodias called them,' Jenyfer replied. 'But he didn't elaborate.' She turned to Jalen. 'You said there were things that no longer existed in the world. Could it mean that?'

'It's hard to say when we don't know exactly where the Treasures are,' Jalen told her, his tone clipped.

'Melodias said the Treasures were sentient, that they had a will of their own,' Ordes explained, taking a seat next to Jenyfer. 'Like calls to like is what he said. Magical things are drawn to one another.'

'Makes sense,' Katarin agreed. 'Let's forget Treasures and guardians and prophecies for one moment. I'm more interested in where the line has been drawn and by whom. Jalen, you confirmed there were two sides to this ... whatever we want to call it. Who is on which?'

'Niniane, the Green Knight and Morrigna on one,' Ordes answered. 'Ankou, Inanna and Ereshki on the other. And Melodias hasn't made up his mind – *if* we believe him.'

Jalen shook his head. 'Inanna and Ankou would not align themselves with the Red One.'

'Wouldn't they?' Katarin argued. 'We don't know what the Old Ones would or would not do, not anymore.' Irritated, she rubbed at her cheek. 'A map, Treasures that we now know are guarded by the Gods only know what, Old Ones with different visions of the future and all of us, stuck in the middle. Did Melodias say anything else that might help us work this shit out?'

'Only that the Red One was not the one to betray the world,' Jenyfer said quietly.

Arthur thought back to his conversation with his aunt. Morgause had told him the disappearance of the Treasures had nothing to do with Ereshki's banishment, but was that another half-truth? *History is written by those who hold power over others, Arthur. The stories that have shaped this world are just that – stories.* Arthur closed the book, sitting up straight. 'I don't think we can come to any conclusions yet,' he said. 'I think we have to make up our own minds about what is happening here. If the stories are wrong and Ereshki did not betray the world but acted out of a different motivation, should we even be looking for these Treasures?'

Everyone sucked in a breath at his words.

'If the Red One was not a betrayer,' Jenyfer said slowly, 'then everything we have been told about her is incorrect.'

'And if that is the case, how many other things are incorrect?' Kat mused.

'One man's truth is another man's lie,' Ordes said. 'It doesn't necessarily mean it's the truth or a lie – it depends on how you look at it, I guess.'

Silence slipped between them; faces were turned to the ground in contemplation, lips were being chewed upon and fingers tapped against thighs.

'I don't know what to do,' Arthur said eventually. 'And *that* is the truth. I don't know what we should do.' He laughed, startling everyone, himself included. 'It was straight forward until this conversation – find the Treasures, find the Grail and do whatever it is we're supposed to do with it, but now ...'

'Now?' Jalen echoed. His voice was still tight; Arthur reached up to grasp the hand that was resting on his shoulder.

'Maybe we need to start asking the right questions, but of whom, I don't know,' he said. 'And, I think it's still important to find the Treasures. Whatever guards them ... well, that will be a problem for another moment, I suppose.'

'Good,' Katarin announced. She stood, arranging her coat and cutlass. 'Then let's get out of this forest and get moving.'

CHAPTER 63

Lamorna gripped at her face, pressing her forehead into her hands. She dug the pads of her fingers against her eyes until light popped behind her lids. Fire Night loomed like a beast in her head.

You wanted it, the wicked little voice whispered. *You liked it, Lamorna. You're a heathen, a blasphemer. A beast. You don't deserve the One God's love. You don't deserve—*

'Shut it,' Lamorna hissed. She sat at the edge of the stream, the water reflecting the trees back at her. She stared and stared, leaning over until it was her reflection peering up at her. Her skin was milk-pale, blue eyes irritated. Shadows rested beneath them.

It was too much.

Mordred. Jenyfer. Arthur. Her aunt.

Servants of the Beast, all of them.

And what are you, then? that voice whispered.

Lamorna sighed. The sooner she left this place, the better. Her belly tightened at the idea of Mordred coming with her, but she was glad she would not be alone for the journey. He had taken care of all the preparations for their trip, telling her not to worry about it. A small part of her wondered if he was trying to make up for what he had done, on Fire Night, but another part of her knew he wasn't. He wasn't like her – he didn't feel any guilt, or remorse, or even worry over what had happened.

She should be mad at him. She should despise him, but she didn't.

Lamorna dipped the bucket into the stream, shattering her reflection and sending the forest rippling away.

After leaving the water at her aunt's kibitka, she went in search of Jenyfer. She needed to see her before she left. She wouldn't tell her sister what she had planned; Jenyfer would not understand. She would try and make her stay, and a part of Lamorna was terrified she would succeed. So she squared her shoulders and lifted her chin proudly, making her way to the far end of the village, where she knew her sister was staying with the pirate. Jenyfer hadn't stayed with her family since Fire Night.

Jenyfer and Ordes' kibitka was much larger than Lamorna's. A pang of jealousy went through her, but she pushed it aside. She swept the canvas flap open and strode in unannounced to find not Jenyfer, but Ordes. He raised his eyebrows and glanced up from his breakfast. He wasn't wearing a shirt, and Lamorna hoped he had at least something on the bottom half of him – she couldn't see his legs behind the table. She closed her eyes as he pushed his plate aside and stood.

'I'm dressed,' he told her, his tone laced with laughter.

Lamorna opened her eyes, her gaze sweeping over him. Where Mordred was all muscle and bulk, Ordes was tall and lean; she could see the muscle beneath his honey-coloured skin. She hadn't really looked at him properly before, not wanting to acknowledge he was handsome in any way, but he was. Not in the same way Mordred was, though.

Ordes pulled a shirt over his head. His hair was messy, hanging in his eyes, and he pushed it away with an irritated expression, tucking it behind his pointed ears.

Lamorna's heart thudded painfully. 'What happened in Lyonesse?' she blurted. 'I want to know. What did … Did *he* do anything to Jenyfer?'

'Nothing too terrible. He likes tormenting people, playing with their emotions,' Ordes said softly. 'You truly don't remember anything? We know you were there, Lamorna.'

'No,' she snapped. 'I don't.'

Water and death and music.

She folded her arms. 'Why did you come here?'

'We needed to find Arthur.'

'Arthur Tregarthen?'

'Yes.'

'Why?'

Ordes gave her an astounded look. 'You have no idea what's actually going on, do you?'

'I do,' she retorted. She knew, but didn't understand. She didn't understand anything. It was another sign that she should return to Kernou. 'Where's Jenyfer?'

'Training, with Melhala. You can wait for her, if you like,' he added.

Lamorna shook her head. 'No. I need to go.'

Whatever he saw in her face made him narrow his eyes. She turned to leave, and found the kibitkas flap closed, and she couldn't open it. Slowly, she turned to face Ordes, swallowing her stomach. Fear closed in on her as she remembered what he was.

'Let me out.'

'What's going on?'

'What do you mean?'

'You look utterly terrified,' Ordes stated. 'I can hear your heart - it's so wild I'm surprised you're still breathing. Your thoughts are swirling around like a storm and'—he paused and took a step closer to her—'Jenyfer would kill me if I didn't ask, so, has someone hurt you?'

'No.'

'Threatened you?'

'No.' She shook her head emphatically. 'I wanted to see her. Now let me out.' She turned towards the flap – she'd rip her way free if she had to – but suddenly Ordes was standing in front of her. Lamorna cried out and stumbled backwards. 'How did you …'

'You can't trust him,' Ordes said firmly.

Her heart increased its rhythm. 'Who?'

'Mordred.'

'Who told you about him?' Lamorna demanded, her voice filled with false bravado. Inside, she was terrified as she realised everyone must know, including her aunt. She hadn't been sneaky or stealthy about it at all.

'Jenyfer suspected, and now you confirmed it,' Ordes said gently, then his expression hardened. 'He's dangerous. He hides his true thoughts but the intent is still there, like a dark cloud hanging over him. He smells of deceit.'

Fear, hot and potent, shot through Lamorna again. 'I don't know what you're talking about.' She made herself hold Ordes' gaze, until he nodded and stepped aside. The flap flew open, the slice of daylight blinding. Lamorna hurried out, and didn't look back.

That evening, she met Mordred in the forest. She could see the village, and her sister's kibitka. Lamorna watched until her eyes were hurting. Night was closing in around them, and she was twitchy, impatient to get moving, but she wanted to see Jenyfer one more time before she left.

A hand closed over her arm and she jumped.

'Are you ready?' Mordred said softly.

She shook her head, not taking her eyes off Jenyfer's kibitka.

Mordred sighed. 'Lamorna—'

'She's my sister,' Lamorna snapped. 'I want to see her.'

'Fine,' he said, his hand coming to rest on the back of her neck. 'You can see her, but don't talk to her. She'll only convince you not to go, you know that.'

She nodded. Her heart gave a little jump as Jenyfer appeared. She was with the water wielder – Melhala. Lamorna had met her once. She watched Jenyfer and Melhala talking for a moment. Jenyfer laughed at something the other woman said, and then Melhala was gone.

Jenyfer ran her hand through her hair and her shoulders slumped; in exhaustion or something else, Lamorna could not tell. She went to step away from Mordred, but his hand tightened on the back of her neck. She swallowed, was about to demand he let her go, when Ordes came out of the kibitka. Jenyfer spun around, a broad smile on her lips. Something he said made her laugh and then she folded her arms around him and he was kissing her, pulling her into his body. He broke away to say something and Jenyfer's head whipped around, as if she was searching for something. She stepped away from him, frowning. He had hold of her hand and gently tugged her back to him, bending his head to talk to her. After a moment, she nodded, and they went into the kibitka.

'Ah,' Mordred said softly. 'The heartfire. It's obvious, now that I think about it.'

'What is that?' Lamorna asked. Mordred's fingers caressed the back of her neck.

'Soulmates. It's a bond that cannot be broken,' he explained gently. 'It means they're destined for one another.'

'Oh,' Lamorna whispered. 'That's not bad, is it?'

'It means you will always be second to him, Lamorna, and there is nothing you can do to change that,' Mordred replied. 'It's how it is.'

Lamorna's shoulders slumped. 'Let's go,' she said, her throat tight.

With one final look at her sister's kibitka, Lamorna turned and followed Mordred into the trees, where his horse was waiting.

CHAPTER 64

After the discussion in Arthur's kibitka, Jenyfer had felt a renewed sense of purpose, but they were still all here. She had imagined them packing up and returning to the ship the following day, but it had been almost a week and nothing had changed.

Except the quietness she could now sense in people. Jalen, in particular. She hadn't seen much of him, but his anger during the impromptu meeting had made her nervous – and even more convinced that maybe her father was right; something else was happening and they were yet to work it out.

Apart from Treasures to track down, Jenyfer missed the sea, the smells and the sounds of the water. There were creeks and streams inland, but it wasn't the same. She missed the sand between her toes. Her song had been unusually quiet in Cruithea, but she could sense it, crooning away unhappily at the heart of her. She had continued her magic practice, leaving Ordes to study the book on the Otherworld, frowning and muttering to himself as he tried to decipher words he didn't know, looking for answers to the questions burning him up.

It was early, not long after dawn. Jenyfer and Melhala were seated near the cooking fires. Cruithea was chilly in the mornings, before the sun made it high enough in the sky to push its way through the trees and warm the world. A bowl of porridge balanced on Jenyfer's knees, but she had barely touched it.

She'd woken that morning with something gnawing at her insides.

Something was wrong, and it wasn't anything to do with Treasures or prophecies or gods.

Lamorna had come to see her yesterday. Jenyfer should have found her last night, as soon as she could. That had been her intention, but after a day of working magic with Melhala, she'd fallen onto the bed and not woken until a few hours ago. It was draining, holding her song back, but that was what she'd been doing since they left Lyonesse. The memory of the power she'd unleashed when she destroyed the watery-replica of Bryn was always tugging at her, as if reminding her of what she could do, if she was brave enough to let it all out.

She hadn't told anyone about that moment.

'Jen! Jenyfer!'

Jenyfer glanced over her shoulder. Her aunt was hurrying towards her, Keraine on her heels. Tamora's face was pale and pinched, and she wrung her hands. 'Thank the seas I found you. Your sister is gone!'

'What?' Jenyfer looked at her aunt, aghast. 'When?'

Tamora swallowed. 'She didn't return after evening meal, but I thought she was sulking again, so I decided to wait, but she didn't come back and—'

Jenyfer passed Melhala her bowl and leapt to her feet. 'Then I'll go and get her.'

'You don't know where she's gone,' Tamora argued. 'She could be anywhere.'

Arthur rushed over to them. He was out of breath, his face worried. He cleared his throat. 'Mordred has disappeared – the Inborn have reported him missing. Morgause told me. He went out on patrol last night but did not return. His horse is gone, and some of his things.'

Tamora's face paled further.

Jenyfer's fists curled as the realisation hit her. 'Where would they go?'

Then, before anyone could speak, she turned and hurried to her aunt's kibitka, snatching a blanket from the bed Lamorna had last slept in. She paused, pulled a shaking breath into her lungs, before running back across the village to where her aunt and Arthur were waiting. Melhala had gone. Jenyfer held out the blanket. 'This will help find her.'

'Jen—' Arthur began.

'Touch magic. Ordes can find her,' she announced, and closed her eyes, sending out her mind. It was strange – she was still unsure of how it worked, and had only done it once before, but he'd been lying beside her then, not ... wherever he was.

The air around her shifted, and when she opened her eyes, Ordes was there, his face folded into a frown. 'What's all the shouting about?' he asked, his eyes falling to the blanket in Jenyfer's arms.

'Lamorna's gone,' she said, and passed over the blanket. 'Mordred too. We need to find them. Can you—'

The moment Ordes closed his fingers over the blanket, his face stiffened. 'Kernou,' he said. 'She's gone back to Kernou.'

'Are you sure?' Tamora asked him.

Ordes nodded. 'She was thinking of Kernou the last time she held this, and,' he paused, 'about Mordred ... going with her. She doesn't fully trust him, but I don't think she knows that.'

'I don't trust him,' Jenyfer said, folding her arms.

'Neither do I,' Ordes agreed.

Tamora gripped Jenyfer's arm. 'Find her,' she whispered. 'And bring her back.'

'Bring them both back,' came a voice. Jenyfer turned to watch as the High Priestess approached, Melhala on her heels. 'I will deal with my son.' Morgause's face was hard, her tone harder, but her eyes glistened.

She collected herself, smoothing the emotion from her face, and turned to Arthur. 'I wish you could stay longer, but you must go. The three of you'—she glanced between Arthur, Ordes, and Jenyfer— 'cannot be apart again. The prophecy has begun. Your journey has commenced.'

'But,' Arthur said, 'I haven't learnt enough. I'm still not able to use my magic properly and I'm not much good with the sword, and—'

She reached out a long-fingered hand and placed it on his cheek; he fell silent.

'You will not be alone. Morgaine will be with you,' she said softly.

'As will I,' Melhala put in. 'Ethinne and I have already discussed it, Arthur. Where you go, we go as well.'

The High Priestess nodded. 'Halymere will accompany you also. This has already been decided. He will continue to train you.'

'We leave now,' Jenyfer cut in. Urgency was filling her up and she was almost bouncing where she stood, her magic rushing and rushing and rushing through her. 'Now!'

'Jen—'

'Now, Ordes! The sooner we get going, the sooner we can find them. If the winds are kind, we'll get there before them,' Jenyfer snapped. She turned and hurried away, not caring that the High Priestess was there, not caring that she might be breaking some sort of Cruithean rule. She needed to find Lamorna.

Your sister is very sweet.

She shuddered, hurrying between kibitkas, her thoughts a swirling mess. The air shifted around her and Ordes was by her side. He didn't say anything, didn't try to stop her, didn't tell her to slow down. He held open the flap of their kibitka for her so she could race inside.

'Good thing we don't have much to pack,' he said, watching her grab their packs and shove whatever clothing she could find into them. She shot him a look, reaching for the book. There was no way she was leaving that behind. When she was done, Jenyfer tossed Ordes his pack, took one last look at the kibitka, at the bed where she had finally surrendered herself to the heartfire – and one part of her fate – then turned and left.

The Excalibur was silent. Arthur lay in his bed, Jalen curled beside him, the timbers of the ship shifting and groaning gently. Arthur blinked. Sleep was rushing towards him, but his mind was busy, his thoughts tumbling over and over like waves crashing against a shore.

It was all happening too fast.

He sighed and tugged at his hair. What game was Mordred playing? He could not work it out. And Lamorna! The knowledge that the two of them were involved with one another was something Arthur was having difficulty reconciling. His cousin, a Cruithean warrior, a powerful Magic Wielder, and one of the One God's most devoted servants?

There was something he was missing, something they all were missing, but he couldn't figure out what. Yawning, Arthur rolled over; Jalen's arm tightened on his middle, making him smile, and before he knew it he was in the Fisher Queen's cave.

It was dark and damp, as it usually was, but the guardian of the Grail was not there. Swallowing, Arthur moved further into the cave, searching for a clue as to where Eseld was. Something glinted white from the ground. Her crown of chipped coral. Arthur picked it up gently, examining it. All the points were broken. He frowned, certain that the last time he had seen it some were still intact.

Wind rushed into the cave, cold and smelling of the ocean, and the crown in his hands trembled. He went to put it down, wondering if he should be touching it at all, when it vanished, and he was left holding a map of Teyath.

Startled, he ran his eyes over it. It was an old map, the edges curling and yellow, the parchment water-stained and slightly damp. There were no towns marked on this map, nothing at all, not even Malist, one of the first settlements. Arthur traced the spine of the Nemhain Mountains with his eyes. He had never seen the mountains except on a map. As he looked, he realised he had been wrong – there was one place marked: Dinas Emrys.

Where the castle that once belonged to Eseld and her brother lay. Nothing but a ruin now, on a barren, cursed wasteland.

Arthur swallowed, tearing his eyes from Dinas Emrys. As his gaze travelled south, his magic tingled, warm and light. He stopped, sweeping his eyes to the east, and his magic became chilled, like the sea on a winter's day. He moved his gaze back to the mountains. Warm and golden light filled him.

North and it grew cold.

South, and it was warm.

'Alright,' Arthur murmured. He brought the map closer to his face so he could see it better. The Faery Forest spread itself between the western and eastern ridges of the mountains, the Banstein and Vinlay Rivers on either side. Arthur stared at the inky forest. What was in there? he wondered.

An image flashed into his mind.

A sword, a white dragon curling around the hilt, the blade inscribed with foreign words.

As he watched, something began to form on the map and the image of the sword pressed into his mind so forcefully it burnt.

There, at the base of the Nemhain Mountains, where the Vinlay River began its journey to the sea, near the treeline of the Faery Forest, was a drawing of a sword.

Arthur sat up with a gasp. Throwing back the bedclothes, he flung himself into the morning, pulling on his clothes so quickly he got tangled in the legs of his pants. Jalen mumbled something from the bed, but Arthur was already rushing for the door. He hurried along the dark passageway and took the steps two at a time, flinging himself across the deck towards the Captain's cabin. He didn't knock, shoving the door open and barging in.

A shirtless Ordes and a wild-haired Jenyfer were standing behind the desk, a map of Teyath spread before them. Neither of them looked up. Arthur swallowed, trying to slow his racing heart as he approached the desk.

Jenyfer's eyes flickered to him, and back to the map.

'The Treasures,' Arthur guessed. 'You dreamt of them?'

'Yes,' Ordes replied. 'The bow.'

'The Singing Stone,' Jenyfer said. 'Makes sense that that one is mine, I guess.'

Ordes murmured his agreement. He picked up a stick of charcoal and carefully drew a bow on the map, in the ocean off the coast halfway between Kernou and Port Leore. '*That* doesn't make sense,' he said, turning to Jenyfer. She had her bottom lip pulled between her teeth, her eyes moving over the map. She held out her hand for the charcoal and bent over the map; when she straightened, she'd made a mark of her own – in the middle of the ocean west of Carinya.

Neither Jenyfer nor Ordes said anything more. Jenyfer simply passed Arthur the charcoal. He swallowed, eyes running over the map, searching for the location he had been shown in his dream. He found Cruithea, and followed the spine of the Nemhain Mountains south, stopping when he reached the headwaters of the Vinlay River. There, he drew a sword.

'At least yours is in a place we can actually find,' Ordes pointed out.

Jenyfer looked at him. 'Maybe we got it wrong?'

'I don't think so,' he said. 'I saw what you saw, remember.'

'Wait,' Arthur said. 'You saw her dream? How?'

'Another little thing about the heartfire no one told us,' Ordes replied. 'I can walk in Jen's dreams, and she in mine, if she wants.'

'The heartfire?' Arthur said. 'What's that?'

'Just a fey soul mates' thing,' Ordes said, slinging his arm around Jenyfer's shoulder and pressing a kiss on her head. 'She's stuck with me now.'

Arthur glanced at Jenyfer, not sure whether her expression meant she was pleased about this, or uncomfortable. He rubbed his eyes. It was early. Apart from the man on watch on the deck, he didn't think anyone else was awake. 'Well, we're closest to Carinya.'

'We're going to Kernou first,' Jenyfer ordered, then turned and left the cabin.

Arthur and Ordes exchanged a look.

'We find her sister, and then we find these Treasures,' Ordes said, following Jenyfer.

Kernou was like a blazing dot on the map. 'Does Lamorna want to be found though?' Arthur asked himself, his eyes lingering on the place of his birth, before joining the others on deck.

CHAPTER 65

The journey back to Kernou was much swifter on horseback. Sometimes Lamorna rode up front, and Mordred let her take the reins and steer the horse. Other times, he walked while she rode, and sometimes, like when they crossed the mountain pass from the Hunter's Forest, they both walked, Mordred leading the horse slowly, making sure the animal did not stumble and break its leg. If that happened, he told her, he would have to kill it.

'A horse with a broken leg cannot survive, Lamorna,' he had said gently, when she gasped and hurried over to rest her cheek against the horse's warm neck. 'He would be in great pain. It is the best way.'

So she'd nodded, and prayed silently to the One God that the horse would not fall.

They passed Camlann, where Mordred stopped and stared at the dead place for a long time, even though he must have seen it before. Lamorna wiped at the sweat on her face. It was hot here, but she did not take off her coat, knowing that once they re-entered the mountains she would need it.

'What's he called?' she asked.

'The horse?' Mordred asked, and she nodded. 'His name is Pellinore.'

'Pellinore,' Lamorna said, trying the name out; Pellinore snorted and tossed his head when she spoke his name. 'I like it.'

Mordred cast her a smile over his shoulder, and then the three of them began the trek through the Nemhain Mountains. This time, Lamorna was not afraid of the slabs of granite that towered above them. She took the time to look at the rock formations, noting the places where the edges were shorn sharp as blades by the wind, and at the places where water had created small crevasses from aeons of run-off. She took note of the trees and shrubs that she had not paid attention to before, and how they clung to the rocks, their roots barely finding purchase against them, but still managing to survive. At night, she slept close to Mordred, snuggling into the warmth of him, enjoying the moment, even though they were sleeping on the ground with nothing but some animal hide to protect them from the rocks. She clung to him, keeping her face tucked into his neck. If he sensed anything was wrong, he did not say.

She knew that once they reached Kernou, everything would change between them; for a moment, she thought that maybe they should turn back, return to Cruithea – or go somewhere else, just the two of them. Mordred could hunt for them, and Lamorna knew how to prepare food. He would have to teach her to make a fire though, and maybe he could teach her how to ride Pellinore on her own.

'Are there faeries here? In the mountains?' she asked Mordred as they were packing up their camp one morning. She had lost track of how many days it had been since they had left Cruithea, and she had feared others would follow them and bring them back, but Mordred had hidden their passage, much like Tamora and Keraine had on the journey north.

'There are,' he told her, helping her onto Pellinore's back.

'What sorts?'

She felt Mordred's surprise but did not look at him, keeping her eyes on Pellinore's soft ears. He seemed to be listening; she reached out and stroked his ears, making him toss his head. When he was settled behind her, Mordred pressed a kiss to the side of her head, making her shiver and smile at how it made her feel.

'Piskies are everywhere,' he said simply. 'And there are sprites – elemental spirits, attached to these rocks. They are shy though – you will not see them.'

'Are there dangerous things, like the colpach?' Lamorna asked.

'There are many dangerous fey creatures in the world, Lamorna,' Mordred said. 'Things like the night criers, and korrigans.'

'My sister spoke with korrigans,' Lamorna told him.

'Did she? Well, she was lucky. They can be very deadly, and don't usually like people.'

'Jenyfer isn't human though, is she?' Lamorna asked quietly.

'No, I suppose she isn't,' Mordred said.

'What else is there?' she asked.

Mordred pulled her against him suddenly. 'Things that would rip your pretty throat out, my love. Things like glastigs and carlings, the washerwomen, black dogs and things you do not want to meet, Lamorna. Things that make the colpach seem as dangerous as Pellinore.'

'Where do these things live?' she asked in a whisper. She wanted him to stop talking, but she wanted to *know* what was out there.

'The Teeth, mainly,' Mordred told her. 'The rocky islands to the north-east of Cruithea. They are ruled by a queen, Medb, who is ruthless and terrible, as are the fey she commands.'

Lamorna swallowed. 'Have you been there?'

'I would not be here with you now if I had,' he responded.

Conversation between them fell away the closer they came to Kernou. As they left the Nemhain Mountains behind, Lamorna realised she could see the sea, and she could smell it, and her heart raced at the familiar scent from a life that used to be hers.

Nothing would be the same for her ever again, she realised suddenly; before she could stop herself, she began to weep.

'Lamorna,' Mordred murmured. 'What is it?'

She sniffed and wiped at her eyes, glad he could not see her face. They were both astride Pellinore, one of Mordred's arms resting lightly around her middle, his chest pressed into her back. Now, at her emotion, he tightened his grip on her and his lips touched her hair.

'It's silly,' she whispered.

'Tell me.'

'Everything will be different,' she said. 'I don't like it when things are different.'

'Cruithea was different,' he reminded her gently. 'You adapted there, so you will adapt again, as I will have to.'

Lamorna swallowed. She had not thought of that. 'Will you be alright?' she asked.

'Me?' Mordred said, chuckling lightly. 'I shall be more than alright, Lamorna, because you will be with me.'

'But I won't be,' she muttered. 'I won't be allowed to be. I will have to stay away from you. Those are the rules.'

'Rules are made to be broken,' Mordred said simply, jabbing Pellinore in the ribs with his feet. The horse snorted but quickened his pace and they slipped beneath the trees.

'The Chif won't be happy with me,' Lamorna lamented. 'I have failed in the mission the One God set me. I was supposed to spread the Word in Cruithea. He will be disappointed.'

'He won't, because you are bringing him something of great value,' Mordred said.

'What?'

'Me.'

Kernou came into view the following morning. Lamorna's heart was stuck in her throat and she had no words. They stood at the treeline of the Vidarra Forest, the Bay of Calledun in the distance, the sea glistening like a jewel. Lamorna could see no boats out on the water, which she immediately thought was strange, but maybe the weather was not right for fishing. She glanced up at the sky – bright blue, achingly so, not a cloud to be seen.

They entered Kernou from the hills behind the town, passing by the stone circle. Lamorna had never seen it, but now she stared at it. She knew this was a place Jenyfer used to go when she snuck around in the darkness. She knew there were faeries here. She wondered what Mordred was thinking about the stones. There were no stone circles in Cruithea that she knew of.

Pellinore kept his feet as they descended the hillside, but his hooves sank into the soft sand. He snorted in displeasure.

'He does not like the sand,' Lamorna whispered.

'No,' Mordred agreed. He pulled on the reins; Pellinore halted immediately. Mordred slid from the horses' back. When Lamorna went to climb down, he shook his head, taking up the reins. Lamorna's return to Kernou, on the back of a great black horse being led by the leader of Cruithea's Inborn, was something everyone would talk about for a long time.

Lamorna directed Mordred to the Chif's house, her heart hammering, her head spinning. She wanted to be sick.

She wanted to turn around and go back.

They were met by Bryn, who was standing guard outside the Chif's residence. His eyes widened and he drew his weapon at the sight of Mordred, but when his gaze fell on Lamorna, his mouth opened in shock.

She realised how she must look. Her hair was unbound, and she was wearing her Cruithean clothes. She guessed her face would be dirty, her hands as well. She made herself remain still as Bryn approached, his Red Hand cloak gleaming like blood in the morning light. He eyed Mordred suspiciously.

'I'd like to get down now,' Lamorna said. Bryn moved towards her, but Lamorna shook her head, and Bryn watched as Mordred reached for her, lifting her down from Pellinore's back. His fingers lingered a little too long on her waist and Lamorna shot Bryn a worried glance. His face was creased in disapproval and suddenly Lamorna was angry, angrier than she had ever been at anything before.

She pushed past Mordred and approached Bryn, not caring that she was breaking the rules, not caring that she was standing close to him. He looked at her in shock, but when he opened his mouth to chastise her, to tell her to step back, she belted him across the face, her hand shooting out before she could think.

The sound of her blow echoed around them.

Bryn made a noise of anger, but when he moved towards her Mordred was there, his strong body between them, and Bryn stepped back. Lamorna glared at him.

'That's for my sister,' she hissed.

Before Bryn could say anything, the door to the Chif's house flew open, and Ulrian Tregarthen was standing in the doorway. His gaze passed over them, stopping on Mordred. Slowly, he made his way down the path, opening the gate, not taking his eyes off Mordred.

'You're excused,' the Chif told Bryn. He did not mention the lurid red hand print glowing against Bryn's tanned cheek. He did not look at Lamorna, or the horse.

His eyes were for Mordred.

When Bryn had gone, the Chif cleared his throat.

'You've grown,' he said.

'Of course,' Mordred answered. 'I was a child when you left.'

'And now, you're the leader of the Inborn, if I am remembering the signs correctly.'

Mordred smiled. 'You are, Uncle.'

'Uncle?' Lamorna gasped. 'What?'

'Didn't I mention that?' Mordred said.

'Yes, but …'

Idiot, she chided herself. How could she have not realised? *Because you were too busy opening your legs for him like a common whore*, the little voice whispered and she went to tell it to shut up, but stopped, realising it was right. She hadn't paid proper attention, too caught up in Mordred, and in her own pleasure.

The Chif turned his attention to Lamorna then, his dark eyes crawling over her, from head to toe and back up to rest on her face, and she felt naked beneath his gaze. 'You were supposed to report back to me,' he said sternly.

'But … I did. I sent letters!' Lamorna protested.

He shook his head. 'I received no letters from you, Lamorna. I did, however, receive some interesting correspondence from Mordred.'

Lamorna swung around to face the Cruithean warrior, hurt ripping through her. 'You wrote to him? And didn't tell me? Or send my letters?'

Mordred's face was the picture of innocent confusion. 'You didn't give me any letters.'

'I …'

'Lamorna,' the Chif cut in. 'You forget your place.'

'But—'

The Chif held up his hand, silencing her. With the other, he beckoned to Mordred. 'Come. We have much to discuss, you and I.'

Lamorna went to follow them inside, but the Chif turned to her, a frown crossing his face. 'What are you doing?'

'Oh,' she said softly. 'I thought—'

The Chif cut across her. 'I think you've been away for too long, Lamorna. I think perhaps you should return home and read the Word. You will wash, cover your hair, and dress appropriately. I fear this time in Cruithea was not kind to you.'

She gasped, then lowered her eyes. 'Yes. You are right. I will go home and pray.'

She sensed Ulrian nod, then the door was closed in her face and Mordred was gone, vanished into the Chif's house.

The cottage was dark and cold and silent, so silent. Lamorna pulled her arms around herself. She had never been alone before. Her sister and her aunt were always present, even if they weren't home. With a sigh, Lamorna found the candle on the kitchen table and lit it; slowly, warm golden light filled the room.

She lit the fire in the stove next, struggling to get it going. Tamora had always managed the fire. With her magic, a little voice inside Lamorna reminded her. She shut her ears against it, blowing gently on the kindling until she could feed in a larger piece of firewood.

In the pantry, she found a few potatoes, withered and full of eyes, and a pumpkin. All the green vegetables were rotten in their basket, so she took them outside and left them near the back door. She would check the garden tomorrow and see what could be salvaged.

Back inside, she swept the floors while waiting for water to boil for her tea. She had no appetite, but knew she had to eat, so she would bake bread for the morning. Setting the broom aside, Lamorna carried the candle down the hall, pausing for a moment in the doorway of the bedroom she had shared with Jenyfer. The room was dark and chilled; the window was open and a sharp breeze shot inside, threatening to blow out the candle. Lamorna hurried over to close it, catching sight of lightning streaking across the sky. The rumble of thunder followed, making her jump, although she'd been expecting it.

Leaves were scattered across her sister's bed. Lamorna picked one up – it was dry and crunchy. She lay it on her palm, staring at the skeletal-like structure, wondering how long it took for the colour to fade and leave this grey husk behind. Lamorna squeezed her fist closed. The leaf crumbled into a million little pieces, which she let fall to the floor.

There were more leaves at her feet, some feathers. Lightning flashed again.

If Jenyfer were here, she'd be sitting by the window with the curtains open, watching the sky. Lamorna swallowed the lump in her throat and headed further down the hall to her aunt's bedroom. She pushed the door open, stopping on the threshold. The girls never went into Tamora's room, but now, Lamorna strode in, false confidence dripping from her. She set the candle on the nightstand and looked.

Tamora's dresser was covered in wild and wonderful things that Lamorna had never seen before. There were colourful feathers from birds she could not name. Dried flowers and crystals. In a small, ceramic jar with a lid, Lamorna found the skull of an animal. It was so delicate looking, so white and gleaming in the darkness she could only stare at it, wondering what it had belonged to and what it was for. She set the lid back on the jar and lifted the lid of another. Herbs, still fragrant even in their shrivelled state. Another lid revealed powdered clay, or dirt – Lamorna wasn't sure. There were ointments and salves, more dried herbs, a stone with a hole in its centre.

Dusting her hands on her skirt, Lamorna turned away from the obvious signs of witchcraft, wondering at her aunt's bravery, to leave them on display like that. She opened the wardrobe, where she stood and stared at the clothing her aunt had left behind, before closing the doors firmly, collecting the candle and hurrying from the room. Tamora would never return here. Lamorna knew that, but still, a little part of her hoped that she'd wake in the morning to her aunt, and her sister, in the kitchen.

Lamorna rubbed at her eyes. She was tired, but wasn't sure where she should sleep. She didn't think she could sleep in her old room without Jenyfer; after her sister had left to marry Bryn and live in his cottage Lamorna had had trouble sleeping, although she told no one. She couldn't sleep in her aunt's bed, either, so maybe the floor in their small sitting room?

Frowning, she stepped into the kitchen and nearly dropped the candle.

Mordred was standing by the stove. 'The water is boiling,' he said simply.

Lamorna hurried over, handing him the candle and pulling the tea-pot away, setting it on the bench. She found the herbs she liked and left the tea to brew, feeling Mordred's eyes on her the whole time.

'What are you doing here?' she asked him, still not looking at him. She was angry with him for not being honest with her, so she watched the storm rolling closer instead; the sky was a show of blue and silver light, bouncing through the clouds with reckless abandon. 'Did anyone see you?'

'No one will see me if I don't wish it,' he replied.

'Where is Pellinore?'

'I let him go. He will come back when I wish it.'

'Why didn't you send my letters?' she demanded. She still didn't look at him.

'It has been a long time since he saw me last. I needed him to trust me,' Mordred replied. He moved closer to her until he was standing directly behind her, the heat from his body warming her back. Lamorna held her breath as he traced the curve of her cheek with the tip of a finger. Slowly, she turned around.

'By making me look like a fool? By disgracing me?'

He chuckled and touched her lips – she pulled away from him. He frowned, then that smile was back. 'You have done a good job of that yourself, Lamorna, don't you think?'

She opened her mouth, and promptly closed it, because he was right. She had. She swallowed and hung her head. Mordred touched her cheek again; this time, she did not move away. His fingers curled around the line of her jaw.

'Lamorna,' he whispered. 'Don't be angry with me. You know I had to do it. I will make it right – I will speak with the Chif and confess my sin. I will tell him I misled you.'

She sighed and shook her head. 'No. You don't have to do that,' she said softly. 'Do you want tea? Or something to eat? I was going to bake bread and there isn't much else but I—'

'I'm not hungry, Lamorna.' Mordred's voice was low and soft, washing over her like the storm washed over the world outside the cottage.

Lamorna could hear the wind rushing through the garden and swirling around the sides of the house. The Chif no longer trusted her. Mordred had lied to her, again. She should be angry with him but, instead, she simply asked him where he was staying. She assumed the Chif would have arranged something for him, but her heart skipped a beat when he shrugged casually.

'I thought I would stay here.'

She stared at him, aghast. 'You can't! It's not proper!'

'No one has to know,' he said, moving away from her to pull out a chair and sit at the table. He looked so big in her kitchen, his body too large for the small space.

She wrung her hands. 'But—'

'Come here,' he commanded. She hesitated for a moment, then went, and he closed his arms around her and buried his face against her stomach. She liked it, she decided, the way he held her. Even though he had deceived her, there was a part of her that still liked this – that yearned for him, aching and burning and tugging at her with longing. Eventually, he sighed, standing and sliding his chair out of the way. Lamorna watched in confusion as he dropped to his knees in front of her. 'Is it time to pray?' he asked. 'Every evening, right?'

'Yes,' she whispered. She went to kneel also but he shook his head, his hands moving beneath the hem of her skirt. She swallowed; the familiar feeling of anticipation and desire flowed through her as his hands moved up the insides of her legs, higher and higher, until he reached the core of her body. She sucked in a breath, biting her lip to stop from moaning as his fingers caressed her.

'Then I'm going to pray,' Mordred said, lifting her skirts up around her middle, his hands gripping her hips. She wanted to protest – this was not praying – but his tongue was on her, and everything melted away.

CHAPTER 66

The *Excalibur* had dropped anchor off the coast of Teyath, the Bay of Calledun several nautical miles to their east. Everyone was gathered in the Captain's cabin, which was suddenly feeling very crowded. Katarin let her eyes move around the room, studying everyone and doing nothing to hide it. Her brother might be destined to be a King, but she was still concerned about his lack of confidence. Since returning to Cruithea she had seen a change in Arthur, but it was small, and didn't leave her brimming with confidence herself.

And then there were the love birds. While she was pleased they had gotten their act together – finally – it was sickening, if she was being honest. Jenyfer was standing with her arms folded, her bottom lip between her teeth. Ordes stuck to her like a burr; some part of him was always touching her. If the heartfire got in the way of things ... Ordes was capable of making dumb decisions without some mind-numbing mating bond messing with his senses.

Kat shook her head, frustrated, as Jenyfer's eyes darted to the window again. Thinking of her sister, Katarin guessed, the brainwashed idiot who decided running away with Mordred was a good idea, giving them all something else to worry about in the middle of everything.

They should let Lamorna rot, Mordred with her. Morgause was furious with her son. Kat had agreed to returning to Kernou for one reason only – Mordred. They were family, but even as children they'd butted heads, both stubborn and prideful. Now, she wanted to know what the fuck he was thinking.

But even if he would see her, he wouldn't tell her anything. She knew that as well.

She'd always known Mordred felt cheated for being born a man in a world where women's power was what mattered. Once it was known Morgause would have no more children, and without a daughter to pass the title of High Priestess to, the Priestesses had told Morgause that Inanna had chosen Katarin to be the next High Priestess. Even though she was only young at the time, Kat could still remember how angry her cousin had been when he found out. It was a sore point between them then, and a sore point now. She'd made sure to stay out of his way whenever she visited Cruithea, and this last time had been no different.

It wasn't like she ever had the chance to fulfil her chosen role; Ulrian Tregarthen had seen to that. And now Kat knew it was too late. The role would pass to someone else, another young woman chosen by Inanna, yet another reason for Mordred to seek some sort of warped vengeance on his mother and the Old Ways.

Kat wanted to slap some sense into him.

Slap that sister of Jenyfer's across her plump little cheek as well.

She sighed inwardly, forcing calm on herself, trying to push some of the tension from her muscles, but it was difficult when a certain Cruithean was standing inside the door, his eyes tracking her as she paced in what little space she could find in the Captain's cabin. She threw him a scowl every now and then, a warning, one that she knew Halymere would heed. She didn't want him here, but could not refuse Morgause's request. The High Priestess was right – Arthur did need training, and there was no one better than Halymere to do it. No one else had the patience needed, especially now, when everything was moving forward.

Kat had heard about the prophecies and the Treasures of the Gods her whole life. The stories were always there, lingering in the back of her mind, no matter where she sailed around the coast of Teyath. Another thing she and Mordred used to discuss when they were children – would they get to meet the promised King? And would he do what the Myrddin said he would?

Arthur and the storm demon stood behind the desk, shoulders touching. Kat bit her lip. There were no demi-gods in the prophecies that she knew of, but when she had asked Niniane was very clear on it – Jalen must be by Arthur's side. Kat let her eyes linger on Jalen's face; the demi-god looked up, met her gaze, and looked away and again, that feeling that there was something she was missing niggled at Kat's belly.

She'd barely begun to shuffle through all the thoughts swirling around her brain since Jenyfer and Ordes dumped that darn book on the Otherworld into Arthur's lap and left everyone with more questions and no answers. If they took a detour to Avalon, would Niniane tell her the truth?

No, Katarin decided sadly, she wouldn't.

The door opened and closed quickly as the Cruithean water wielder and the Priestess entered. More unasked-for participants on their journey. Katarin knew she should be grateful – Arthur was grateful – but people were something she didn't deal with well. She rolled her shoulders and folded her arms, her eyes falling to the Captain's chair behind the desk. Would she get to sit in it again? Although *The Excalibur* was not *The Night Queen*, she was a ship's Captain. Without a ship. Anxiety gnawed on her belly. Who was she without her ship? Her crew? Her thoughts drifted briefly to Aelle, and quickly away again.

When everyone had settled themselves, Arthur cleared his throat, gesturing to the map. 'I don't pretend to know what I'm looking at here.

Just after we left Cruithea, the three of us had a dream – all separate, yet all similar. We dreamt of the location of the Treasures of the Gods.'

Silence answered him.

'An exact location?' Iouen asked slowly.

Ordes shook his head. 'We each saw separate places, and we have marked these on the map of Teyath.' He moved closer to the table and the map; Iouen rose from his seat so he could see the map better. 'But, as you can see, there is only one of the three locations that is an actual specific place. And that is Arthur's Treasure, the Sword of the White Dragon. And,' Ordes said, picking up the map of Teyath and moving it out of the way, 'we still have *this* mystery to solve as well. This is a copy of the map that was on mine and Jenyfer's skin.'

Katarin made a noise of annoyance, raising her eyebrows at Ordes' irritated look. She still thought him and Jenyfer were fools for handing it over to the God of the Seas without a fight.

'Wait …' Iouen said, eyes on the map. 'Can I see that?'

Ordes stepped back.

Iouen took up a stick of charcoal and Ordes tensed. 'I won't destroy your work of art, don't worry,' the quartermaster said, grinning. Muttering to himself, Iouen returned the map of Teyath to the centre of the desk, studying the places they had marked as the locations of the Treasures. Frowning, he stepped back, then reached for Jen and Ordes' map, rolling it up and carrying it over to the window.

'What are you—' Katarin began, but the sailor shook his head at her. She bristled but bit the words back.

'We've been looking at this wrong,' Iouen said. 'I don't know why I didn't realise it before. I have a rather useless skill,' he added, grinning at the blank looks on their faces. 'I can read backwards. Words, numbers, whatever. Backwards. Makes as much sense to me as it does the right way around.'

'Backwards …' Arthur murmured, then a smile spread across his face. 'Show us.'

Iouen unrolled the map, and held it up against the glass. The sun crept through the parchment, illuminating the lines Ordes had so painstakingly drawn. 'Hold this, will you?' Iouen asked Tahnet, who hurried to help him.

With one hand holding the map in place, Iouen pointed to a location south of Teyath. 'We're here right now,' he said, indicating where they had decided the Bay of Calledun was on the mystery map.

'Yes, and?' Katarin said. She had gone over that map a thousand times already, while anchored halfway between Lyonesse and Teyath, needing to do *something* while waiting to see if she'd made the biggest mistake of her life in leaving Ordes in Melodias' realm.

Iouen shook his head impatiently. He took the map down, turned it around and then, with Tahnet's help, held it against the glass once more. 'We should be here,' he said, tapping the area roughly off the coast of Malist.

'Why?' Katarin demanded, arms folded. 'That doesn't make sense.'

'We've marked the Treasures on the wrong map,' Iouen said calmly. 'If I use the same locations from the map of Teyath, and add them here—'

With Tahnet holding the mystery map, Iouen placed the regular map over it. With the sun behind both maps, he traced over the locations of the Treasures again, leaving an impression on Jen and Ordes' mystery map. Letting the regular map of Teyath flutter to the floor, Iouen carefully traced the impressions of the Treasures on the mystery map. 'See? With the map in reverse?'

Ordes grinned. 'You're a genius, Iouen.'

'Oh,' Jalen breathed. 'Malist. The Bow is in Malist.'

Arthur was frowning. 'We need to avoid Malist and the Sacellum.'

'No, we don't. We need to walk straight into that cesspit of a city and find your Treasure,' Iouen said. His eyes met Ordes'. 'I know that city. I have friends there. I can't promise you they're upstanding citizens though,' he said. 'You want to stay undetected? With your fancy tricks and my connections, we can do this.'

Jenyfer had moved closer to the window and the illuminated map. 'And the Stone is now on an island in The Teeth,' she said softly. 'Arthur, your sword is still in Faery Forest, at the base of the mountains.'

'Alright, let's—' Arthur began.

'What about Lamorna?' Jenyfer interrupted, turning from the map. When no one said anything, her expression grew hard. 'I'm not leaving her. If I have to march into Kernou myself and get her, I will.'

'No,' Ordes said. She glared at him, then stormed from the cabin. He followed. For a moment, no one moved, then Katarin pushed herself away from the bulkhead, hurrying out onto the deck to see Jenyfer moving towards the railing, the coast of Kernou visible in the distance. Ordes vanished, reappearing in front of her, blocking her path. Jenyfer's fists clenched; Katarin held her breath, waiting, as everyone rushed out of the cabin.

'Move, Ordes,' Jenyfer growled.

'I won't let you go.'

It was the wrong thing to say, especially with Kernou lingering in the background. Jenyfer's face tightened. 'Won't?' she repeated, voice low, cold – deadly. 'You won't let me? Is that right?'

'Jen—'

'Try and stop me,' she seethed. She attempted to push past him to the railing, but he blocked her path at every step, not relenting even when she drew her dagger. Katarin tensed, her hand dropping to her own weapon. Arthur caught her eye and shook his head.

'Ordes, move! She's my sister! I won't leave her there with him!' Jenyfer shouted.

'I know how worried you are, but this isn't the way,' he said.

'Move.' The syhren's voice was as chilled as the ocean in winter.

Ordes shook his head and Katarin wanted to sigh. 'Sing me to sleep then, Jen, because it's the only way I'm letting you go back there.' With his back against the railing and her dagger not far from his neck, Ordes undid the buttons on his shirt, placing his hand over his chest, above his heart. Slowly, something slipped free of his skin and he held it in his palm. Kat sucked in a breath – she could feel the magic in the charm from where she stood. Ordes glanced at it quickly, then back at Jenyfer, before he tossed it over his shoulder and into the sea.

Jenyfer's hand trembled, the dagger lowering an inch. Kat hurried up to the quarter deck. She could feel her magic shifting beneath her skin. Exchanging a look with Kayrus, she let her magic pool in her palm.

'What are you going to do with that?' the helmsman asked her quietly.

'What I have to,' she replied, not taking her eyes from Jen and Ordes. '*If* I have to.'

'Sing to me,' Ordes said softly, his voice managing to echo around the deck.

Everyone tensed; some of the crew slammed their hands over their ears.

Jenyfer opened her mouth – the air around her shifted, but she crammed her lips shut and then screamed in frustration. Ordes closed his arms around her. 'We'll find another way,' he promised. Jenyfer sniffed and nodded, burying her face in his neck.

Jalen cleared his throat. 'I'll go.'

Jenyfer and Ordes both turned to look at him. The storm demon ignored Arthur's objection. 'I'll be in and out before anyone realises I'm there. You want to know how your sister is?' he asked Jenyfer, who nodded. 'Then I'll find out for you.'

He was gone, vanishing from the deck of *The Excalibur* in a swirl of clouds and lightning.

'If you're all done with the drama,' Katarin called and Kayrus chuckled. 'We have choices to make. We need to work out where we will go first.'

Arthur was standing with his back to them, arms folded, his gaze facing Kernou. 'We need to keep going. I think we try and find the sword first – we're closer to the Faery Forest than the capital,' Arthur declared. 'Once we have it, we'll head north, to Malist, following the path laid out on the map. It will save us doubling back.'

'I am looking forward to visiting the Sacellum.' Halymere cracked his knuckles.

Arthur gave the Cruithean a wry smile. 'I expect none of this will be easy.' He moved away from the railing, running his hand through his hair. 'After Malist and the bow, we'll head to The Teeth,' Arthur said, his eyes moving over them. 'I don't suppose any of you have ever been there?'

Katarin's blood ran cold. 'No one goes to The Teeth.'

'Why does that sound ominous? And why does my Treasure have to be there?' Jenyfer muttered. They lapsed into silence, the only sound the waves as they tongued at the hull.

Arthur was frowning. 'What will we find there, Kat?'

Katarin was silent for a long moment. She used to think she was fearless, but the idea of them going that far north made the hair stand up on the back of her neck. 'No humans live there,' she said eventually. 'The islands of The Teeth are inhabited by faeries. But,' she said, 'these are not the faeries you're used to. The faeries on Avalon are wild, yes, but in comparison, the faeries of The Teeth are—'

'Feral,' Halymere cut in. Kat shot him a grateful look and nodded. 'They do not like people crossing their territory.'

'You've been there?' Arthur asked Halymere.

'No one goes there and comes back,' the Cruithean said, his voice low. 'You do not want to meet whatever will be guarding the Treasure in The Teeth.'

Iouen groaned.

Jenyfer cleared her throat. 'It's my Treasure. I'll go.' She pulled away from Ordes. 'And I'm not fully human, so maybe …' her voice trailed off and she shrugged. 'Maybe they'll let me in?'

'I'll go with you,' Ordes said. 'Goerika told me I wasn't human at all.'

'You're both fools if you think it will be so easy,' Katarin argued. 'These aren't piskies or the Night Riders, Ordes. I'm talking carlings and kelpies, the widows, boggarts and asrai, and creatures that have never been named. These are the beautiful and terrible things our demon friend was talking about.'

'It doesn't matter what they are,' Arthur said before anyone could reply. 'We need the Stone.' He cleared his throat and raised his voice so everyone could hear him, including *The Excalibur's* crew. 'I won't lie to any of you on board this ship. What we are about to do will be dangerous. The voyage we are about to embark on will be perilous. Whatever the waves throw at us will be the least of our worries.' He moved until he was standing near the main mast and then climbed on top of a barrel that rested there so everyone could see him.

'I'm not going to make any of you come with us if you don't want to. We will let you off at the next safe place.'

Katarin's heart swelled at her brother's words.

'We're sworn to this ship,' Iouen said loudly. 'And whoever is her captain,' he added and the men around him nodded. 'I'll stay.'

Murmurs of agreement rushed through the crew.

'A question,' Kayrus asked, his low, rumbling voice washing over them. 'Who do we defer to as Captain on this ship now?'

'Me,' Katarin said firmly. She met Ordes' gaze, held it.

Let me have this. Please let me have this.

When nobody spoke, Katarin put her hands on her hips, her eyes moving over everybody. 'Do we need to put it to a vote then?'

Ordes smiled in understanding. 'The ship is yours, Katarin.'

CHAPTER 67

A storm washed over the town. It's as if the world is drowning, Lamorna thought, her eyes drifting to the window and the rain that slid down the glass. Mordred's fingers trailed down her arm. Was it only yesterday that she returned?

'You're worried about your sister,' Mordred stated. It was early morning. They were in her aunt's bed, which Lamorna decided was now her bed – hers, and Mordred's – at least for the moment. In the back of her mind was the little voice, telling her to make him leave, but she wasn't listening to it, not now. She burrowed a little closer to his warmth in defiance.

Mordred repeated his question.

Something sharp pinched in Lamorna's chest. 'Yes.'

'Do you want to see her?'

'She's in Cruithea,' Lamorna answered. She sat up, wondering where her clothes were. Mordred sat up also, his arms sliding around her middle, his chin resting on her shoulder.

'Do you want to see her?' he said again.

'How?' Lamorna breathed. Out over the ocean, lightning flashed, followed by the rumble of thunder. She wondered absently if the fishing boats would be out there, getting tossed around.

'I can show you,' Mordred said, his breath, then his mouth, touching the shell of her ear, 'with magic. But'— sighing lightly, he lay back and chilled air slipped between their bodies— 'you won't want that. Especially now.'

'I do,' Lamorna said quickly, then bit her lip and hung her head. 'I do.'

'Do you have a mirror?'

'There are no mirrors here,' Lamorna answered. Mordred climbed from the bed. He didn't bother to dress, stretching his arms above his head. It was dark still, so he lit a candle with the click of his fingers, his body gleaming golden in its light. She tried not to look at him – she should be cross at him, wanted to be angry with him, for lying to her, for making her fail in her mission – but she couldn't help it.

'A bowl of water will do,' Mordred told her. Lamorna nodded, scrambling from the bed. In the hall, she found her dress and hurried to pull it on. She then fetched a large bowl from beneath the sink. She went outside to the tub that sat near the back door, and was soaked by the time she returned, the bowl full to brimming.

'It needs to be boiled before it can be drunk,' she said.

Mordred chuckled. 'We're not drinking it,' he told her. 'I need a knife. Sharp.'

Lamorna nodded, setting the bowl on the table, her heart pounding, her head screaming a warning. She found a knife – the one her aunt used to cut herbs. It was small, the handle well worn, but the blade was sharp. She passed it to Mordred and sat opposite him at the table, water dripping from her sodden clothes to pool on the ground at her feet. 'Now what?'

'In Cruithea,' he said, twirling the knife between his large fingers. 'There is magic that is not practised anymore, not in the village, and not by my mother or the Priestesses. Once, long ago, the Red Ones performed the Blood Rites. They could see the future, the past, and they could speak with the dead. But my mother, when she became High Priestess, sent them away; for years they have lived in the Dead Woods, in the Ossuary, the House of Bones. It is forbidden to speak with them, and forbidden to visit them. We are not to seek them out.'

Lamorna swallowed.

Mordred looked up and met her gaze. 'But I am not good at doing what I am told. Give me your hand.'

'Why?'

'Blood magic requires blood, Lamorna.'

She clutched her hands tightly in her lap and shook her head.

'You wish to see Jenyfer? She is your family. I need your blood for this to work. Only a few drops. It won't hurt,' he assured her. 'The Red Ones worship Ereshki, the Dark Mother, she who brings death – but death is part of life, and we enter this life in blood, do we not?'

Lamorna thought about her mother, whose blood was given so that she would live. 'Yes,' she whispered.

Mordred smiled. 'Then hold out your hand.'

The knife was sharp – Lamorna already knew this, having sliced her finger on it once while cutting herbs – but it felt sharper when wielded by someone else's hand. She tried to pull away, to nurse the sting in her palm, but Mordred held her hand tightly, and slowly turned it to the side so her blood fell against the clear face of the water in the bowl that waited between them. He released her and she went to stand, to find a cloth to press against her wound, but he shook his head and indicated the bowl.

'Watch.'

As words she didn't know left his lips, Lamorna did what she was told and watched the water in the bowl, her heart beating painfully in her ears as the shame, the sin, of what she was doing sank inside her, burning and twisting and mingling with all the sins she had committed since arriving in Cruithea.

Since meeting Mordred.

She risked a glance at him, finding him looking at her, his lips moving quickly as those strange words raced into the space between them. Hurriedly, Lamorna dropped her eyes to the bowl. Slowly, the water began to swirl, the bright red of her blood flowing like streamers, and she was suddenly looking at her sister.

Lamorna gasped, her wound and its bite forgotten. 'It's …'

'Yes.'

'Can I talk to her?'

'No. That requires more than blood.'

Lamorna swallowed, not wanting to ask what he meant, but wanting desperately to know. She couldn't take her eyes off Jenyfer's face, the fierceness of it, the way her features were set firm. Jenyfer opened her mouth to speak to someone, but Lamorna could not hear the words. She was on a ship, Lamorna realised. She could see the sails straining in the background. She stared and stared until the vision faded and it was just her and Mordred, who practised Blood Magic and sin, and the storm raging outside.

By that afternoon, Lamorna knew she could put it off no longer. She needed to go into town. Hunger was gnawing on her belly, so she took the last two jars of honey from the pantry and found her basket. Mordred sat at the kitchen table, watching as she bustled around, making a mental list of all the things she would need. They, she corrected, sneaking a glance at him. He gave her a smile.

'I won't be long,' she said, picking up the basket and heading towards the door.

'Haven't you forgotten something?' he asked, holding out his hand.

Nestled in his palm was a bundle of white.

Her cap.

Lamorna reached up to touch her hair. She had forgotten.

Mordred unfolded the cap and held it before his eyes, frowning. 'It's a strange thing,' he mused. 'This rule about hair. Does it not bother you?'

Lamorna said nothing, taking the cap from him and securing it over her hair.

Without another word, she left, not knowing if he would be there when she returned or not. They had not discussed it. It would be better if he was gone, she thought. She would not have to explain it to anyone when they asked why he was staying in her home.

Because they already know, the little voice said.

Lamorna slowed her steps. Did they? She wondered. Would people truly be able to look at her and *know* what had happened? She pushed the worries aside. She would deal with them later. She would deal with the whispers later, because if there was one thing she knew for certain about Kernou, it was that there were always whispers.

They had never been about her, not until she'd returned from beneath the water; that had been bad enough, but she knew that, this time, the whispers would be different.

There were not many people in the town square. The market stalls were set up, everything in the same position it had been before she left for Cruithea, but it was very quiet. And, she realised as she headed towards Mr Chigwidden, something else was different.

Every woman in the square was accompanied by a man, and the Red Hand stood guard at the perimeter. Lamorna swallowed, her steps slowing again. Mr Chigwidden, she realised, had averted his eyes, not looking at her like he used to. There was no smile of welcome on his chubby face as she approached him.

Lamorna reached into her basket for a jar of honey. 'I would like carrots, tomatoes, potatoes, and beans, please,' she told him, making sure her tone was polite. He said nothing, indicating she was to put the honey on one of his wooden benches. She did so, her heart thundering, as he gathered her produce in his large hands. She passed over the basket, and when he had filled it, turned and hurried away. She wanted fish, so she made herself stand up straight and walk across the square.

Denny was behind the counter. His eyes widened when he saw her, and colour sprang to life on his cheeks. Lamorna gave him a small polite smile.

'Where is everyone?' she asked, indicating the almost-empty market area beyond the bakery door.

'You don't know? A lot of people have left, like you did. Only they haven't come back,' Denny said.

'And it's good they didn't,' a voice said firmly. Margaret appeared from the back room, wiping her hands on her apron. She eyed Lamorna with distaste. 'Denny isn't to speak with you.'

Lamorna swallowed. 'Why not?'

'Because you've been with *them*,' the woman said spitefully.

'I was on a mission for the One God—'

Margaret laughed scornfully. 'You were on your back, more like,' she said. The blood drained from Lamorna's face as the woman went on, enjoying her nastiness. 'We've all seen him, that Cruithean. How do we know he won't murder us in our beds?'

'Trust me,' Lamorna snapped before she could stop herself. 'Mordred wouldn't go anywhere near your bed!'

She could still feel Maragret's eyes burning a hole in the back of her head as she hurried away. Lamorna was almost running by the time she reached the edge of town and the path that led to her cottage. In the distance, somewhere out in the hills, she heard the whinny of a horse. Pellinore. She hoped he was happy. Margaret's horrible words were swimming around her head, making her stomach churn.

Someone stepped out from behind the last building, blocking her path.

Bryn.

Lamorna gasped and almost dropped her basket.

'Where is your heathen bodyguard?' he asked her, his tone hard.

She said nothing.

With one hand, Bryn reached up to touch his cheek, the one she had smacked; the other made a show of pushing back his cloak so she could see the dagger at his hip. He ran his fingers over the hilt.

Lamorna's blood ran cold. 'What do you want?'

'Aren't you going to ask me what I've been doing while you've been gone?' he asked, then went on before she could say anything. 'I've had many adventures, Lamorna. Did you know that catching a faery isn't that hard? You have to go about it the right way. Did you know piskies have green blood? Imagine that.'

'What ... what do you mean?' she stammered.

Bryn's fingers continued to stroke the hilt of the dagger. 'The Red Hand regularly travels to other towns. We are asked to come, you see. If it isn't Magic Wielders we are hunting, it's faeries. Don't you want to know how I catch them? I'm very good at it.'

'No,' Lamorna managed. She thought of the piskies she had seen in Cruithea.

Piskies were gentle. Harmless. They liked the horses, like she did.

'Where is your sister?' Bryn asked. He took a step closer to her. Lamorna wondered how quickly she could run if she dropped her basket. Would he catch her? Of course he would, she thought.

'I don't know,' she said. 'Why?' She kept her voice steady. She would not show fear. She had spent a night alone in the forest in Cruithea. She had travelled for weeks through the wilderness. She had survived being attacked by a colpach. But Mordred had been there then, she remembered. Now, she was alone.

Bryn's smile became wicked and cruel. 'You should not have raised your hand to me, Lamorna.'

'Get out of my way,' she commanded, feeling the muscles in her legs prepare to run.

The smile dropped a little. 'You have forgotten your place,' he said. 'You need reminding of how things are here.'

'You won't touch me!' she hissed, her grip on the handle of the basket tightening. She might not have a dagger, like him, but she was certain she could smash his face with the basket if she timed it right. She planted her feet as her mouth went dry. She did not take her eyes from Bryn's, even when a fierce wind rushed in from the ocean and pulled her cap free. Her hair billowed around her face like a golden cloud.

Bryn laughed. 'Enjoy the rest of your walk home, Lamorna,' he said, pushing past her and heading towards the town.

Lamorna did not move until she was certain he was gone, and then she ran, her thoughts tumbling over one another until she was dizzy and breathless, standing outside her cottage. Before she pushed open the gate and hurried inside, the wind increased, until it wrapped itself around her, digging at her. She blinked, pushing the hair out of her eyes. For a moment, she thought she saw a face appear – blue eyes, sandy hair – and then, it was gone, and she was left with a thundering heart.

CHAPTER 68

The mists were a thick, grey soup, wrung with water and chilled to touch. They closed around him as he planted his feet firmly on the pebbled shore. He pulled a deep, steady breath of the morning air into his lungs, held it, and let it out, lifting his hands as he did so.

His power rose like a great snake at his call, dormant for too long. It soared and swirled and carved its way free of him. With the flick of a wrist, a wall of water rose from the sea, arching high into the sky. Another twist of his fingers and it froze, a great wave suspended mid-break, sea foam twinkling like stars on its peak. With both hands he brought it down; it crashed into the sea, but made not a ripple as it vanished.

He laughed, and his power welled inside him, clamouring to be let out once more. Delighted, he swirled both hands through the air – a plume of fire shot from his fingertips to curl into a ball, which he sent flying across the water to be eaten by the mist. Then it was the water again, bubbles of it rising from all around him. He held them in the air, juggling them, before he let them go as well and turned his attention to the sky.

A slice of blue was visible through the mist; he waved his hand lazily and storm clouds swooped in, preternatural darkness closing in on the world. Another wave and it was lightning. He let the sky be, and bent to place his palms on the pebbles at his feet. The waves lapped gently at the shore as he sent his power out. The earth beneath his feet shuddered and when he opened his eyes, a land bridge extended far out to sea, swallowed by the mists. He wondered how far it went.

'I trust you'll put my island back the way it was when you're done playing,' a female voice said. The bridge fell beneath the surface of the water with hardly a splash.

'Of course,' he said, standing and holding out his hand. She drifted closer, closing her fingers around his. 'Why give it back to me now?'

'Born of a mortal woman, fathered by something not of this world anymore – you will need your powers for what is to come. You know this.' Niniane shrugged, a graceful lifting of slim shoulders. 'And, I felt it was time.'

'Time? It's been thirty years, woman.'

The smile she gave him was rueful but not apologetic. 'What is thirty years to ones like us? You will need them,' she repeated softly. Then, 'I can't sense them, any of them. Where are they?'

Merlin closed his eyes, and his power flowed from his body to soar into the world, skimming the surface of the ocean. It raced through the mists and out over the open water, moving inexorably closer to land. It rippled past fishing boats and crested the shore on its own wave, moving through a village, then over grass that swayed in the morning breeze. Here, it paused, before shooting off to the south, back over the water, where it locked on to a man with silver eyes and the wind in his hair. There was a woman with him, dark hair flowing over her shoulders, and a man with messy brown hair and soft eyes. They faded away, becoming first a blur, then nothing but empty space as the magic came racing back across the water.

'The syhren is with him.'

'The Grail bearer?'

'He is there.'

'You need to get them all in the one place at the right time,' Niniane said simply. 'One foot on the land, one in the sea and one with a foot in both worlds. Only then can the Once and Future King be—'

'Can I ask that you don't claim my prophecies as your own?' he interrupted.

She smiled. 'Yes alright, but I swear, in the hundreds of years I have known you, you've never been this moody.' When he didn't respond, she squeezed his hand. 'Start with the Sword. I trust they know where to look?'

'They do.'

'And you won't say where?'

'No.' Merlin did not look at her when he spoke, closing his eyes. He could see the sword, the dragon that curled around the hilt, and the words engraved on the blade - "for the serpent to become the dragon, it must consume itself and be reborn."

He liked that one for the poetry, but not for the gravity those words carried.

He could feel the sword's weight, its power, strangely comforting. His fingers twitched, but it was not his to hold. It never had been.

He had never liked this part of the plan, but Niniane had assured him it was necessary – Gawain would give up the right to the Sword, as she would give up her Bow, and Melodias ... Merlin frowned. Even he had not seen what the God of the Seas would do next, but he could not worry about Melodias, not now.

'If they discover we've tricked them ...'

A small frown graced Niniane's face. 'We deal with that when, if, it happens.'

They watched the mist swirl over the surface of the water.

'He really is my greatest creation,' the Goddess of Magic said softly. 'I can see that, now.'

'You can't tell him the truth. He can't know where he came from. He can't know *why* he is.'

'I won't.'

'I mean it, Niniane. Leave it to me,' Merlin said sternly. 'Ankou?'

Niniane sighed, rubbing at her cheek with delicate fingers. 'Ankou, as you well know, is more concerned with the balance than anything else. He may yet be a problem.'

'Have you sensed anything? Any stirrings?' Merlin asked, and his magic shifted beneath his skin, a stirring of its own. He held it steady; it writhed like a living thing in protest.

'No, and I don't expect to until the Treasures are recovered,' Niniane replied. 'Another thing we will deal with when it happens. Safe travels, my love.' Her voice was sad. He touched her cheek and kissed her gently.

A click of his fingers and a twig was resting between them. He tossed it into the water, where it grew and twisted to shape itself into a small ship, enough for one person to manage. The vessel bobbed impatiently, the movement sending minute waves rippling gently against the shore. He could change his shape he supposed, but he'd grown used to boats.

As the sun broke through the wall of grey, Merlin parted the mists of Avalon and walked out into the ocean.

ACKNOWLEDGMENTS

I would like to acknowledge that *A Song of Magic* was conceptualised and written on the lands of the Widjabul people. I acknowledge and pay my respect to the traditional custodians, past, present and emerging, of the Bundjalung nation, and their continuous connection to the landscape and the rivers of this ancient place.

I have to thank my family first. We have been through a lot of upheaval over the last twelve months, and you still found a way to give me the time and space I needed to write. I don't have enough words to truly thank you for this – I love you guys.

My editor, cover designer, cartographer and blurb writer. Danikka, you are the best editor I could ever hope for – you seem to share my brain and know exactly what I want to say when I can't seem to find the words. Thank you for all your work and for your support. I am grateful to be able to call you a friend. Fran, my wonderful cover designer – once again you have come up with the most glorious cover for my book! Thank you for taking my weird scribbles and ramblings and creating this work of art. Rachael, my cartographer – your art and your skill brought my world to life. My map is beyond amazing – it is perfect! Thank you so much! And to Jessie at Book Blurb Magic – thank you, once again, for untangling my tangly plot and making my blurb the best it can be!

My online friends and the writing community – I could not do this without you all. I feel privileged to receive such support and encouragement. I am so thankful for all the time and effort members of the online writing community put into supporting each other, whether it be sharing tips or tricks or just simply offering feedback. You guys are amazing. Writing is a solitary pursuit, but I do not feel alone.

My beta and ARC teams – there are way too many of you to mention by name, but please know how grateful and thankful I am that you gave up your time to read for me, and for your support of me and my story.

To Skye, for your help with all things Jarthur. Thank you so much!

And lastly, to you, the reader, for diving into this world with me. I hope you enjoy your journey. The story will continue with Blood on the Earth, book three in The Grail Cycle.

ABOUT THE AUTHOR

KATE SCHUMACHER is the author of *Shadow of Fire* and *Heart of Flame* (The Fires of Aileryan series). Her latest series, The Grail Cycle, is a reimagining of Arthurian legend. *The Call of the Sea*, book 1 in this series, was published in 2023. *A Song of Magic* is the second book in the series.

When she isn't writing, Kate is reading her way through an ever-growing TBR pile. She has wanted to be an author since she was a child, and finds time to write in the in-between moments of life.

Kate completed a Bachelor of Arts in Creative Writing and Journalism, and an Honours degree in Screenwriting, followed by a Graduate Diploma in Education.

She lives in Northern NSW, Australia, with her partner, two children and three very spoiled cats.

Follow her on Instagram @kate.schumacher.writer
or visit her website kateschumacherauthor.com